ALB

Also by Patrick McCormack

ALBION

The White Phantom

Patrick McCormack

Robinson
LONDON

Constable & Robinson Ltd
3 The Lanchesters
162 Fulham Palace Road
London W6 9ER

First published in the UK by Robinson, an imprint of
Constable & Robinson Ltd 2000

A copy of the British Library Cataloguing in Publication
data is available from the British Library

ISBN 1-84119-051-9

Typeset by Hewer Text Ltd, Edinburgh
Printed and bound in the EU

DRAMATIS PERSONAE OF ALBION

Addonwy Dumnonian warrior, member of Gereint's warband. Old friend of Nai.

Agricola, or Aircol High Lord of Dyfed in Arthur's day, father of Vortepor.

Ambrosius The Elder and the Younger. Father and son who opposed the policies of Gworthigern and refused to acknowledge his authority.

Amren Son of Bedwyr and Garwen.

Angus Abbot of a monastery visited by Nai. In his younger days he served as a warrior with the High Lords of Dumnonia, and with Arthur's Companions at Eidin. Kin to Lleminawg and Eremon, married Custennin's sister.

Anir Arthur's son, killed by him.

Arthur Emperor or Amherawdyr of Albion.

Atlendor One of Arthur's Companions. Accompanied him to the Iardomnan and was later at Eidin.

Bedwyr One of Arthur's Companions. He and Cei were Arthur's oldest friends and chief Companions.

Bodgath Master of the horse herd at Mordav's villa, and friend of Seradwen.

Bran The Crow Lord. Father of Llew in the tale told by Regin.

Budoc Name used by Bedwyr after Camlann, while he was a monk in Brittany and a hermit in Dumnonia.

Cadlew Dumnonian warrior, member of Gereint's warband. Old friend of Nai.

Cadwallon Lord of Gwynedd during Arthur's later years, father of Maelgwn.

Cadwy Legendary hero of Eastern Dumnonia.

Calpornia Member of a Christian community in Isca.

Catraut Ruler of Calchwinyth at time of Camlann.

Cei Called 'the Long Man' because of his great size. With Bedwyr, the chief of Arthur's Companions.

Celemon Daughter of Cei and friend of Gwenhwyvar. Disappeared after the disaster of Camlann.

Ceolric A young Saxon who aided Bedwyr and Nai in their struggle against Eremon.

Cerdic King of the West Saxons or Gewisse.

Coel Rival of Gworthigern in the lands to the south of Hadrian's Wall.

Cunedda Ancestor of the rulers of Gwynedd, originally from Manaw in Gododdin.

Cynon One of Arthur's Companions.

Cynrig Saxon, leader of Cerdic's warband.

Cunomorus, or Kynfawr Ruler of Dumnonia in Arthur's day, father of Custennin.

Custennin, or Constantine High Lord of Dumnonia in succession to his father Cunomorus.

Diffeidell In the tale told by Regin, one of the three sons of Dyssinendoth who led the invading Peryth.

Dirmyg One of the Clan Menestyr.

Dovnuall A follower of Eremon. He killed Erfai and was himself slain by Gorthyn.

Eleuther Ruler of Eburacum. Led his men to Eidin at Cei's command.

Eremon Outlaw of Irish descent. Foster son of Gereint and kin to Lleminawg and Angus. Slain by Nai.

Erfai Bedwyr's nephew and follower of Gereint. Father of Gorthyn and foster father of Nai.

Eri Member of Custennin's warband and friend of Isgofan.

Eurgain Girl from the village of Porthyle who aided Bedwyr and Nai in their struggle against Eremon.

Fferog One of the Clan Menestyr. Son of Peythan.

Gall In the tale told by Regin, one of the three sons of Dyssinendoth who led the invading Peryth.

Garwen Bedwyr's long-dead wife.

Gereint   Minor lord in Dumnonia, served by Nai. Also, common name in Dumnonia.

Glewlwyd   Originally Gatekeeper to Gwenhwyvar's father. Later Gatekeeper to Arthur.

Gorthyn   Dumnonian warrior, member of Gereint's warband. Foster brother of Nai.

Greid   One of the Clan Menestyr.

Grugyn   Llew's war leader in the tale told by Regin.

Gurfelling   High Lord of Eidin in Arthur's day.

Gwalchmei   The Hawk, one of the Companions and kin to Arthur. Accompanied him to the Iardomnan, and later led the Army of Albion to Gododdin.

Gwaredur Bow-back   One of Arthur's Companions who followed Medraut to Camlann. Father of Morfudd.

Gwenhwyvar   Wife to Arthur. Disappeared after the disaster of Camlann.

Gwilym   Old fisherman at Porthyle.

Gworthigern the Thin (Vortigern)   'The High King': Vitolinus, who first invited the Saxons under Hengist to Britain, to help fend off the attacks of the Picts and Scots.

Gwydawg   Son of Menestyr, killed Cei.

Hengist   Leader of the original Saxon mercenaries invited to Britain by Gworthigern.

Heuil   Pirate and reiver whose lair in the Iardomnan was destroyed by Arthur.

Hoewgi   The oldest of Mordav's cousins and heirs.

Iddawg   Once one of Arthur's Companions, opposed him at Camlann, and died there.

Isag   Monk at Angus's monastery.

Isgofan   Member of Custennin's warband assisting the Clan Menestyr.

Llacheu   Arthur's son, killed by Cei.

Lady, The   In the tale told by Regin, the Mother of All.

Lasrian   Monk at Angus's monastery.

Lleminawg   The Dancer, one of Arthur's Companions, descended from Irish settlers along the River Oak in Dumnonia. Accompanied Arthur to the Iardomnan and did not return.

Maelgwn   Lord of Gwynedd, son of Cadwallon. Young rival to Vortepor of Dyfed.

Magnus Maximus Or Macsen Wledig   Roman General of Spanish origin. While serving in Britain he declared himself Emperor of Rome in 383. He invaded Gaul, and was defeated and executed in 388. Many later British rulers claimed some connection with him.

Medraut Once one of Arthur's Companions, opposed him at Camlann and died there.

Meirion One of Mordav's cousins and heirs.

Melwas The Young Prince. Lord of the Summer Country, formerly betrothed to Gwenhwyvar.

Menestyr The name of a clan of tattooed men from the far north, the Sons or Children of Menestyr, and of its leader: Pedrylaw Menestyr 'The Skilled Cupbearer'.

Menw One of Arthur's Companions. Accompanied him to the Iardomnan and was later at Eidin.

Morfudd Abbess of St Helena and daughter of Gwaredur Bowback, one of the Companions who followed Medraut to Camlann.

Mordav Husband of Seradwen. Farmer and horsebreeder, who died very suddenly.

Nai Dumnonian warrior, member of Gereint's warband.

Ogrvran Gawr Father of Gwenhwyvar.

Pedrylaw See Menestyr.

Peythan One of the Clan Menestyr and father of Fferog.

Pryderi Legendary hero who gave his name to Prydein.

Regin Wandering bard from Dyfed.

Seradwen Horsebreeder and farmer. Widow of Mordav, and old friend of Nai.

Soemil First Saxon king of Dewr and grandfather of Wulfstan.

Syvno One of Mordav's cousins and heirs.

Teilo Steward of Angus's monastery.

Teleri Bard and daughter of Pedrylaw Menestyr. Once loved by Bedwyr.

Vitolinus See Gworthigern.

Vortepor High Lord of Dyfed, son of Agricola.

Vortigern See Gworthigern.

Wethenoc Monk at Angus's monastery.

Wulfstan Saxon, grandson of Soemil, king of Dewr. Friend of Llacheu, accompanied Angus to Eidin.

Ysgafnell In the tale told by Regin, one of the three sons of Dyssinendoth who led the invading Peryth.

For my parents

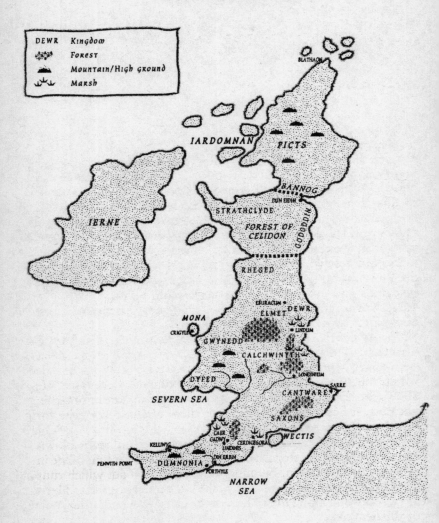

A MAP OF ALBION
AND THE ADJACENT ISLES

DEWR   Kingdom
        Forest
        Mountain/High ground
        Marsh

BLATHAON

IARDOMNAN   PICTS

IERNE

BANNOG

DUN EIDIN

STRATHCLYDE

FOREST OF
CELIDON

GODODDIN

RHEGED

EBURACUM   DEWR.

MONA   ELMET

CRUGYLL

LINDUM

GWYNEDD

CALCHWINTH

DYFED   LONDINIUM

SARRE

SEVERN SEA   CANTWARE

SAXONS

WECTIS

CAER
GADW

KELLIWIC   CERDICESORA

LINDINIS

PENWITH POINT   DUMNONIA   DIN EIRBIN

PORTHYLE

NARROW
SEA

PROLOGUE

Early in the morning he comes, riding the raised Roman causeway across the bleak countryside, his pony's hooves loud in the stillness. The fields below the embankment are patterned with drainage ditches, their edges limned with glittering ice harsh on the eye, and in the ditches sits water so black and heavy it seems incapable of movement. The sky is white and hard, huge all around him, and the marshy moors are silver in the cold clarity of morning.

The old man shivers, huddles into his cloak, but the cold bites deep into his bones, finds his scars and makes them ache, numbs his hands and feet despite the gauntlets and boots.

He had forgotten this, the bitter chill of the margins of the Summer Country in winter.

The paved road is fissured and broken, worn by rain and frost. The horse crunches and slithers on the ice that scums the puddles spilling across the stones, then splashes through in sheets of pale water, the droplets freezing as they cling to cloak and mane. He allows the creature to take its time, for there is no need of haste, not now. It has been ten years since there was last any need for haste along this road.

Faintly and from far away he hears the wail of gulls blown inland by the winter storms. Otherwise there is not a hint of life in all this vast desolation. Nothing moves on the road, which runs straight in either direction for as far as the eye can see. He is alone, crawling along the ribbon of the causeway under the vault of the heavens.

I

At length the monotony is broken by a low range of hills. One is higher than the rest, a whale-backed colossus towering above its fellows, the summit white with frost. He urges the horse forward, suddenly eager, and comes to a familiar branching in the road. He takes the southern fork, leaving the old Roman way to run unswerving to its destination, and turns onto a grassy track between high earthen hedges.

Signs of neglect are everywhere. Twice he is forced to dismount where the banks have slipped and buried the surface under a pile of earth and rocks. Once he fords a stream of which he has no recollection at all, though its course is well defined and clearly not new. If he did not know better, he would say nobody has travelled this route in decades.

The hill looms ever larger. From a distance it seems nothing has changed, except that smoke no longer curls across its heights. He can see the dark shapes of the buildings, and between them the main street winding up the slope to the Great Hall at the summit. He can see the winter green of the gardens and the pastures, the square of the practice grounds, even the wooden ramparts standing atop the drystone wall ringing the perimeter.

For a moment hope leaps in his heart.

From a distance, he thinks, from a distance one can delude oneself all is yet well with Caer Cadwy: that Glewlwyd of the Mighty Grasp still keeps the gate, announcing new arrivals; that the Companions still foregather in the Great Hall every evening to boast of battles fought and battles won; that Arthur, Emperor and Warlord of Albion, still sits in the High Seat dispensing justice to petitioners.

So he rides a little closer, and looks again.

Brush and saplings cling to the foot of the hill amidst the rotted stumps of their predecessors, dead these forty years or more. Long yellow grass has rooted in the rubble bank, blurring the once crisp outline. He casts his gaze upward and examines the decay in the timbers of the palisade, the red and black stains where the nails are slowly rusting into dust.

He shakes his head, follows the rutted track, the surface lost under mud and silt from the hillside, till he reaches the entrance tower. It looms above him, dark and forbidding; unadorned now, though once pennants would have fluttered from the platform. The great gates have gone, carried away for their timber and the iron bands which bound their planks together, leaving open the yawn of the tunnel beneath the tower.

The old man hesitates in the shadows at its foot, uncertain, a tremor in his hands where they clutch the leather reins. For this he has ridden miles through winter weather, and it would be easy, so easy, to turn again and ride away, leaving the ghosts undisturbed, leaving Caer Cadwy untouched in his memory . . .

He flings back his hood and squares his shoulders, preparing himself as once he prepared for battle, while the pony fidgets beneath him.

Then he rides through the tunnel, horse's hooves clattering in the darkness, and comes again into the grey winter light, and the road winds as it always wound, up the hill ahead of him.

The trees have grown. This is the first thing he notices. The young saplings have thickened and broadened, so the bare branches reach much farther than he remembers. The horse pastures beyond them are empty, the long grass ungrazed, white and withered by the winter winds.

Ten years of rain and snow have cut deep grooves in the surface of the road. New potholes have appeared, and old ones have reopened. The houses too have fallen into ruin. The thatched roofs are green with moss, and much of the render has fallen from the walls, exposing the timbers to the elements. Some buildings have already tumbled in upon themselves, collapsing under their own weight. Those that still stand will soon follow.

It was a mistake to come back.

These ruins were the dwellings and workshops of the crafts-men, the potters and smiths, the carpenters and horse-doctors – the huddled wreckage to his left, forlorn in the winter light, was surely where the cobbler who made such sturdy boots carried on his trade, and the fire-blackened shell beside it was the saddler's. The open ground beyond was where the markets within the walls were held, where one could barter for fish and fresh produce from the surrounding countryside, or jewellery both good quality and gimcrack, or clothing both elaborately beautiful and severely practical.

If he closes his eyes the old man can see it as it was, hear the hustle-bustle of a busy town neither Roman nor native British, but something in between. Here one might meet with big fair men and women from eastern and central Britain, descendants of the Gallic tribes; with the smaller darker folk of the west whose

3

forefathers are said to have come from Spain long before the twins dug the first foundations of Rome; with raw-boned redheads from the Caledonian Confederation north of the great Wall; with people of all sizes, shapes and colours whose ancestors had come to Britain from within the bounds of the old Roman Empire; and with the newcomers, the blond giants from beyond the Rhine, not all of whom were blond, and not all of whom, despite the rumours, were giants.

But when he opens his eyes again all he can see are the ruins, and the dead leaves and the long grass stirring in a bitter breeze. A tree squeaks in the background, one branch rubbing against another, and a sudden flurry flings a handful of rotted thatch across his path.

There is nothing here for him. This place is shunned, even by the locals, shunned as the haunt of ghosts and failed dreams.

He follows the road (having come this far he will continue to the end) while the wind rises around him. As he climbs the land unfolds, and rather than see what lies ahead he twists in the saddle to look behind.

The weather is altering. Black clouds scud across the sky, pregnant with sleet or rain. A flock of dark birds fight the wind, sink defeated to the woods below. Gulls cry, closer than before, wailing like the souls of the damned. The light has changed, and shadows chase each other across the countryside. The hills beyond the Black Moor are almost luminous, standing out with such clarity he can perceive details usually lost in the blue mists of distance.

He does not turn until he reaches the summit of the hill, the plateau where the Great Hall and its attendant buildings wait, abandoned these last ten years.

Here, if anywhere, was the heart of Albion. This fortress town of Caer Cadwy was the symbol of Arthur's power and majesty, the creation of his mind and will, much imitated by his rivals though never surpassed. And the Great Hall on the heights of the hill dominated the town even as Arthur dominated Britain, the lesser buildings spread around it like fledglings nestling in their mother's shadow.

Now there is nothing to dominate. The town of Caer Cadwy is empty, its roofs fallen, docks and brambles growing on the hearths. The kitchens reek of damp and decay where once fine cooking scented the air and roused the appetite. The chapel is deserted, the bishops and the priests are dead or long gone, the altar exposed to the wind and rain.

In his mind twenty or thirty years of memories meld, so that in the kitchens he sees red-faced Fracan running with sweat while cool Maia watches with detached amusement, though the two never worked together; and in the chapel he sees Bishop Enoch (whom he disliked with an intensity verging upon hatred) celebrating mass in company with the priest Kebi, who was not ordained until after Enoch's death.

Here if anywhere was and is the old man's home. This is the place whose image appears in his mind when he thinks of home, conjured in a way that the monastery in Armorica and the hermit's hut by the sea will never be conjured. This is the place where he loved and lost and loved again, where he found friendship truer and more lasting than love, where he tasted fear and enchantment, wonder and adventure, and savoured them all. This is the place where he found scholarship and learning mixed with knowledge and understanding, so that every day seemed to bring a new fascination. (Or so his memory tells him, though memory is notoriously fickle, and his has played him false before now.)

And thus he comes to the Great Hall itself. He dismounts, tosses the reins over the pony's head, leaving it to browse, and on stiff legs limps the last few paces to the entrance door with its ramshackle porch. Gulls scream above him, swoop and tumble around the sharp edges of the roof.

Again he hesitates, fearing that within he may see the shades of old comrades: the Long Man, Cei the Fair, the battle pillar of Britain, the best and bravest of Arthur's Companions; Gwalchmei the Hawk, the handsome man with the golden tongue; Lleminawg the Fated One, the Dancer by whose skill and courage the Sovereignty of Albion was brought to Arthur, its rightful owner. And perhaps he will see the shade of great Arthur himself, who was his friend, keeping court as he kept it in his prime, with Gwenhwyvar his lady at his side.

Or does he hesitate for fear that he may not see them, that all he will find within is an empty hall with a leaking roof, black mould staining the walls, the hearths long cold and the splendour long forgotten?

If he enters and finds the hall desolate (and in his heart, truly, he knows it will be so, for how could it be otherwise after all these

5

years?) then some part of his hopes will die. In his dreams this place has remained untouched by time, preserved like a leaf in amber: not as he saw it at the last before he rode forth to the final battle, but as it was when Arthur's empire was at its height, when the land was at peace and it seemed that though Rome might have failed Albion would rise like a phoenix from the ashes of the diocese of Britannia.

The rekindled flame burned only briefly. In the midst of the happiness the seeds of Camlann lay waiting, so now, looking back with the hindsight of another decade, it seems to him that Arthur's fall at the last battle was inevitable, that everything which happened led to that single moment. Perhaps the glorious time of Albion and empire was nothing more than an interlude in the civil wars which have rent this island these past hundred years or more (and for all he knows may rend it for the next hundred). Perhaps the realm he served so faithfully never existed outside the heads of a few deluded souls, perhaps it was never anything but a dream.

The door has dropped on its hinges. He lays his good hand upon the catch to lift it free, and pauses. The gulls circle frenziedly overhead, calling and calling in tones tinged with desperation.

The old man turns and looks behind him, standing on the high hilltop with the western lands spread at his feet. The wind is in his face, the sky black with the threat of rain. Here and there a shaft of sunlight shoots through the clouds and briefly illuminates a hilltop or a valley before being swallowed by the darkness. One such shaft moves along the causeway as if tracking his morning's journey, but is snuffed before it reaches the fork leading to Caer Cadwy.

In his mind he can hear Arthur's voice, oddly gentle, speaking the words he spoke on that last terrible night before they rode forth to fight and die at Camlann, the night when they knew that all those among the Companions who were still loyal were already within the walls of Caer Cadwy and there were no more left to come. He remembers looking around and seeing how pitifully few they were, realizing that on the morrow they must face the combined hosts of the traitor Medraut and his Saeson allies and that they would be overwhelmed by sheer numbers. It was then, in that moment of despair, that Arthur laid an arm across his shoulders and said: 'We are not quite done.'

At the time he was heartened, thinking the Emperor had some

plan, some stratagem of war as yet unrevealed. (After all, this was Arthur who spoke: Arthur, who knew more of warfare than any other then living in the island of Britain; Arthur, who had never been defeated in battle.) And indeed in a sense they did win Camlann, in that Medraut, Iddawg and the rest were slain, their armies annihilated, their ambitions thwarted.

But since then, in the long and lonely years spent first as a monk in Lesser Britain and then a hermit by the sea in southern Dumnonia, he has often pondered the Emperor's words, wondering whether he meant anything so simple. Arthur must have known, as did the rest of the Companions, that whatever happened on the morrow Albion was doomed. A decisive victory like Badon was beyond their grasp; the best they could hope for was that a handful of them would be left holding the field.

They were not even granted that. (Which is why of course nobody won Camlann, why it is a nonsense to think in those terms.) Arthur took one last terrible head wound and vanished from sight, falling into the turmoil of mud and hooves as the survivors forced flagging horses to lumber in a final mockery of a charge through the thickening mist and rain.

(And yet there were victors of Camlann: the ones who did not themselves take part but sent support to Medraut in more subtle ways, men like Vortepor of Dyfed and Cerdic of the Saeson Gewisse, men who have prospered since that time. And this too Arthur must have known.)

The storm beats down upon him. A shingle clatters down the roof until it reaches the eaves, where it hurls itself into space. The pony, which has huddled in the lee of the Great Hall for shelter, starts and whinnies. The old man wakens to the present, to his soaked face and hair, the winter cloak hanging sodden and heavy on his shoulders. The rain sweeps across the plateau, blots the decaying remnants of the town from view, and he is not sorry that it should be so.

'We are not quite done.'

Did Arthur mean anything beyond momentary encouragement to a faltering comrade? Is it wishful thinking to believe otherwise?

Or was there some hidden meaning? Did he somehow know that against all odds one man at least would survive the last battle? Was he saying that there would be a future after the morrow, that all would not be lost?

And now, as the old man raises his face again to the heavens

7

and the rain streams down his cheeks mingling with his tears, he knows it does not matter, for regardless of Arthur's meaning it is true.

'We are not quite done.'

As the wind and rain abated Bedwyr left the hall behind him, walked down the slope towards what had been his house, his feet finding the path though the cobbles were buried under a coating of slick grass and mud.

In his mind he pictured the plateau as it had been in the very early days, forty years ago, when Arthur first refurbished this ancient site. This area was planned in detail, the shape of each building pegged out before the work began, and though later changes and additions blurred the symmetry, one could still see its outlines – perhaps all the more clearly because now it lay in ruins.

(A cluster of workmen around Arthur and Gwenhwyvar on the summit of the hill, debating how the hall should lie, and the tall figure of Cei wandering away from the crowd with his infant daughter perched on his shoulders, urging her to choose a site for their house, their very own house. And Celemon, face solemn as only a child's can be, picking the place.)

Forty years ago. And though time had dimmed his memory, those broken walls with the leafless branches of a hawthorn poking out above them must have been Cei's house, on the very site Celemon chose that spring day, only a short distance away from his own.

The winter grass was wet and dark beneath Bedwyr's boots. The path was steeper than he recalled. The wind soughed through the ruins as he stumbled the last few steps to the ivy clad mound which had once been his home.

He could not enter.

The doorway – a mere gap in the humped and rounded walls – was full of rubble and old wood. The space beyond seemed tiny now it was open to the sky, far too tiny for the house he remembered. The enclosure smelled of winter damp and decay, was choked with brown ferns and briers growing from a mat of rotting thatch. He gazed at the tangled undergrowth filling the hollow where he had dwelt with Garwen his wife, where later (for a few short nights) he had brought his lover Teleri, and realized there would in any case be no purpose in entering. What there

8

was to be seen could be seen from where he stood, and the spirit of the place had long since departed.

Head bowed, he regarded the ruin a while longer. To an onlooker it might have seemed as if he was deep in prayer, but in fact his mind was empty of all coherent thought, lost in a jumble of images from the irretrievable past: Teleri's strong-boned face in the winter firelight; Garwen laughing uneasily as she handed him a bowl of broth; Amren their son turning angrily in the door to fling a final word of defiance; Cei stooping beneath the lintel, carrying an old sword he had captured from a Saeson and brought to show his friend; Celemon daughter of Cei proffering a bunch of primroses . . .

At length he straightened, lips moving silently, and stared at the building which loomed on the slope above. The long, high roof dominated the skyline, plain and unadorned in comparison with the halls of the Saeson lords – there were no carvings on the end gables, no antlers nailed to the porch – for this had been the hall of a civilized man.

Bedwyr sighed. Now that he was here his long pilgrimage seemed pointless, an exercise in melancholy. Slowly he retraced his footsteps up the hill, following the old path between the ruins, and he came again to the broken porch with its leaking roof. Water from the storm was running down the walls, and a puddle had formed where the passage of many feet had worn a hollow outside the door. Suddenly weary, he put his hand upon the latch, lifted the door and pushed it open.

Inside was darkness, and the now familiar smell of damp and rot. Glimmers of light came through the roof, and at first that was all he could see, chinks like stars above and the great gloom stretching out before him. He stood in the doorway, listening to the steady drip of water falling from the roof both inside and outside, and as his eyes began to adapt he saw that the hall was empty of all furnishings. The long tables, the bronze hanging bowls, the fleece-covered benches and couches, had gone from the body of the hall, and the walls, which had been lined with fine needlework or decorated with shields and highly polished parade armour, were bare of decoration.

To his left was the partition wall, carved with images of the great hero Cadwy whose hilltop this had been long before it became Arthur's. (Some said that Arthur was Cadwy come again, and certainly the exploits of the two were often muddled in the

9

tales told around winter firesides.) In the dim light from the doorway he could see a grey bloom on the surface of the wood. He ran his gauntleted hands across the closest panel, breaking the sheen of the mould, traced the outline of Cadwy battling the water-horse on the banks of the River Isk.

He took a pace deeper into the darkness, strained his eyes against the shadows. In places the plaster had fallen from the walls, leaving oddly shaped black patches like charts of unknown islands. Over in the far corner, near the dais where Arthur and Gwenhwyvar had sat when holding court, was a trail of pale grey splatters that culminated in a black mound on the floor; his gaze followed the trail up into the rafters and found the huddled form that perched there, light from the broken roof striping the soft body with bars of gold.

He moved forward, skirting the row of empty hollows that ran down the middle of the hall, the hearth-pits which had once provided the inhabitants with both heat and light. His feet crunched across the debris littering the floor: shards of pottery, lumps of old clinker from the fires, the bones of small animals.

A round eye opened, stared down through the gloom. The head unwound on the body, and the hooked beak flashed from darkness to light as the great white wings stretched, unfurled, flapped in disapproval at the intrusion, the feathers sharp along the lower edge like serrations on a knife blade.

The owl hissed, revolved its head, and slowly settled on its perch, though the eye remained fixed upon him.

(Once, scrying in a pool of water for some sign of Gwenhwyvar, he had seen a vision of a white owl roosting in a tree, and had laughed to himself, knowing that wherever she might be the Lady was well protected.)

'Where?' he said to the bird, to the hall, his voice hollow in the emptiness. 'Where is she?'

The owl drew itself to its full height, seeming to double in size, unfurled its wings a second time and beat them rapidly in the air.

'Where did she go?'

The bird snorted contemptuously, then whistled at him.

He clutched the sword hilt under his heavy cloak with the broken claw of his left hand, and strode the length of the hall, leaving the owl muttering to itself among the rafters.

He knew the story – who did not? – of what had happened when news of the disaster at Camlann was brought to Caer

Cadwy. Fifty or a hundred times he had heard the tale told in the refectory of the monastery in Lesser Britain, told by every wanderer eager to pay for a night's hospitality, had heard the endless speculation about where she had gone, the fairest woman in all Prydein, the white phantom, Gwenhwyvar, Arthur's Queen.

Ten years ago, on a dull day in early autumn after one of the worst summers in living memory, Arthur had gone forth from Caer Cadwy, taking with him every able-bodied man. The Emperor's enemies were gathering fast: a horde of Saesons had come up from the south to meet with Iddawg and his British force on the edge of the sea marshes which protected the north-eastern flank of the Dumnonian peninsula. Now they awaited the arrival of the third part of their army, led by the arch traitor Medraut, which was rapidly approaching from the heartlands of Britain. The conspirators believed they had caught Arthur una-wares, held him pent in Caer Cadwy, cut off from all his supporters save those in western Dumnonia.

But Arthur marched, and fell upon them before their hosting was complete. He destroyed Iddawg and his Saeson allies before Medraut could reach the field, then turned like a great bear brought to bay to face Medraut and his cohorts. By the time darkness came on the day following the Emperor's departure from Caer Cadwy it was all over.

For those who remained behind those two days of waiting were the worst they had ever known. All the menfolk save the very old or very young had gone with the warband, with the Companions. Even some of the merchants from the town below the Great Hall had found a spear or a long knife and marched with the foot.

At first Gwenhwyvar busied herself in organizing the defences – there was always the possibility Medraut would take the gamble of avoiding Arthur and laying siege to Caer Cadwy instead – but that did not occupy her for long. The old men, semi-crippled and infirm though they might be, were veterans of the Emperor's campaigns. In the present emergency old rivalries and dislikes were forgotten, so men who had not spoken to each other for half a lifetime stood shoulder to shoulder on the walls, watching and waiting.

Then she visited the infirmary, but here too all was in a state of readiness. It might have been nearly fifteen years since a major battle had been fought on the soil of Albion, but the old skills had not been forgotten. Those doctors who had not accompanied the army were prepared for the influx of wounded, were well supplied with herbs and dressings, with cloth for bandages and blankets. Their tools were freshly polished and sharpened, laid out neatly on the tables, and they say Gwenhwyvar shuddered at the sight before commending the surgeons on their foresight.

After that all she could do was wait.

A few of her ladies stayed with her. The Court had scattered during the bad summer, gone home to their own estates to do whatever they could to help as the poor harvest was gathered in, and most had not had the chance to return. When word spread that Iddawg and Medraut were on the march, those still loyal among the Companions had ridden day and night to reach the Emperor, but they had left their womenfolk behind.

Celemon daughter of Cei was there, a big woman who had inherited her father's bone structure and colouring. Her yellow hair was threaded with silver at the temples now, and she was more solid than she had been in her youth, but the years had brought her dignity and great presence. She and Gwenhwyvar were old friends: at one stage she had been a kind of surrogate daughter, but as the years passed so the gap between their ages had seemed to close.

Nobody ever received false comfort from Celemon. Others might prate of how all would be well at the end, of how Arthur had never been defeated in battle, of how the Kings of Britain would ride to the Emperor's aid – 'What, let the Amherawdyr fall, and go back to the bad old days of Vitolinus the High King? They'll never allow it!' – while Gwenhwyvar sat and listened, knowing full well that the Princes of Prydein would not only allow it but that most of them actually wanted it, though they lacked the courage to strike as Medraut had struck.

Celemon was aware the Companions had gone to almost certain death, was aware there was little hope of Arthur returning victorious. She was no stranger to tragedy: her father and brother had been cut down before her eyes fourteen years earlier, and few were now living of the men who had ridden her on their shoulders when she was a child. Her talk was therefore practical, suiting Gwenhwyvar's mood, and on that first night the two of them sat late in the Lady's own chambers, making and discarding plans.

Thus they were still awake when the messenger arrived, and

told them of Arthur's movements, of how the Emperor had come unseen to within a few miles of his enemies, and of how on the morrow he intended to take Iddawg by surprise.

'And Medraut?' demanded Gwenhwyvar.

'He is close, Lady, close,' replied the messenger, 'but he cannot reach the field until noon at the earliest. The Amherawdyr plans to give Lord Bedwyr command of the army for the first part of the battle, while he himself waits with the reserves. Bedwyr will destroy Iddawg and his Saeson allies, then be left sitting like a fruit ripe for the plucking when Medraut arrives. Once Medraut is embroiled, Arthur will strike!'

The women nodded, seeing that it might work. Arthur's sudden arrival on the field would give his tired men new strength to counter Medraut's fresh troops.

'Bedwyr,' Celemon said, with affection. 'Loyal to the end.'

'They planned it together,' the messenger said proudly, 'Bedwyr and the Amherawdyr. I saw them both, sitting beneath an old thorn tree like men with not a care in the world, laughing and joking as they contrived their design.'

The women exchanged a glance. The messenger saw the expression on their faces and realized his attempt to cheer them had failed. All three in that room were well aware of why Arthur and Bedwyr sat joking in the public gaze, displaying themselves before their troops.

'And the mood of the men?' asked Gwenhwyvar.

'They are confident, and determined.'

'Truly?'

The messenger met her eyes with his own, returned her steady stare unwavering. 'Lady, they will not fail him, not now or ever. The Companions will fight because it is their nature to fight, without questions or doubts. The foot will fight because they love him, because he is Arthur, because his dream of Albion is what has kept this land safe and secure these past twenty years or more. They love him because he can sit under a thorn tree on the eve of what may be his last battle, against odds so overwhelming most commanders would abandon their men to their fate and seek safety in flight, sit and laugh with his lieutenant.'

'We always knew,' said Gwenhwyvar, 'that the greatest danger would come from within. It was not the Saesons we feared, but the Princes of Britain.'

'Many are still loyal,' the messenger said eagerly. 'Cunomorus marches from the west. He should arrive on the field late tomorrow. We believe others are coming from the north and east, though the enemy lies between and it is hard for word to reach us.'

'What is it called, this place where the battle will be fought?' asked Celemon.

'Camlann.'

The word echoed round the room.

'The crooked bank.' Gwenhwyvar's voice was soft. 'In years to come they will speak of the three futile battles of the island of Britain: Cat Achren, where the trees fought at the behest of the ancient lords of the land; the fight at Velenrid, where the hero Pryderi was slain by the wiles of an Enchanter; and Camlann, where Arthur and Medraut . . .'

She choked and did not finish.

The messenger was sent away to rest a while before he returned to the emperor. Gwenhwyvar and Celemon remained alone in the Lady's private quarters, and perhaps they slept a little, or perhaps they passed the night in talking – nobody knows, for there was no one to see. Shortly before dawn they appeared together on the walls of the fortress, bearing bowls of hot broth for those standing guard.

'Today will be the day,' said one of the veterans, as he drained the bowl and limped stiffly across the parapet to give it back to Celemon. 'The Amherawdyr will not fail.'

Gwenhwyvar smiled, but her countenance was drawn and lined in the pale light.

'I remember how we fought in the Hills of Agned on a morning much like this,' said the old man, turning his face to the dawn. 'Mist and rain, worsening as the day went on. We were outnumbered then as well, and facing an alliance of Saesons and Painted Men from the far north. But we hit them before they could unite: caught the Picts in disarray while they were still on the road, then swung south to deal with the Saeson dogs.'

He laughed, chewed his lip. 'Fast and furious, it was. I remember your father, Lady Celemon, remember him standing head and shoulders above the rest, his horse killed under him, laughing at the Saesons as they ran at him, desperate to bring him down and thus blunt the force of the Companions' charge. Ha! Small hope of that! "When Cei came into battle, he slew as would a hundred," the poet says, and rightly, rightly.' He nodded to himself.

'But Cei comes into battle no more,' murmured Celemon.

'Bedwyr is there,' the old man returned sharply. 'And many of the younger generation.'

She put a hand on his arm. 'Yes, of course. Forgive me, old friend. I thought merely of my father.'

Mollified, the veteran smiled. 'It will not be long now. Perhaps they will parley first – it would be the Amherawdyr's way to give them a chance to go home in peace, even at this late hour. But soon the horns will be blowing and the drone will be rising in the throats of the Companions, and there will be red blades along the banks of the River Cam.'

As he spoke he took his spear, jabbed and thrust at imaginary foes, and all the while the light strengthened, though the mist hung thick and heavy from the sky.

Gwenhwyvar gathered together the remainder of the bowls. 'Come, Celemon, we must be about our business,' she said, and moved to the steps leading down from the wall.

'We shall not forget, Lady,' called the old man. 'On this day, this dire morn, you fed us with your own hands. God's blessing upon you, Lady.'

His comrades echoed him, and they say Gwenhwyvar's cheeks, hitherto pale from lack of sleep, were flushed as she descended the steps.

There is another gap now, a gap of several hours during which perhaps she slept (though this seems unlikely, given that she must have been coiled tight with anxiety). More probably she passed the time in prayer or contemplation, as did many others throughout the town. Indeed, there was a heavy silence upon Caer Cadwy that grey day, a silence so deep one would have thought it already the ghost town it was to become in later years. Even the little children were hushed and solemn at their play, taking their lead from their elders, and when one fell down and cut his knee his cries echoed through the empty streets and a dozen women sprang from their homes to his aid, where normally there would have been too much noise for anybody to notice the minor distress of one small boy.

At length another rider came, pushing a tired horse to its limits, making for the north-eastern gate. The sentries saw him through the mist and fine drizzle, called down from the battlements, and soon gathered a crowd which lined the roadway.

He rode through the gates, reeling with tiredness, his cloak ripped and muddied, his tunic stained with blood. But there was a grin on his face, and he shouted to the silent crowd the moment he was through the tunnel:

'The day goes well!'

A huge sigh went up from them, and they followed him up the hill to the Great Hall, where Gwenhwyvar awaited word of her lord.

The veterans had to lift him from the saddle, for his legs would not obey him. They half carried him into the hall, and the crowd entered after them, shuffling through the doors and spreading into the brightly lit space as a flood of water spreads across a floor.

Gwenhwyvar was upon the dais, seated on the High Seat she shared with the Emperor, and Celemon stood to her right as Cei had once stood beside Arthur, and there they waited, the two golden ladies of Albion, while the old men brought the second of Arthur's messengers to them.

'Greetings, Lady. I bring tidings from Arthur Amherawdyr Albion, Master of the Armies of Prydein,' he began formally, then choked and fell into a coughing fit.

'Bring him a chair, and wine,' commanded Gwenhwyvar. Only her hands, white where they gripped the arms of the throne, betrayed the tension within her as she waited for the messenger to continue.

'It goes well, Lady,' said the man after a while. 'We caught them at dawn, as we had planned, took them by surprise. Bedwyr led us, Bedwyr the Swift, the one-handed hero, brought us surging down the hill onto Iddawg's cavalry in a single glorious charge that cut them to pieces. Then – and I do not believe any other man in all the world could have done it, unless it was Arthur himself, for you know what it is like when the horns are blowing and the hooves are drumming – he made us rein in, reform as if we were on the parade ground, and start upon the Saeson foot where they waited like dogs in their pen.' He shook his head in admiration, added gleefully: 'What a man he is, Bedwyr Bedrydant, Bedwyr of the Perfect Sinews. He took Iddawg himself, smote him from the saddle with a single blow.'

'And Arthur?' The Queen leant forward, her hair golden in the torchlight.

'Ah, there is the cleverness of it! Arthur waits upon the hill, waits for the traitor Medraut, and the sight of him in his cloak of royal purple adds the strength of ten to our arms. When I took this – ' he indicated the bloodstain on his tunic '– we were still softening the Saesons, but the final blow cannot have been far away.'

'So still no word of Medraut?'

The messenger sobered suddenly. 'No, Lady, not when I left. But by now . . .' He glanced at the roof rafters as if trying to estimate the time, shrugged.

Gwenhwyvar bit her lip, turned to Celemon as if seeking support. But before the younger woman could react she seemed to gather herself, the momentary weakness forgotten.

'See to his wounds,' she said, signalling to the servants.

They came forward to carry the man away to the infirmary, and he went protesting that he must return to his lord while she watched grim-faced. When he had gone she murmured so softly only those at the very forefront of the crowd could hear: 'At least I have brought one man alive from Camlann,' and then she rose in a sudden movement that caught them all by surprise, and departed to her own quarters.

The day wore on, interminably slow, and the weather worsened steadily. The drizzle turned to real rain, the kind that soaks through cloak and tunic alike, and the mist thickened as the light failed so dusk came earlier than usual, though it did not seem early to those who waited at Caer Cadwy.

One of the old men slipped on the greasy wood of the walkway while patrolling the wall and broke his leg. Gwenhwyvar and Celemon visited him in the infirmary, found him sitting up cracking jokes about the attention he was receiving, all those idle doctors and surgeons dancing attendance on their second patient of the day.

'We must do something about the walkway,' said Celemon as they left. 'Spread ash or grit to make it less slippery.'

Gwenhwyvar was walking with her hands clasped behind her back, lost in thought. When she made no reply, Cei's daughter frowned and repeated her remark while studying the older woman out of the corner of one eye.

Gwenhwyvar shook herself, like one roused from a deep reverie. 'I am sorry?' she said vaguely.

Celemon repeated her remark for the third time. Gwenhwyvar nodded absently. 'Yes, I suppose we should, though it does not matter much now. See to it, if you will.'

She raised her face to the sky. 'The wind is rising. I think the last of Arthur's messengers will arrive soon.' Shivering, she turned to Celemon. 'It is finished. Arthur is gone.'

There were tears running down her cheeks, and Celemon, usually so calm and competent, quailed before the other's certainty.

'How . . .?'

'Can you not feel it?' Her voice was cold and hard. 'All day the land has wept for what must come. Now darkness has fallen, and the realm of Albion is lost.'

Filled with sudden purpose, she strode across the yard between the infirmary and the Great Hall, leaving Celemon standing in the open space, while the wind blew away the low cloud that had hung about the hilltop since the dawn.

All the accounts agree that when the third and final messenger came, riding through the twilight as if a host of Saesons were on his heels, Gwenhwyvar was waiting on the ramparts. This time there was no ceremony. The rider flung himself from his mount while Gwenhwyvar descended the steps, and they met at the foot. Torches flared as men came running, and by their light she heard the news. (If indeed it was news to her, who seemed to know already.)

The threefold battle of Camlann was over. Both Arthur and Medraut were lost, and scarcely a man was left unhurt. The remnants of the Companions held the field, said the messenger, and awaited the coming of Cunomorus. The survivors of Medraut's followers had fled into the night, a broken rabble.

'And Bedwyr?' demanded the Lady when he had finished.

The messenger shook his head. 'I do not know. He was alive when the Amherawdyr fell, but after that . . .'

His voice trailed away. The torches crackled and spluttered, flickered in the wind. Gwenhwyvar looked round at the ring of stunned and silent faces, waiting for her to give them the lead.

'It is finished,' she said loudly. She took a step, seemed to stumble, regained her balance. The crowd stood unmoving, not understanding.

'Why do you stare at me so?' she cried, and put her hands to her face.

They shuffled uneasily, their own shock so great none of them knew what to do, or how to comfort her.

'Do you not see? Nothing remains.'

18

One of the veterans made a half pace forward. 'Lady, you are still the High Queen, still the Empress,' he pleaded.

Ashen in the torchlight she reached out to touch his arm, drew him close. 'There is no Empire.' He flinched away from the intensity of her words, but she continued relentlessly, speaking to them all:

'Albion is fallen. Without Arthur we will return to the bad old days of Vitolinus and Ambrosius, become a mass of minor states and petty princelings constantly quarrelling one with another. For twenty years, Arthur has held the Sovereignty of Albion. Now he is gone, and he leaves no heir, for our sons are dead. Had Medraut not proved so impatient he might in a few years' time have had for the asking what he sought to take by force of arms.'

She choked, swayed beneath the yellow torches, recovered. 'Perhaps it would have been better if Arthur had abdicated in Medraut's favour rather than force the issue.'

'Never!' called someone from the back of the crowd, and the rest growled in agreement.

'Nobody would have followed him,' shouted another. 'Medraut the Traitor.'

'Curse him, curse him,' cried a third.

'But what is done is done,' she said as if none of them had spoken. She ran her hands through her hair, looked about her like one waking from a dream. 'Celemon will give you your orders.'

She walked through them, slowly, carefully, and they parted before her as cattle might part before a herd-dog. Because they were still half dazed by the news from Camlann, they did not realize what she was doing until she had brought the horse, black as midnight, out from the shelter of the building where she had hidden it, and swung herself into the saddle.

The horse stretched and leapt forward. The crowd scattered, suddenly awakened to life, buzzed like a hive of bees as a few foolhardy souls grabbed for the reins and missed. The hooves clattered on the cobbles, left sparks glowing briefly in their wake.

'Wait!' somebody shouted, but she paid no heed.

The black horse was through the gate and running down the road with the wind at its back, and all that remained to the crowd was the memory of the High Queen, hair wild about her face, riding into darkness like a creature out of legend.

And they say that no man knows where she went or what became of her.

Bedwyr studied the carved screen which divided the hall into two parts. In one panel the hero Cadwy stood on a hilltop with a handful of followers, facing the host of his enemies. In the next, the hero gave voice to the great shout which shattered his enemies' swords and spears to fragments. Bedwyr pulled off his gauntlet and touched the hero's face, remembering the bright summer morning when the craftsmen fixed the panels to the wall. The wood was smooth to his fingers, smooth and hard, the hero's cheek swelling in a sudden fierce curve that ended in the gape of the open mouth.

It was not true that no man knew where Gwenhwyvar went when she left Caer Cadwy. He knew, because she had come to him.

He turned and studied the aisle posts supporting the roof. In his mind he saw them adorned with whitewashed shields, with iron parade armour gleaming blue in the light from the central fires and the bronze hanging lamps. Now they were black with ten years of dirt and grime, festooned with thick threads of cobweb.

Frowning, he let his gaze roam up from the shallow footings of the posts to the crossbeam which bound them together, and thence into the tracery of rafters which held the roof. The hall was the work of skilled carpenters, who had chosen to use cunningly crafted joints rather than nails, who had set timber into timber to create a frame that relied upon the sum of its parts for its strength, a mass of stresses and strains kept in perfect balance. If, as was often said, the builders of Rome had been masters of stone, then the builders of Albion had been masters of wood.

The owl had decided this lone human was harmless and settled back to sleep on its perch above the dais. Bedwyr stared at the shapeless huddle, knowing there must be meaning here even though he could not fathom what that meaning might be, and shook his head.

The latch clicked quietly into place as he lifted the door shut, leaving the hall to its ghosts. The pony nickered a greeting from beside the wall, returned to its grazing. The storm had blown over but the sky was grey with layers of cloud, the lower levels thin wisps moving rapidly to the south-east, writhing like dragons, while the higher levels were still and stately banks piled one atop another, reaching to tremendous heights. Yet within this solid seeming mass there must have been tunnels and deep chasms, for rays of sunlight played upon the face of the clouds and upon the ground, lighting the way north-east.

Bedwyr sighed. That was the direction he had intended to travel, though not with any eagerness. If he had been loath to visit Caer Cadwy, he was even more reluctant to take the next step.

For a final time he looked across the ruins of the town, fixing them in his mind: the dark buildings, the brambles and the weeds growing in the streets, the air of desolation and abandonment. All his life melancholy had infested him as marsh fever infests a man, so that every time he thought himself cured it swept through him afresh, and if any scene could be described as melancholy it was this.

Yet what he felt now was not melancholy but an emotion so unexpected he did not at first recognize it, though he felt it opening within him like a tightly furled flower unfolding its petals to greet the sun, or like a white bird waking from sleep to loose its wings and beat the currents of the air, felt it coursing through him with such force he stumbled and nearly fell.

It was joy, unconditional and unalloyed, joy that bubbled within him so he turned his face to the wind and laughed aloud.

CHAPTER ONE

1

Nai pulled the spears from the ground, straightened and stood for a moment studying the shadow of the winter clouds on the hillside across the estuary. The day was chilly and the wind was strong, carrying the roar of the sea to his ears. Far away inland was a hint of white under the grey sky, as if there might be snow on the high ground. He shivered at the thought, drew a deep breath, the air cold in his chest.

Turning, Nai was aware of how awkward the shield felt on his left arm. The months spent recovering from the wounds of the summer had left him unaccustomed to its weight: his body was unbalanced, top heavy. Gritting his teeth, he glared towards the target, growling softly.

It was tiny and seemed a very long way off. With the trees tossing behind it, the sack – stuffed full of ferns to make the shape of a man – looked like some monstrous creature that had ventured out from the woods in search of prey.

The spears were in his left hand and the wind was at his back. Nai grinned to himself, his flash of temper gone, and rolled his torso a few times to loosen the muscles. He took a few more deep breaths to fill his lungs, then started his run down the slope.

His shield arm came up and passed the first spear to his right hand. He was running very upright, chest full and proud, head level, eyes following his left side as that shoulder came forward.

His right shoulder went back, he rose on his legs and heels without breaking stride, using the line of his shield arm to sight and aim.

As he threw the first javelin his left hand dropped the next into place, to be seized by the other hand and whirled back over his head. There was a feeling of smoothness and rightness to the movements, and he knew that to an observer it would seem as if his arms were part of a great wheel, relentlessly lowering and launching spears.

These were lightweight spears, so he held them a third of the way down from the head, resting the shaft in his palm, fingers curled around the wood in a grip relaxed but firm, thumb along the length, hand turned inwards to create the best position for his elbow and shoulder. Light javelins had a long reach but tended to wander off target, at the mercy of the wind and any imperfections in their own design. Even a slight warp in the shaft could render a spear almost useless except at point blank range.

But today the wind was behind him, pushing both him and the spears towards the trees. The sixth and last javelin left his hand, and still without breaking stride he brought the shield up and over his head to cover his back. The spears were falling beautifully on the target, bursting through the old sacking and ferns to land quivering in the ground. He drew his war-knife and returned the shield to its normal position, then cut and slashed at the imaginary foes from whom he had been guarding his back. A pulse pounded in his ears as he twisted and turned to avoid their counters, the shield and the long knife weapons alike as he smote his way through a host of enemies, until at last he collapsed panting on the ground beside the straw dummy.

His strength and stamina were returning. There had been days when he had wondered whether it was worth the effort, but now, lying with the winter grass damp against his cheek and the breath wheezing in his lungs, he knew the answer.

Yesterday he had run the perimeter of Sanctuary Wood in his warshirt of hammered iron links, with his shield on his back and his foster brother Gorthyn's sword slung from his shoulder, and that was a feat he could not have managed before. At the end he had been staggering like a drunken man, and it had been a long time before his limbs had stopped shaking, but he had done it.

Nai rolled over and stared up at the target. Looked at from below the sacking bore no resemblance to a human being. The spears had opened fresh rents in the material, and sprigs of the bracken he had used to pad the sack poked through the holes. He rose, freed his arm from the shield straps and hung the shield on his back where it would not get in the way. Then he fiddled the stuffing into shape again, closing the wounds with his fingers and debating whether he needed to take a needle to the sacking or whether it could withstand a few more rents.

Behind him a flock of rooks lumbered into the air, shrieking loudly. They wheeled once around their roosting place and scattered across the forest, croaking and calling their complaint.

He scanned the dark outline of the trees, a spear in his hand though he had no memory of plucking it from the ground. A row of scraggly pines protected the wood from the worst of the storms blowing in off the sea. From where he stood on the slope of the hill he could look between the thin trunks and into the depths of the forest, a wintry tangle of dead leaves and black branches reaching to the low grey sky. Of whatever had aroused the rooks there was no sign.

In the distance he could hear the rhythm of the sea beating on the cliffs. All around was the rustle of small creatures scurrying through the brittle brown undergrowth. The wind whispered in the pines, whispered of old battles and comrades long dead.

The hairs were bristling on the nape of his neck. Somebody was close, somebody who did not wish to announce their presence, but who had been careless in passing near the rooks. Not a friend, seeking to surprise him, for it was only three days since Cadlew and Addonwy had last ridden out from the garrison at Penhyle. They would not be back so soon, and he could think of nobody else who would not have announced themselves by now.

Nai wrenched the remaining javelins from the earth and ran down the slope to the wood, his tiredness forgotten, the shield bouncing on his back, the scent of pines in his nostrils and the shouting of the rooks in his ears. He did not stop until he was safely beneath the shadow of the firs.

Six spears, war-knife and shield. He was wearing leathers, not mail, though leather did at least have the advantage of blending into the background. With luck this was a false alarm – or, failing that, he would be able to avoid his visitors in the depths of the wood. But he needed to know who they were and what they wanted.

At this time of year it was unlikely they had come from the sea, which in turn meant they were unlikely to be Scotti or Saesons, the twin scourges of the coast. So if not raiders from the sea, then what?

He shifted uneasily, snuffed the air like a dog, and went silently between the trees (his trees, was how he thought of them now), walking on the edges of his feet, checking every step for twigs that might snap under his weight, moving with a rolling rhythm through the obstacles, slipping from side to side through the brambles, one spear in his right hand and five clutched in his left.

The woods were still green despite the lack of leaves on the trees. Moss flourished everywhere, on rock and bark alike, while ivy thickened the boles, clung to the branches, trailed between the saplings, narrowing the view down to a matter of a few paces. He crouched low, slid beneath the hanging boughs, feeling the fragile winter twigs dragging at his hair, rubbing on his shield.

A motionless man always has the advantage over a man who is moving, so from time to time Nai stopped to listen intently, staring about him for some sign of movement. The longer he looked without finding his unexpected visitors the more convinced he became that they must be hostile.

He guessed they would have come along the track from Penhyle, the settlement at the head of the estuary. They would have followed the ridge until the track dropped down into the ruins of what had once been a village beside a creek. There, almost certainly, they would have taken the fast fading traces of the path leading from the village to the Sanctuary in the wood. Somewhere near the Sanctuary enclosure they had disturbed the rooks. After that true paths would have failed them – though there were plenty of deer trails wandering towards the cliffs.

So where were they?

Nai pressed his back against a beech tree (the rim of his shield cutting into his shoulders) and quartered his surrounds. To his left two birds were quarrelling noisily. A robin watched him from a fallen tree buried in a veil of brambles. Something small scuttered through the dead undergrowth. A horse bridle jingled far off to his right, in the direction of the Sanctuary.

He ran, wishing Gorthyn were with him. The two of them had ridden and fought as a pair all their lives, and it seemed unnatural to be alone. Grief for his friend awoke within him, like an old wound that one had thought healed suddenly breaking out afresh, and he almost missed his footing as the cold wind made his eyes water.

Soon he saw the straight boughs of the ancient oaks that ringed the clearing at the core of the woods. He slowed his pace, slid silently across the thick mulch of dead leaves, eased his way up the earthen bank that surrounded the Sanctuary, using the roots as footholds, and merged his body with the rough bark of an oak. Bending low, he slipped his head around the trunk, his movements slow and deliberate so as not to attract attention.

Three horses grazed idly near the middle of the clearing, their flanks still streaked with drying sweat. One man stood beside them, his face turned away from Nai, stamping his feet and beating his arms about his torso to keep warm. Behind the man were the broken fragments of the basin that had channelled the spring which rose in the centre of the lawn. Now the water seeped aimlessly across the grass, turning the heart of the Sanctuary into a muddy bog.

The horses seemed normal enough: shaggy-coated and rough-maned ponies, with the customary collection of gear slung from the saddles and blankets. There was nothing about them to give any clue to their origins. The man also was what one might expect: long-haired and bareheaded despite the wind, clad in a faded tartan cloak and a dull brown tunic.

Nai took a deep breath, shifted his grip on the javelin in his right hand, and slid down the bank into the enclosure, careless of the noise.

'Welcome!' he called as he found his footing on the lawn.

The ponies started at the harsh sound of his voice, moved from hoof to hoof, snorting and rolling their eyes. The man swung, hand going to the long knife at his belt, tossing the folds of his cloak back over his shoulders out of the way.

Nai froze at the sight of the stranger's face.

It was green and blue between the black hair and beard, monstrous and inhuman, like something out of a tale told to frighten children, a demon from the deep forests. The creature was rushing towards him, war-knife drawn and ready, and he was standing useless with his mouth wide open, unable to move, while the hideous face loomed larger and larger, slim braids bouncing on either side of the head.

He threw at the last moment and leapt aside.

The man stumbled past, crumpled in the middle and crashed into the bank. The spear shaft snapped with a report that echoed round the enclosure and set the horses dancing. Nai stood still, staring at the body as it trembled with the passion of death (the fingers scrabbling among the leaves), himself shaking with the suddenness of what had happened.

When it was finished he rolled the body over. The head flopped back into the dirt, revealing the face. The skin was dark, dark as his own, and the black beard was well greased with animal fat. On either cheek was a spiral pattern drawn in green and blue. He rubbed at one to see whether it would come off, and felt the ridged scars under his thumb. A shudder ran down his spine, and he glanced behind him at the horses.

There were two more of these Picts somewhere nearby. He was alone, and not so fit as he had been in the summer when he had last fought for his life. If he took the horses, he could be halfway to Penhyle and the safety of its garrison before the strangers realized he was gone.

The prospect was tempting. What dissuaded him was pure sentiment. Gorthyn's sword was hanging on its hooks in the hut, and he would not leave without it. The tattooed men must have found the hut by now; in fact it had probably been their objective all along. No doubt they were waiting there for his return – or rather, for its occupant's return. He did not think they were seeking him, Nai mab Nwython. Much more likely they wanted the hermit of Sanctuary Wood, the man who had called himself Budoc, the man who had lived in the hut until the events of the summer had driven him away.

Nai dragged the body up over the bank (aware of a faint pull from the old wound in his flank) and pitched it down the far side. He scuffed out the marks the man had made in his death throes, then jumped down after the corpse and did his best to bury it under a pile of gold and yellow leaves, not stopping until he was satisfied the body was well enough hidden to fool all but the most conscientious searcher.

A crow flapped through the treetops as he moved away from the Sanctuary, and he smiled at the omen, for its course led straight and true to the clifftops where the little stone hut huddled in the shelter of a hollow. He followed, moving quickly though not at the full run he had used earlier. Now that he knew where his enemies were there was no need for great haste.

At the edge of the wood he slowed his pace. Here there was no line of firs to mark a clean break between the forest and the meadow: instead the trees gradually grew further and further

27

apart until suddenly they came to an end. Nai eased his way through stands of brown bracken, following a deer trail that wound between the ferns, and hunkered down at their edge.

The wind stirred the dark green grass. He could see two lines of bruises leading away from his left towards the hut; the pale outline of the new thatch was just visible from where he squatted. There was no sign of his enemies, and no sign that they had returned to the wood: only that double track running across the grass.

He waited, wondering what to do next. The meadow was open and exposed, and though he guessed the Picts were hiding inside the hut (which was what he would have done) their tracks seemed too obvious an invitation, almost as if that was what he was intended to think. A gull waddled through the grass, the fierce beak stabbing at the ground, criss-crossing the footprints. Above him more gulls wheeled and soared, their cries drifting mournfully across the cliffs. In the distance he could hear the roar of the breakers. Still he waited.

After a time the cold wind began to bite through his leather jerkin. His hands were going purple and numb where they gripped the spear shafts, and his calf muscles were stiffening. If he did not move now he would never move, so he rose from his crouch, shaking his legs to loosen them, and stepped out into the meadow.

A twig snapped behind him.

He turned, too late, and something hit him very hard behind the left ear.

2

Seradwen stretched wearily, hands in the small of her back, and surveyed the horse pastures. Despite the weather the men were still working on the fence where the white stallion had broken it down the previous morning. She blinked against the persistent drizzle, trying to see how far they had reached, but the mist from the river was rising to join the low cloud blowing in from the hills, rendering it impossible to discern any detail.

'Soon be shortest day,' murmured Bodgath.

She grunted, glanced down at him, a little brown nut of a man, sturdy and independent as the horses he watched over. He would never meet another's gaze, his eyes wandering everywhere but towards the face of the person to whom he was speaking. When she had first married and moved to the farm she had taken this to mean he was untrustworthy. The years had proved her wrong.

'January, the black month,' he added. 'Always think the worst is passed once the days begin to lengthen, but not so, not so.'

'Will you walk the fields with me?' she asked.

His eyes darted from side to side. 'Walked them this morning with Hoewgi. Walk them again with you if you wish. Set your mind at rest.'

Seradwen frowned at the mention of the eldest of her late husband's four cousins. 'He did not tell me.'

Bodgath stared at the mist curling from the river. 'Searching for someone to blame,' he said, and his tone of voice made her smile.

'You?'

He shook his head vehemently. 'Bigger fish than old Bodgath.' He pointed a crooked finger at her chest, though his gaze remained fixed on the river mist. 'You, Lady. All your fault if Whitey damaged the mares or foals.'

She laughed. 'He is a vicious beast, but not with the mares or the young. He has done no harm, just stirred them up a little.' She shrugged, began to pace the line of the first fence. 'What intrigues me is how he escaped from his pen.'

The little man trotted along at her side, barely reaching her shoulder. 'Not hard to answer,' he said solemnly, giving the ritual formula used by somebody offering the solution to a riddle. 'Meirion's boy, at the behest of his uncle.'

Meirion was the second of her husband's cousins.

'Which uncle?' she asked, there being three to choose from, and either of the younger pair to her mind possible candidates for mischief.

Bodgath grinned. If he had been less dignified he would have scampered around her like a puppy to show his delight at holding knowledge she did not possess.

She decided to ignore him. He would tell her in his own good time, tell her for her own sake and for the sake of the herd. 'A weakness there,' she remarked, indicating the fence.

He paused to examine the spot. The fences were post and rail, and many of the posts were coming to the end of their life. The previous generation had been careless in their use of timber, often choosing pine rather than a hardwood. Keeping the fences in good repair was a constant battle, and a stallion on the rampage was capable of wreaking a great deal of damage.

She smiled fondly at the top of Bodgath's head as he bent to assess the post's footings, prodding with the hawthorn stick that had become his constant companion during the last few months. His scalp gleamed white where wind and rain had plastered the greying hanks of hair to his skull. When she had first come to the farm, nearly six years ago, his hair had been thick and black.

He straightened, glared at the dark outline of the woods beyond the meadows, snatched a shapeless cap from inside his tunic and jammed it on his head.

'Syvno,' he said, and spat.

The youngest of the four brothers, then, and the one who actively hated her. The others disliked her, but she could cope with that, even work with them if necessary. She turned the implications over in her mind, the fence forgotten for the moment.

Despite the five years of their marriage, Seradwen and her husband Mordav had never been blessed with children. The irony of this, two people keeping a stud farm yet being unable to produce young of their own, had not escaped them, but it had not seemed important. They were young, they had plenty of time.

Then one evening Mordav came home complaining of pains in his chest. Three days later he was dead, and everything changed.

The rules of inheritance were very clear. Land and buildings belonged to the family. Under normal circumstances the house and a few acres of land would go to the youngest son, together with the most important of the household tools, on the assumption that the older brothers would already be established in homes of their own. The younger son would divide the remaining land into equal portions, and let his brothers choose in turn, the eldest going first. Thereafter they might work the land together or separately, depending upon their natures and whether they were friends as well as kin.

When a man died without sons matters grew more complicated. Inheritance always passed from father to son, or son to father, never between brothers or cousins. A man inherited from his brother simply because they were both sons of the same father. Thus the property was deemed to have reverted to the father, even if the father was no longer living, and thence passed down again to another son. Where there were no brothers, the descendants in the male line of the grandfather inherited: first the uncle, and failing him, his sons, the cousins of the deceased. The limit was four generations, reaching back as far as the great-grandfather if no closer kin could be found.

Seradwen's husband Mordav had outlived his brothers, both of whom had died childless. His father was long dead, and had likewise been the sole survivor of his generation. The grand-father's line having thus failed, the farm had reverted to the great-grandfather. The great-grandfather, who had been dead for so long not even the oldest inhabitant of the farm could remember him, had produced two sons, Mordav's grandfather and another. This great-uncle had fathered numerous daughters and a single male child, and in his turn the male child had produced four boys. These four, Mordav's second cousins, were the legal heirs to the farm.

But only the farm: only the houses, the barns, the stables and the family land. Half the adjoining estate was held direct from the local lord, Gereint mab Cadwy. The rent for this was paid in kind, in horses, and the agreement was subject to revision every five years. The present tenancy had two more years to run, and Seradwen had no doubt Gereint would renew on similar terms provided she herself continued to oversee the herd.

The herd itself was hers and hers alone. Stock, whether sheep, cattle or horses, were the property of the individual, not the family group. The horse herd had been owned jointly by Mordav and Seradwen, and before his death he had willed his share to his wife. The prosperity of the farm sprang from the horses, from the five stallions and the fluctuating group of some seventy mares and foals. Without the horses it was no different from any other large farm in the district; with them it became one of the wealthiest holdings in this part of Dumnonia.

So the brothers needed her. Remove her, and their new found estate would both halve in size and lose its source of revenue. All that would remain would be a few acres of enclosed ground (not much, divided four ways) and the buildings. The buildings admittedly were worth having, and were the reason the brothers had abandoned their own farms to stewards or tenants and settled themselves and their families here, with her. As yet they had not asked her to move out of the quarters she had shared with Mordav, but she knew it was only a matter of time.

Seradwen frowned, walked on across the pasture with Bodgath

at her heels. The men had finished working on the fence; she could see their distorted outlines moving towards her through the river mist. The mares ignored them, stood or grazed quietly, though a few of the younger colts and fillies frisked around their mothers.

'Been a good year,' said Bodgath.

She grunted, strode to the gate leading to the next paddock.

'For the stock,' he added hastily, realizing he had been tactless. 'A good crop, and more to come.'

'How did you know it was the boy?' she asked, suddenly curious.

Bodgath fiddled with the rope halter that fastened the gate. 'Caught him smirking. Lammed him with my stick and he confessed.'

'He will tell his father.'

The old man grinned. 'Might do, might not. Told him I'd teach him about horses if he stopped his fooling around.'

She nodded thoughtfully. 'Do you think he will?'

'Yes.' Bodgath poked the ground with his stick. 'Not a bad boy, just bored in a strange place and scared of the beasts.' He raised his eyes to the wooded hills beyond the pastures. 'Scared of you too. Ice Lady, they call you.'

'Amongst other things,' she said drily.

'Said you might teach him too, if he asked you.'

'You did, did you?'

'They are not going to go away, Lady.' His attention remained firmly fixed on the middle distance. 'Mordav is dead, and they are his legal heirs. None of us like it, but we must live with it.'

She sighed, ran her hands through damp hair. 'I know. Often I have thought of taking the herd and leaving, going back to my father's lands, but it would be no better. My brothers are married with families of their own, and their wives would not welcome me. Oh, they are friendly enough if I visit, but to stay, that would be a different thing.'

'This is your home, Lady.' He shook his stick. 'The men work for you, because you know what needs to be done. They will not work for the cousins.'

'They know about sheep and cattle.'

'They think they know about everything,' muttered Bodgath. He cupped his hands and called: 'Finished then?'

The foremost man waved a sledgehammer in the air. 'Old

Whitey'll not get through there again in a hurry.' He saluted Seradwen, added: 'Back to start on the stables, Lady.'

'Well done,' she said. 'Watch out for Whitey's hooves when you come to his stall!'

He laughed and went on his way with the others.

'You see?' Bodgath said quietly. 'They are yours, as they were Mordav's. Hoewgi is not a complete fool. He sees it, and when he has swallowed his pride he will deal with you fairly.'

'Not easy, learning a new trade at his age,' she murmured reflectively. 'But how long will it take him to swallow? And Syvno is simply dangerous. I will not tolerate anyone playing games with the horses.'

'Let me deal with Syvno.'

'And break your bargain with the boy?'

The old man shook his head. 'You know me. I can be crafty when I must.'

She hesitated, nodded. 'Very well. You handle him.' She turned and stared up the river valley at the complex of farm buildings.

Smoke from the cooking fires billowed across the roofs to mingle with the mist. Dusk was gathering and the farm looked at its best. In broad daylight one saw how patched and repaired the buildings had become, what a strange mixture of styles and materials they were. No two roofs were of the same height or pitch, no two walls were the same colour. The older parts were a mixture of unrendered brick and stone; the more recent were of wood, sometimes exposed and sometimes plastered. Some roofs were thatched, some shingled; the verandah which ran along the front of the main house even retained its original pink tiles, chipped and broken but still capable of keeping out the rain.

But in the dusk none of this mattered. When the lamps and torches were lit, the complex came alive. There were two court-yards: the outer, between the barns and what had once been the workers' bathhouse, all now used for stabling or storage; and the inner, the squared U of the old villa and its two wings. At one time the villa had been a single residence; now it was subdivided vertically and horizontally into smaller units, with a refectory hall occupying most of the right wing. After dark, lamps glimmered from the windows and doorways, and during the breeding season the yards were busy with the passage of grooms back and forth from stable to stable, since most mares chose to give birth at night.

33

Bodgath waved his stick at the mares. 'They seem happy enough. A couple might need to come indoors if it turns cold, but they're all right for now.'

Seradwen nodded absently, and the two of them retraced their route through the various paddocks. Bodgath unlatched the solid door in the wall of the outer courtyard, drew in his breath in a hiss of surprise as he pushed it open and saw what lay beyond.

'Visitor,' he muttered before stepping aside to let her enter first.

In the middle of the yard stood Hoewgi, the eldest of her husband's cousins, talking with a stranger. Sensing her approach, Hoewgi broke off his conversation and waited for her to join them. As befitted his new found importance as the most senior of Mordav's heirs, Hoewgi had taken to dressing well, in a style more suited to a minor lord than a working farmer. His tunic and cloak were of fine wool, the colours a co-ordinated russet and yellow. On each wrist he wore a bracelet of polished copper, and his cloak was fastened with a magnificent silver disk brooch.

By contrast the stranger was wrapped in a travel-stained cape of no particular colour, much patched and darned. In one hand he clutched a leather bag containing the unmistakable outline of a harp.

'A bard!' exclaimed Seradwen. 'Welcome, thrice welcome!'

'Lady,' said the bard, his voice a rich bass that made her toes curl with delight. 'Lady,' he repeated, gazing directly into her eyes, 'your husband has bidden me dine in the hall this night. May I dare hope you will grace us with your presence?'

She felt herself blushing. 'Hoewgi is not my husband.'

'The Lady Seradwen is not my wife,' Hoewgi said in unison, and she stifled an urge to laugh at the expression of horror on his round face.

'Forgive me,' said the bard, and such was the magic of his voice that she did. 'I am Regin of Dyfed, and I have been too long from civilized company.'

'You have travelled far since you left Dyfed?' she inquired politely.

'The breadth of western Prydein,' he said proudly. 'I have seen the seas breaking on the Promontory of Belerium, have sung before Custennin in his great hall at Kelliwig, where the emperor Arthur once feasted the Warband of Albion.'

'Custennin was not civilized company?'

'On the contrary!' he protested, then realized she was teasing.

34

'What I intended was that I had spent overlong on the byways between Kelliwig and this delightful haven.'

'Where are you bound?' demanded Hoewgi, not approving of their mild flirtation.

'Din Erbin, where I hope to find Gereint mab Cadwy. A few days ago I visited a place called Penhyle, where his men were kind to me. I understand Gereint is the ruler of this Portion of Dumnonia?'

'Indeed. A just lord, and a generous one,' Hoewgi said stiffly. His cold eyes strayed towards Seradwen. 'Some say too generous.'

'Only a very few.' She turned to the bard. 'Has my kinsman shown you the hall? You may sleep there with some of the grooms if you wish, but they will probably be coming and going during the night. We have a couple of sick horses they will be checking on. If you prefer we can arrange a private room where you can sleep undisturbed.' She kept her tone brisk and business-like so he would not make the error of reading an invitation into her words.

'Lady, I thank you. Private quarters would be the answer to my prayers. Too many nights of late have been passed trying to sleep against the sound of another's snores.'

'Good.' She linked an arm through his, drew him away from Hoewgi. 'Tell me, who did you meet at Penhyle?'

He kept pace with her across the outer yard, waited with the harp cradled against his chest while she opened the door in the wall leading to the inner court.

'A man named Addonwy, and a savage little fellow called Cadlew.' He smiled ruefully. 'Cadlew did not approve of my material.'

'Yet you say they were kind to you?' She ushered him through the doorway and he gasped at the sight of the verandah with its torches sputtering in the damp evening air.

'This is civilization indeed!' Regin paused to take in the scene. 'How old is it?'

She shrugged. 'Nobody knows. My husband used to say parts went back hundreds of years.'

The bard cocked a dark eyebrow. 'Used to say?'

'He died.'

'I am sorry.' The words sounded heartfelt, but the man was a professional entertainer. 'And then his heirs moved in?'

35

'His distant cousins.'

'Not easy.' His voice was sympathetic, understanding.

'Not easy,' she agreed.

She led the way up the steps to the portico, brushing past the ivy clinging to the pillars, and made to enter the house proper before she realized the bard was not following. He had stopped to admire the portico floor, which was paved with tiles set in a herringbone pattern.

'Ear of corn,' he said, giving the pattern its Roman name.

'Cracked and worn, like the rest of the house,' she said, and clapped her hands together, startling him.

One of the household women appeared from the direction of the kitchen.

'Sometimes it works,' Seradwen said lightly over her shoulder. 'Blanith, make ready a room for our guest. And perhaps a glass of wine in my study to wash the dirt of the road from your throat before we dine, Regin?'

'I would be honoured, Lady Seradwen.'

'Show our guest where everything is, Blanith, then bring him to the study. There is a while yet before the meal will be served.' She turned to Regin, who seemed larger here within the confines of the house. 'Simple fare, but wholesome.'

'Lady, any meal prepared within these walls will be immeasurably superior to last night's supper.'

'Which was?'

'A dry crust washed down with stream water,' he said smoothly, and she gave him the laughter he expected.

CHAPTER TWO

The gulls wailed above Bedwyr's head. He gazed once more around the ruined town, seeing how badly most of the buildings on the exposed plateau had deteriorated compared with those further down the slope. The exceptions were the Great Hall and the Guest House, both of which had been built to endure. Ordinary dwellings were not expected to last longer than a generation even when in daily use, and these had suffered ten years of neglect.

He raised his eyes from the remnants of the town, resisting the eagerness in him to be gone. From here one could see for miles in every direction except the east, where the view was blocked by a line of rolling hills. In the north-west was the unmistakable landmark of Ynis Witrin, rising from the icy marshes like the breast of a goddess. To the south was the great vale of Lindinis, dotted with farmsteads, their smoke curling and dissipating in the wind.

Everywhere he looked reminded him of some incident in the past. Ynis Witrin was where Melwas Lord of the Summer Country had held court, and Melwas was the man to whom Gwenhwyvar had been betrothed before Arthur stole her away. One of the farms to the south had been the home of Glewlwyd of the Mighty Grasp, who had kept the gate of Caer Cadwy. Both men were long dead, but they had left sons and grandsons behind them. If Bedwyr were to ride down to the farm he would find a welcome and a warm bed; if he were to ride across the marshes to

Ynis Witrin he would receive a very different greeting, for the lords of that place had no reason to love Arthur and his followers.

And there was the road from Lindinis, halfway between the farm and the tor, the sunlight playing on the causeway, and there were the dark shapes he had been expecting, moving slowly towards him like a pack of hounds sniffing out an uncertain trail.

He smiled, fetched his pony and walked towards the far gate, being careful to leave plenty of good hoofprints in the muddy ground.

He had seen them first in Isca.

After three years as a hermit, he had grown unaccustomed to cities. He had found the press of people, the sheer number of strange faces, confusing. Rather than be alone in the multitude, he had sought shelter with a group of Christians living around the old market place. They were not a monastic community, for they took no vows and had few rules, but a gathering of like-minded citizens more devout than their fellows.

Here he had found peace during the summer and autumn, earning his keep by copying texts, assisting the priests and deacons in their ministry, being useful without being obtrusive. The community had accepted him as a former monk who had returned home from Armorica to die in the land of his birth, and had not asked too many questions. Several of them had lived very different lives before receiving the call. If the elderly ex-monk had no desire to discuss his past, he was not alone in that. They were content to take him as he was, not worry about what he might have been.

Two days ago one of the women had returned from the new market and sought him out where he sat trying to decipher an account of Bishop Germanus's visit to Britain a century earlier.

'Adherents of the Pelagian heresy were distinguished by the richness of their dress,' he remarked as she entered. 'Beware, my dear Calpornia, lest you be taken for one of them.'

'I do not think I am in any danger,' she said, glancing down at her grey gown, 'but you may be.'

'I? How so?' he said lightly. 'Like a good son of the Church, I accept the doctrine of original sin, though I suppose I do veer towards believing a good life and good works will count for much when the time comes. Certainly I do not credit the opposite, that Grace and Grace alone will save us from damnation, which seems to be what Germanus was arguing.'

'I am serious,' Calpornia said brusquely. 'There was a stranger going among the stallholders in the market, asking if anyone had seen an old man with one hand, calling himself Budoc or Mab Petroc, a recent arrival in the town.'

Bedwyr stiffened. 'Indeed?'

'Since the name you gave us is Petroc, and since you could be loosely described as having one hand –' She looked meaningfully at the way he held the scroll.

'What kind of man was this stranger?'

'A dark man, a warrior, with a sword and knife at his belt. Not a godly man, and not one I would care to meet in a lonely place.'

'A dark man? Did he speak awkwardly, as if his voice had been damaged?'

'No. He had a northern accent, but there was nothing wrong with his voice.'

'Not Nai, then,' Bedwyr muttered to himself. 'Was he alone?'

'I was coming to that.' She pulled up a stool and sat facing him, her eyes intent upon him. 'When he left the market I followed him. I do not know why, unless it is that once long ago when I was very young I saw one of Arthur's Companions ride past my home on his way to Kernow.'

'One of the Companions?' He laid the scroll aside.

She nodded. 'Bedwyr mab Petroc was his name, and my father told me to remember it was through the courage and skill of men like him that little girls like me were safe in our beds at night.'

'Ah,' he said with a faint smile. 'There your good father erred. For as Bishop Germanus would doubtless have said, only by the Grace of God are we any of us safe. To believe otherwise is a form of vanity.'

'Perhaps. But it is notable that while Arthur and his Companions ruled this land I was safe. It was only when Arthur had gone . . .' She shuddered, dropped her gaze.

Bedwyr waited, and after a moment she continued.

'I followed the stranger down the hill towards the River Gate, and along the way he met with two friends. One was a man much like himself. The second was bundled in a hood so his face was hidden.'

'They did not see you?'

Calpornia shook her head. 'Women over a certain age are invisible to men of that kind. If they noticed me at all, it was as a drab female on her way home from the market, one among many.

39

I pretended to have forgotten something, and searched through my basket in case I had by chance remembered it after all. The three were deep in conversation. The one who was wrapped in the hood had to let the folds fall so he could speak.'

'Yes?' prompted Bedwyr.

'His face! One hears of such things – and I have seen sailors with tattoos upon their arms, even their chests – but on his face! So ugly!'

Bedwyr let out a long breath.

'That decided me,' said Calpornia. 'No man who desecrated his appearance in that fashion could possibly be up to any good. I thought you should be warned. Besides –' she hesitated, blushed '– Petroc, Bedwyr mab Petroc. Once you rode past a farmhouse and a father held his little daughter up to see, and you waved.'

'Did I? I am glad.' He bent forward and kissed her cheek.

She sat very still. 'Who are they, and what do they want with you? Where have they come from?'

'They have come from the far north, out of my past.' He ran his left hand through his hair, cut short in the Roman style. 'As to what they want: information, certainly, and probably revenge.'

'Revenge?'

He nodded. 'I would think so. Long ago I did a thing of which I am ashamed. I slew one of them very slowly.'

Her eyes widened. 'You mean you murdered him?'

'In effect, yes. Oh, he had a sword in his hand, but it made little difference. I was at the height of my powers, and angry, for he had killed Cei. I forced him to fight when he wanted to surrender, kept him alive when he wanted to die.'

She watched him closely. A barrel rumbled over the cobbles outside and a voice shouted directions, but neither moved.

'If the heretic Pelagius was right and our salvation depends upon good works, then I fear that I am damned,' he said quietly. 'I have not lived a good life.'

'We are all of us poor sinful men and women. I too have done things of which I am not proud.' She shifted uncomfortably on the stool. 'Not always of my will – or rather, often through a lack of will, through a failure to say "No, this is wrong!".'

A second barrel rolled across the cobbles with a sound like thunder. Bedwyr waited until it had passed.

'I must leave. By staying here I bring danger on you all.'

'Can we not have the city magistrates restrain these people?'

'We have no grounds. They have done no wrong.'

'Suspicion is often enough,' she said, rising to her feet. 'Besides, you are Bedwyr mab Petroc. If you tell the magistrates who you are, they will believe you.'

He laughed, his face suddenly lightening. 'Thank you for that, my dear Calpornia. But it is better if I leave.'

With her help he gathered equipment and provisions, saddled the pony which had once belonged to his nephew Gorthyn mab Erfai. The wooden box that contained all he owned he left with her, after removing the sword he had carried at Camlann and a handful of bronze pins and barter tokens.

'If I do not return, use what remains for the good of the community,' he said.

She stared at the bundles of cloth that hid the contents. 'I will.'

'There is a set of fine glasses and a chalice of Scythian make which is valuable. Enough to endow a chapel, perhaps.' He grinned. 'If the tattooed man comes calling, you might offer the chalice to him in trade. He would be interested, I think, until he saw it.'

'Where will you go?'

'Down through the city first, for a glimpse of these strangers. Then away east in search of one who was lost long ago.' He clasped her hand in farewell. 'Pray for me, Calpornia.'

'Always, my lord Bedwyr,' she said, and there were tears in her eyes.

He had ridden through the town in the early afternoon, the sword concealed under a thick winter cloak, his hands disguised by heavy gloves. The streets were less crowded than when Calpornia had done her marketing, and it had not been hard to pick out the men loitering on the street corners, their dark eyes scanning the passers-by.

They had seen him and marked him as a possible. One had strolled after him, very casual, pausing to admire the porch and steps of a newly completed building when Bedwyr halted to let the pony drink from a trough, hastening when the pony moved into a brisk walk.

He had passed through the red walls of the city in the company of other travellers hurrying on their way before the early dark. The man had broken into a run as Bedwyr joined the throng, appeared panting at his saddle bow.

'Your pardon, sir, is this not yours?'

He held out a yellow cap, his cold eyes studying Bedwyr's face, the gloved hands on the reins. Bedwyr glanced down indifferently. 'Mine? No. Yellow does not become me.'

'Are you sure? I thought it fell as you passed.' He shoved the cap forward.

Reining in the pony, Bedwyr reached for the cap with his left hand, twirled it on his fingers, returned it to the man. 'Not mine.'

'Perhaps you should take it, lest the weather turn cold. You are going far?'

'Far enough.'

'It may be we shall meet upon the road,' said the man, and slipped away through the crowd.

The man had recognized him. He had cut his hair and shaved his beard during his time in Isca, which had the effect of making him less like the hermit Budoc from Porthyle, and more like Bedwyr the companion of Arthur. Calpornia had known him, but then she had had several months in which to study him. The man had recognized him after a few brief moments.

The man. Call him by name. He was an Attecotti, one of the old race who claimed to have ruled the whole island of Albion in the very dawn of time. The Attecotti, sometimes confused with their kinsmen the Picts because both groups adorned their face and bodies with painted decorations, inhabitants of the far northwest, rumoured to be cannibals and masters of dark magics: a fierce and proud people who never forgave an injury.

One could be even more specific. The man was not simply an Attecotti. He was one of the Children of Menestyr, the leading clan of the Attecotti. And his presence here in the south, as far from his home as a man could travel and remain within the island of Albion, meant that Bedwyr's worst fears were realized.

He had seen five or six in Isca. More than that number followed him from the city, staying behind him even when he made the awkward circuit around the walls to put him on the road to Lindinis in the east.

At least he had led them away from the community. The thought of the Children of Menestyr extracting information from his friends in Isca made him shudder.

The first night he spent crouched in the ruins of an old way station, shivering with cold, not daring do more than doze. At

42

first light he was moving again, and now he tried cunning, turning off the road and waiting for his pursuers to pass. They did not come. When he returned to the road he saw them behind him, black dots in the distance, too far to make out their numbers. Later he abandoned the highway altogether and struck out through heavy woodland. For a while he thought he had lost them. Then he heard the birds shouting in alarm and knew they were still with him.

In Lindinis, near dusk, he glimpsed the man with the yellow cap, and any faint hope that he might have been imagining things, that he might have mistaken several different groups of innocent travellers for his enemies, vanished absolutely. They knew him and they were after him.

Yet they were unsure of themselves. Although he had ridden hard, he had not run at full speed. They could have overhauled him had they wished, brought matters to a conclusion in some quiet corner of the road. For the present they were content to watch him flee, to see where he went.

He had departed from Lindinis before dawn, sneaking like a thief through a gap in the ancient walls, and ridden for Caer Cadwy.

And now they were again upon his trail, which was good, for this was country he had ridden and hunted over for decades, country with which he was intimately familiar.

He left Caer Cadwy by the same route as the one Gwenhwyvar had taken ten years earlier, though he did not travel with her haste. Instead he walked the pony calmly down the slope to the north-east gate, leaving plenty of tracks to show where he had gone, not mounting until he was back on level ground.

He travelled in this fashion for the rest of the day, riding or walking as the fancy took him, rarely moving faster than a trot. The countryside was lush in contrast to the marshes which lay behind him, and warmer. The hills were wide and green, thickly wooded with all manner of trees, and small muddy streams flowed along the valley bottoms. At first he kept to the Fosse Way, but as the afternoon wore on he left the road and cut across country, fording the streams and climbing the hills, until he came to a track that ran along the ridges.

Here he paused a while, looking back the way he had come, watching for some sign of pursuit, chewing on a piece of dried

43

venison while the pony grazed on the long grass growing along the verge, studying the landscape from the vantage of the ridge as the light left it. Darkness pooled in the hollows, thickened the leafless woods into solid bands of blackness, and still he saw no sign of them. Perhaps he had already lost them when he left the road and cut across country, though it seemed unlikely the people who had followed him from Isca to Lindinis could be so easily fooled.

At last, before the light faded altogether, he abandoned his watch and led the pony a short way along the track to where a stand of firs crowned the brow of the hill. He pushed between the springy branches, holding them clear of the horse's face, winding between the trunks until satisfied both he and the horse were hidden from the path, and settled for the night.

Sleep did not come easily. Pine needles pricked him, the pony stamped its hooves or blew loud breaths down its nostrils. The wind soughed in the trees. Just as he was dozing off he was pulled back to wakefulness by a vixen screaming like a dying woman, somewhere over the hill. Cold, he burrowed deeper into his cloak, debated rising to fetch the spare blanket from the saddle pack, but could not be bothered.

Gwenhwyvar.

Ten years since he had seen her last, a lifetime since he had seen her first.

They had all loved her on sight: loved her but known she was not for them. She was Arthur's, and Arthur was hers, from the very beginning . . .

So long ago that now in memory they seemed impossibly young: a time when they had believed they could change the world, change the greedy self-serving nature of people, cut through the jealousies and the petty hatreds, build rather than destroy.

Memory? His first sight of Gwenhwyvar had ceased to be a memory and become a story like the tale of her final departure from Caer Cadwy, a story in which the characters – even himself – were creatures of the imagination, phantasms not flesh and blood. Had they really ridden through a perfect summer day with the skylarks trilling above them and the cattle lowing in the pastures? Had they truly agreed to an abduction which could have sparked a minor war, with no more thought than that Arthur asked it, and therefore it would be so?

*   *   *

44

In those days Ambrosius commanded the Army of Prydein and the young Arthur was merely one of his officers. Ambrosius had led an embassy to the lands of the Durotriges, taking Arthur with him. On his return Arthur burst into the quarters he shared with Bedwyr and Cei.

'I have seen the woman I am going to marry,' he announced, flinging his saddlebags across the room.

Cei, imperturbable, looked up from the mailshirt he was relacing. 'Oh yes? Who is she?'

'The most beautiful woman in all the world,' said Arthur.

'Naturally. And her name?'

'Gwenhwyvar verch Ogrvran Gawr.'

Bedwyr laughed. 'Your host's daughter? Surely she is betrothed to Melwas of Ynis Witrin.'

'True,' said Arthur. 'A marriage of convenience. Their territories march together, and Gwenhwyvar is Ogrvran's heir. Any child of the union would inherit a great swathe of land.'

'Ogrvran Gawr,' mused Cei. 'Ogrvran the Giant. An ambitious man.' He turned the mailshirt in his hands. 'What is he like?'

'A big man, though not so big as you; very forceful, decided in his opinions. His hair is grey now, but they say when he was young it was black as a raven's wing, and thus his name, Keen-raven. Odd his daughter should be so fair.'

'Hence her name, I suppose,' said Bedwyr. 'Gwenhwyvar, the white phantom.'

'She is no phantom, my lad.' Arthur lifted his hands and began to describe her virtues.

'Have you spoken to her?' Bedwyr asked slyly.

Arthur looked offended. 'Of course. And wonder of wonders, she feels as I do. The first night we were in Ogrvran's hall, I was sitting near Ambrosius, listening to the talk going back and forth and nothing being said – you know how it is with these lesser lords, how they never commit themselves – when I looked up stifling a yawn and our eyes met. I knew then, in that very instant. It was as if it were meant, as if we were two parts of a long sundered whole.'

'God save me from lovers,' said Cei, who was older than the other two. 'You all think you are the first to feel as you do.'

'What of her father?' said Bedwyr.

'Not good. I asked him for her hand on the last day, and he laughed in my face.' Arthur frowned at the memory.

'Ogrvran Gawr.' Cei laid the mailshirt aside and stood, his head brushing the ceiling. 'He holds his lands through his wife, though he has added to them at the expense of Lindinis.'

'He came from the east, driven from his home by the Saesons, which is why Ambrosius had hopes he would allow us to establish a fortress in his territory.'

Cei smiled coldly. 'I take it he refused? Ambrosius is a single-minded man. In his intensity, he forgets others do not see the Saesons as the only threat to their security. If I were Ogrvran, I would not be keen to have a thousand trained warriors under another's command sitting on my land.'

'Our general is not a diplomat,' conceded Arthur. 'But he is right all the same. We must establish a stronghold in the south where we can train undisturbed, a safe distance from the deba-table frontier, yet not so far away we cannot react to trouble.'

The talk turned to matters of strategy and tactics, and if Arthur did not respond with his usual enthusiasm, the others assumed he would recover in a day or so. The young men of the Army of Prydein were constantly falling in love or lust with chieftains' daughters, and as a rule none of the affairs lasted very long.

In this, as in so many other things, Arthur was different.

Even then Arthur was being groomed by Ambrosius as a possible successor. Having himself failed to convince Ogrvran Gawr of the necessity for a fortress in the latter's territory, Ambrosius entrusted the task to the younger man, without any great expectation of success, reckoning the experience would be good for him.

Over the next few months Cei and Bedwyr saw little of their friend. He would appear from time to time, always in haste, grab fresh clothes and confer rapidly with the general, then vanish again.

'We have found the perfect site,' he said one day while strug-gling into a clean tunic. 'Din Cadwy, not far from Lindinis.'

'We?' Cei inquired drily.

'Gwenhwyvar and I. Only one drawback – you can see Ynis Witrin from the hilltop, a reminder that time is short and summer comes apace.'

'Her father does not object to you spending time in her company?'

Arthur grinned crookedly. 'We are never alone. The wedding is set for the summer, Cei.'

'So you have said.' *Often*, he might have added.

'What am I to do?'

'Well,' said Cei, half joking. 'If Ogrvran will not change his mind, you will have to steal her away.'

And so the plan was born. Like all of Arthur's plans, it was essentially simple. They would wait until the wedding day, when Ogrvran's hall would be filled with strangers, bluff their way past the entrance, seize Gwenhwyvar and be gone before their host and his guests realized anything was amiss.

'Would it not be easier to arrange an ambush in the next few weeks?' Bedwyr asked.

Arthur shook his head. 'Too much risk. Somebody might be hurt and we must avoid bloodshed. These are our people, not our foes.'

'They might be hurt at the wedding!' objected Bedwyr.

'We will carry no weapons within. We will go as guests, not warriors.'

'Not easy, to gain entrance,' said Cei. 'Ogrvran's gate is kept by Glewlwyd of the Mighty Grasp. I have heard of him. They say no man may pass uninvited through any door he guards. He will know you and guess why you have come.'

'I shall be disguised.'

Cei snorted. 'Glewlwyd is no fool. He will recognize you whatever you do – he must have seen you often enough these last few months – and I do not think he is a man who can be bribed.'

'We must do what we can,' said Arthur. 'Perhaps fair words will win him to us.'

Early on a midsummer's morning, a dozen of them set forth in silence through a dawn of liquid gold, trailing a single spare mount. They rode in pairs, and an observer would have thought them on their way to a burial, not a wedding. Only when the sun was well into the sky did they begin to speak, and then but softly to their partners.

The day was beautiful, with a sweet-scented breeze wafting across the downs and a hint of a heat haze in the distance. Cattle watched them curiously from every hillside, for this was good grassland, heavily grazed, and the farmsteads they passed were prosperous, the people friendly.

Bedwyr rode beside Cynon, as was his custom. 'You were raised near here. Do you know this Gwenhwyvar?' he asked after a while.

47

Cynon shook his head. 'I saw her when she was a child.'

'Was she fair?'

'Fair of hair, certainly. Of face and form?' He shrugged expressively. 'Too long ago. She would have been about ten, at a guess. I will tell you one thing though.'

Bedwyr waited. Cynon turned his pale gaze upon him.

'Even in those days she was promised to the heir of the Summer Country.'

A dragonfly shimmered between them, startling the ponies.

'You do not approve?'

Cynon spat. 'They are a strange breed, the Lords of Ynis Witrin, nestling in their old villa in the shadow of that misshapen tor. They are a secretive lot, cold and unfriendly to strangers. If I had a daughter she would not marry among them.'

'One hears tales of magic.'

'They say the tor was a great shrine once.' Cynon shifted in the saddle. 'I do not fear much, cousin. But I do fear Melwas and his kin, even here in broad daylight. If I were Arthur, and if we succeed today, I would guard against their curse.'

Towards midday they came within sight of a green hill crowned with a bank and palisade. The lane wound through neatly fenced paddocks, crowded now with lines of tethered horses. One field was given over entirely to the carriages of the wealthier guests. Cei sniffed the air. 'Can you smell the feast? Beef and pork.' The Long Man smacked his lips hungrily.

Arthur swung himself from the saddle. 'Two of you stay here with our ponies. Mael, Pabo, cut loose the horses, as many as you can manage.'

'There are grooms among them,' said Pabo, peering at the paddocks.

'Then you will have to be subtle,' said Arthur. 'Remember, nobody is to be hurt.'

He strode up the hill, and the rest of them followed him, ignoring the stares from the servants left to guard the guests' possessions.

Bedwyr walked with Cynon, trying to look as if he belonged here, feeling naked without the sword that was hanging on his saddlebow.

'What if Glewlwyd refuses us entry?' Cynon muttered anxiously as they came to the gate.

Only the postern was open. Through it Bedwyr could see a

brightly-coloured crowd moving towards whitewashed buildings. He could hear the hum of conversation, the shouts of greeting, the laughter and chatter of the wedding guests. He swallowed, his mouth dry.

'I had sooner ride into battle,' he whispered, and regretted the words the moment they left his mouth. Cynon glanced at him quizzically, shook his head.

A darkness blocked the entrance. A burly man stepped through the postern, pulled it shut behind him, stood with folded arms blocking the way.

'Glewlwyd,' murmured Cynon.

The Gatekeeper studied the small group of latecomers with care. A strange company they must have seemed: Bedwyr with his mutilated left hand; Cynon with his villainous grin; Cei towering above them all – and to their fore Arthur himself, dressed like a lesser lord from the Summer Country, crying 'Open the door!'

'I will not,' said Glewlwyd, and smiled upon them.

'Why not?' demanded Arthur. 'The feast has not yet begun.'

'Knife is in meat, drink in horn, and a thronging in the house of Ogrvran Gawr. Save for the son of a rightful ruler or a craftsman who brings his craft, the door will not open.'

'I am a craftsman,' said Arthur.

'What is your craft?' asked the Gatekeeper, stretching lazily.

'Two crafts have I: the fighting of battles and the wooing of a fair woman. And a third craft I possess: the making of friends.'

'Useful skills all three,' answered Glewlwyd. 'And the breeding of heirs, is that a craft you possess?'

Arthur grinned. 'That I know not, not yet.'

The Gatekeeper grunted, dropped the formal pose. 'You remind me of a fellow I have seen, a puppy of Ambrosius, save that his hair is auburn while yours is dark, he is bearded while you are clean shaven.'

'I would account it an honour to be mistaken for a man of the Magister Militum.'

'Would you, by God? There are some in this house who do not agree with you.' His gaze wandered over the rest of the troop. 'Enter then. You are not too late for the feast.'

They passed through the postern and stood in the shadow of the palisade among the crowd of privileged servants, watching the colourful array file into the hall. A large grey-haired man was greeting the guests at the porch, and near him were two smaller figures in their wedding finery, bowing and smiling to the steady stream of well-wishers.

'What now?' asked Bedwyr.

Arthur laughed and stepped out into the sunlight. 'Cei!' he called.

Cei moved beside him, towering over him though Arthur was not a short man. There they stayed until the last of the guests had entered the hall, and Ogrvran with the bride and groom had followed after them.

'She saw us,' Arthur said confidently. 'She will slip away in the confusion while they find their seats.'

'What would you have done if I had refused to accompany you?' demanded Cei.

'Made Bedwyr sit on Cynon's shoulders. But I knew you would come.'

The servants drifted away about their business or to their own lesser feast, but the companions remained, waiting, listening to the sounds of merriment from the hall. Suddenly they saw her sprinting towards them across the court.

For years afterwards that was how Bedwyr pictured her whenever he heard her name: a golden woman running through sunlight, her face alive with happiness, her hair in disarray where she had pulled fresh clothes over her head, bubbling with excitement.

'It worked!' she exclaimed breathlessly. 'I like you without the beard, but I prefer auburn to black. Quick, before they miss me. Some old fool cracked a joke about brides and nerves that made the bishop frown. Was Glewlwyd all right? Cei is even bigger than I thought: I knew who he was at once and that you must be here.'

Bedwyr was not sure what he had been expecting. That she should be fair of face and form was predictable. That he should like her upon sight was a surprise.

'Now I understand,' he whispered aloud.

'Too good for Melwas,' said Cynon. He eyed his friend. 'Cousin, your mouth is open.'

The Gatekeeper held the postern for them. They went hastily through, Gwenhwyvar bestowing a kiss upon his cheek which made him blush. Outside Cei paused and turned to Glewlwyd with a frown.

'Why?'

The Gatekeeper shrugged. 'I serve the Lady, as I served her mother before her. She chooses for herself.'

'Will you not come with us?'

'No. I shall stay at my post.'

'It will not go easy with you. They are young, these lovers, and take no heed for the consequences to others.'

'Do not begrudge them their time. They will have cares and responsibilities enough in later years. You know that.'

'I do,' said Cei, and clasped his hand. 'Seek me out if you ever have need.'

Below was chaos. Horses and men dashed to and fro in the pastures, while one of the carriages had somehow become overturned and blocked the path at the bottom of the hill. The party scrambled through the debris, disregarding the cries around them, found their mounts and departed with all speed. If there was pursuit it did not catch them.

As Cei had predicted, the Gatekeeper suffered for his part in the escape. He was cast into prison by Ogrvran, who would have done worse had he dared. But as Glewlwyd pointed out in his defence, he had only been obeying the commands of his lawful mistress, and Glewlwyd had many friends among the followers of Ogrvran.

Glewlwyd was not released until Arthur had succeeded Ambrosius as leader of the Army of Prydein. Then he came in triumph to Caer Cadwy, the very fortress whose proposed construction had been the root of the matter, and Arthur raised him up to be his own gatekeeper at Caer Cadwy as a reward for his faithfulness. And Glewlwyd's first loyalty lay always with Gwenhwyvar.

Bedwyr could remember the dry amusement with which Ambrosius had met the news that Arthur had eloped with Gwenhwyvar. 'An extreme way of ensuring we one day obtain our stronghold,' he said. 'Marry the heiress, eh? Well, I wish you joy.'

Despite his dryness Ambrosius had protected them from the wrath of Ogrvran and Melwas. Soon afterwards the Saesons broke out of their eastern reservations and ravaged almost as far as Aquae Sulis, and all else was forgotten in the dark days that followed.

Bedwyr stirred on his bed of pine needles, listened to the wind sobbing through the trees.

She had won them all, even the hard and cynical veterans of Ambrosius's guard, men who had been with him throughout the long struggle, sometimes winning and sometimes losing the battles but always giving ground. She had brought them a new hope, a sense that Prydein, Britannia, with its endless squabbles and petty hatreds was still a place worth fighting for. To the older men she was a daughter, to the younger a sister. To them all she brought joy.

From the time of her coming among them the Army began to win: not at once, but little by little, a lengthy chain of engagements that would eventually culminate years later in the great victory of Badon Hill. She was their Luck, the Luck of Britain; a blessing brought from Heaven.

Meanwhile the love between Arthur and Gwenhwyvar waxed ever stronger with the passing years, so that the old saw about being two halves of a single whole seemed in their case to be true, and by its strength others judged their own affairs, rarely to their advantage.

Yet even in those early days she had needed her protectors. Cynon had been right to fear Melwas, to warn of the necessity to guard against his curse.

One afternoon in that first winter Bedwyr had returned to the house he now shared with Cei alone, and found the Long Man brooding by the fire.

'What?' he said.

The other's face was grim. 'A message came from Ynis Witrin for Gwenhwyvar. I took it from the man, though he was not happy that I should have it. He had been told to place it into Gwenhwyvar's hands.'

'From Melwas?'

Cei nodded. 'Not a pleasant message.'

'What does it say?'

'Read the thing for yourself.' He passed across a small tablet.

It was unexpectedly heavy. Bedwyr moved closer to the fire so he could read the letters, frowning with the effort.

'This . . .'

'Is written backwards,' said Cei. 'And by a practised hand at that.'

The tablet was of lead, the letters lightly inscribed in a flowing script unlike the sharp capitals used on stone. Each word was reversed.

'D.M.' Bedwyr spelled out the heading, stared at Cei in puzzlement. 'D.M.? Dis Manibus? What has this to do with Gwenhwyvar?'

'A curse. Have you not seen such a thing before?' The Long Man closed his eyes and quoted from memory.

'"Dis Manibus. To the Divine Shades. May the union of Gwenhwyvar and Arthur evoke the displeasure of the gods. May they outlive all that springs from their union. May nothing they make achieve maturity."'

The heat from the fire seemed to fade. A shudder passed down Bedwyr's spine and his vision blurred.

Cei stirred the fire with a foot, held out a hand for the tablet. 'Say nothing to either of them.'

Bedwyr shook his head, bemused. 'Supposing Melwas sends more?'

'I told the messenger to bring them to me, or if I was not here to you.' Cei's smile was hard and cruel. 'I think the man will obey me.'

'What shall we do?'

'This!' said Cei. He took the lead tablet in his fist and squeezed. Bedwyr saw the cords of his wrist spring into prominence, saw him frown with the effort. The tablet buckled, lengthened, and Cei shifted his grip, compressing the thing upon itself until he had reduced it to a shapeless lump, which he cast aside with a snarl. 'That goes to the metalworkers tomorrow. They can melt it into something useful.'

He flexed his fingers, stared challengingly at Bedwyr. 'You and I, we know, do we not? The others do not recognize it, not yet, not even Ambrosius, but with every day it becomes clearer. Arthur is born to rule, with Gwenhwyvar at his side.'

'He is born to save this land,' Bedwyr said with the fervour of youth.

'We too have our part. We are the Companions, and our task is to guard them from filth like this –' he nudged the lump of lead with his foot '– to guard them while we have breath in our bodies.'

Bedwyr nodded.

'There will be others, cousin.' Cei's face was sombre as he stared into the fire. 'Melwas is nothing, less than nothing, a little man thwarted in his desire. One day you and I will pay him a visit and persuade him to desist. But in the years to come Arthur and

Gwenhwyvar will arouse stronger hatreds. Their opponents then will not be the kind to be frightened by a hard blow or the threat of a sword. We must be ready for them.'

By the light of the fire the two of them had sworn to defend Arthur, Gwenhwyvar and their unborn family against any who wished them harm, to keep them safe to the best of their ability.

Yet it had been Cei himself who had given Arthur's heir his deathblow. And if Llacheu had not died, they would never have come to Camlann, and the rest of Melwas's prophetic curse would never have been fulfilled.

CHAPTER THREE

Nai lay on the ground, aware of what was happening but unable to move. Rough hands turned him, fumbled at his belt for his war-knife and the little blade he kept for cutting his food; the shield strap was lifted over his head and the shield itself was tugged clear.

'Greid!' shouted a voice above him. 'Greid!'

He heard feet pounding towards them from the direction of the hut. His captor said something unintelligible, and the newcomer laughed. Nai opened his eyes.

Two figures towered against the grey sky, their hair wild and unkempt, slim braids dangling on either side of their faces. On each cheek they bore spiral tattoos in blue and green, and at first sight he could see nothing to distinguish between them, except that one was leaning on a spear.

They spoke again, and he wondered whether the blow had knocked the sense from him, for the sounds they made were gibberish.

'You are not the hermit.' The speaker prodded him with the spear butt.

With a sense of relief he realized they had been using some other tongue before, and he remembered what Budoc had said, that the tattooed men of the far North had some secret dialect or language of their own.

'The hermit is gone,' he replied.

'Gone where?' demanded the same man.

'I do not know,' he said, which was true, and did his best to seem both surprised and puzzled.

The second man bent forward and seized Nai's hair, lifted him by it so his whole torso was off the ground and shook him as a dog might shake a rat. Nai gave a cry of pain and sat up hastily.

'Who are you and what do you want?'

'You are a feeble fellow for a warrior,' the first man said contemptuously, levelling the spear so it pointed at Nai. 'Let him go, Greid.'

Greid grunted and released Nai's hair. 'We want the hermit. Budoc, he called himself.'

'He is long gone.' Nai rubbed his head. 'May I stand?'

'What is wrong with your voice?' Greid demanded suspiciously.

Nai blinked, then flung back his head to reveal his throat. 'This,' he said, indicating the scar, at the same time drawing his legs under him and rising awkwardly to his feet, taking his time about it so they could see he was no threat. 'A spear point from a former friend. A finger span to the side and I would be dead.' He flung his arms wide and grinned at them. 'I was lucky that day, do you –'

Mid-sentence he kicked with his right foot, catching Greid on the kneecap, grabbed the spear shaft a little behind the blade with his left hand, and twisted. Greid went down with a shout. His comrade gaped in astonishment and allowed the spear to be wrenched from his grasp.

Nai swung the weapon like a staff and cracked Greid across the temple with all his strength. The Pict folded and was still. The other jumped aside out of reach, drew his war-knife, and made a dash for Nai's shield lying on the grass.

'Not so feeble as I thought,' he panted as he slid the shield over his arm. 'Fferog! To me, Fferog, to me!' The woods gave back the sound of his bellow.

'Fferog is not coming,' Nai said quietly, holding the spear level and advancing his right foot.

The tattoos did not seem so terrifying now. As he pushed forward with the spear, careful not to overreach himself, Nai could see the sweat glistening on the other's brow. He brought his left foot up to match the right, and stepped to the side, threatening the shield, forcing the Pict to turn in response.

'Fferog!' the other roared.

'Fferog is dead,' said Nai, jabbing at the face, seeing the fear in the dark eyes.

'Fferog!' There was desperation in the shout, and for a moment the man was distracted as he jerked his head away from the spear-point.

Nai let the shaft slide through his hands, lengthening his grip, then thrust home under the rim of the shield in one quick movement. The Pict went down and did not rise again.

Nai released the spear. His hands were shaking and the old wound along his ribs, which he had strained while moving Fferog's body, was hurting so badly he half expected to find it torn open anew. His head was tender under his probing fingers, and he felt a sudden rush of fury at what had happened.

From behind him came a groan. He strode across the grass and found his war-knife, then crouched beside Greid, who was beginning to stir. He seized the matted hair and wrenched it tight, paying the man back in kind for his earlier treatment, a small part of him surprised at the strength of his own anger.

'Give me a reason not to kill you.'

The black eyes blinked, struggled to focus. 'You are a dead man walking.'

'A threat?' He twisted the hair tighter, watched the pain flash across the eyes, hoping to provoke a response.

'The Children of Menestyr avenge their own. We will come for you, Southerner, and your dying will not be easy.'

Nai laughed and struck the man across the face. 'What did you want with Budoc?'

'Something he stole from us,' snarled Greid, and lunged forward, hurling his whole body into the air like a salmon leaping a weir.

But Nai was expecting it – it was only a variant of the same trick he had played himself – and twisted clear, the war-knife ready in his hand.

Greid slumped, his breath coming in short sharp pants.

'An old hermit stole something from you?' said Nai, pressing the point of the knife to the nape of the other's neck.

'When he was young.'

'Tell me.' He pressed harder.

'A rumour reached us that the hermit known as Budoc was once Bedwyr mab Petroc, the greatest of Arthur's warriors.' The words came bubbling out as if a dam had been breached. 'Years

57

ago Arthur and a handful of Companions stole away our birth-right. Bedwyr, if it is Bedwyr, would be the last of those Companions left alive.'

'So you came here to a strange land and attacked me without warning, on the grounds that I might know the whereabouts of an old man who may have been one of Arthur's Companions?' Nai snorted contemptuously. 'I have heard more likely stories.'

'It is true!' Greid cried in protest. 'I do not know whether it is true the hermit was once Bedwyr, but we were sent here to find out.'

Then he added something which made Nai laugh aloud. 'We have the authority of your overlord Custennin to question whomsoever we need.'

'And his Household warriors to hold your horses, no doubt.'

'Doubt me if you wish,' returned the other, 'but we are men of distinctive appearance. How long do you think we would last in a strange land without the approval of its ruler?'

A shiver of horror ran through Nai. The claim had a ring of truth about it. The tattooed men were unmistakable, would stay in the minds of all who saw them, which would make it hard for them to move around the countryside unseen. Furthermore, Greid did not have the look of a man who had been camping out or living on hard rations for the last few nights: his clothing was too clean and he seemed too well fed. The Pict had been sleeping in houses or halls, guesting with the local lords. And besides, it was a strange claim to make unless it was indeed true.

'How many of you?'

Greid smirked. 'Many, which is why I say you are a dead man walking. If my kinsmen do not make an end of you, your own overlord will ajudge you a common murderer.'

'It would need many of your kind to make Bedwyr Bedrydant answer your questions,' Nai replied absently, his mind occupied with what he was going to do with the man. He could have killed him in the heat of the moment, but not now, not in cold blood.

'You cannot do it, can you?' Greid said mockingly, reading his thoughts.

'No,' said Nai, reversing his knife and hitting the man hard over the back of the head with the hilt, 'I cannot.'

He needed time to consider. It was quite possible Greid would die anyway – he had seen that oddly unfocussed look in other men's eyes after severe blows to the head, and not all of them had lived – but at least Nai would not be the direct cause of his death.

That the Children of Menestyr had discovered Budoc the hermit might be the same person as Bedwyr the warrior was disturbing. Only three people knew for certain that it was true: Nai himself, the young Saeson Ceolric, and the girl Eurgain. So far as he was aware Ceolric and Eurgain were safe in the lands of the Gewisse, several days' journey to the east, and in any case they were unlikely to have had dealings with the Children of Menestyr. Since it had been clear Bedwyr preferred to keep his continued existence a secret, none of them had spoken of the part the old warrior had played in the events of the summer.

Nai shook his head, which ached, and concentrated on slicing the dead man's belt into strips of leather he could use to bind Greid's hands and feet. He would have to leave the Pict in the hut, otherwise the man would probably die of exposure. The corpse could go over the cliff, and he supposed he should collect the other body from its hiding place beside the Sanctuary. Their weapons and jewellery he would take with him, but now he had seen their clothing up close he reckoned it was of too distinctive a weave. A bronze brooch could be bartered, but a cloak or tunic of unusual style was likely to provoke questions. His belongings he could load on the ponies, and he had enough food to keep him going for some while.

It seemed his time at Sanctuary Wood was at an end.

Leaving was harder than he had expected.

He had come to the hut in late summer, knowing it was empty, knowing that Eurgain's village was now a deserted ruin, knowing he would be more alone than he had ever been before. His closest friend was dead, he himself had slain his oldest enemy, and he felt himself to have come to a turning point.

Gereint mab Cadwy, his lord and master whom he had served since childhood, had allowed him to return to the Porthyle estuary once the worst of his wounds were healed. It was Gereint's hope that Nai would rejoin the warband after a few months' rest. Gereint accepted that Nai felt himself too old and battered to continue playing the same active role in the warband as before, but hoped a period of seclusion would change his mind. At the very least, Nai could take over the training of the young-sters in the Boys' House.

But as the days grew shorter and the trees shed their leaves, Nai settled into a routine. He spent much of his time visiting the Sanctuary, where he had buried the amulet containing the fragment of wood that Bedwyr had told him was a piece of the True Cross. His voluntary exile was enjoyable and free from care. Gereint's men had provided him with a plentiful supply of food and firewood, and every so often somebody would ride out from the newly installed garrison at Penhyle to check on his needs.

To the younger members of Gereint's warband Nai had become a hero, the man who had finally defeated the renegade Eremon in single combat. Of his contemporaries, only Cadlew and Addonwy were still alive (another reason for his reluctance to return to his old life: his luck could not last much longer), and only they treated him like a flesh and blood human being. Perhaps by living in exile he made it worse; perhaps if the younger men had seen him getting drunk in the Hall of an evening they would not have held him in such reverence, but he had no desire to put it to the test.

His chief purpose during these months was to become fit again. He had still been an invalid when he arrived, panting for breath after walking a few paces, with no strength in his arms or legs. Now he was closer to what he had been, though the older he grew the harder he found it to come back from an injury.

He was not ready to leave. Meeting Bedwyr had been the most extraordinary experience of his life, and it was here that it had happened. Whatever the youngsters of Gereint's warband felt for him was but a tenth part of what he felt for Bedwyr.

Reluctantly he pulled himself up into the saddle of the lead pony, and took a last lingering look at the hut lying in its hollow. The light was starting to fail and a small voice was telling him it would be wise to be well clear of the wood before nightfall, but he could not go until he had fixed the image of the place in his mind. He needed to know that he would able to recall the pattern of the green stones at will: to remember that this one near the door was twice the size of its fellows, and fitted thus between two thin slices in which ran veins of yellow that always made him think of weeds waving under water.

(And that patch of ground by the doorway was where Gorthyn had taken his death wound. For a moment Nai saw it again, his friend wrenching a javelin from his side and wrestling with a moon-silvered hound while the blood poured from the wound and two Scotti danced around him searching for an opening . . .)

He wheeled the pony, the others tugging reluctantly on the leading rein, and rode away at a fast trot without a backward glance.

Over the years he had learned it was wise to pay attention to inner voices, and his was telling him not to take the obvious route through the woods to the remains of Eurgain's village by the water, but to skirt around the western edge of the forest. It would mean a slower journey, for the landscape was criss-crossed with deep coombes and he would have to dismount and lead the ponies up and down the steep slopes, but if the three men had been part of a larger group it would be much safer.

This part of the wood had been coppiced in the distant past, so the trees grew thin and many-trunked: hazels, hornbeams and alders mixed with sessile oaks. There was little undergrowth, only an immense carpet of lightly curling leaves through which it was impossible to move without noise. The ponies' hooves made a steady pitter-patter as they shuffled through the debris, but at least the pair he was using as packhorses were now following his lead without balking, as they had at the start.

After crossing one deep valley and fording the stream at the bottom – fighting to prevent the ponies from bloating themselves on the cold water – he kept to the very edge of the wood, under the trees and slightly down slope from where they came to an abrupt end, so that the darkening sky above him could have been the rim of the world. The light was going fast, the darkness rising between the trees, welling from the hollows further down the hill, and it was becoming increasingly difficult to pick the best route between the low branches. In places the trees were long dead, had fallen or been uprooted in a gale, and now lay propped at fantastic angles against their fellows, so they seemed to be leaning on them for support as if tired or wounded in some long struggle.

Away in the depths of the forest a bird shrieked in alarm. Nai reined in his pony, waited a while, listening. It might have been nothing – a fox out hunting, another bird trespassing – but he feared the worst. The shriek came a second time, and a long chattering that carried on the still air of the wood. He was sweating inside his heavy winter cloak, and he flung back the fur-lined hood to hear better, the cold like a balm on his cheeks.

Suddenly he was positive that he was no longer alone in the

wood, that somewhere over to his right others were making their way through the trees, moving quietly but not so quietly they were not disturbing the wildlife. Had he dared he would have run for it, perhaps even abandoned his coffle of ponies, but the ground was too uncertain.

He loosened Gorthyn's sword in its scabbard and checked the supply of javelins in their quiver before urging the horses on through the drifts of dead leaves, clucking gently between his teeth to encourage them. They came on without any difficulty, which made him wonder whether he had imagined the presence of others in the forest, but these were well-schooled beasts, and of a better quality than he had at first thought.

In fact the very quality of the animals – the one he was riding was trained to battle unless he missed his guess – made him think that Greid had been telling the truth about the tattooed men having the assistance of Custennin the High Lord of Dumnonia. The ponies were too plump to have been ridden very far. They were of local origin, and although it was possible Greid and his comrades had either bartered for them or stolen them, it was much more likely they were a gift. Trained war steeds were prized possessions, rarely traded and always well guarded. Only a powerful and wealthy chieftain could afford to part with them – Nai's own lord, Gereint mab Cadwy, was notorious for valuing his horses more highly than his children – and there was no greater praise of a man's generosity than to say he was liberal with the fruits of his horse herd. These mounts were surely from the stables of Custennin himself.

As the gloom thickened Nai began to see shapes among the trees, a man crouching here, another leaning there, shapes that resolved themselves into stumps or odd growths when he came closer. At times he was forced to dismount and find a passage through the network of small branches that barred their way, the horses patiently following in his wake despite the twigs that scraped at their faces and flanks. The obstructions meant noise, and it seemed to him they were crashing through the woods so loudly nobody could miss them. Whenever he dared he stopped and stared about him, thinking how much easier this journey would be with a companion to watch his back, but he saw nothing except the thin trees.

After scrambling across another deep coombe he realized there was a lightening of the darkness ahead of him. A faint wind had sprung up, rustling the leaves of the holly beside which he had paused to catch his breath, and it brought with it the smell of open ground and the sea. Behind him the horses snuffled and stamped their feet, sensing the end of the wood.

He mounted and walked the horses forward, knowing he should come out on the heath, with a ridge to his right cutting him off from the estuary and the track leading to Penhyle, while the ground to his left would fall away in a series of long terraces to the cliffs on the western side of the peninsula. The ridge should hide him from prying eyes, and a short ride would bring him clear of the peninsula and give him room to manoeuvre without being trapped against the sea.

The horses pushed through the winter-brittle brushwood, snapping shoots and stems, while he peered anxiously ahead. Something twitched beyond the final veil of scrub: he reached for a spear, panic rising in his throat, sharp twigs stabbing at his face and hair, then heard a sound which was neither quite cough nor bark, and saw prick-eared triangular heads turned towards him. The deer bounded away through the dusk in a huddle that gradually formed into a column.

They raced up the slope of the ridge and suddenly halted. The rearmost gazed anxiously back in his direction, but the foremost were intent on another threat beyond the skyline. He could see them fretting like black shadows along the ridge, casting this way and that as they sought an escape. Then the leader burst for freedom over the horizon and the others flowed after, leaving the ridge empty.

Nai brought the horses out into the open, hoping they would be hidden by the dark bulk of the wood behind them. He was closer to the ridge than he had intended, but perhaps that was no bad thing, for it meant he had more space between him and the cliffs to the west, and was less likely to be pinned against them.

The only movement along the ridge was the winter grass waving in the breeze from the sea. The deer might have been spooked by some other animal. Now the villagers had gone, slaughtered during the summer by Eremon and his Scotti reivers, the larger predators were moving into the area. Several times he had seen traces of wolves in the forest and once he had found the fresh paw prints of a bear, though he had never seen any sign of the animal itself.

Even so, he hesitated for a while, listening for sounds of

something creeping through the fringes of the forest behind him, watching the heath and the skyline for a sign of movement. The heavens darkened, and the long dusk turned to true night. The waxing moon was high, but the cloud cover was heavy and it did not give much light.

At last he was ready. If there was anybody on the far side of the ridge, the chances were good they would not see him – by now he could scarcely see the way ahead himself. He had done his best to muffle the harnesses, and though the wind was blowing from the west and thus towards his enemies, the jingle might not carry.

His mouth was dry and he was sweating. Every moment he waited made moving seem more daunting. For all he knew, the three men had come alone and not as scouts for a larger party. Even if there was anyone lurking in the woods behind him or on the heath before him, they would surely not be so foolish as to ride roughneck across uncertain ground in the darkness.

An owl hooted in the woods. Nai heeled the pony into a trot as a second bird replied. The packhorses pulled reluctantly on the lead rein, and then they were all committed, out in the open with the faint roar of the sea to their left and the susurrations of the wind in the trees to their rear, and the horses' hooves were thudding on the hard turf, and he was riding blind, relying on his pony to pick the best route.

By the time the moon cleared the clouds he was well away from the peninsula, circling westward to avoid being caught against the mudflats of the estuary to his east. This was strange country to him, a place of open heaths and rough pastures interspersed with scrub woodland. At night one patch of wood was much like another, and he deliberately stayed clear of the hilltops, keeping to the valley bottoms or sides, seeking cover wherever possible, but his sense of direction did not fail him.

While he rode Nai settled to thinking seriously about what he was going to do. He was Gereint's man, a man with a name for loyalty and steadfast service, but Custennin was Gereint's overlord, and there was no love lost between the two of them. Gereint would do what he could to protect him, he had no doubt of that, but he also knew that if it came to the point Gereint would have to give him up to Custennin's justice. And in Custennin's justice Nai had no faith at all.

The obvious place to go was Penhyle. It was garrisoned by

friends, and anybody seeking out Sanctuary Wood must surely have passed through it. There, if anywhere, he could rely upon receiving honest answers to his questions. The only disadvantage was that it was so obvious it would be the first place any pursuers would seek him.

Yet he should be ahead of them, if they even existed. Despite his circuitous route, he had not really ridden so very far out of his way. He could cut back now for the track leading from the ruins of Eurgain's village to Penhyle, and reach the town before it settled for the night.

His mind made up he turned the ponies towards the north-east and the road along the ridge. With the thinning of the cloud cover the crescent moon cast a pale light on the long white grass. Looking back he saw he was leaving a trampled swathe behind him. Now he was further inland, the soil in the damp valley bottoms was a heavy marl that clung to the horses' hooves, and he feared it would be easy to follow his trail all the way from the wood.

Again an owl called, startling the horses, to be answered by another from somewhere within the black outline of a nearby copse. A third hooted behind them, and the ponies frisked uneasily, rolling their eyes and showing the whites. Nai reached for a javelin and steered his coffle down a steep slope – travelling faster and more noisily than he liked – into a long gully which would hide them from view.

The spear was a comfort in his hand. He wished he had donned his mail shirt before leaving the hut, but at the time it had seemed much simpler to roll it up and put it in a saddlebag. His shield hung in its customary place on his back and he decided to let it stay there, guarding his shoulder blades. The war-knife was ready at his belt, as was the long sword he had inherited from Gorthyn. (One day he would stop thinking of it as Gorthyn's sword, and then it would truly be his, instead of a weapon borrowed from a friend.)

All along the rim of the gully the owls hooted, back and forth, and to his ears some sounded real and others sounded like poor imitations. He drove the horses hard along the course of the brook in the valley bottom, thankful for the moonlight, splashing through the muddy water, careless of the ring of iron-shod hooves on the pebbles littering the bank, riding upstream for all he was worth, and still the owl hoots followed him.

The gully petered out in a marshy cleave. His mount struggled clear of the wet ground, dragging the others behind it, and he found himself exposed in the open under the pitiless glare of the moon, which suddenly seemed very bright. The hooting stopped. He stared around him, saw nothing except the moon-frosted grass and the dark trees of the copse waving in the night wind behind him, urged the horse on using the butt of the javelin as a crop.

They galloped wildly across the heath, the ponies close to panic, the thunder of their passage loud in the empty land, his seat slipping in the saddle and his calves knotting with the strain. Ahead of him the ground rose and he pulled himself forward, aware his balance was precarious and that he was treating these animals with an abandon he would never have countenanced had they been his own.

Then they were at the top, and there spread below him were the pale grey waters of the estuary glimmering in the moonlight, and, glowing against the darker outline of the shore, the red lights of the settlement at its head. With a sob of relief, he swung his horse's head onto the track and gradually slowed the animals to a walk.

Nothing moved behind him.

Feeling slightly ashamed of his fear, he wiped the horse froth from his cloak and eased his legs, which were wet with both his own and the pony's sweat.

The remainder of the ride was uneventful, in so far as riding at night can ever be said to be uneventful. He came within sight of the stockade surrounding the settlement at about the time the moon was swallowed by a heavy bank of cloud, and the last part of his journey was spent on foot, feeling his way across the ruts and pits in the road.

Finally the horses' hooves rang on the cobbles which led to the entrance gate. The moon reappeared as a sleepy voice cried a challenge, and the freshly-cut timbers of the wooden palisade suddenly loomed very white before him. He could remember hearing them being raised into place with much banging and cursing as he lay in the grip of wound fever after being brought here from the beach where he had slain Eremon, his childhood friend and foe . . .

'Who comes to the gate of Penhyle?' The challenge was repeated impatiently.

'Nai mab Nwython, of the household of Gereint mab Cadwy,' he called to the half-seen figure leaning over the stockade.

'Nai?' the sentry said in puzzlement. 'Wait!'

Feet clattered above him. He waited, shivering, watching the empty road behind him and the cloud shadows dipping across the line of the ridge.

'Nai?' said a familiar voice. 'Nai, what brings you here?'

'The need for shelter. May I enter?'

Addonwy pulled the gate open and ushered him through.

'By God, cousin, I had not thought to see you in Penhyle. And a cavalcade of horses! Where did you find them?'

'A long tale,' he said, abruptly exhausted.

'Come inside, come inside. I'll call one of the boys to take them away. You have ridden hard,' Addonwy added, feeling the flanks of the lead pony.

'Wait,' Nai said with difficulty, his tongue seeming swollen in his mouth. 'Who knows I am here?'

Addonwy caught him as he swayed. 'Only Evrog and I. Evrog will not talk if you do not wish it.' His bearded face loomed large in the moonlight. 'Gently, cousin, gently. Sit here for a while and I shall stable the horses myself. None will see them, and I can tend to them properly once you are settled.' He turned to the sentry on the platform over the gate. 'Not a word of this to anybody, do you hear me?'

Nai did not catch the reply. He was slumped on a mounting block in the shadow of the palisade, so weary he could barely keep his eyes open, thankful that Addonwy was a quick-witted man. Perhaps he dozed, for it seemed to him the other returned in no time at all.

'Can you walk?' A strong arm slipped round his shoulders. 'Come, Cadlew and I have been sharing a hut – you can hardly call it a house – but I dare say we could squeeze in a third, provided he's an old friend.'

The stream of inconsequential chatter kept him moving though the strength seemed to have left his legs, moving down a narrow street between thatched buildings, some built of stone and some of wattle and daub.

'In here,' said Addonwy, opening a flimsy wooden door. 'Mind the step.'

Nai stumbled down into an oval room lit by a central fire and a solitary taper. One wall was taken up with bedding; against the other was a rickety table. Sitting at the table with his back to the door was a short stocky man engaged in mending a broken belt.

'Cadlew, find a stool for our guest,' Addonwy said cheerfully.

'If you are here, who is on guard duty?' growled the stocky man. He swore loudly as the heavy needle pricked his finger. 'Can she sew leather, whoever she is?' he demanded, and whirled round on his stool.

'Well,' he said after a moment. 'You are not a woman, that's for sure.' He dropped the belt and needle, ran a hand through thinning fair hair. 'What is the hermit of Sanctuary Wood doing in our hovel in the middle of the night?'

He rose and flung his arms around Nai, half carried him to the stool, held him upright and helped divest him of shield, cloak and sword (Cadlew's eyes briefly lighting at the sight of Gorthyn's blade), then helped him sit.

'Food and drink!' said the stocky man. 'Stay there and I shall find you some.'

Cadlew bustled about the hut while Addonwy cleared a space on the table, then the two of them watched as Nai forced himself to eat the bread and cheese. At first the mead made his head spin, but he sipped it slowly and after a time began to feel better.

'Tattooed men,' Nai said through a mouthful. 'Did they pass through Penhyle?'

The pair exchanged a glance, then Addonwy pulled his stool closer to the table.

'They did,' he said. 'We wondered what they would make of you.'

'You told them about me?'

Addonwy nodded. 'They came to us yesterday at dusk and stayed the night. We were hard pushed to find room for them all.'

'How many?'

'A dozen, and four of Custennin's men as their escorts.'

Nai raised an eyebrow. This was worse than he had thought. 'Tell me.'

'Did you not meet with them?' interrupted Cadlew, bursting with impatience.

Nai nodded. 'But tell me what they told you.'

Addonwy shrugged, reached for a wooden goblet and filled it from the mead flask. 'Evrog can keep the gate alone a while longer,' he remarked absently. He took a swallow, said:

'They themselves told us nothing. A clannish group who

shunned all contact with us. But the leader of the escort was Isgofan mab Banon, and him I have met before. Do you know him, Nai?'

Nai shook his head. 'I have heard of him.'

'A smooth-talking dog,' said Cadlew, the dislike thick in his voice. 'Fancies himself a swordsman. Keeps a baton at his belt with a notch for every man he has killed.'

Addonwy smiled faintly. 'Like all Custennin's men, he looks upon those of us who serve Gereint as half-trained provincials, and makes no effort to hide his opinion. At all events, he explained these strangers were from an island in the far North, which I must say seems probable since no civilized man would scar his face in that manner.'

'Not all of them had scars,' objected Cadlew.

'No,' acknowledged the other, 'not visibly. But remember what Nai told us of the magic man Eremon had with him last summer: he had a small tattoo concealed on his shoulder. I suspect these were the same.'

He took another pull at the goblet. 'Isgofan span us a tale, and I do not know whether he himself believed it or not.'

'Thought it good enough for us, though,' growled Cadlew. 'Moonshine!'

'Peace, cousin,' Addonwy said with a grin. 'I must admit, it had an air of moonshine about it, but who knows what barbarians might believe, up there in the darkness of the far north. According to Isgofan, the northerners have been charged by their King with the task of finding a hermit who lives in a woodland sanctuary beside the sea. The King's son is dying of some illness. After much fasting and prayer the King was vouchsafed a dream, and in the dream he learned that only this hermit can cure his son.'

Cadlew snorted, and even Nai managed a wan smile.

'Groups of them are scouring the coastline of Prydein, but this particular party had approached Custennin himself, bearing gifts from their northern king, and sought his help and advice. Sweet Custennin, being the kind-hearted and open-handed fellow he is –' here Cadlew laughed aloud '– at once assigned Isgofan to bring them to the Porthyle estuary.'

'What did you tell them?' asked Nai.

Addonwy refilled his goblet. 'You would have been proud of me, Nai. I was stricken with grief, and bade Isgofan convey my sorrow and regrets to the strangers. I said the hermit was dead, slain during our troubles in the summer with Saeson pirates and Scotti reivers. Perhaps Isgofan had heard of what happened?'

'And?'

'Isgofan looked wise, nodded sadly. A terrible thing, but a great triumph for Gereint's men: two of them against such a host! And yet – here he cocked his head upon one side, gave me a penetrating stare – was it possible there might have been some mistake in the initial reports? It must have been a very confused time, with the one reliable source so badly wounded we all feared for his life. What was his name again? Nai mab Nwython? An old friend of mine? What could be better, what could be better. Did I know where you were now? And the other survivors, the Saeson boy and the peasant girl from the little village? Did I know what had befallen them?

'I hummed and hawed. Gereint had bound me to secrecy, he must understand. On the other hand, Custennin was Gereint's overlord, and obviously the secrecy did not apply to him, nor by extension to Isgofan his deputy. I bound him with solemn oaths not to reveal a word to any save Custennin himself, and told him that the two youngsters had gone east to the Saeson lands. You had chosen to take the hermit's place at the mouth of the estuary. As for the hermit himself, to the best of my knowledge he was dead.'

'You have shortened the tale, cousin,' said Cadlew. He turned to Nai. 'They kept me awake half the night with their gabbling. And the upshot, to my mind, was that my dear friend was too clever for his own good.'

Addonwy raised a rueful eyebrow. 'Isgofan wanted to know why the need for secrecy. I answered that Gereint preferred not to have it bruited about he had aided a Saeson, and Isgofan looked puzzled. Surely, he said, though the boy may have entered our land as a foe, he departed a friend? Was not the whole point that this lad had stood shoulder to shoulder with Nai and the late lamented Gorthyn against Eremon's Scotti? Where was the shame in helping him return to his own people?'

'How did you reply?'

Addonwy spread his hands in a disarming gesture. 'I simply said the ways of princes are beyond my ken.'

'Was he satisfied?'

'I doubt it. But there was nothing he could do without calling me a liar, and Cadlew was sitting in the corner sharpening his war-knife, muttering under his breath about people disturbing his rest.'

'My knife was blunt,' said Cadlew. 'And besides, this room has no corners, being an oval.'

'What happened next?'

'Isgofan left to sleep —'

'Praise God!' interjected Cadlew.

'In the morning they divided their party. Some went south to find you and hear from your own lips what had befallen the hermit. Others rode west in search of another holy man who is said to dwell near the mouth of the Avon.'

'How many came to find me?'

'Isgofan and his comrade Eri, together with six of the tattooed men.' He regarded Nai steadily. 'And now, cousin, I think it is time you told us what has befallen you since we last met.'

Nai wet the tips of his forefingers and rubbed them across his upper eyelids, an old trick to stave off drowsiness he had learned from his foster-father.

'They must have divided again before they reached me,' he said. 'I only saw three, though there may have been others nearby.'

He gave them the whole story from the moment the rooks in the wood had disturbed him to the hooting of the owls along the rim of the gully. At the end of it his voice was raw with talking and he drank deep from his cup to ease his throat. 'I think now that they were merely owls and nothing more, but at the time . . .' He shuddered.

There was a long pause while his friends considered what he had told them. Eventually Cadlew rose with a grunt and threw another log on the fire.

'They already knew the hermit was dead. Why then did they let you think they had mistaken you for him? And where were Isgofan and the rest of them while all this was happening?'

Nai shook his head. 'Perhaps they did not believe Addonwy.'

'Perhaps.' Cadlew frowned, said carefully: 'The first man. He attacked you without warning?'

'Yes. I gave him greeting, and he came at me directly, without speaking.'

'Mmm.' Cadlew kicked at the fire, sending up a shower of sparks. 'I have heard your greetings before, cousin. Your voice can be rough, especially if you have not used it for a while.' He kept his face turned to the fire.

71

'And the others,' said Addonwy in measured tones. 'One caught you spying on the hut. Perhaps . . .'

Nai slammed his fist onto the table. It creaked alarmingly. 'What are you saying? That I acted too hastily? They tried to kill me!'

'Ye . . . es,' said Cadlew. 'But did you have to bring their God-farting horses here?'

Nai stared at him angrily. Cadlew returned his gaze, and suddenly both of them were laughing.

'The horses!' exclaimed Addonwy. 'I must see to them.'

'No.' Cadlew straightened, wiped his face. 'I will do it. Better you stay and talk with Nai. I'll wake one of the others and tell him you are unwell, persuade him to take over your guard duties. Evrog must be lonely by now.'

The stocky man patted Nai on the shoulder, nodded to his comrade and left. Addonwy waited until the sound of his footsteps had died away, then said:

'So what do you think the tattooed men wanted?'

'They wanted the hermit. The man known as Budoc.'

'Why?'

'Because they believed that years ago Budoc had helped steal something from them.'

'Had he?'

'No.' Nai hesitated, frowned. 'Or at least, from their point of view perhaps he had, though it was not theirs to keep.'

Addonwy tugged at his beard. 'I do not understand.'

'Neither do I, not altogether.'

The taper guttered and went out, leaving them with only the firelight.

'How much do you know about the events of last summer?' asked Nai.

Addonwy leaned back on his stool. 'Not enough, it would seem. I take it this Budoc is still alive, whereas Gereint gave me the impression he had died during the fighting. I knew our old friend Eremon had some link with Vortepor of Dyfed – which reminds me of another thing I must tell you – and through Vortepor with some group of tattooed men from the far North, but to be frank the whole affair was so convoluted and so garbled I never really understood what it was all about. How did the Saesons become involved?'

'The Saesons blundered in by chance, though they were the

reason Gorthyn and I came to Porthyle.' Nai closed his eyes wearily. 'Two things Gereint told us before we left his hall: Eremon mab Cairbre had been plotting with Vortepor of Dyfed, and a Saeson ship had been sighted sailing west in search of new lands. Gereint sent us to keep watch on the ship. When we reached the estuary we discovered the Saesons had anchored and been overwhelmed by Scotti raiders.'

He went on to explain how he and Gorthyn had crossed the estuary, suspecting that the raiders were led by the renegade Eremon. Eremon had been fostered by Gereint, but had turned reiver once he reached manhood. Five years ago Gereint had summoned his warband and driven the renegade from his lands, but not before Gorthyn's father (who had treated the orphaned Nai as his own son) had been tortured to death by one of Eremon's followers. Nai himself had been wounded in the throat by Eremon during the fighting, and since that time had found speech difficult.

'Gorthyn was eager to cross,' said Nai. 'He wanted vengeance on Eremon and Dovnuall the torturer.'

'And you?' Addonwy's face was gentle in the firelight.

'I was afraid, cousin.' Nai rubbed at the scar on his throat. 'Eremon had come close to killing me on the last occasion we met.'

'I remember.'

'But I could not let Gorthyn go alone. And I was caught up in his fury.'

On the far side of the estuary they had met with three people: Budoc the hermit of Sanctuary Wood; Ceolric the sole survivor of the Saeson ship; and Eurgain, likewise the only survivor of her village, which had been seized by the Scotti. Gradually Nai had come to suspect that Budoc the hermit had once been Bedwyr, the chief of Arthur's Companions.

'Bedwyr!' exclaimed Addonwy. 'I thought he died at Cam-lann.'

'That was what we were supposed to think.'

'Why?' Addonwy sat forward in excitement. 'And surely, Gorthyn was kin to Bedwyr?'

'He was, just as Eremon was kin to Lleminawg the Dancer, the Fated One. I do not think it was mere happenstance that brought us all together.'

'Lleminawg? Eremon spoke of him sometimes when we were

boys. He was another of Arthur's Companions.' Addonwy's brows wrinkled in thought. 'I cannot remember how he died, though he must still have been a young man when he fell.'

'His death was a mysterious one. I heard the tale of it from Bedwyr himself, and I do not pretend to understand it fully.'

Bedwyr had told Nai of how a female bard had come to Arthur's court at Caer Cadwy in the years following the last great victory over the Saxons at Badon Hill. In those days Arthur was leader of the warband of Prydein, Magister Militum per Britannias in the Roman style, but his army was drawn from the disparate forces of the Princes of Britain, who had acknowledged no master since the death of Vitolinus the High King decades earlier. Some were Arthur's keen supporters, knowing that without him they would soon be swallowed by the Saesons in the east or the Scotti out of Ireland in the west. Others hated and feared him, and one of these was the young heir to Dyfed, Vortepor.

The bard, Teleri, had evoked the oldest of all names for the island: Albion. She persuaded Arthur the time had come for the Britons to unite behind a single ruler, and offered him a trial at the Sovereignty of Albion. On an isle to the far north-west of Britain was a labyrinth guarded by a clan of tattooed warriors known as Plant Menestyr, the Children of the Cupbearer. Rumour had it only the sovereign lord of all Albion could walk the labyrinth and live.

'But Arthur was wounded before he could make the trial,' said Nai. 'Lleminawg was his substitute.'

'He succeeded? He must have done, since Arthur became Amherawdyr.'

'He did, at the cost of his own life. Arthur brought home a chalice, the symbol of sovereignty, and became Emperor of Albion. He ruled for twenty years until he was brought down by his enemies.'

'Medraut,' breathed Addonwy.

'Medraut was the instrument. But others were the prime movers, and chief amongst them was Vortepor, by now High Lord of Dyfed.'

Arthur and Medraut had fallen at the disastrous battle of Camlann. The warband of Britain had been shattered, never to ride again. Nobody left alive had sufficient prestige to claim the throne. The symbol of sovereignty was spirited away by Bedwyr and the Lady Gwenhwyvar, Arthur's wife.

'So the tattooed men are the Children of Menestyr,' said Addonwy.

'Yes. They want the chalice, and they are not alone in their desire. Eremon was sent by Vortepor to find it. Being Eremon, he thought to cheat Vortepor and keep it for himself on the grounds that he was the heir to Lleminawg. Vortepor had given him one of the tattooed men to advise him. Eremon disposed of the tattooed man and replaced him with a druid from Ierne. The druid also proved to be a member of the clan.'

Addonwy laughed. 'Poor Eremon. He was never as cunning as he liked to think himself.'

'Eremon and his Scotti trapped us in the hermit's hut. We fought, and Gorthyn was slain. Bedwyr saved us.'

'How?'

Nai rubbed at his face. 'You, Cadlew and I: we three are good warriors, yes? I mean, we know how to use our weapons, when to fight and when to run. We may be afraid but we do what is needful.'

Addonwy nodded, his eyes on his friend.

'Bedwyr is an old man. His left hand is a stiffened claw. He is not a tall man, nor is he very broad. At first sight he is not impressive. But I tell you, cousin, the three of us together could not stand against him for longer than a few heartbeats. Our only hope would be to find him already exhausted, for age has stolen his stamina.' Nai shrugged, half smiled at a memory. 'And even then I am not sure.'

'And after that?'

'Bedwyr drove off our attackers. We gathered ourselves and fled. We had not gone far when Eremon challenged me to single combat.'

'Ever one for the grand gesture.'

Nai grinned. 'He agreed to give the others – Ceolric, Eurgain and Bedwyr-Budoc – safe passage while the fight lasted.'

'He thought he would win?' Addonwy caught the look on Nai's face. 'No, I mean more than idle flattery. In a real fight, one to one, I would always have backed you. Not on the practice ground, no; but when it mattered, yes.'

'Would you?' said Nai, surprised.

'Yes, cousin, I would.'

Nai shook himself. 'Anyway, you know the rest. I killed him and collapsed. Ceolric and Eurgain met Gereint's force coming to our rescue and guided them back to me. The remains of the Scotti fled and were hunted down.'

'And the hermit? Bedwyr?'

'He left, avoiding Gereint's men. He feared that if he stayed he would become a counter in another's game. Too many people would have a use for the one-time captain of Arthur's warband. And besides, there was the matter of the chalice.'

Addonwy frowned. 'Yes, the chalice. That is the part I do not follow. How could a cup confer the Sovereignty of Britain? And why was Vortepor of Dyfed working with these Children of Menestyr? What did he stand to gain from it?'

'It puzzled me also. Obviously Vortepor wants the chalice for himself. He has ruled for longer than any other prince in Britain, so I suppose that might give him some claim to seniority over the rest. I think he needed the tattooed men to confirm that he did indeed have the right chalice, was not being palmed off with an imitation. The first man, the one Eremon murdered, Vortepor knew about. Whether he knew about the second, the druid Eremon found in Ierne, I am not so sure. They were allies, all of them, but allies of convenience, not conviction.'

'One betrays the other, and Eremon seeks to cheat them both.' Addonwy pushed back his stool. 'And the chalice, cousin? How does it convey Sovereignty? And where is it now?'

'I do not know.' Nai's voice was so hoarse the other had to strain to hear him. 'All I know is what Bedwyr told me. After Camlann, Gwenhwyvar kept the chalice. I made him a promise. If he fell to Eremon's men, I was to seek her out.'

'Gwenhwyvar?' Addonwy whistled softly. 'As well to seek the golden apples of the sun. The Princes of Prydein have sought Gwenhwyvar for ten long years, and never found a sign of her. You know the saying, cousin. "Three things not known: the grave of Arthur, the grave of Medraut – and the whereabouts of Gwenhwyvar" .'

The door swung open and Cadlew returned, grunting under the weight of Nai's saddlebags. He kicked the door shut behind him and dumped his load on the earth floor.

'God and his angels!' he said, sagging at the knees. 'Did you bring everything you own?' He staggered to the table, filled a goblet with mead and tossed it back.

'I have moved the ponies, divided them between the other stables. As a group they are obvious to anybody with half an eye.'

'Well done,' said Addonwy.

The stocky man stretched, refilled his mug. 'Then I brought Coal from his stall and left his harness beside him. Your warshirt is hanging on the hook above the saddle, Nai. It was too heavy to carry back with all the other stuff.' He prodded a bag with his foot. 'Your loot I shoved into the thatch. Not very original, I know, but the best I could manage.'

'Did you say Coal?' said Nai, blinking at him.

'Yes, Coal. Used to be your horse, I believe? If you don't want him, have another one. Help yourself. If none of ours match your fancy, I daresay somebody else will come wandering into Penhyle before long and you can bash them over the head and have theirs. The countryside seems uncommonly busy for the time of year.'

Nai had known Cadlew all his life, but he still found it difficult to tell when the stocky man was joking and when he was being serious.

'You mean you have Coal here?'

'No, no, of course not,' Cadlew snarled sarcastically. 'He's sitting in Din Erbin with Gereint awaiting your return.'

'We brought him with us,' said Addonwy. 'Gereint thought he might tempt you back to life.'

'You did not tell me.'

'You were not ready.'

'We were saving him as a surprise,' said Cadlew, 'hoping you would one day say you were bored with the hermit's life. Then we were going to produce Coal on our next visit, and see what happened.'

To his horror Nai felt tears pricking his eyes. He looked up and saw both men watching him sympathetically.

'You should sleep,' Addonwy said kindly. 'When you wake we can discuss what to do next.'

Nai stood, swaying with tiredness. Addonwy pulled back the covers for him and he collapsed onto the bedding, rolled over once and was instantly asleep.

CHAPTER FOUR

'So you met with Cadlew and Addonwy in Penhyle?' said
Seradwen, pouring the bard a goblet of wine.

'You know them?' He tasted the wine, smiled with pleasure.

'For years, though I have not seen them for a long time. My
father's lands are near Din Erbin, so before my marriage I was
often at the fort.'

Regin nodded. 'No doubt you had many suitors.'

She ignored the compliment. 'Tell me, did they speak of a man
named Nai? Nai mab Nwython?'

'Nai?' he repeated, wrinkling his brow and settling back in his
seat. His gaze wandered around the room, taking in the wall
paintings and the neat line of scrolls stacked in their alcove above
the writing desk. 'I do not think so.'

'A pity,' she said lightly. 'An old friend, badly wounded during
the summer. Rumour had it he had taken himself off to the mouth
of the estuary to recuperate.'

'Ah, wait,' he said suddenly, setting his goblet down on the
little table by his chair. 'Yes, there was some mention of a
comrade living like a hermit. Near a woodland sanctuary, is
that right?'

'It could be.' Seradwen tried to keep the eagerness from her
voice.

'Addonwy and Cadlew were planning a visit. I had the impression they keep a close eye on him while trying not to
interfere.' He shook his head. 'But I regret, I can give you no

news of him, other than that he is alive and well. I am afraid their talk did not mean much to me. Had I known you would be interested I would have paid more attention.'

'It is not important.' She waved a hand airily. 'You said Cadlew did not approve of your material?'

Regin laughed. 'By God, that man is fierce! No, he did not approve, and he made his disapproval clear.'

'What was his objection?'

The bard leant forward. 'As I told you, I come from Dyfed, across the Severn Sea. Our traditions are slightly different from yours. You may be aware that our Protector, the High Lord Vortepor, was never so keen a supporter of the Emperor Arthur as the rulers of Dumnonia.'

'Kynfawr, Custennin's father, was Arthur's man through and through.' She sipped her wine. 'I am not sure about Custennin himself.'

'Well,' shrugged Regin, 'it is ten years or more since Arthur fell at Camlann. In those days Custennin was but a boy, doing as his father bade him. My point is that Vortepor always believed Arthur threatened the power of the individual rulers of the regions.'

She made to protest, but he raised a hand to forestall her.

'Rightly or wrongly, it matters not. But as a consequence, our version of events in Dyfed is often rather different from the one you may have heard here in Dumnonia. For example the song I sang in Penhyle told of a quarrel between Arthur and Cei. In Dyfed, it is said that Arthur caused Cei's death, and that is a tale not told in these parts – as I discovered!'

'And what will you give us tonight?' she asked, suppressing a grin at the thought of the notoriously foul-mouthed Cadlew remonstrating with the urbane and self-possessed bard.

'A few safe favourites. The Hunting of King Boar is always popular.'

'And news? What news do you bring?'

He ran a hand through dark hair, grimaced. 'Nothing good, I fear, though at the same time nothing which immediately affects us here in the south west. The West Saesons wage war upon each other, and the winner will become a power to be reckoned with. At the end of last summer Cerdic's war-leader, Cynrig, attacked the Isle of Wectis.'

'Wectis is under the sway of the Ytes, yes?'

Regin lifted his brows. 'You are better informed than I had expected.' There was a hint of condescension about his voice, rapidly concealed.

'These things interest me,' she said coolly. 'If I remember rightly, Hengist the conqueror of the Cantii was a leader of the Ytes.'

'The Half-Danes, they call them sometimes.' He drained his wine, placed a hand over the top in refusal when she offered more. 'Cerdic declared himself Cyning last summer. Now he flexes his muscles, for a cyning must have a cynedom to rule.'

'Cyning?'

'In Latin, Rex. In our tongue, Brenhin. Vortepor and Custennin are cynings; Dyfed and Dumnonia their cynedoms.' This time the condescending tone was not so well hidden.

'I understand. And why does Cerdic move first against the Ytes of Wectis?'

'He rules a precarious alliance of settlers. By waging war he will unite them behind him. Wectis is rich farmland; once he has its revenues he can think of expanding on the mainland, towards Sarum and the lands east of the great forest they call Sallow Wood.'

As an answer to her question it was incomplete, but she could see his point, and the danger Cerdic represented. Thirty years ago Arthur had destroyed a generation of Saeson warriors at Badon Hill. Ten years ago their successors had allied with the traitor Medraut and marched to Camlann. Again a generation was slaughtered, in what was said to be the bloodiest battle ever fought on British soil, a fight in which hundreds if not thousands had died on both sides. Arthur himself was slain, and the Warband of Albion was lost, but the Saesons fared no better. Since that day they had remained bound on their eastern reservations, licking their wounds, so that men still spoke of the Amherawdyr's Peace as if Arthur yet lived. Now Cerdic threatened to disrupt that peace, and Seradwen had no doubt that if he was successful others would follow his example.

'Cerdic did not fight at Camlann,' Regin said softly. 'Some of the chieftains he has now brought under his rule sent men, but he himself was wise enough to steer clear. He was not tainted with the disaster.'

'And of course the failure of his rivals at Camlann is one of the things which has allowed him to become dominant.'

He was impressed by her acumen. She could feel him reappraising her, tilting back his head and surveying her down the hook of his nose.

'Exactly,' he said. 'Exactly. For years Cerdic has sat quietly in a corner weaving a fabric, interlacing the yarns here, snipping a loose thread there, and all the while we have thought him harmless, no danger, a good example of the kind of Saeson lord with whom we can deal as with one of our own, and all the while his cloth has grown till now it threatens to smother us.'

'Us, Regin? I can see he might be a danger to eastern Dumnonia and the Summer Country, but surely Dyfed is safe?'

'Two things I would say to that.' He held up a long-fingered hand and counted them off. 'First, if Cerdic moves north successfully the other Saeson tribes in the east will imitate him, and the heart of Prydein will fall to them. Second, if Cerdic is successful then either in this generation or the next his people will reach Aquae Sulis and sever the land link between Dumnonia and the rest of Prydein.'

'Which would have far-reaching effects,' she said absently, thinking it through.

'It would be the end of Prydein, the end of any hope that one day Arthur's empire of Albion might be reborn. Custennin's hold upon Dumnonia is not strong. Some in the eastern part of the region might welcome a new master, even a Saeson.'

'There were rumours in the summer of an attempt to overthrow him.'

Regin grinned, revealing strong white teeth. 'The rumours are true. The affair is still too fresh to be much mentioned at Custennin's court. From what I gathered, the leader of his warband plotted to take Custennin's place. This man, one Angus, either is or was married to one of Custennin's sisters – or perhaps it was one of his aunts, I don't quite recall. Whichever, that gave him a close enough connection to the royal kindred to garner some support, and then I suppose as leader of the warband he had trained most of the household warriors.'

'What happened?'

'Somebody betrayed the plot before it came to fruition. A few people were executed, a few imprisoned. Angus himself, because of his connections, was sent into exile. A monastery in the wilderness.'

Seradwen straightened in her seat. 'Now that is interesting. I have heard of a new monastery somewhere on the moors, but nobody seems to know much about it.'

'Perhaps it is the same one,' Regin said lightly. 'Mind you, most religious houses are built in awkward places, to aid the inmates in their withdrawal from the world. I wonder at the urge myself.'

He was interrupted by a knock at the door.

'Dinner,' said Seradwen. 'Perhaps we shall continue later.'

'I should enjoy that, Lady.' He rose to his feet and swept her a bow. 'It is rare to meet so fine an intellect outside a royal household.'

And it is even rarer, she thought as she led the way to the refectory, to meet a travelling bard with such strong opinions on the present state of Britain. Regin sounded more like a leader of men than a praise-singer.

Mordav had always insisted they should eat most nights in the communal hall. Some of the workers and their families preferred to eat their own food, especially on the long summer evenings, but in the depths of winter most people took advantage of the warm and well-lit refectory with its hot meals. Hoewgi and his family had followed Mordav's custom, dining in hall perhaps five times out of seven. The other brothers were less regular in their attendance, but the promise of a bard bearing news and gossip from Custennin's court had brought them in tonight, together with their wives and older children.

It had also brought almost everybody else who worked on the estate: Seradwen could hear the hubbub as they approached along the corridor between the kitchens and the hall. The night was mild and the windows had been left unshuttered, so the noise spilled out across the inner courtyard.

'I had no idea the farm was so large,' murmured Regin, hesitating in the antechamber.

Seradwen frowned to herself. There was something odd about that statement, something she could not quite bring to mind. Then it was too late, and they were through the double doors and inside the crowded room, negotiating a route between the closely packed tables, further conversation impossible until they reached the haven of the dais where the family sat.

'Grief, and it's warm,' said the bard. 'Where is your place, Lady?'

Hoewgi was beckoning to him, indicating the seat of honour at his right hand. With all the family present the High Table was crowded, but certain of the older retainers had refused to give up their jealously guarded privilege of dining on the dais.

'My friends will have kept me a seat,' she said, and pushed him towards Hoewgi.

Bodgath, by dint of snarling at anyone who came near, had managed to save a space at the end of the table.

'Handsome man,' he remarked as she squeezed in beside him.

'Striking, I would say.' She looked around the company, grinned. 'Not my kind. Talks too much.'

They relaxed, grinned back at her. 'Stick with old Bodgath, Lady,' called one of the women.

'Get on,' she said. 'All he ever talks about is horses.'

'Worse things than that,' Bodgath said with dignity. 'Besides, sometimes I branch out into the weather. Speaking of which, they tell me it will be colder after the next moon.'

'About time,' grumbled someone else. 'This winter's been so mild it's not been winter at all.'

Hoewgi beat upon the table with a mallet he kept for that purpose until the noise died away. He stood, clearing his throat, and announced in a reedy voice:

'Knife is in the meat and drink is in the horn.'

'Not over here it isn't,' growled Bodgath.

'And a fine craftsman bringing his craft honours us this night: Regin the bard from Dyfed.'

'Thinks he's the Lord Gereint, he does,' snorted a woman. 'Sit down, you.'

As if he had heard, Hoewgi abruptly subsided, glaring at their end of the table.

'That it?' said Bodgath. 'Can we eat now?'

Seradwen kept her head bowed, understanding how they felt, knowing her intervention would make matters worse. Mordav had kept the customs of his fathers, treating the farm as a community with himself the first among equals. Hoewgi preferred a formal style, but lacked the force of personality to carry it off.

The servitors brought food and drink, and the company fell to their meal, eating ravenously like a horde that had not been fed in days. From where she sat Seradwen could see the bard's hooked profile between the movements of the other diners, and she noticed he ate sparingly, sometimes seeming near to choking on a mouthful. She recognized the signs of nervousness, and wondered a little, for Regin had seemed like a polished performer, a man accustomed to reciting in front of far larger and more sophisticated audiences than this gathering of farm workers.

When the remnants of the meal had been cleared away and the wine passed round again (for the presence of a bard from far off Dyfed made this a special occasion), Regin rose and strolled to the front of the dais, strumming casually on his harp, bringing it into tune.

'Let us begin with a song we all know,' he said, his deep voice filling the hall, and suddenly he launched into The Dream of Macsen Wledig, the long fingers gliding across the strings.

They listened, all of them absorbed in the familiar tale, and when he finished they beat upon the pinewood tables and demanded more.

He blotted the sheen of sweat from his brow with one sleeve, drank thirstily from a beaker of plain water. His eyes roved the room, assessing the mood of the crowd.

'Here is a new song. I heard it first in the hall of the High Lord of my people, in the hall of great Vortepor the Protector of Dyfed, and I deemed it worthy of adding to my store. I hope it will please you also.'

He drew his hand across the harp, sending a cascade of notes shimmering through the chamber like droplets of water falling from a fountain, then laid his palm flat on the strings. Into the silence came his voice, deep and confident, surging as might the sea at dawn.

He sang of a woman with a form like gossamer, one of the three shining ones who inherited the beauty God bestowed upon Eve. There was Diadema the mistress of Achelarwy White-Shield, there was matchless Elen on whose account Troy was destroyed, and there was this one, the most beautiful of them all after Mother Eve herself, a woman of fair and light form like summer sunshine.

She lived with her husband, this woman, and bore him two sons. Her beauty did not fade with the years but rather grew greater, and with it grew her fame, till her renown spread throughout the land. The love she and her lord bore each other became a byword through all Prydein, so that to speak of steadfast or constant lovers was to speak their names.

Now it happened that before her marriage she had been wooed by the young prince of the Summer Country, a man of birth and

84

breeding similar to her own, a man whose suit found favour in the eyes of her father. But she preferred the one who became her husband, a junior member of a family which had prospered under Roman rule, though he himself at that time lacked either fame or fortune. She spurned the young prince, with his ancient lineage stretching back into the dawn of time when Pryderi the Strong first named the rivers and hills of Prydein, spurned him and married instead the red-handed warrior, who with the collusion of her father's gatekeeper stole her away from her family and friends on her wedding day.

(The audience laughed and nudged each other, for this part of the story they recognized.)

This much is well known, a tale oft told at the expense of the young prince. After the abortive marriage feast, when his bride was plucked from under his very eyes, he retreated to his own domain. A strange place, the Summer Country: a place of lagoons and marsh, of small islands rising like hummocks above the flat calm of reed-strewn lakes; a place where water mirrors and reflects, flings sky and cloud to cloud and sky. In winter it broods emptily, the haunt of fish and fowl; only in summer do men enter the Levels. Thus the name, the Summer Country.

Melwas the young prince shut himself away in his brooding land for many years, while the tale of his humiliation grew in the telling. So too did Gwenhwyvar's beauty and Arthur's prestige, but Melwas never faltered in his resolve that one day the woman would be his, in accordance with her father's promise. A recourse to arms would have been futile, for he was not a warrior, like Arthur, nor could he command a following to match the Warband of Albion. That power was not his, for his power was of another kind.

A strange place the Summer Country, a place of wind, wave and water. Winds blow on the hills, scudding clouds across the heavens. Waves from the salt sea lap the edges of the marshes, ripple the surface of the silent lakes. Fresh water bubbles from the earth; stagnant water stands in black pools scummed with green where long weeds trail. There is power in land, power in sea, power in water running or still.

And Melwas Lord of the Summer Country lived on the margins of the world, in a place that was not land, not sea, not lake, but all three of these, a place which could be reached only at certain times of year, and then only by one who knew its channels and byways. Down the long years he meditated on his country, till its powers were his, and then he was ready to seek his vengeance.

So the Lord of Summer clad himself in his cloak of green and went forth from his watery land at the end of the world. Wherever he went fresh flowers sprang up behind him and the earth groaned under the weight of fruit and crops. Green was the forest through which he travelled, and high his road among the many-branched walls of the treetops where he walked unseen. He came to the house of Arthur the soldier, a well defended house with guards set all about, and chief among them were her two sons, the brave warriors Llacheu and Anir.

Melwas passed above them in silence, walking on the branches of the trees over them where they kept watch – keen their eyes and keen their spears had they but raised their heads – and crept through the window of the chamber where Gwenhwyvar slept. Away he stole her, and whether she went willingly or not who can say?

(The audience rumbled in surprise.)

Back to the greenwood he took her, the fairest of women, Gwenhwyvar of the golden hair, beloved of Arthur, beloved of Melwas the magician. Long had she lived with Arthur the Roman, two sons she had borne him. Now perhaps it was in her mind to try the old ways, the ways of her father's people . . .

(The rumble grew louder, angrier. Regin faltered, missed a note. 'That's a lie,' somebody bellowed from the rear of the hall.)

. . . For half a year she stayed, living in the forest with her new lover who was her old lover come again, while Arthur and her sons scoured the land for some sign of where she had gone . . .

'You have muddled your stories, minstrel,' called a woman. The audience whistled and shouted in agreement, stamped their feet and pounded on the tables. Regin glanced behind him at Hoewgi his host, who bit his lip worriedly and shook his head. The bard ducked as a lump of bread flew past his shoulder. Flustered, Hoewgi half rose, thought better of it, shot a look of appeal along the table at Seradwen.

For a moment she was tempted to ignore him, pretend she had not seen, but the room was near riot. If she did not act all the tensions and petty resentments which had built up over the last year since Mordav's death would suddenly come to the fore. Words would be said that could not be unsaid, and deeds done that could not be undone.

She stepped out beside the bard, who looked relieved, and spread her arms wide.

'Now I see how you annoyed Cadlew,' she whispered as she waited for the audience to calm.

'Strong feelings you have in Dumnonia,' he said shakily.

'Strong loyalties,' she corrected, and raised her voice to address the hall.

'He hoped the song would please us. Well, it did not please you, my people, and it did not please me. Nor did it please my cousin Hoewgi, who joins with me in demanding a halt to this calumny.'

She drew breath, knowing she had them with her now. 'A tale worthy of the traitor Medraut, and one I had not thought to hear in this hall. Gwenhwyvar unfaithful to Arthur? As well say grass is red, or geldings sire foals. A nonsense tale, not a true song at all. If we are to hear nonsense, let it at least be nonsense that amuses us. So sir bard, finish the evening with a song to undo the harm you have wrought. Give us "The Hunting of King Boar"!'

Shakily, Regin began to play, and the crowd took up the rollicking beat, carrying the tune where he could not. Once she was sure the song was safely launched Seradwen squeezed back to her seat. After a moment Hoewgi slipped from his couch (the master's couch, which had once belonged to her husband) and came to squat beside her.

'Well done,' he said.

These were the first words of praise or encouragement he had ever offered her. From the corner of her eye she could see Bodgath's mouth agape in astonishment.

'The bard told me his songs did not sit well with Gereint's men at Penhyle. My old friend Cadlew took offence at a tale concerning Arthur and Cei. He promised me he would give us a few safe favourites tonight.'

'Perhaps his definition of "safe" is different from ours,' Hoewgi said gravely.

'It must be.'

'I am sorry we did not save you a seat with the rest of the family. The blame is mine.' He spoke stiffly, and she realized how hard it must be for such a proud man to admit a fault, especially to a woman he disliked. 'Forgive me. It will not happen again.'

She waved a hand dismissively. 'It is not important. I am

content here among my friends, and besides, the farm is yours now, not mine.'

Hoewgi took a deep breath. 'You are kind. It has not been easy for any of us, the aftermath of Mordav's sudden demise. We did not expect to inherit, and you did not expect to be displaced.' His tone changed, became less formal. 'Bodgath tells me you have agreed he may teach Meirion's boy the business of caring for the herd.'

Beside her, Bodgath coughed, caught unawares.

'Bodgath too can be kind,' she said, kicking the little man under the table. 'He can also be headstrong. Over the years I have found he often does what he wishes, rather than what I wish.' She allowed herself to smile. 'But in this instance what he proposes is the wish of us both, and I am happy that any of your family who want to learn about the horse herd should receive instruction.'

'That is most generous, Lady Seradwen, most generous.' For once there was a faint hint of warmth in his frozen eyes. 'And please –' he laid a hand on her sleeve '– let it be our family, not your family. We are all one kindred now.'

'I shall try to remember,' she said, privately vowing to do no such thing.

She waited until Hoewgi had regained his seat before turning accusingly on Bodgath. 'Quick work on your part.'

The little man shrugged. 'He was angry when you took the bard off to the house. Thought it his place to offer hospitality. I distracted him.'

'And now he would be friends.'

Bodgath opened his mouth in a silent grin, rocked back and forth in time with the music. 'The horses are your property. If you took a liking to the youngsters . . .'

'Having no children of my own, I might name one of them my heir,' she completed the little man's sentence. 'Is he that calculating? We must work together if the farm is to prosper. He was making overtures of friendship.'

'Do you trust him?' Bodgath's face was serious.

She thought about it. 'I would trust him to keep his word.'

'I did not hear him give it,' said Bodgath, and turned his attention to the music.

Left alone, she let her thoughts drift as the hunting song came to an end and Regin began to play a lament for young men fallen in battle. Had things been different, had she not resolved to make her own decisions rather than allow others to make them for her, that might have been her, lamenting a young warrior slain in the endless round of raid and counter raid. (Instead of which she sat here mourning a farmer dead before his time.)

She had been fortunate in her marriage, more fortunate than most. It had been a meeting of like interests, based on hard work and mutual affection. (How different the carefree wooing of her girlhood among Gereint's warriors: Nai's slow smile across the hall, the mead flowing freely, the boasting of great deeds, Gorthyn's laughter ringing among the rafters.) Mordav had come in search of a wife and she had been ready to marry: a farmer's daughter, knowledgeable where horses were concerned, accustomed to ruling her father's household, an eminently suitable bride. (Nai had never asked, though they had lived together for a time.)

And now she was a wealthy woman. A wealthy woman with no home of her own, no children, no lover, forced to deal with a marriage kindred who regarded her as an obstacle. If there had been anywhere else to go she would have gone, walked away from everything and relied upon Gereint (who had always liked her and whose warband was kept mounted by her efforts) to see that she was not cheated of her share.

But for all her wealth there was nowhere she could go, unless she was prepared to abandon everything and become a beggar-woman dependent upon the charity of others. Somehow she must reach an accommodation with Hoewgi and his brothers, must learn to work with them. After tonight that did not seem quite so unlikely as before, though it would still not be easy. She knew there would be many false starts along the way, many difficulties, much hatred and resentment to be overcome. But it might be possible for them to work together, which was something she had come to doubt.

And yet . . .

Did she truly want to remain here? Sometimes in the dark hours before dawn she woke and lay thinking about the bleak future, her future: about the long and lonely vista of the years ahead. She would grow old, unloved and unloving, while the estate workers who had known her one by one died and were replaced by a new generation. The memory of Mordav and his pretty young wife would fade in the communal mind of the farm, and all that would remain would be the ill-tempered old woman, wrinkled and toothless, sitting by the fire like a household ghost, another useless mouth to feed while her heirs waited impatiently for her to die.

CHAPTER FIVE

Nai dreamed he was walking along a track at dusk, between two earth banks, the fields on either side a deep green, the trees in the distance bare branched and black against the darkening sky.

In his dream he knew this was the lane leading to Eurgain's village, though it looked quite different in waking life. The wind moaned down the funnel of the banks and he quickened his pace, eager to reach the safety of the village before it became aware of his presence.

Overhead, starlings wheeled and gathered in a great curve of broken lines, descended on the black copse to his right. Rooks rose from the trees to drive them off, and battle was joined. The rooks seemed heavily outnumbered and clumsy in comparison with the smaller birds. But after several forays the starlings whirled away into the sky, screeching loudly. One by one the rooks settled, crowing in triumph.

The pale track narrowed before him as the high hedges closed in on either side. Suddenly he was walking on paving stones. Brambles trailed down from the banks, caught and tugged at his clothes. Not far away he could hear the gush and tumble of water, which his dream knowledge told him must be the brook where the washerwoman waited for the unwary.

Something was approaching along the lane, a tall dark shape keeping close to the hedge, stepping from shadow to shadow. He could hear his own footsteps, hard on the paved surface, and their muffled echo rebounding from the high banks. Between footstep and echo came another sound, the pad and click of some great beast with soft paws and sharp nails, walking on its hind legs.

He came to a gap in the hedge and glanced through. There squatted the washerwoman, dragging a tunic back and forth in the brook. On the bank beside her lay what he knew to be Gorthyn's cloak. Into the air she raised the tunic. Water streamed from it in a long trail of shining droplets, and he recognized it for his own.

Behind him the great beast drew closer. Impotent, unable to move or cry out, he waited for it to reach him with his eyes screwed shut. He felt the hot breath on his cheek, smelled the rank odour. He opened his eyes to see the hairy muzzle looming before him, and hidden beneath the lupine features was the green and blue face of the Pict he had killed in the Sanctuary.

'You are a dead man walking,' said a voice. 'You should have killed all three.'

'You should have killed all three,' repeated Cadlew.

Nai groaned, clutched at the coverlets as the stocky man pulled them back.

'Wake, Nai! Quick! They are at the gate.'

He came to with a start, found himself staring into Cadlew's worried face.

'They have the man you left in the hut, and he has given them your description. Addonwy is talking with them now, down by the gate.'

'Do they know I am here?'

'Not yet. They lost your trail last night. But they want us to take the wounded man.' Cadlew began gathering Nai's possessions. 'If they bring him inside – and Addonwy can hardly refuse – Isgofan is bound to visit this house. He knows Addonwy and I have quartered ourselves here, and he also knows we are old friends of yours. He will want to warn us in private not to give you any help. We must move, and fast.'

Nai staggered groggily to his feet. 'Where are we going?'

'Where are you going, you mean. I must be here when Isgofan arrives.' Cadlew slung Nai's shield over his shoulder. 'You have everything? Come then.'

Cadlew opened the door and Nai followed him out into a cold brightness that made him blink. It was not long after dawn, and the sun was very low and weak. The ground was covered with frost. The roofs seemed to be steaming with the mixture of smoke seeping through the thatch and ice melting from the straw. Moisture dripped from the eaves.

'Pull your hood over your head,' hissed Cadlew.

He obeyed. As a disguise it left much to be desired, though it did have the advantage of warmth.

The town was larger than Nai remembered, but then the last time he had been here, recovering from the wounds inflicted by Eremon and his reivers, he had not been very interested in his surroundings, and had spent his convalescence sitting by the waterside with the old men. Most of the inhabitants lived by a combination of fishing and farming, but a number were also craft workers of one kind or another: weavers, potters, leather-workers, whitesmiths and blacksmiths. Penhyle lay at the head of the estuary, so anybody travelling east or west along the coastline was bound to pass through it – unless they were prepared to bargain for a ferry – which made the town a natural meeting place. As a result, Penhyle was the local market for the surrounding farms and communities on both sides of the water.

The house in which he had slept lay near the main entrance. Cadlew led him deeper into the town, threading between the dwellings, workshops, granaries and storage huts, crossing the open-air workfloors, picking through the frozen mud that lay off the main thoroughfares, steering a course which kept them away from the majority of people. They passed an old man chewing a straw in his doorway, his gaze fixed on the sky: he grunted a greeting as they drew level but showed no other interest in them. They skirted a courtyard where a group of women wrapped in shawls sat weaving, defying the cold in their determination to use every moment of daylight. They passed chickens and a sow grunting happily in her pen, dogs running loose and others leashed to posts, a pair of semi-wild cats disputing their territory, two small boys so busy arguing over a sling they were able to slip by unnoticed, and a little girl with a dirty face and one thumb in her mouth who stared at them curiously.

'She will remember,' muttered Cadlew, dragging Nai into the shelter of a storage hut.

'Does it matter? What did she see, except two men walking through the town?'

'It cannot be helped.' The stocky man shrugged, turned and grinned at Nai. 'We have made such a circuit that none save the child could guess where we were going. It was the only way to avoid the open ground in front of the gate.'

He walked around the hut, crossed a cobbled yard and made straight for what appeared to be a solid wall. At the last moment he ducked under a leather hanging, and Nai following hard on his heels realized they were in a narrow passage between two buildings. The eaves on either side almost met, leaving only a ribbon of sky down the middle. Unable to see either the ground or Cadlew ahead of him, Nai kept his eyes fixed on this ribbon and trailed one hand along the nearest wall like a blind man.

Cadlew touched his arm. 'Hold still while I see if the way is clear.'

Nai smiled to himself. The stocky man was enjoying this scurrying back and forth. Nai had by now lost all sense of direction, something which only ever happened to him among buildings and never in the open or among trees. From time to time during their wanderings he had caught a glimpse of a long grey sheet of fractured light, bound between banks of white-rimed sedge, which he knew to be the estuary, but latterly he had seen nothing to act as a landmark.

'Come,' called Cadlew, holding back another leather curtain. He waved Nai across a paved enclosure – Nai thankful there was nobody else in sight, for if ever a man looked guilty it was Cadlew as he hopped from foot to foot trying to shield Nai from view – and into a small stable.

It was dark inside, and the smell of horse was strong. Nai could hear the animal shifting within its stall as he waited for his vision to adjust. The pony nickered, swung its head, gazed at him with a soft brown eye, nickered again, wrinkled a velvet lip.

'Coal,' he whispered, and let himself into the stall.

Cadlew gave them a moment alone then propped Nai's warboard against the wall and cleared his throat noisily.

'Why did you not kill the third man, cousin?' he said plaintively.

Nai released his horse's muzzle and peered at his friend. 'I could not, not in cold blood. Besides, I reckoned it made no difference. They would have known it was me.'

'With no bodies?' scoffed Cadlew. 'No proof? You could have denied everything.'

'I do not think these are the sort of people who require proof.'

'Maybe not, but your denial would have been enough for Gereint.'

Nai said nothing, merely looked at him. Cadlew blushed slightly.

'Very well. I dare say I would have done the same thing myself.' He fiddled with the door latch, then burst out: 'But oh, cousin, how much easier it would have been for us to defy them. As it is I do not see what help we can give you. We cannot hide you forever.'

'You will not need to. You have given me shelter, returned me my horse.' He smiled, reached out and touched the other's shoulder. 'Yesterday I was confused. Today I am myself again.'

Cadlew grunted, recovered himself. 'Stay here till one of us comes,' he said briskly. 'If anything goes wrong and they find you – well, at least you have Coal. But I do not think they are confident enough to try a house to house search.'

He slipped through the door, latching it behind him.

Left alone in the dark with Coal, Nai busied himself with a curry-comb, muttering nonsense words of love under his breath as he groomed the horse from head to tail. The pony had been well fed since he had seen him last, and well exercised too, for he could feel the muscles tautening and loosening under the wiry winter coat.

Somehow Nai had to reach Lindinis, several days journey to the east, find the Convent of St Helena and begin his search for Gwenhwyvar, without bringing Isgofan and the tattooed men down upon her. That was the danger: that by the very act of seeking the Lady he would lead her enemies to her door.

And Bedwyr. Bedwyr must have gone upon the same quest. The old man had foreseen that the tattooed men, the Sons of Menestyr, would move in search of the chalice once they heard that he still lived. What Bedwyr had not foreseen was that they would suborn Custennin, High Lord of Dumnonia – Nai wondered what promises they had made to Custennin – and thus raise the countryside against him, and against those who sought to help him.

The first step was to escape from Penhyle. Isgofan clearly suspected something – bringing those ponies back to the settlement had been a mistake – and would have set a watch upon the two gates. Nai played with schemes of riding out in the midst of a patrol, or of walking out disguised as a peasant while Cadlew left Coal tethered at some prearranged spot, but all his ideas seemed obvious, the very things for which any watchers would be waiting.

There was of course a third way through the palisade surrounding Penhyle. These days it was used only by fishermen, for it led nowhere except to the estuary. A gap in the wall rather than a true gate, in times of danger it could be blocked with a barricade of brushwood, but otherwise lay wide open with only a pair of Gereint's men to act as sentries. Beyond was the embankment of wood and stone the inhabitants of Penhyle had created over the generations to keep the creek from flooding the settlement. Where the embankment ended the mud began: on one side the silt surrounding the mouth of the stream that flowed into the creek; on the other the thick and impassable ooze of the estuary limits. A number of landing stages projected from the embankment, giving access to the deeper water in the middle of the channel.

Nai had spent long periods of his convalescence sitting with the old men watching the water. In the past boats would have been the chief method of transport up and down the estuary, but nowadays most people came by land. The locals fished from tiny coracles with scarcely enough room for their catch, let alone a passenger, and in any case the last of the small communities living by the sea had vanished during the summer – the one near the Sanctuary had been destroyed by the Scotti raiders, and the inhabitants of the village on the eastern shore had wisely fled inland.

Surely nobody would expect him to escape by the water? Even if he was wrong, and his enemies were watching the estuary, it still seemed to him to offer a better chance than either of the alternatives. To go by land was to deliver himself directly to his foes, whereas to go by water at least seemed to open a choice of routes, depending on where he came to land.

Crooning a tuneless song of affection, Nai checked Coal's hooves. They had been freshly shod, with good iron shoes. Then he inspected the horse-gear hung about the stable. The thick padding which went under the saddle to soak up the mount's sweat and prevent chafing, besides helping to spread the weight of the rider, had never been used. The saddle blanket, fringed with strong thongs for carrying possessions, was also too clean to be anything except new, without even the shadow of a stain. But the saddle itself was his own: battered, worn and familiar, smooth and supple with years of polish, tailored to the size and shape of his seat. Nai checked the stitching, ran his hands over the soft leather. Under his fingers he could feel the nicks and scrapes in the surface that were the mementoes of old fights, for this was a war-saddle. From each of the four rounded corners a short horn curved bluntly up to hold the rider to the horse's back. The horns always reminded Nai of a double-headed snail peering in both directions from under its shell.

The pair at the front bent outwards, and enabled you to lean and slash with sword or knife at an opponent – a precarious matter at the best of times, and all the more so if the opponent was on your left side, where you were already top-heavy with the weight of your shield. By locking your thigh around the horn, you compensated for the loss of balance. You could also rise and brace yourself against the horns before throwing a spear, which allowed you to put real strength behind the cast.

The rear horns angled slightly inwards. These stopped you from being pushed out of the saddle by the impact of a lance or the force of your own blows. They also prevented slouching, the mark of a slovenly rider, and helped hold you upright with a deep seat, since you were obliged to ride almost on your pelvic bones with straight legs hanging down in close contact with your horse. As many commands were signalled by leg pressure, this close contact made it easier to guide and control the mount.

Some people disliked war-saddles, claimed they were desperately uncomfortable. But to Nai the advantages of a well-made saddle designed to fit the rider far outweighed any minor discomforts, and the advantages were not to the rider alone. The saddle would take the pressure of his body off the horse's spine and transfer it to the upper spring of the ribcage. It would distribute his weight more evenly than a simple pad or blanket, and stop much of the inevitable chafing which could lead to deep and incurable sores on the horse's back.

Besides, discomfort was a matter of what you were used to. Since he had not ridden for a while – apart from the madness of the previous night – Nai knew he would suffer for the first few days until his muscles grew accustomed to being on a horse again. But once his body had adapted, the saddle would seem comfortable enough.

The wide girth with its pair of leather fastening straps was new, the leather oiled and supple. The breastcollar, which prevented the saddle slipping backward, and its companion breeching, which went around the horse's rump to stop the saddle slipping forward, were also new. Tears pricked at Nai's eyes as he handled the leather.

While he waited for one of the others to release him from his hiding place he divided his belongings into two piles: things he would need on the journey, and things he would not. For the most part the choice was simple: he would take his weapons, a small supply of food, a change of clothes, and a few goods for barter. He hesitated over his mail shirt: it was heavy, and took up space unless worn all the time. On the other hand it gave good protection and was extremely valuable. In the end the weight decided him: he wanted to travel fast and light, and his leather jerkin would be armour enough.

The war-knives he had taken from the tattooed men were buried in the thatch immediately above a manger. Being taller than Cadlew (who had doubtless believed he was concealing them in an inaccessible place) Nai was able to reach them without difficulty. In his confused state the previous day he had not had a chance to examine them properly, so he carried them over to where a chink in the door let in a ray of light.

His own knife was the length of his forearm. These were shorter and thinner, reminding him of the weapons carried by the Scotti. The workmanship was good: he guessed the blades were formed from a skin of steel over a wrought-iron core, a method which gave both strength and flexibility. Although to his eyes the knives seemed small, like children's toys, the single edges were lethally sharp, and the metal seemed to be of a uniform quality. The handles were plain and unadorned, with wooden grips slightly roughened so they would not slip when the palm began to sweat. They were tools for killing, and a shudder passed through him as he recalled yesterday's events.

Coal whinnied softly. Nai shoved the blades deep into the thatch, pulled wisps of straw over the hole.

'Nai?'

Beard jutting, Addonwy strode across the uneven stones of the paved area, red cloak billowing around him with the force of his passage. Even through the chink in the door Nai could see that his old friend was angry, angrier than he had seen him in years.

Addonwy unlatched the door and stormed into the stable. 'Isgofan says that unless you surrender yourself to Custennin's

98

justice, he cannot undertake to keep the painted barbarians from killing you.'

'Do they know I am here?'

'No.' Addonwy slammed a hand into the roof post, startling Coal. 'They suspect I have helped you, but Isgofan does not believe I would be mad enough to hide you on my own doorstep.'

'You have been too long with Cadlew,' Nai remarked mildly.

'Cadlew suggested we gathered a few loyal men and arranged an accident.' Addonwy swung on his heel, pounded the post again. 'Half a year ago you defended this land against invaders, were feted as a hero. Now you are supposed to be a ruthless murderer, to be handed over without a hearing.'

'It is a bluff, cousin,' Nai said calmly. He squeezed past Addonwy, set about saddling Coal. 'They want me alive, and they want you to talk me into surrendering.'

'Alive? What about yesterday?'

'Easy, easy,' he hissed as Coal twitched impatiently. 'I have had time to think. The first man panicked when I appeared behind him. He moved to capture me with his knife drawn, and I killed him. It is possible he intended no more than to disable me. When they had the opportunity they took me alive.' He heaved the girth tight, added with emphasis: 'They must want me alive.'

'Why?'

'Because I am their only link with Bedwyr.'

Addonwy frowned. 'That does not mean they will keep you alive once you have told them what they want to know.'

He groped behind him until he felt the manger and slowly subsided onto its edge, where he perched awkwardly. 'Their behaviour puzzles me. I had already told them the hermit was dead and you had taken his place, however temporarily. Yet you say they seemed surprised to find you.'

'Perhaps they did not believe you. Or perhaps they did not believe you knew the whole truth.'

'They were right,' Addonwy said drily.

'They may have thought Bedwyr was hiding with me: after all, what safer place to hide than the very place you are supposed to have left? And for the same reason some of them rode to the mouth of the Avon, in case he had merely moved a few miles to the west. I think in doing these things they were making sure they covered every possibility, but I am certain their prime hope was to trick or coerce me into revealing where he had gone.'

'Do you know?' Addonwy asked, then at once raised a hand to ward off an answer. 'No, don't tell me. Better you keep it to yourself.'

Nai fiddled with coal's bridle. 'I do not know, not for certain. But I do know what Bedwyr wanted me to do if I survived Eremon's attack and he did not. Unfortunately –' he loosened one strap, tautened another '– I cannot do it if Isgofan and his men are on my trail.'

'Where was Isgofan yesterday?' Addonwy said suddenly. 'Why did he allow half his party to go on ahead?'

'I have wondered that too.' Nai hefted the saddlebags and tied them into position. 'To make me run?'

'To make you run?'

'Where did Cadlew put my quiver?' Nai cast around the stable until he found it hanging from a nail, the javelins invisible against the dark wood of the wall. 'Will you keep my mail shirt? And my other things?'

'What do you mean, to make you run? They took you prisoner.'

'Yes, but was that what they were intended to do? Or did they panic when I did not act as they expected? Why allow three men with tattooed faces to sneak so clumsily through the woods – I was bound to fear the worst. Better surely if Isgofan himself had come, announcing himself from a distance like a civilized man. We may not have any great love for Custennin's followers, but the laws of hospitality would have made me greet him as a guest – and thus I would have fallen straight into their hands.'

'I have not heard you talk so much since Eremon stuck his spear in your throat,' Addonwy said distractedly. 'Nai the Silent, they call you.'

'I had Gorthyn to speak for me.'

There was a moment's silence. Addonwy shifted uncomfortably on the edge of the manger. 'You think they were beaters sent ahead to flush the game.'

The other nodded.

'So why not simply capture and torture you until you told them what they wanted to know?'

'I would have told them Bedwyr was in Gwynedd or Gododdin, somewhere far away.' Nai shrugged. 'By the time they discovered the truth I would have been long dead.'

Addonwy steepled his fingers. 'What would happen if you did as Isgofan demands, and surrendered to him?'

Nai hesitated, rubbed the scar at his throat. 'The one thing I learned from Bedwyr about the Children of Menestyr is that they are a people who believe in vengeance. Blood for blood, a life for a life. And they have a long memory. Yesterday they wanted me to run, in the hope I would lead them to Bedwyr or the chalice. Today – today I am not so certain.'

'Neither am I,' Addonwy said quietly. 'I think they will kill you, cousin, and not quickly.'

'They must catch me first.'

'They will be waiting for you. Isgofan said they would retrace their steps, search for your tracks. If I were him, I would keep a close watch on the town as well. He must guess you cannot be far away.'

'He did not demand more men to help in the search?'

'No. He realizes any men of mine would be a hindrance.' Addonwy gestured helplessly. 'They will take you the instant you leave Penhyle. Isgofan will have set a watch on both gates.'

'I shall not go by the gates.'

Addonwy stared. His face furrowed and he tugged at his beard. 'You will go by water then? But how? And where will you go?'

'If I escape from here they will be on my trail at once. I must disappear for a while.'

'Not easy, this time of year. It has been a soft winter so far, but the weather must change soon. You cannot live in the woods like a wild man.'

'No. I must find a haven.' Nai buckled his shield to the crupper, the leather strap running from the saddle to Coal's tail.

'If Custennin is against you nowhere in Dumnonia will be safe. For all his power is on the wane, nobody yet dares defy him openly.'

'None wish to be the first,' Nai said sourly.

'Who can blame them? To throw off his yoke the lesser lords must act in concert, and they are not ready for that. If they act alone he will crush them, as he crushed his sister's husband last year.'

'Gereint cannot help me.'

'It will be the first place Isgofan looks. In times of trouble a man seeks shelter with his lord.'

'I thought of Seradwen.'

'Seradwen?' Addonwy blinked, caught his balance on the edge of the manger. 'Seradwen,' he repeated, and whistled softly.

'I can trust her.'

'Ye-es,' the other said doubtfully. 'You can trust Seradwen. But she does not live alone.'

'True.'

'Are you going there because you believe it safe, or because you want to see her?' Addonwy's eyes were hard.

'You were always shrewd,' Nai said affectionately. 'Does it matter?'

Addonwy twisted his beard around his fingers. 'No, I suppose not. More to the point, how do you intend to cross the water? What about Coal? You cannot swim him through the mud.'

'When I was here in the summer I sometimes sat with the old men of the town. They will help me. And yes, there is a boat big enough to carry a horse.'

Nai spoke confidently to allay his friend's fears, though in his heart he remembered the look of the hulk moored to one of the landing stages, and wondered whether the bottom would not simply fall out under the weight of the pony.

'The palisade will hide me until I am well out into the water. The tide is high so we shall make the shore without being trapped by the mud. With luck the watchers will not see me.'

He turned, smiled. 'It crosses your mind I may be mad?'

Addonwy took a long moment to reply. 'Yes, cousin. Driven mad by grief for Gorthyn and months of solitude. Of course it has crossed my mind, and I confess your tale of cups and emperors did little to satisfy me otherwise. Isgofan is very convincing. Arrogant, but convincing.'

He rose from his perch, rubbing his backside where the rim of the manger had left a groove. 'Two men have vanished, and one is so badly battered about the head he may die. By your own admission you killed the two missing men and cast their bodies over the cliff into the sea. You tell me they attacked you. Their comrades say they merely sought to ask you some questions in peaceful and friendly fashion. If you were anyone else, anyone else in the world . . .' Addonwy shrugged, managed a weak smile. 'But I believe you. I believe you though I do not understand. If I dared, I would give you open escort out of Penhyle. As it is I have delayed the departure of our usual patrols. They will ride forth when you leave, and they may serve to distract your enemies for a short while.'

'My thanks.'

They regarded each other in the dim light of the stable, then embraced, making their farewell.

Coal nickered and swished his tail impatiently. Nai soothed him.

'One more thing,' he said, remembering. 'What were you going to tell me last night?'

'Last night?'

'When I mentioned Vortepor of Dyfed.'

'Ah yes, I had forgotten,' said Addonwy in surprise. 'Perhaps it is not important, but a wandering hedge bard, from Dyfed by his speech, stopped here a few days ago. Not many bards visit Penhyle, which made me wonder. He stayed the night and entertained us with a song I had never heard before.'

Addonwy pulled at his beard, assembling his thoughts. 'What he sang makes more sense now I have heard your story. The bard told of a quarrel between Arthur and his Companion, Cei the Long Man. Cei had slain Llacheu, Arthur's son. Some say it was an act of mercy, that Llacheu was dying of his wounds and Cei killed him to ease his pain.' Addonwy shrugged. 'We have all done that, given a mortally-wounded comrade the grace. The bard hinted at another reason. Jealousy, or a feeling the Warlord had raised himself too high when he declared himself Emperor.'

Nai listened intently. The presence of a Dyfed bard in Penhyle was so unlikely it had to have some significance, though what it might be for the moment escaped him.

'Anyway,' continued Addonwy, 'as a result of Llacheu's death Arthur slighted Cei in some fashion, and the Long Man withdrew vowing vengeance. Later Arthur had Cei killed because he no longer trusted him, and Cei knew too much about a certain voyage to the far north, a remark which meant nothing to me then.'

'How was the song received?'

A smile flashed across Addonwy's face. 'Poorly, cousin, poorly. Cadlew was for hanging the fellow up by his heels, and some of the youngsters came near to throwing him in the creek. I took the man on one side and warned him that in this part of Dumnonia we liked our tales simple, unsullied by any nonsense. Next he would be telling us Gwalchmei was a coward or Bedwyr a traitor.'

'And?'

'He blanched, and gave us the Siege of Badon Hill, which

mended matters. Even Cadlew calmed enough to give him a trinket as reward.'

Nai took a last look around the stable to be sure he had everything he required. Addonwy watched him sadly, then pushed open the door. Light flooded in, revealing the black ropes of ancient cobwebs under the eaves, the swirling motes of dust rising and falling to the floor. Coal snorted, eager to be gone.

'Give me a while to send out the patrols. I will make plenty of noise about it,' said Addonwy. He strode away, boots loud on the cobbles, or perhaps he was slamming his feet down with greater force than usual.

Nai waited, cradling Coal's muzzle in his arm. There was a gleam in the horse's eyes which had not been present earlier. A shudder ran through the barrel body, and Nai caressed the shaggy coat, combed his fingers through the coarse mane before leading him out into the yard.

A pair of leather gauntlets waited in a saddlebag, but for now he wanted the touch of bare skin on the reins. He hitched his cloak out of the way over his shoulders and heaved himself up into the saddle, suddenly clumsy, the scar tissue along his ribs catching his side and adding another ache to those of yesterday's bruises.

Coal sidled, disturbed by his master's awkwardness. Nai let his legs dangle while he settled into the saddle, at once familiar and strange. The settlement was livelier now the sun had burnt away the morning frost: from his vantage point on the pony's back he could see people going about their business in the courts between the buildings. The air had a clarity about it which was often a sign of rain, and he could not decide whether rain would be good or bad. It would conceal his tracks, but it would also make the going more difficult, and at the moment he wanted speed, to carry him clear of Penhyle and its environs.

Behind him he heard a commotion of hooves and shouting, then Cadlew's voice raised above the rest, bellowing curses. He smiled to himself and set his heels to Coal's flanks.

The horse sprang forward, bounding across the paving stones in a surge of energy. Nai reined him in, feeling the urgency shuddering through the pony's body. They squeezed through the gap between a round house and an oblong barn (the house wall curving away behind them) and startled a tethered goat from its grazing in a patch of muddy grass. Three women glanced up in surprise and a small child ran across Coal's path; the pony checked then gathered speed again when the way was clear.

The wind had died. The smoke from the outdoor cooking fires rose in straight plumes to the heavens, while the seeping fumes from the houses drifted aimlessly across the rooftops. Sound carried, even here in the town (it would be worse on the water), so he could hear the clatter of the looms from the doorways around him and the rattle of horses and men from the main gate behind him. Ahead of him was the lap of water on stone and the creaking of small boats, and he felt the wildness rising in his blood.

Coal pounded past a baking hut (the aroma of fresh bread hanging in the air) and crossed a series of workfloors, narrowly skirting a potter busy selecting clay from a pile, frightening a woodworker engrossed in carving a door latch. The smell of fish grew stronger as the scent of bread was lost. They shot through the alley between some storage sheds, the fern thatch scraping Nai's hair, and swung hard right along the line of the palisade. Faces gaped, words were called, but nobody moved to stop them.

Ahead were the sentries, drawn by the noise. An old man mending a net looked up and grinned, his expression changing to a frown as he realized horse and rider were aiming for the gap in the timber wall. The sentries moved to bar the way, leapt aside when they saw Nai did not intend to slow.

'You cannot –'

'It does not –'

He brought Coal skidding to a halt, laughter boiling within him. Their faces were familiar, though he could not call their names to mind.

'Do you know me?' He flung back his head to show the scar at his throat.

'Nai?' said one. 'Why are you here?' He glanced nervously towards the main gate. 'We heard Custennin's men are after you.'

'More than Custennin's men,' he said solemnly, though the joy still bubbled below the surface. 'Vile creatures from the far north, monsters in the shape of men.' He let Coal sidle towards them, and they drew back. 'Do you trust me?' he demanded.

'Yes,' they answered, keeping a nervous eye on the pony.

'Then you have not seen me.' He turned to the fisherman, who sat cross-legged listening avidly, net forgotten in his lap.

'Do you remember me, friend? In the summer, the wounded

warrior who sat watching the water with you and your comrades.'

The old man blinked. 'I do.'

'Is the old ferry still usable?'

'The ferry?' Startled, the old man looked at the net in his hands as if he expected to find the answer in its mesh. 'The ferry?' He blinked slowly, rubbed at his eyes with a blackened finger.

'In the summer it was moored at the end of the longest jetty,' prompted Nai. 'Pride of place, and you and your friends kept it bailed of bilge water.'

'She,' returned the old man absently. 'Not it, she.'

Nai grinned, and the old man cackled, for this was an argument they had had many times before, during the long days of summer.

'Well,' he said. 'Usable. She floats, if that is what you mean. But that great beast of yours.' He shook his head dubiously. 'Whether she will take that is a different matter.'

'Him,' said Nai. 'Not that, him. Or Coal, if you prefer, which is his name.'

The old man sucked in his breath to acknowledge the hit. 'Still,' he said, brightening a little, 'she used to carry livestock from the settlements near the sea. And a horse is livestock of a kind.' He rose to his feet, folded the net and left it in a neat pile.

'You had best hurry if you are going,' said the guard, still glancing uneasily in the direction of the main gate while his fellow shuffled awkwardly from foot to foot at his side. 'Custennin's man accuses you of murder. If he orders the town searched, not even Cadlew will dare forbid it.'

'Custennin's man!' the old fisherman cried scornfully. 'A murrain on him, and all his kin! Where were Custennin and his bright warriors when the sea raiders threatened us last summer, hey? Sitting feasting in their nice hall, that's where, while this lad and his friend did all their work for them.'

He marched angrily through the gap in the palisade, beckoning Nai to follow, calling at the top of his voice: 'Gwilym? Gwilym! Wake up, idle one, I have need of you!'

Nai winked at the guards and urged Coal in the old man's wake.

The light from the inlet was blinding. He swayed in the saddle, Coal snorting and shying beneath him, dazzled by the shifting patterns of the waves. The old fisherman strode along the deserted quay bellowing for his friend, his voice oddly flattened by the open water. Nai screwed up his eyes against the glare and soothed the pony.

The jetties were more fragile than he remembered, narrow platforms that seemed to float upon the tide. The ferry was moored to the far end of the longest stage, just as he recalled, and he swallowed at the thought of persuading Coal to walk out across the water.

A gull swooped overhead, screaming. Here in the shadow of the palisade he was hidden from both shores, but once the boat pushed away from the jetty they would become all too visible. His scheme seemed like madness.

'Are you ready?' said the old man. 'Let us go first, then bring on the horse.'

Nai watched them go, two elderly men unusually animated, carrying an oar each. They moved quickly along the landing stage, which bounced alarmingly under their weight, and stepped into the boat, a kind of flat-bottomed barge, arguing fiercely about who should bail and how the horse should be stowed.

With another mount he might have wrapped his cloak around the head and guided the animal blindfold to the boat, but his was Coal, who was perfectly accustomed to the ferry across the River Oak. He nudged him forward onto the platform, thinking it would be easier to ride him, and at once wondered whether he would have room to dismount when he reached the far end.

Coal's hooves rang hollow on the wood, the pony lumbering as he strove to keep his footing on the slippery surface. The water was slack and still, only a few dead leaves slowly drifting to mark the outflow of the stream down the middle of the creek. The wooden structure was vibrating beneath them, and Nai could see the ripples spreading out from under the stage.

'Steady then,' he murmured in Coal's black ear, and felt the pony gather himself, blindly trusting in his rider.

The end of the jetty drew nearer and nearer, and suddenly it was upon them, the dark water waiting, the boat looking as if it might sink at any moment.

'Stand,' he said, and slithered from the saddle, clutching the pony's shoulder to avoid falling from the stage.

The old men watched open-mouthed as he eased himself around Coal's bulk, praying the horse would not choose now to toss his head. Grabbing the reins he hopped down into the boat.

'Come,' he said gently, and Coal balked for an instant, then stepped sweetly over the side and allowed himself to be led into the middle of the space.

Gwilym grunted in triumph and pushed them off. The old man began paddling with an oar, working their nose out into the current. 'Sit, you,' he snapped impatiently at Nai. 'How far would you go?'

Nai squatted beside Coal, ignoring the dirty water swilling around his feet. 'The shortest route to dry land. There are watchers on the hills searching for me.'

'From the noise they were making by the main gate, not all are on the hills.' The boat swung into the stream current, which was stronger than it had seemed from the jetty, and the old man grunted with satisfaction. 'Beyond the reed beds. The ground is solid there.'

Nai glanced over his shoulder. The two sentries watched from the wharf, but nobody else seemed to have noticed their departure from Penhyle. At present the curve of the palisade still hid them from the hills where Isgofan and the Picts would be waiting, though if they continued to be carried downstream they would soon come into view. He waved at the sentries, and after a brief hesitation they waved in return.

It was quiet on the water except for the sounds of their passage. The old men were letting the current carry them down towards the bank, drifting past the winter sedge with only the occasional twist on the oars to correct their course.

'Light,' said Gwilym.

Nai followed the direction of the fisherman's gaze. They were beyond the shelter of the palisade now, moving faster than he had thought, and the hills on the far side of the estuary bulked large, green and brown in the winter sun. A flash of reflected light came from a tumble of rocks and brambles on the edge of a leafless wood.

'Are they signalling, or careless?' said Gwilym, pulling on his oar.

'Signalling, I fear.' Nai gnawed at his lip, ran his hands through Coal's coarse mane to calm them both as the pony picked up on his nervousness and began to fret.

'We can land you here,' said the old man from the bows.

They had passed the reed beds and were opposite a place where the bank was high and the trees and undergrowth grew thick to the shore, impenetrable even at this time of year. A heron flapped from the water's edge, crying in alarm, and looking closely Nai saw the mouth of a tiny stream, half hidden behind a dam of driftwood and dead leaves.

'Ach!' exclaimed Gwilym in disgust. 'Pass me your shield, warrior, and I will beat a tattoo upon it in case any of them have missed us.'

The boat grated smoothly to a halt. The old man grinned at Nai. 'Move fast and they will not find you. Follow the stream inland till you can climb out.'

'My thanks,' said Nai, handed him one of the brooches he had taken from the Picts, then jumped over the side.

Freezing water instantly filled his boots. He tugged at Coal's reins, clucking encouragingly. The horse moved, and the boat tipped so far over the side was in danger of going under.

Coal lurched for the stream-bed, floundering in a mist of spray, droplets showering around him. The boat righted itself and floated free, the old men using their oars as poles to push themselves back into the current. The pony staggered, caught in the mud, then his hindquarters bit on solid ground and with a great surge he hauled himself clear, Nai pulling on the reins and ducking beneath the overhanging branches as they fought their way into the mouth of the stream, careless of the noise they were making.

Behind them the old men began to row in earnest. Nai waved a farewell, and then the boat was hidden behind the screen of trees and bushes. He shivered, suddenly feeling very alone, and urged Coal on until they came to a place where they could scramble up the bank.

Temporarily safe under the cover of a stand of pines, Nai paused to pour the water from his boots and take stock of his position. Coal seemed unworried by his adventures, tossing his head briskly back and forth, eager to be moving. Nai gave him a few moments to recover then led him through the trees to the edge of the stand. Keeping well back in the shadows, Nai surveyed the eastern side of Penhyle and the low wooded knoll where he suspected Isgofan's watchers would be waiting.

Three riders trotted slowly across a meadow where sheep were grazing. At this distance he could not make out their faces, but he guessed they were one of Addonwy's patrols. A movement on the knoll caught his attention, and a fourth rider came galloping down the slope, bringing his mount skidding to a halt in a flashy display of horsemanship. The three conferred with the newcomer then continued on their course. The fourth man waited until they had gone a short distance then raised a spear above his head as a sign to the unseen watchers on the mound.

If the flash of light across the water had also been a signal – and he found it hard to believe any of his pursuers could have been so clumsy as to betray themselves unintentionally – then its recipients must know that he was here somewhere. If he had had charge of them, they would be beating the shores of the estuary in search of him.

But they were not, and that was a very curious thing.

Nai nodded to himself and retreated through the pines, the needles crunching underfoot and Coal nudging at his back, till he came to the far side of the copse.

A moment of indecision caught him as he gazed down into the narrow valley below. His natural inclination was for caution. By all means he should move quickly during the remainder of this day in order to escape the net Isgofan had flung around Penhyle, but thereafter he should travel slowly, staying under cover until he reached the haven of Seradwen's farm. By then, with any good fortune, his hunters would have decided he was long gone, would have turned their attention elsewhere. The alternative was to strike hard and fast direct for Lindinis, relying on speed to lose his pursuers – and that, surely, was what they would be expecting him to do. They might not know his destination, but they would be waiting for him to run.

His first thought was best. He would go to ground, and they could follow if they dared.

As he pulled himself into the saddle to begin his journey it came to him suddenly that he had not felt so alive for months.

CHAPTER SIX

Lying under the firs, Bedwyr waited for sleep. The world seemed to conspire against him. From somewhere close by came a quavering, bubbling sound that startled him fully awake. The owl was answered by another and a duet began, that ended as the nearer bird took flight, crying *kiwack kiwack*.

Bedwyr rolled over and closed his eyes, but instead of sleep he fell into a semi-daze, a waking dream in which the chill of this night merged with the bitter cold of a night ten years gone, when he had thought himself dying.

In his mind he heard again the wind blowing off the margins of the lake, the rattle of the reeds, the whistle and groan of the sedge mingling with the moans of the dying. Huddled shapes stalked the darkness, murmuring softly as they looted the dead. Occasionally a scream marked where they hastened the passing of some unfortunate they had reached too soon.

He could not move. He lay and watched the mist rise from the marsh, the drifting tendrils blowing out to hide the dead, and near at hand he heard the scrabbling of a fox or wolf feeding on a corpse. A horse whinnied where it stood guard over its master, lashed suddenly with an iron-shod hoof to send a grey form yelping. Pennants flapped and cracked from the butts of spears abandoned in the ground. The moon broke from behind streamers of black cloud, and he closed his eyes, not wishing to see what it would reveal.

Later there were torches, pale haloes of light shining through the mist, and the sound of voices moving confidently among the bodies. It seemed to him it did not much matter who reached him first: the scavengers, human or otherwise, who would at least give him a quick end; or the rescuers, who must be the men of Dumnonia come too late to the field, who would no doubt seek to delay the inevitable.

He had lost all sense of place. It would have pleased him to think he lay beside Arthur, or among old friends, that his death might come upon him in good company, but he could not remember how the battle had gone in those last moments before his fall. One of Medraut's men had struck him down, and from the feel of it had continued to hack at him after he lay senseless, but how far from where Arthur took his death wound he could not tell. Everything was different in the dark, and the ground so churned by the day's fighting that none of the morning's landmarks remained.

Except the tree, a thin and scraggly thorn bent by the winds, its leaves already half fallen so the network of branches was clear against the moonlit sky. And that, surely, had been well behind the Saeson foot when they drew up in their battle-pen – he remembered being surprised they had not formed up around it, since it made a natural mark in the landscape of the kind they often used as a rallying point. But it had been too far back, and would have left too great a gap between them and Iddawg's cavalry – though as things turned out they were small help to the horsemen, or the horsemen to them.

So the fighting must have moved much farther across the field than he had thought. Arthur's last charge had bowled Medraut's newly arrived cavalry back into the Saeson dead – and now he thought on it he remembered how his tired mount had sidled and sidestepped to avoid trampling the corpses.

The thorn tree fascinated him. The narrow branches interwove like a net, and in their sharp and spiky mesh they caught the stars, or held the clouds against the wind. A pity all was ended. He would have liked to have lived among trees, to have followed them through the dance of the seasons, through their cycle of little death in autumn to glorious rebirth in spring – and what sight finer than young leaves in sunlight? But it was too late now, too late for everything.

By the time the hands reached him he had traced every out-stretched twig, every joint and juncture in the branches. At first he

112

barely noticed how his body was being turned, tipped over on its side, how the hands were reaching for his belt, fumbling for the brooch at his throat. This was all part of his long dream of dying, was happening elsewhere to the husk he had cast off and left behind.

Then a voice shouted, angry in the night. 'Get away, you ghoul!'

He groaned, protesting the disturbance.

A torch flared. The light hurt his eyes. A narrow face bent over him, the cheeks hollow, the mouth a black hole without teeth.

'Away with you, or you'll feel my sword's edge!' the voice bellowed.

Even in his dying he recognized the accent and would have smiled had he been able, for it had never occurred to him that the denizens of Heaven would speak with the tones of a Dumnonian, and yet truly how could it be otherwise, for were not the lands of his birth the nearest thing in all Albion to Paradise?

The face snarled and vanished from his vision. Other hands, larger but gentler, seized him, eased him upright. He squinted against the red glare, felt himself moan as the air left his lungs, began to shiver uncontrollably.

'To me, to me!' shouted the voice.

The hands stretched across his body, found his left arm and began to unbuckle the shattered remnants of his warboard. More light came, and other voices muttering instructions.

'Fetch Erfai!' said the first voice, low and urgent, and as the darkness took him he laughed at the thought of one of these angels bearing the same name as his nephew, his brother's son.

Bedwyr jerked awake and sat up, listening intently. The wind was rushing through the pines like the roaring of the sea. The pony stamped its hooves and snorted softly. It too was listening with all its might. Glancing across through the gloom, Bedwyr saw its ears twitch back and forth as the long muzzle swung this way and that.

The howl came, hanging between the trees like a veil of sound. And another, chilling his blood though he knew he had nothing to fear from anything that hunted on four legs. Far off, something thrashed through the undergrowth. The wolves had started their prey and would now chase it until they ran it down, unless it quickly showed it could outdistance them.

From the noise it was making their victim was already lame. He guessed it must be a deer from the series of rhythmic crashes that seemed to mimic the leaps and bounds of a small doe. The wolves were silent now, preserving their breath for running, though he could hear the quick susurration of their passage behind their prey.

They must have chased it across the track and on through the edge of the woods in which he had made his camp, for suddenly the sounds were all around him, and the pony was snorting and dancing closer to him on the end of its tether, and his sword was in his hand and he was wide awake, straining his eyes to see, though there were only dark shadows which might have been anything or nothing at all, and once, fleetingly, the gleam of yellow eyes, though that might have been imagination.

Then they had gone, leaving only the wind rustling the trees. 'The wolves are running,' he muttered, and rolled himself afresh in his cloak.

The men of Cunomorus had established their camp on the far side of the hill where Arthur had waited with the reserves for Medraut's arrival. The Dumnonians carried him to the edge of the encampment, to the tents set aside for the surgeons' use. All night long they had been bringing the wounded to these tents. The ground was covered with bodies laid out in neat rows, graded according to the seriousness of their injuries, and the longest rows were of those for whom there was no hope.

The noise was dreadful. In the dark one could not see too much of the injuries, but nobody save the deaf could have missed the anguished drone that rose about the place like the clamour of bees, composed of hundreds of individual mumbles and groans, with the occasional agonized scream from within the tents as the surgeons set about their work.

Bedwyr regained consciousness when they carried him through the tent flaps. This time his mind was clear: he knew precisely where he was and what was happening. The sight was a familiar one: the leather tent and the oil lamps carefully placed to give the maximum light with the minimum danger of fire; the trestle table arranged in the middle where there was the most headroom; the buckets of water with the steam gently coiling; the bundles of bloodstained rags lying in the corners; the surgeon and his assistants, their faces drawn with tiredness, bending over the unfortunate on the table.

'No,' said the surgeon, and stepped back.

The orderlies took the body by its head and feet and carried it outside, brushing past the men who held Bedwyr.

'Bring him up,' said the surgeon. 'Strip the mail from him.'

Then there was pain, and a leather strap thrust in his mouth for him to bite on, and more pain, and the surgeon's shadowed eyes, and a voice murmuring 'Not long now, not long, hold on, hold on,' while he fought to breathe against the agony, and great weights held down his arms and legs so he could not even struggle.

'Best I can do,' the surgeon said from far away. 'Not much chance. Not a young man.'

'But a hard one,' said another. 'He will come to my tent. I'll not leave him to lie outside with the rest.'

'As you wish,' the surgeon said indifferently. 'Let me know if he lives through the night.'

Again he felt movement, and he was borne from light to darkness to light, and in one way it seemed the journey lasted forever, and in another it was over almost before it had begun. He was set down upon a soft pallet of straw spread with rugs, and for the first time felt warm, though he was vaguely aware his body had run with sweat while the surgeon worked on it.

'Bedwyr, can you hear me?'

His nephew Erfai's face blurred in and out of focus.

'You are safe, do you understand? Safe in my tent, with your wounds dressed and bandaged.'

He tried to raise a hand in acknowledgement, failed and tried to blink instead, but once his eyes were shut it seemed too much effort to open them.

He woke afraid in the darkness, thinking himself still on the battlefield waiting for the scavengers, shadows all around him and drums beating in the distance, burning with the heat in his side, lost in the night. Somewhere nearby was the marsh, filled with Saeson dead, their pale faces floating to the surface of the stagnant water, lips writhing in unnatural curses before they sank back into the depths. Above him the sky frayed and a black raven poked its head through, fixed him with a beady eye, the sharp beak opening and closing in anticipation, croaking of the dead and the mighty feast awaiting . . .

'Bedwyr. Bedwyr.'

He knew that voice, though it was one he had not thought to

hear again, and he sat outside himself wondering who would appear next in this strange version of the Halls of the Dead.

'Bedwyr, you must wake!'

She leant across him and he caught the familiar odour of her scent: lavender, but overlaid with the smell of a hard ridden horse, and damp. This was a good part of the dream, and he was not afraid any more. The rain was drumming on the walls of the tent, which explained why she smelled damp, and a candle was burning behind her, so her face was in shadow.

'Bedwyr! Listen to me! What happened to Arthur?' The words were soft but insistent.

'Falling, falling,' he answered, seeing it again, the grey blade coming down on the unprotected head, and Arthur toppling from the saddle. 'Under the hooves of the horses.'

'What did he say?' demanded Erfai. 'Lady,' he added belatedly as he remembered to whom he was speaking.

'That Arthur fell under the horses' hooves – which is why nobody has found him. The body must have been trampled beyond recognition.'

'Is he dead then?' asked Bedwyr, raising his head from the pillow.

Erfai hissed with surprise, and would have moved to his uncle had Gwenhwyvar not forestalled him.

'Dead?' Her voice was strained. 'Dead? Say not that he is dead, say rather that by the Grace of God here in this world he has changed his life.'

A gust of wind caught the tent flaps and forced them asunder. The candle flickered and went out. The sound of the rain dulled to a faint patter then stopped altogether. Gradually the tent filled with moonlight, a cold white glow with no warmth to it, so that for an instant Bedwyr feared the tent and all within it were phantoms of his dying, and that he had indeed been lying delirious on the field all this while.

Her face was like marble, with not a trace of colour, and her hair hung dripping about her shoulders, plastered flat on the crown of her head. Deep fissures ran from her nose to her mouth like natural faults in the stone, and she was silver in the moonlight as she bent over him and spoke in tones he had rarely heard her use during all the years he had known her:

'Live, Bedwyr, live. You must not die, do you understand? You swore an oath to the Emperor, and an oath to me, and I will not release you from it no matter how grievous your wounds.'

Her eyes studied him dispassionately. She took his good hand in hers, and he could feel the strength flowing out of her into his battered body, so he gasped aloud at the force of it.

She stayed with him for hours while he drifted in and out of consciousness. Sometimes the two of them were alone; sometimes Erfai was there as well, burly and bearlike behind the Lady's slender form. Wind and rain blew against the walls of the tent; the candle guttered, was replaced with another. When he slept he dreamed, nightmarish sequences filled with menace and foreboding, but always her hand clasped his and dragged him free, as a drowning man might be pulled from beneath the surface of the waves by the grip of a friend, and always her voice followed him however deep he went, cajoling and commanding, demanding he fight.

'It breaks now,' he heard her say. 'He will live.'

'By your will he shall live,' said Erfai.

'And his own.'

He groaned, struggled against the covers. The light hurt his eyes.

She squeezed his hand. 'Lie still, cousin.' She pressed a cup to his lips and he drank gratefully, peered around him at the tent.

'Nephew,' he said, and tried to smile. 'Gwenhwyvar.'

She mopped his brow with a cloth, cool against the hot skin. 'I cannot stay much longer. Erfai can keep a still tongue, and the others who saw me did not recognize the Lady of Albion in the becloaked and mud spattered figure who asked directions to your kinsman's tent, but I must be gone before dawn.'

'You will hide then?' he said weakly.

'I must.' She studied him gravely. 'You know that.'

He nodded feebly. They had discussed this, Arthur, Gwenhwyvar and he, during the dark days preceding Camlann. They had agreed that if anything befell Arthur, and if the Companions were broken as an independent force, then she must go into hiding. Without the Companions to protect her she would become a counter in the games the Princes of Prydein played among themselves. Whoever held Gwenhwyvar would hold a powerful claim to be Arthur's successor, and the Princes would fight rather than allow one of their number to become dominant. Some – perhaps many – would find it preferable that Gwenhwyvar should die quietly, if the alternative was that she should fall into the hands of a rival.

'I shall go to the Convent of St Helena outside Lindinis. Celemon will come to you; I charge you in our Saviour's name, take what she gives you and keep it safe.'

'Yes.'

Their eyes met and she smiled. 'Most will think you dead. Better perhaps if you stay that way. Erfai tells me those who found you are close friends of his. The surgeon was too busy with your wounds to worry about your identity, and besides, he does not expect you to survive. If we hide your scarred hand under a swathe of bandages to make it seem a new injury, there will be no reason for anybody to connect you with Bedwyr mab Petroc.'

'I understand.' He also would be much sought after if it was known he had survived Camlann. His support – voluntary or otherwise – would add substance to any usurper's claim, and his presence in a warband would lend a spurious legitimacy to suggestions it was the Army of Albion reborn.

'You will know when I need you. Come to me then.'

He fought for speech. 'How shall I find you?'

'Begin your search at St Helena's.' She released his hand. 'But you will find me, when I need you. I shall draw you to me, as once your woman drew Arthur's Companions to the islands of the north-west.'

And thus set us on the path to glory and to ruin, he thought, but all he said aloud was: 'She was not my woman.'

Gwenhwyvar rose, looked down upon him. She seemed taller than he remembered, though perhaps it was just his own weakness and the angle from which he saw her, taller and very straight of back. Her hair was dry now, showing more silver than gold, and her face was scored with lines and wrinkles.

'For a time she was, Bedwyr. And if she had remained your woman, or you her man, we might not have been brought to this.'

He shook his head, lacking the strength to argue.

She regarded him fiercely, then suddenly relaxed, bent forward and brushed his cheek with her lips.

'Fare you well, cousin.'

She turned, her shadow huge in the candlelight, patted Erfai on the arm, and was gone through the flap of the tent before either man had the chance to speak.

It was fortunate, thought Bedwyr as he lay under the pine trees waiting for sleep to claim him, that Erfai was a man of his word.

He had sworn to keep silent about what had passed in the tent that night, and had told no one, not even his son. So far as most people were concerned Bedwyr mab Petroc had died with the others at Camlann. There were rumours, of course, perhaps because one of those who found him on the battlefield had talked, but few paid much attention.

For a time he had become a monk in Brittany, and there he had heard the tale of the Seven Survivors of Camlann. Sandde Angel's Form escaped because of his beauty; Morvran son of Tegid the Bald because of his ugliness. Kynvelyn escaped because of his red horse: 'Kethin Kiflym, the ruddy one, running across the grassland under the thighs of the generous lord, swifter than the fleeting cloud shadows'.

Those three (and the horse) were much older than Arthur: if they had lived at all it was in a past so distant only vague memories remained.

Cedwyn escaped because of his luck; Dervel the Strong because of his strength; Geneid the Tall because of his speed. These three he had known, and if they had indeed survived, he had no idea what had befallen them since.

The seventh and last name was his own, or more exactly it was his father's name, which he had often borrowed when he did not wish to be recognized. 'Petroc of the splintered spear, Petroc Paladrthellt, fought his way clear by his skill with his weapon.' None of the Companions at Camlann were called Petroc, though Petroc was a common enough name, and the tale made it clear this one had fought for Arthur, not against him. He had always assumed it referred to him – a thinly-veiled reference, perhaps, by somebody who knew the truth but did not wish to spread it too widely. But perhaps that was only his vanity . . .

He shook himself. During the summer he had come perilously close to being ensorcelled by a druid. The will had been drained from him, as the blood might drain from a dying man taking with it all vitality and purpose. Already weakened by illness, he had found himself slipping into an endless round of daydreams, so that at a time when he should have been acting, fighting to protect his land and people, he had lain in a waking sleep, lost in a past which had seemed more real than the present.

He had roused before it was too late, and that particular druid would cast no more spells. But the effects remained with him: a tendency to slip into a past so vivid he could taste the food on the platter, smell the scents on the breeze, feel the texture of the cloth under his fingertips. Even now, when he was fully awake and conscious of his surroundings, of the wind soft among the fir boughs, of the pony wheezing and whuffling a few paces away, he could recall Celemon's face as he had seen it last: the tawny hair tangled, the tear tracks down her cheeks, the mole beside her upper lip dark against skin pale with exhaustion; call it to mind so perfectly she might have been standing before him in the darkness.

She was not beautiful, either by the standards of Rome he dimly remembered from his boyhood, or by the standards of his contemporaries. She had too much of her father in her for that.

Dio Cassius in his Roman History gives a description of Boudicca, the Queen of the Iceni who led the famous rebellion against the rule of Rome. 'She was very tall, the glance of her eye very fierce; her voice harsh. A great mass of the reddest hair fell down to her hips. Around her neck was a large golden necklace, and she always wore a many-coloured tunic over which a thick cloak was fastened with a brooch. Her appearance was terrifying.'

Other than the colour of the hair, this could have been Celemon. She too was tall and fierce of eye, and her voice was capable of being harsh if the need arose. When Bedwyr read about Boudicca, or about that other British Amazon, Cartimandua, Queen of the Brigantes in the days of the Roman Conquest, who handed the British leader Caradawg over to Rome and banished her husband Venutius, it was Celemon's face and form he gave to them.

Celemon was not beautiful, yet she never lacked for suitors. Some, of course, desired her simply because she was the daughter of Cei, thinking of the prestige and power such an alliance might bring. Others desired her for herself; when she was in a room lesser women paled into insignificance, however classic their beauty, because her wit and conversation outshone other women as the sun outshines the moon. All manner of men sought her hand: princes and kings, heroes and wise men, warriors and farmers. Yet she never married, perhaps because none of the suitors could match the wild exuberance her father had brought to the daily business of living.

She had come to Bedwyr while he lay sequestered in the tent, struggling to accept the fact that he had survived the ruin of his world. Erfai had ushered her through the flap (kindly Erfai, who would die a hideously painful death on the banks of the River Oak five years later) and though he was a massively powerful man whose physical size usually dwarfed those around him, he seemed quite ordinary standing beside her.

'I did not think to see you again,' she said, leaning down to kiss Bedwyr. Her eyes were wet with tears.

'I did not think to be seen,' he said weakly, trying to make her smile.

'Without Gwenhwyvar you would not have been,' Erfai said soberly. 'The wound fever had you in its grip and would not have released you. She fought for you as I have never seen anybody fight, willing you to live, commanding you to live, calling you back from the very gates of Heaven.'

'She has need of you.' Celemon's face was sorrowful. She stood beside the bed, her hair brushing the ridge of the tent, and Bedwyr thought that he had never seen her in such distress. 'Those last hours at Caer Cadwy. She was stern and cold, almost broken under her grief – she knew Arthur was gone, knew before the messenger arrived bringing word of the disaster – dazed and uncertain one moment and filled with purpose the next.'

' "We are not quite done," ' Bedwyr murmured softly.

'What do you mean?' A shiver ran through Celemon's body.

He shrugged, winced as the pain lanced through him. 'I do not know. They are the words Arthur spoke to me on the last night before we left for Camlann. They mean something, but I do not understand what – or even how they can have any meaning.'

She wrinkled her brow, shook her head. Behind her Erfai made a face, as if worried his uncle was relapsing into fever.

Celemon gestured towards the entrance of the tent. 'I have brought a few of your things. Gwenhwyvar seemed to think it better you did not return to Caer Cadwy.'

Erfai looked surprised. 'You have seen her? Rumour around the camp has it that she has vanished.'

'No. We arranged this before she departed Caer Cadwy.'

Frowning, Erfai said: 'But how?' His voice trailed away as his gaze travelled from one to the other, from the tall woman at his side to the man on the bed.

'She seemed to know he would survive.'

The words hung in the air between them. Erfai swallowed,

pulled at his beard. 'This is too deep for me,' he said unsteadily. 'I am only a simple warrior. I –' He waved a hand in the air, helplessly, and subsided slowly to a stool, where he sat and watched the others.

'I did not believe her,' Celemon said calmly. 'I did not believe her at all.'

'Yet you did as she wished,' said Bedwyr.

She nodded, her eyes full of unshed tears. 'What else could I do?' Erfai made a strangulated sound in the background.

'What did you bring?' asked Bedwyr, ignoring his nephew.

'Whatever I thought you might value. Fresh clothing and your red parade tunic, some brooches and arm rings, the glass goblets you used to let me play with when I was a child – a trusting man you were –'

'With reason,' he said, sketching a grin.

'– your copper and enamel bowl –'

'Ah, cunning,' he muttered. 'Some may mistake it for that other bowl.'

'– the wooden cup Teleri gave you, the amber beads you took at Badon Hill, and –' She hesitated, glanced at Erfai on his stool.

'Go on.' Bedwyr's voice was stronger now, and there was colour in his cheeks. 'Trust him, as I do.'

'And the amulet containing the fragment of the True Cross.'

Erfai sat bolt upright. 'What! The fragment of the Cross Arthur carried at the battle of Badon Hill? You have it here?'

'Hush, nephew, hush! Leather walls may hide our bodies, but they will not hide the sound of our voices.' Bedwyr waited until the big man had control of himself. 'We agreed it would be safer with me.'

Erfai looked at him, lying almost helpless on the bed, and raised an eyebrow. 'Safer?' he repeated slowly. 'Safer than what?'

His uncle ignored him, spoke directly to Celemon. 'I think it would have been your father's place, if he had lived.'

The sorrow welled in her again. 'But he did not. If this, if that. There are so many ifs.' Her expression hardened. 'If Medraut had never been born, if Iddawg had not been gifted with a silver tongue . . .'

'I killed Iddawg,' Bedwyr said with surprise, remembering how the blade had bitten the hated face to the bone. 'I had forgotten that, till just now.'

'Good,' she said savagely.

'What will you do?'

She shrugged. 'What can I do? Like the rest of you, I will be sought by those who think themselves Arthur's heirs. Retire from the world in a house of religion, I suppose. I might as well follow Gwenhwyvar to Saint Helena. What choice do I have?'

'I am sorry.'

'We are all sorry, Bedwyr. But sorrow does not mend matters.'

'No.' His left hand – heavily bandaged, as Gwenhwyvar had suggested, to disguise its old scars – plucked at the covers. 'I do not think the realm of Albion can be mended in our lifetimes. The circle is broken, and all that remains is to live out the rest our lives in whatever peace we can find.'

Erfai grunted impatiently. He was still comparatively young, and had never been, as they had, part of Arthur's Court. Though he sorrowed, his grief did not run as thick or as heavy as theirs.

'You could come home with me, Bedwyr,' he said after a moment. 'Gereint is a good lord, without ambitions of his own, beholden to nobody except Kynfawr his overlord.'

Bedwyr shook his head, slowly, sadly. 'Kynfawr, Cunomorus, is also a good man. But he will not live forever, and his son Constantine is not of the same mettle. Dumnonia will not be safe for me.'

'If not Dumnonia,' spluttered Erfai, 'then where? Here at least you would be among friends. What part of Britain could be safer?'

'None.' Bedwyr's eyes met Celemon's. 'I must leave Britain.'

She nodded in resignation, recognizing the truth of his words.

'Leave? Leave?' Erfai was red with indignation. 'Where will you go?'

'Armorica. Brittany. It is still a civilized land, and many of our people have taken refuge there over the years.' He sighed. 'I shall find a monastery and pass the remainder of my days in prayer, for there is much blood on my hands, and many sins.'

'But you are Bedwyr mab Petroc,' expostulated Erfai. 'After Arthur himself, the most respected man in the island.'

'That is why I must leave,' he said wearily. He settled deeper into the bed, closed his eyes. 'And besides, I am so very tired of being Bedwyr mab Petroc.'

The pony moved, stamped its hooves. Tendrils of mist crept between the tree trunks. Bedwyr shifted on his couch of needles, gazed up at the glitter of stars, at the familiar outline of the Bear, its tail dangling towards the earth, remembering with something like longing the snug warmth of his sickbed in Erfai's tent.

It had taken a while for Erfai to see that nothing would sway his uncle from his course. The big man had tried all kinds of blandishments, even lost his temper on several occasions, but Bedwyr had been obdurate. To stay in Britain would mean becoming another's tool, and having served Arthur he had no desire to answer to a lesser master.

Bedwyr was never sure how long they remained camped on the field of Camlann. During the day the tent filled with a soft brown light which did not change until dusk, when candles or lamps were kindled. Other than this duality of light and dark there was nothing by which to measure the passage of time, and one day blurred into another. He knew the camp was gradually shrinking from what Erfai told him and from what he himself could hear of the outside world: little by little Cunomorus's followers were drifting home.

Everything was drifting. Cunomorus was an able ruler of Dumnonia, but he lacked wider authority. Once the battlefield was cleared – the dead buried or burned, the wounded cared for or given the quietus, the still usable equipment salvaged – there was nothing left for his army to do. Nominally, this was still part of Dumnonia, but in practice the area had been under the Emperor's rule for more than a generation. The lords of Ynis Witrin and the lesser landowners hereabouts had paid their taxes directly to the Amherawdyr. Now Arthur was gone they had no intention of acknowledging Cunomorus as their new overlord, and thus would not cooperate with him, even over minor matters.

'What of Caer Cadwy?' Bedwyr asked one evening.

Erfai paused in the act of lighting an oil lamp. 'Deserted, apart from a handful of servants who refuse to leave. The lower town is still occupied, but fast dying. The craftsmen and women are packing their belongings.'

He put the taper to the wick just as the flame began to scorch his fingers, hastily shook it out. A gentle golden glow danced through the tent as the wick caught and steadied.

'One cannot blame them,' he added. 'They need custom, and they will not find any in Caer Cadwy.'

'Cunomorus does not plan to occupy it?'

'How can he?' Erfai shrugged expressively. 'His army dwindles with every passing day. You need men to hold the fortress, plenty of men. And if he does take Caer Cadwy, it will be assumed he sees himself as Arthur's successor. That will bring more fighting down on our heads: Vortepor of Dyfed, Cadwallon of Gwynedd, Catraut of Calchwinyth will not permit Cunomorus to set himself in the Emperor's place.'

'Would Cunomorus wish to do so?'

Erfai smiled mirthlessly. 'I would not have thought so, but who can tell for certain what another man desires? Ambition takes people in odd ways. Still, he is no fool, and must realize the task would be beyond him.'

He busied himself about the tent, tidying corners. Bedwyr watched him affectionately, thinking how strange it was that this bearlike warrior should have lavished such care and attention upon an uncle he scarcely knew, save by repute. Gwenhwyvar might have pulled him back from death by the force of her will, but it was Erfai who had dealt with the unpleasant routine of caring for a bedbound patient, Erfai who had cleaned and fed him without complaint.

'I keep returning to the same thought,' the big man said over his shoulder. 'If only Arthur had left an heir.'

'Medraut was his heir.'

'Medraut!' Erfai made the name a guttural sound from deep within his throat. 'I meant an heir of his body.'

'If only,' said Bedwyr. He lay back on the pillows, sighed. 'The hardest thing of all, to my mind, to transfer power.'

'What do you mean?'

'It was where Rome failed. Think how many Emperors of Rome were slain by their own Imperial Guard: Caligula, Galba, Vitellius, Domitian, Commodus, Pertinax – the list is endless. Think how many Emperors took the purple by force of arms: from Augustus himself, through Vespasian, Severus and the giant Thracian Maximinus, down to the chaos of the later years, when every minor general with a legion to back him was likely to claim the throne.'

'Who was the giant Thracian?'

'Hmmm?' Bedwyr glanced up, saw the expression of puzzlement on his nephew's face. 'I am sorry. I was thinking aloud. The Thracian Maximinus was Emperor of Rome nearly three hundred years ago. He was renowned for his size and strength, but was brought down by a succession of rebellions and eventually murdered by his own troops.' He ran a hand across the heavy stubble on his chin. 'A familiar story. At least the end was quick for Arthur.'

He fell silent, and Erfai waited patiently for his uncle to speak again.

'What I was thinking,' the older man said after a while, 'was that the weakness of Rome was its inability to ensure a stable transfer of power from one ruler to the next. It worked if the dynasty was secure, which was why so many emperors made co-rulers of their sons, that the succession might be easier.'

'And if they had no son?'

Bedwyr smiled. 'Then they adopted a suitable heir, just as Ambrosius the Younger adopted Arthur. As a system it sometimes worked, sometimes did not. Too often it led to palace intrigue and large numbers of unexplained deaths, much use of poison as a weapon of statecraft.'

Erfai grunted. 'Not unknown today.'

'Yes. It is a weakness we inherited from our forebears. When Agricola of Dyfed went to his rest – may Heaven receive his soul, for he was a good man – many of his sons fell prey to mysterious maladies. Only Vortepor survived unscathed.'

'Vortepor!' Erfai spat contemptuously. 'As gross in mind as body. I notice none came to this place from Dyfed, though every other region sent somebody, even if it was only an emissary to say their forces had mobilised too late to be of use in the strife and now must look to their own borders. At least they kept the pretence of being loyal to Arthur.'

'Indeed? Interesting Vortepor alone did not bother with the courtesies.' Bedwyr frowned, shook his head. 'Still, there were plenty of Dyfed men at Camlann, both among the Companions and among the followers of Medraut. Perhaps he feared to favour one side or the other, lest he spark a civil war in Dyfed itself.'

'You seem much stronger today,' Erfai remarked after a time.

'I am, thanks to your care.'

The big man seemed uncomfortable. Watching, Bedwyr half expected him to start wriggling or hopping from foot to foot like a small child reluctantly confessing to some misdeed.

'As you know, the camp is shrinking. There is no purpose in staying, and the lesser lords are worried about their own lands. My own lord, Gereint, is suggesting we should leave soon. Gereint does not know,' he added hastily, 'that you are alive.

I told him I was caring for an old family retainer, who had accompanied you to the battle and been badly injured.'

'Did he believe you?'

'Gereint is a good lord. He trusts me, and does not ask too many questions.' Erfai shuffled from one leg to the other, and Bedwyr stifled a grin. 'He still believes in the virtues: in loyalty, honour, duty.'

'A naive man?'

'I do not find him so. He offers you a place with us, when you are well enough to travel.'

Bedwyr shook his head regretfully. 'It would not work, kinsman. My foes would sniff me out. Give Gereint my thanks – or the thanks of the aged retainer – and say I feel the burden of my sins pressing upon my soul. Truly did the psalmist write: "*viri sanguinum et doli non dimidiabunt dies suos*" – "Men of blood and craft will not live out half their days." I must retire from the active life, spend whatever time God allots me in prayer and contemplation.'

'In that case,' said Erfai, 'what shall I do with this?'

He reached behind him and produced Bedwyr's sword with a flourish. The mud of Camlann had been cleaned from the leather sheath, and the bronze chape had been polished until it gleamed in the lamplight. As Erfai drew the blade – the blue-grey steel rasping on the wooden frame of the scabbard – Bedwyr saw that this also had received much care and attention. The nicks of battle had been lovingly ground from the edges, and the hilt had been refurbished, a fresh piece of roughened leather bound into place with new wire for the grip.

'I would hardly recognize it,' he said, his voice thick with emotion. 'I . . . I do not know. I do not wish to carry it, not now, yet I am reluctant to leave it behind. Especially after all that you have done.'

Erfai's face clouded, then brightened again. 'I have it!' he exclaimed triumphantly. 'I shall put it in the chest of your belongings that Celemon brought you. Then it will be with you without being in the way, if take my meaning.'

'I do, and once more I thank you.' Bedwyr inclined his head gravely, thinking to himself that he could always give the thing away once he reached Armorica.

Yet somehow he never had.

* * *

It was with him now as he lay beneath the pines awaiting sleep, the heavy pommel pressing into his side below the ribs. During the years in the monastery he had taken it out of the chest from time to time, cleaned and oiled it, because it had once served him well and deserved better than to rust away from neglect, then carefully wrapped and replaced it. The act was always performed in private, a ritual of which he was ashamed; not even Winwalloe, his closest friend in the community, knew what dark secret was hidden away in the carved wooden chest he kept under the truckle bed.

That was how he thought of it, as a dark secret.

In one corner of the monastery library was a pile of mouldering scrolls not considered worth the effort of copying, a collection of moral tales written by an early Christian. The unknown author had borrowed from many sources, Virgil's *Aeneid* and Petronius's *Satyricon* among them, but the common factor in the stories was a character with a dark secret. Sometimes they were an escaped slave trying to enter high society, sometimes they turned into a slavering beast when the moon was full, sometimes they had been promised to an obscure pagan sect when a new-born child. In each case the illuminating power of Christ was turned upon their dark secret, and they saw the error of their ways, to live happily ever after as a servant of the one true God.

Bedwyr – or Budoc, as he then called himself – found the stories oddly touching, and he recognized that for all their trite simplicity they contained a lesson from which he could profit. He had renounced the sword, renounced the way of blood and violence he had pursued all his adult life. Yet he could not bring himself to take the final step and dispose of the blade he had carried at Camlann – the last in a long line of blades he had carried since he became a man. He could not even admit to his fellow monks, let alone the Father Abbot, that he had a tool of death and destruction hidden among his few possessions.

And when he left the monastery, took ship for Britain and landed on a quay in western Dumnonia, the sword went with him, concealed in the wooden chest. There it stayed while he wandered through the land, answering the call that came to him, and it was with him when he reached the hermitage at Sanctuary Wood, the Nemeton of Porthyle.

Here too, in the privacy of his isolated hut, he had from time to time taken the sword from the chest and performed the ritual cleansing, losing himself in the beauty of the cold grey blade with its sheen of blue as it caught the light (so, playing along its length like cold fire), twisting and turning it in his hands, seeing the pattern of hammer strokes from its forging faint under the skin, a ghostly series of rippling indentations undetectable to the touch.

It was a modern blade, a blade of Albion not of Rome, forged in the fires of Caer Cadwy and presented to him by Arthur himself. The old Roman cavalry had used the spatha, the double-edged long sword, but that weapon was cumbersome and ill balanced, designed for slashing and little else. Oddly, it was from the Saxons that the smiths of Albion relearned the art of making good swords that tapered to a point, of twisting and hammering metal to form the core of the blade, to which the hard cutting edges were then welded. Saxon swords had light pommels, which left them blade heavy; here the smiths of Albion improved upon the original, countering the weight of the blades with cunningly crafted nuggets of iron.

Sometimes he would stand in the rough grass above the cliff-tops, the surge of the sea in his ears, the sword unsheathed in his hand, and he would move, slowly at first then with gathering speed, move as he had once moved among Arthur's enemies, acting out the terrible beauty of the dance of death.

Afterwards he would pray, beg forgiveness for this the greatest of his sins: not the pride he took in his ability, not the joy he felt in the flow when man and blade became one, but the overwhelming desire to kill, the desire which for more than half a lifetime, ever since the battle of Badon Hill, had too often mastered him.

For ten years he would have been happier if Erfai had left his sword forgotten in the chaos of Camlann. For ten years he had shut it in a box like a guilty secret, only bringing it out when he was alone. With each passing year it seemed less likely he would ever need to use it again. As his own inevitable death loomed larger in his mind, the sessions of cleaning and exercise grew in intensity, for this was the part of his life he was most reluctant to leave behind.

Then on a summer morning Scotti raiders had come to disturb his solitude, destroying the village beneath the Sanctuary Wood, hunting for the chalice they believed Arthur and Gwenhwyvar had entrusted to his keeping. In the wake of the Scotti had come two British warriors: Gorthyn son of Erfai and his foster brother Nai. With the Saxon boy Ceolric and the girl Eurgain, the sole

129

survivor of the village, they had formed an alliance of five to thwart the Scotti.

He had not revealed himself to Erfai's son, and sometimes now he cursed the pride which had made him continue to play the part of Budoc the monk turned hermit. Nai had guessed the truth, but Gorthyn had not believed his foster brother when the latter told him of his suspicions. So far as Gorthyn was concerned Bedwyr mab Petroc had died at Camlann. Had not his own father attended the field of slain, helped gather the bodies for communal burial? If Bedwyr had lived, Erfai would have known, and if Erfai had known, he would have told his only son.

But Erfai had kept his word and held his peace. Gorthyn had fought the Scotti in the moonlight outside the hermit's hut all unwitting that the old man he strove to protect was his own kinsman. Bedwyr had fumbled with the fastenings of the chest, hesitated to unsheath the blade Erfai had restored to him, and while he hesitated Gorthyn had died, dragged down by a dozen lesser men.

For ten years Bedwyr had nurtured the sword, tormented himself with guilt, and then when at last he had needed to use it he had acted too late.

He was not a fool, was aware there were good reasons for his fatal slowness. He had still been recovering from the fever which had nearly killed him not long before. The magic of the Scotti's druid had come perilously close to destroying his will, reducing him to lethargy by trapping him in a long dream of the past, a dream from which even now he was not entirely free.

Most important, what was done was done. He could not call Gorthyn back to life or change what had happened. Already the big man's face was blurred in his memory, overlaid with images of Erfai, whom he had closely resembled. All Bedwyr could do was ensure that never again was he caught so helpless, and as part of that the sword would no longer languish in a trunk but stay with him, close by his side.

Eventually he slept, and woke to morning, the cautious notes of the first birds and the mists curling between the trunks of the trees. Moisture dripped from the branches, and he lay shivering in the cold grey light, struggling to summon the strength to rise.

It was the cold that drove him forth. A curious thing, and one he had often noted, was that one might be perfectly warm wrapped in a cloak while one slept, but the moment one wakened the chill began to bite.

Bedwyr dealt with the pony first, leading it through the trees till he reached a small meadow bordered on all sides by woodland, the long grass white with frost. Here the pony seemed happy to browse, and he left it there knowing it could not be seen from any vantage point.

Then he returned by way of his campsite to the track he had crossed the previous night, moving through the morning mist like a ghost, using the boles of the trees for cover, parting the branches with great care, never hurrying. Around him the birds continued to sing, undisturbed by his presence, and his feet made no sound in the thick black mulch that underlay the thin carpet of brown needles.

When he came to the edge of the track Bedwyr waited for a long while, motionless among the firs, scanning his surroundings. He did not believe he had lost his pursuers. He had given them plentiful indications of the direction he had taken after leaving Caer Cadwy, and he was certain they would have noted the place where he had abandoned the road.

He hoped they would assume he was making for Camlann. So far they had predicted his every move with unnatural accuracy, and he had indeed toyed with the idea of visiting the battle site, on the grounds it was the last place he had seen either Gwenhwyvar or Celemon.

But now he had decided it was unnecessary. He would learn nothing from the site his own memory could not tell him. The time had come to find Gwenhwyvar, and there was small purpose in finding her if all he accomplished was to bring her enemies down upon her. His first task must be to lose his pursuers, once and for all, and this was the ideal country in which to achieve that: well wooded and sparsely populated.

The mist was rising from the hills and valleys like smoke, as if the very land itself were smouldering with slow fire. Here and there he could see a dull gleam of water in the pale morning light, but otherwise the ground was veiled. The dark branches of the naked trees emerged above the grey cloak as if they had been overwhelmed in some great flood, and while he watched four or five black specks took flight from a nearby copse.

Something had frightened them, but he could not see what it was. He squatted behind the fir bough, his damaged hand resting

131

on the hilt of his sword, and waited, his eyes scanning the area around the copse. Perhaps it had been a wild beast, a boar stirring with the dawn, or the wolves he had heard last night, returning to their lair.

The birds circled in the air – their crowing came to him faintly across the valley – then settled again in their original place. The mist was thinning, blown away by a wind rising from the north, and he could catch glimpses of the ground now, sloping down from the copse through dark patches of brushwood and shri-velled bracken.

Bedwyr reached out to the verge of the track, moving slowly so as not to agitate the fir boughs and betray his presence, and plucked some grass stalks. His fingers were clumsy with cold, and his left hand had in any case never been much use in situations like this. Laboriously he wound the stems together, in and out, up and over, till he held three platted wands.

Then he bowed his head in silent prayer and cast them into the face of the wind. One blew over the far verge and vanished down the hillside. One fluttered to the ground no more than a spear's length from where he squatted. The third caught the breeze, floating like a gull riding the currents of the air, and climbed above the level of the trees until it was lost from sight. With a smile of satisfaction he eased himself back into the cover of the firs and settled to his wait.

For an age nothing happened. The sun's rays strengthened and the frost continued to melt, dripping from the boughs around him. The wind ruffled the grass, tried and failed to shift the wand on the track, carved great swathes through the mist on the nearby hillsides. He loosened the sword in its sheath, felt the heavy iron pommel cold beneath his fingers, the shagreen of the hilt rough in his grasp. A mouse foraged along the far verge, rustling through the dying brambles.

Metal rang on stone somewhere out of sight down the slope. A voice cursed, once, softly, and was silent. Listening, he could hear the grunt of horses being forced to climb a steep hill, hear the creak of leather, feel the vibration of their passage coming to him through the ground. They were good, and had one of them not lapsed for a moment and allowed his horse to strike a rock with an iron-shod hoof, he might not have sensed their presence until they were upon him.

He drew the sword and lay it on the ground beside him. He

hoped that his three braided wands would send his pursuers in the wrong direction, but the magic of the Dlui Fulla, the fluttering wisp, was not always reliable and it was as well to be prepared.

The sounds grew louder and suddenly they were there on the track to his left, seven men on horses, looming large in the limited space. They reined in and let the ponies recover from the climb, their cold eyes raking the trees where he crouched. The seven were dressed alike in simple tunics and dull cloaks with all the colour weathered out of them. Each had a small round shield slung on his back, a quiver of throwing spears hanging from the saddle cantle, and a sturdier lance in one hand. Six were bare-headed, their black hair hanging to their shoulders. The seventh, in the middle of the group, wore a hood that disguised his face.

The man Bedwyr had seen in Isca and again in Lindinis rode beside this hooded figure, whom he took to be the leader. The two conferred in whispers while the others waited; a quick gesture, and the cowl was flung back.

Dark eyes, cunning eyes, swept across his hiding place, halted and returned, searching, penetrating. He froze, crouched un-breathing among the fir boughs, which seemed suddenly thin and flimsy. Plumes of steam rose from the panting horses. Moisture fell steadily from the trees. The sword hilt was hard in his hand as he prepared for the shout of discovery. The eyes seemed to be boring directly into his own; the creature could not possibly miss him.

Unable to look away, Bedwyr stared in fascination.

At this distance the man appeared to be wearing a mask painted with green and blue designs, but Bedwyr knew from experience that this was no mask, to be doffed at will. The man had willingly undergone the painful process of having the soft skin of his cheeks scarred by dozens of needle-pricks. Woad dye had been rubbed into the fresh wounds, and the result was this permanent and terrifying disfigurement.

One of the others spoke, and the spell was broken.

The words were incomprehensible but the meaning was clear. (He had never been certain whether they spoke a language of their own, a truly alien tongue like that of the Seasons, or whether their dialect had simply shifted so far from the common speech that like some versions of Irish it could no longer be understood by outsiders. Whichever, they could speak true British when they chose.)

The tattooed man waved his spear, indicating the track. The speaker slipped from his mount and surveyed the ground, obviously searching for prints. The rest waited, watching him, keeping out of his way as he crept forward pace by pace, pausing now and again to examine some sign he had found.

Once he said something, and the others chuckled quietly in their throats. One near the back raised fingers to his head in imitation of prick ears, and howled softly, like a wolf. The tracker scowled, and the man hastily dropped his fingers.

As the tracker progressed the mounted men followed, bunching together on the confines of the path. The horses shifted restlessly, bared their teeth and snapped at one another. When they drew level with Bedwyr's hiding place a bay pony launched a kick at the grey crowding on its heels; the grey's rider jerked his own leg aside just in time, and the kick landed hollowly on the horse's ribs. The grey bucked and plunged while its rider shouted angrily at the man on the bay, and for a glorious moment Bedwyr thought the two would come to blows.

The leader turned, barked a word of command. The two men subsided, muttering furiously. The rider of the bay swung his pony's head sharply around, jerking the reins with more force than was necessary, and jostled his way to the rear. His companions glared at him, shook their spears menacingly.

Bedwyr watched with interest. There was a discord here which went deeper than an unruly horse. It was a pity he could not understand what they were saying. He would have liked to have known whether the rider of the bay was unpopular because of his character, or whether there was some more fundamental difference between the men. He was well aware of the strain living in unnatural circumstances can put upon a group. These people had been following him through potentially hostile territory for several days, and seeking him for Heaven only knew how much longer. By now habits which would normally seem mildly annoying, like talking too much or always breaking wind after eating, would have assumed infuriating proportions.

Probably that was all it was: the man constantly picked his nose, or whined about the weather. But there was always the chance that what he was witnessing did indeed run deeper, that there were factions among the Children of Menestyr just as there were factions among other men. And if that were so, it was worth remembering.

The tracker turned his horse till it was broadside across the path, pulled himself up into the saddle and signalled to his companions. The tattooed leader raised a hand; the faint mumble of discontent quieted at once. They all listened to what the tracker was saying, even the rider on the bay, who had been studiously ignoring the others. He spoke for some time, his voice rising and falling with the wind, and only one word made sense to Bedwyr crouched in the firs, and that a word often reiterated:

'Camlann!'

Abruptly the man wheeled his pony and set heels to its flanks. The troop followed, and Bedwyr's last sight of them was of the rider on the bay horse ducking under an overhanging branch as they rounded a bend in the path.

CHAPTER SEVEN

'That was foolish,' said Seradwen.

She had brought the bard back to the study where they had sat earlier. The man still seemed shaken by the hostility he had aroused in the hall: as she poured him a beaker of wine she noticed that his hands were trembling slightly.

'I thought you were going to avoid controversy.'

He took the wine gratefully, nodding his thanks. 'I had intended to,' he said. 'But it is a good tale, with beautiful words. I was tempted and I fell.'

She raised an eyebrow. 'The old excuse.'

Regin smiled shamefacedly. 'True.' He sipped his wine, glanced around the room.

'You are Christians here?'

'Yes,' she said, surprised by the change of subject.

'All of you? The farm workers as well?'

'When a priest or the bishop come visiting.'

'And the rest of the time?'

She shrugged. 'They have their own beliefs. Bodgath – the master of the horseherd – once told me that big gods are not for the likes of him. The common people have their own gods, small gods, gods of springs and woods.'

'You sound envious.'

'Do I?' She considered for a moment. 'Perhaps I am. I see no harm in propitiating the spirit of the place. And belief in the

Hoofed One, the Horned One, the Lady of Horses, is strong here. I suspect it is one reason they accept me as mistress.'

'Epona,' he said softly, twisting the beaker in his hands. 'Rhiannon.'

'Although I am mistress, Bodgath is the one they really listen to. He is their leader, and I think the closest thing they have to a priest. I see the way they look at him sometimes. Cautiously, as if it would not do to offend him.'

'One hears of such things.' He drained the beaker, looked at her from under his eyelids. 'Lady, is there anything I can do for you?'

She felt herself blush, held her breath till it had passed.

'Yes,' she said, aware of her own daring. 'Tell me a tale. An old tale, not one of your Dyfed calumnies.'

He grinned lazily, his eyes assessing her. 'An old tale? No shortage of those. Let me think.'

While he considered she poured more wine, sat back and sipped it slowly, enjoying being alone with him. The fact the brothers and their wives would not approve, would imagine the worst, added to her pleasure.

'I know,' he said. 'It is not a woman's tale, this, but it is strong in my mind, demanding to be told. Perhaps it is right for you.'

Regin picked up the harp, ran a fingernail across the strings. 'You must understand that there is only ever one hero, and that he is the hope and glory of his people. The hero tales we tell are of three kinds, but they all follow the same pattern. The first deal with the conception, birth and childhood of the hero. The story may describe how his parents met and how they overcame the obstacles placed in the path of their eventual union, or it may relate how he was stolen away as an infant and rescued by his kinsmen.'

He laid the harp aside. The oil hissed in the lamp, and its scent came to her nostrils as she studied his face, waiting.

'The second kind,' Regin continued after a moment, 'which are the most numerous, are those that describe his exploits, the deeds that made him a hero. They may include the wooing of his wife, or his several wives; they will certainly tell of the slaughter he wreaks upon the enemies of his people. These are the simplest tales, the ones we bards most often sing within a hall of warriors, the ones which please our audience most easily.'

The deep burr of his voice filled her with delight. She closed her eyes and listened.

137

'The third kind of tale is the death tale, for every hero must have a death to match his life. He must fall in a struggle against overwhelming odds, fighting both men and magic, and if he goes forth to his last combat knowing he must die, yet still determined to defend his honour or protect his people, then so much the better.

'It is easy to treat these matters as entertainments, and perhaps for many people that is all they are. But to become a bard, a true bard as opposed to a mere gleeman, one must learn the five-times-fifty Prime Stories, and the twice-fifty Secondary Stories which are not to be recited in public. One must immerse oneself in the lore of the island of Prydein, in tales of cattle raids and courtships, of feasts and elopements, of voyages and expeditions.

'Now, you know as well as I do that certain tales are appropriate to certain times. Just as a Christian priest when baptising an infant will tell of Christ's baptism in the waters of Jordan, so too there are stories which should be told on first crossing the threshold of a new house, or before setting out on a long journey.

'The reason for this is not, as some might say, that our lives are ruled by ritual. As a youth I did not understand this, for I was raised in a household which paid lip service to Christianity, and I regarded these things as a superstition, a hangover from our barbarous and unenlightened past.'

She opened her eyes. His gaze was fixed upon the lamp flame, his expression pensive.

'After I had received my bardic training, been buried alive in darkness for a night and a day while I composed my own poem and thus passed from pupil to master, I came to have a different appreciation.' He rolled the beaker so the surface of the wine caught the light, glanced up, his eyes meeting hers.

'How can I explain it to you?

'There are – and you should find this easy to follow, dealing daily with a man like your herdmaster Bodgath – two kinds of time. One is the Roman kind, the hours measured with sundials and water clocks, or sands running through a funnel, every falling grain a reminder that time is like a river always moving forward and we are being swept along with it, growing older with every fleeting moment.

'The other is the eternal present, moving through the pregnant spring to lush summer to barren winter in the great round of the year, a time in which what matters is not a material achievement

138

but the manner in which it is done, not the building but the *rightness* of the act of building.'

'I know,' she said quietly.

'Do you?' He peered down his hooked nose.

'We stand outside it.' She frowned, groped for the words. 'Those of us in Roman time, I mean. We look at it from outside, whereas Bodgath is inside, part of it.'

Regin smiled. 'Yes. *Inside.* That is how I feel when I am telling a tale, how great warriors feel as they wield their blades, how your friend Bodgath no doubt feels as he watches over the mares and foals. One becomes part of what is happening. It is a different way of seeing things, neither better nor worse than the Roman way – simply different. One perceives the richness of the world. Or to put it another way, people like Bodgath do not "have" a religion, in the sense that you and I have Christianity – their religion pervades everything, from the grass on which the horses graze to the moon in the sky at night.'

He raised long fingered hands. 'That is the key to understanding our stories. That is why they follow the same pattern, why the hero is born under unusual circumstances, brings hope to his people, performs remarkable feats, dies in battle not in bed. The hero belongs to that other time, to the heartbeat of the world, to the harmony that binds all things together.'

'And?' she prompted.

The fingers tugged at an eyebrow. 'What I am talking about is a way of seeing the world. Our forefathers, living cheek by jowl in their cities, forgot it, or looked upon it with amused condescension, as something fit for children. But the country dwellers, the pagans, never lost that way of seeing. You or I, I think, can never altogether capture it, because we are the product of civilization – which by definition is based upon the city – and therefore are always outside, looking in.'

Regin leant forward, speaking urgently, as if willing her to understand. 'Yet it is *true*, in a way that our measurement is not. Our lives are lived in mythic patterns, patterns that repeat from generation to generation. I will grant you the match is not always exact. Sometimes the story does not work itself out in the life of a single man, sometimes it takes more than one generation.'

Taking up the harp again, he played a series of notes that fell into the silence of the room like ripples in pond, spreading and merging as they echoed from the walls. Then he laid a hand flat against the strings and said in the voice used by bards to command quiet in a noisy hall:

'Listen!'

The story he told her then remained with her for the rest of her life, so that years afterwards when she was an old woman (and she lived to be a very old woman) she would wake in the watches of the night to dream of chariots raising plumes of white water as they splashed through fords, of a young hero coming down from the mountains to save his people, of a talking head bringing destruction on its foes.

The significance of what Regin was telling her did not strike her that night, though she realized from his long preamble that this was no simple entertainment, that he had some purpose beyond the desire to amuse or impress her. Only several days later was she to capture the full import of what he was trying to say, and even then she was never certain she entirely understood.

Sitting in the quiet room that had been Mordav's study and was now hers, she listened as Regin spun his story, sometimes chanting in tune with the harp and at other times speaking in normal tones, and the deep richness of his voice held her engrossed from beginning to end.

In the beginning of the world the People lived in scattered communities under the trees of the great forest that stretched between the mountains and the sea. Their lives were simple, their needs few. They had no enemies: to the north was Worethia, the great river arm of the sea which protected them from the wild tribes of the highlands; and to the south across the barrier of the bare moors were the kindred folk of Dewr.

Then the invaders came. The newcomers crossed the great ocean to the south in hollowed logs, chanting their name songs as they scooped their paddles through the water. They called themselves Peryth, the Lordly Ones, and they bore spears of holly tipped with cold blue metal that burned like ice, and grey swords that never blunted however many times they struck the foeman's shield. The Peryth conquered the folk of Dewr, made them their slaves, took the women for their concubines. As a sign of their wealth and power they raised great barrows over their dead, making the land their own. The People beyond the moors they despised, calling them *Weidhel*, a word that in their dialect meant 'Forest Dwellers', by which they meant 'those who live beyond the margins of the world in the lands that no right thinking person could or would want'. It was a term of deep contempt. The Weidhel were less than human to the Peryth, creatures to be slain on sight.

The People took counsel among themselves, fearful for their own fate. It was clear to them that the Peryth would breed like the maggots spawned in rotting meat. Soon the newcomers would be too many for the land of Dewr, and then their attention would turn to the Weidhel.

The People agreed they could not fight the invaders. There were brave men among the People, men skilled with sword and spear, with the use of the tathlom ball cast from a sling, but most of them were farmers or fishermen, hunters or trappers, not warriors. The newcomers fought from fleet chariots pulled by fast ponies, and their weapons were strange and cold, said to suck the soul of a man from his body.

It seemed to them in that hour that they needed the aid of one more powerful than themselves. The druids made sacrifice, studied the conjunctions of the stars and the bodies that wander through the heavens. They donned their animal costumes and danced in the circles of stone raised by the old ones their ancestors. They cast great treasures of gold and bronze into the gaping maw of the waters. They beseeched and they pleaded, gave blood and flesh and bone, burned bale-fires on the hilltops. They called on the Lady in whose body they lived, the Lady from whom all good things flow, called on her by her many names, her many aspects. And they called on the other, the Crow Lord her Lover whose name is rarely mentioned, the harbinger of death, Bran Brennos the Dark One, seeking to wake him from his deep slumber in Dun Dewed.

'And they were answered,' said Regin. 'They were answered, though many of them doubted the wisdom of calling upon the great powers. Chief among these doubters was a man called Grugyn the Strong, who might have been a leader among the People had things been otherwise. To his mind, calling upon the gods, the old gods of Albion, was a serious matter, not one to be undertaken lightly. Even the druids did not know how a prayer may be answered. Many have asked for some blessing in their lives – a good crop, a high reputation, fat kine, plentiful children – and have received the blessing they sought. But the blessing does not always come in the manner expected, nor bring the happiness hoped for. A good crop may arouse the envy of neighbours. A high reputation brings deep responsibilities. Fat kine may be sickly. Too many children may bring famine and suffering, early death. It is never wise to ask for things without considering the consequences.'

Regin's fingers slipped across the harp strings, and in the music he made Seradwen heard the sound of the sea and the wailing of gulls as he sang of the coming of the perfect youth, the golden hero, across the sea in the hour of the dawn, across the waves where the early light broke and glittered in a thousand pieces.

He set foot on the strand, stretching like a young lion, and the People waited to greet him. Forward he led them, out into the cleared land where sunshine and cloud shadow played across the fields the People had wrung from the darkness of the forest. Out he brought them, to where the warm winds of summer blew over the open ground, to where the great slab of rock stands alone in the plain, the slab which would ever after be known by his name: Llech Llew, Llew's Rock.

'Here we shall begin,' he said, and there he raised the stronghold which has stood through all the ages of the world, Dun Eidin, carving steps in the living stone, and there they came to love him, even those who had doubted the wisdom of seeking aid from the old gods.

For he was a god among men, was Llew, the desire of women, and in those early days at least the beloved of the whole tribe. He was master of all arts. He was a bronze-smith and a metal worker, a carpenter and a shipwright, a harper and a poet. He was a cupbearer and a scholar, a sorcerer and a leech, a swordsmith and a spear-maker. He was a charioteer and a horseman, a warrior and a champion. He knew when to plough and when to sow, when to reap. He was a maker of incantations, a singer of spells. At his command the mountains would dance, the rivers and lakes would hide their waters. At his will fire might fall from the heavens in showers of light. At his bidding the beasts of the forest would flock to the huntsman's spear.

Many things he taught the People, things which strengthened their homesteads and set the boundaries of their lands firm and unassailable. Today we remember him as a warrior-mage, the leader of the warband, lord of chariots and breaker of shields, feeder of ravens. But the People in those days were not warlike, for it was the coming of the Peryth that forced them to take up arms. Much of what he taught was more practical and of longer benefit: secrets of working metal, bone and horn; ways of delving far beneath the skin of the earth in search of minerals. He showed the People how sheep would quickly grow fat in the marshes they had thought wasteland; demonstrated better ways of ploughing fields and planting corn, so the land groaned with the Lady's bounty.

And Grugyn the Strong, who had doubted the wisdom of what the druids did, Grugyn who might have been his rival, Grugyn he raised to be his second in all things.

'Llew,' breathed Seradwen.

'Llew Lord of Light,' said Regin. 'The Young Son, heir of the Crow Lord, master of all arts.'

'But he died,' she said, remembering the story though she had never heard it told like this.

'He did,' acknowledged Regin. 'He died because Grugyn was jealous. It is an old tale, well known, of the man who is raised above the herd by his lord, who has praise and wealth and power lavished upon him, yet still desires more. Llew taught the People the use of chariots, that they might meet with the Peryth on equal terms, and he made Grugyn the leader of his warband, master of his chariots. Yet Grugyn was not content, for the world had changed with the coming of Llew. Instead of being a confederation of like-minded kindred, living in small households and calling no man master, the People had become a nation, ruled by a single lord from his great fortress of Dun Eidin. And if the People were to be ruled by a single lord then Grugyn saw no reason why it should be an outlander, however mysterious his origins and however golden his looks.'

At Llew's command Grugyn fought against the Peryth when they came raiding across the boundaries set by the Lord of Eidin. Many were the battles he fought, and at the last, using chariots and horsemen as Llew had taught him, he won a great victory over the Peryth, driving them back across the moors in confusion.

Then he went home to the champion's portion at the feast, to drink mead from a spiral horn of gold, to recline on a sheepskin couch in the place of honour, while his enemies lay sightless on the cold ground, food for the Crow Lord.

For three nights in Eidin's hall Grugyn was the toast of the People.

Grugyn was the toast, but it was Llew who was the saviour. What Grugyn had done, he had done at Llew's behest, with men and horses trained by Llew, following strategies dictated by Llew, defending the borders ordained by Llew.

So Grugyn was praised and Grugyn was feted, but only as the servant of his master. The true success belonged to Llew, and the People did not forget. Grugyn watched from under lowered lashes as the fairest maidens flirted with the Lord, and it was not lost upon him that only after Llew had smiled upon them and gently shaken his head did they turn to him. He was second-best, and for so long as Llew sat in the high seat he could never be anything except second-best, however many battles he won and however many foemen he put to flight.

At that time the chief power among the Peryth lay with three brothers, the sons of Dyssinendoth: Gall, Ysgafnell and Diffeidell. They were mighty warriors with spear and shield, riders of the swaying war-cart, masters of the wheeled chaos. But that was not all. They were also skilled in the magics of their tribe, in the casting of spells that bound the poisonous urine in the bodies of their enemies, that sapped the strength and will of a man to fight.

They wanted vengeance. Their defeat had damaged their standing, both among the conquered folk of Dewr, who now saw the invaders were not invincible, and among the lesser lords of the Peryth, who questioned the brothers' fitness to hold the rule. This time the brothers must lead their war hosts to victory.

Before the brothers mustered their hosts, they sent messengers to Grugyn the Strong, begging him to meet with them at the Ford of the Spears.

Grugyn went, and no man save the four of them ever knew what passed between them, there at the ford where the water had so recently been reddened with the blood of the fleeing Peryth.

Remember though, in Grugyn's defence, that the brothers were skilled magicians, and that there were three of them. While one spoke, two could croon meaningless little chants they could if challenged pass off as hunting or cradle songs. When Grugyn took his turn to answer whatever they asked him, all three could weave a tuneless web of sound around him, working the rush of the river and the song of the birds into their incantation. First they would have wrought a spell of binding, so he could not leave that place till they had finished, and then they would have wrought a spell of confusion, so he knew not what he did.

The sun was low in the sky when Grugyn departed, driving north at speed for his own dun where the warriors of the borders awaited his return. He told them that Llew himself had summoned him for a private meeting, and that together they had devised a new stratagem to make an end to the threat posed by the Peryth. The warband would withdraw into the high fells of the west and allow the Peryth to cross the river unopposed. In their arrogance the Lordly Ones would assume the People had lost the courage to resist, would march straight for Dun Eidin and the army of Llew. Then the warband would sweep down in their rear, cutting them off from Dewr, and the Peryth would be ground between the pestle of Llew and the mortar of Grugyn, with no means of escape.

They believed him. Perhaps he even believed it himself.

Three days later the full host of the Peryth crossed the river, turning the plain black with their numbers. The earth groaned under their weight, and the sky was clouded with dust. Carrion birds flocked above, crying the news to others of their kind.

Llew looked forth from Dun Eidin. He was his father's son, and the speech of crow and raven was easy for him to understand. The birds told him of the coming of the Peryth, of a mighty army striking for the very heart of his kingdom.

'Has a battle been fought then?' he asked, thinking Grugyn must have fallen.

'Not yet, not yet,' cried the crows. 'Soon, soon.'

With their words he knew Grugyn must have betrayed him, and somehow persuaded the men of the borders to betray him also. Llew glanced around at those of his warband who had remained with him in Dun Eidin, and saw that they were not enough. The best and greater part of his army had gone with Grugyn to the border watch where they were needed most; those who had stayed were the older men and the youths.

He could hold Dun Eidin. Even the host of the Peryth would not be sufficient to take the fortress on the rock if he chose to defend it. But this would profit him nothing. The enemy would ravage the kingdom, carry the People away into slavery while he watched with his household from the safety of the fort, in hollow

145

mockery of all the promises he had made when first he crossed the sea.

'We must fight,' he said to his warriors, and they, who had confidence in him, grinned and whetted their blades in readiness.

They rode forth, what force he had with him, rode down through the groves of Eidin and across the meadows where the horses graze in more peaceful times, and so to the ford of the Shining Water, which was the last river between them and their enemies.

Llew issued his orders and made his dispositions, then crossed the ford alone on Marchlew his steed. He went cautiously, wary of danger, and not the least reason for his going was to search for some sign of Grugyn and the warband of the borderlands. Instead he found the army of the Peryth, and this was the way of it.

First came a crashing and a leaping and a bounding, and all around him the woods were alive with animals, deer and wolf and boar running together, fleeing as they would flee a wild fire. Then came a mist, flowing between the trees, and from out of the mist came rumbles of thunder and flashes of lightning, and a great blast of wind which almost tore him from Marchlew's back.

And he knew that the mist was caused by the panting of the Peryth as they rushed to war. The thunder was the rumble of their chariots and horses, the lightning the flashes of their naked swords and spears. Soon they would be upon his own small band of warriors, and brief would be the slaughter.

His anger rose within him at the thought of what would happen to the People, who had trusted him. He strapped his shield to his arm and set his heels to Marchlew's flanks. In his hands were his slender silver white spears with their heads of red bronze, and at his side a golden-hilted sword.

Thrice round he rode, casting his spears which went whistling through the air, and every time he threw they struck their target, and never did he have less than two spears in his hands. For a time he amused himself thus, and then when the full battle fury fell upon him he rode into their midst with his sword drawn, throwing down whole companies of his enemies, and Marchlew trampled them under his hooves.

For the Peryth, it was as if a second sun had risen and dispelled the mist in which they had been hidden. Some of them panicked, swung their war-carts this way and that to avoid the onslaught, and thus collided one with another. Others sought to flee, crowding against the rear ranks of their own army, and thus reduced the march to chaos. Through that chaos rode the shining one, the lion of light, and wherever he rode men died by his burnished bronze blades.

The sons of Dyssinendoth, Gall, Ysgafnell and Diffeidell, were in the leader's place at the head of the march, free of other men's dust. They saw what horror Llew wrought upon their host, knew their chariots could never match his slender steed – for a well-trained horse and rider may swing on their tracks in the space of a heartbeat, but a war-cart needs more length if it is not to overturn and crush its occupants.

They called out to their men to make the spear hedge behind a wall of shields, and the warriors strove to obey, though it was hard amidst the madness. Horses ran loose, or dragged splintered chariots behind them, cutting swathes through the army. Friend struck at friend, believing they were being attacked by a mighty host and not recognizing old comrades in their mutual terror. The dead lay heaped upon the ground, and the shield wall swayed and bent as the warriors stumbled over the corpses of their kinsmen.

At last Llew's fury lessened, and he realized not even he could breach the spear hedge the Peryth had made, not without others to back him. He withdrew to the ford of the Shining Water where his followers awaited him.

'Cross now,' he said to his chariot men, 'before they rally and fall upon us. Spread out, and make for the hills of the west. Find me my warband, which I entrusted to Grugyn the Strong, and tell them I have need of them.'

They would have argued, not liking to leave him facing his enemies with nothing save a few foot to defend him, but when they looked upon his face they did not dare. Instead they splashed through the ford, sending up a spray of water, and scattered across the forefront of the Peryth. One chariot was brought down in a tangle of horses and smashed cart when it passed too near their line of march, but the others made it safely by.

'Now we must hold,' said Llew to the handful of warriors still with him. 'Do you guard my flanks, slingers and spear throwers to the fore. We must teach them they may not pass.'

Many are the fights at fords in the long story of Prydein, many the heroes who breathed their last defending or assaulting a river crossing. But when people speak of The Fight at The Ford, they mean the battle waged by Llew and his followers against the hordes of the Peryth.

All the long day they held them. First they taught them the way was not open to chariots, a lesson not learned until the far bank of the river was strewn with kindling and broken wheels revolving slowly in the summer breeze. Then they showed them the way was not open to horsemen, and the screams of the steeds mingled with the groans of the dying. Finally they demonstrated the way was not open to men afoot, and now the Shining Water flowed dull and red, her currents choked with the bodies of the slain.

But each time the Peryth attacked, one of Llew's followers fell. Little by little his numbers were whittled away, and in the gaps between the assaults the survivors looked ever more desperately for some sign that their chariots had found the warband.

The sun was red in the west when Gall rode forward in his war-cart, his brothers on either side, and offered to make terms.

'You have fought well and bravely,' he said, 'too nobly to deserve death. Let us end this slaughter.'

'Not hard,' said Llew. 'Turn and go back whence you came!'

Gall laughed. 'I think not. But there is no reason why you should not do that very thing, taking these your dogs with you. Leave Eidin and the lands of men to us, and retreat into the mountain wastes beyond Bannog.'

Llew shook his head. The golden hair was matted with sweat and blood, the handsome face strained with exhaustion, the tunic with the gold threads ripped and torn, yet still there was more nobility in his little finger than in the whole body of the Peryth Lord.

'No,' he said.

Gall grimaced, glanced at the sun where it balanced on the treetops. 'A challenge then. You and I alone, here, while the light lasts.'

'You think it will take so long?' said Llew.

The other made no reply as he dismounted from his chariot. Behind him his men drummed their spears on their shields till the whole valley rang with the sound, drowning the cries of Llew's followers as they shouted encouragement to their champion. But Llew, who was sharp-eyed even now, noticed that Ysgafnell and Diffeidell did not join in. Their lips moved, though no words could be heard above the racket, and their hands made strange gestures, but they did not beat a rhythm with the others.

148

And by this token he knew that although only one brother faced him in the water, in truth he fought all three.

A sore oppression to him were their magics. His limbs felt heavy, his movements slow. His feet slid on weed-clad stones where a moment earlier, he would have sworn, had been firm gravel. Gall rushed at him behind upraised shield, stabbing with his spear; Llew gave ground, struggling for balance, fending off the thrusts with his own shield, sadly hacked and much shrunken from the long day.

A wounded pony, cut loose by a kind hand from a shattered chariot, blundered into the stream, frightened by the drumming of the host. Gall skipped lightly aside and smote the beast on the flank, driving it at Llew; he dodged, and in the same instant Gall's spear slipped through his guard and grazed his ribs.

'First blood, first blood,' crowed the watching Peryth, while Llew's men paled and bit their lips.

Sluggishly, Llew regained his stance. Gall advanced, confident, the many coloured boss of his shield dazzling in the dying sun. Llew stumbled, and the spear point scored his shoulder, darkening the fair tunic.

'Second blood, second blood,' chanted the Peryth, beating on their shields with renewed vigour.

Llew cast his spear with all his failing strength. Hard it went, piercing Gall's shield just above the boss, where it hung quivering angrily. The son of Dyssinendoth tried to tug the blade free, snarling with rage; the head held fast, and he fiddled frantically with the buckles of his shield, for the weight was dragging down his arm.

Drawing his sword – red fire in the setting sun – Llew hurled himself upon the Peryth Lord. Before and behind him he could hear great shouts and the clamour of arms. Ysgafnell and Diffeidell were whipping their chariots forward through white wings of water. Gall dropped his shield, face twisted with fear, and levelled his spear. Llew butted it aside, leapt high in the air and smote with the full force of his falling body.

'Third blood!' he cried, as the sword cut through flesh and bone to find the heart. 'Third blood to the victor!'

Gall crashed down into the foaming water. The chariots passed, one on either side of Llew where he straddled his defeated foe, and as they passed a tongue of blue-grey lightning licked forth from each to meet in his body.

He swayed but did not fall. The chariots swept through Llew's followers, brushing them aside as a bull might brush aside a cloud of gadflies, and jolted up the bank to vanish behind a screen of bushes. Llew's men ignored them, intent upon their lord and upon what was happening on the far side of the river.

The swords had sliced deep with the speed of the chariots behind them, one into his left flank and one into his right. Even as his men raced towards him, Llew sank to his knees in the cold water, watching his lifeblood stream away on the current.

'What passes?' he asked as the first man reached him.

'Grugyn has arrived at last, catching the Peryth unawares.' The man frowned. 'Yet they still outnumber us, and they are rallying from the shock. My lord . . .'

He tried to staunch the wounds but the cloths quickly turned red and sodden. More men came and lifted Llew from the river, laying him out on the northern bank, where they stood fearfully regarding the ebb and flow of the fight to the south.

Llew's sight was fading fast. He could hear his men muttering doubtfully. Grugyn's force, its impetus spent, was being driven back to the river, and it seemed as if the long day's work would have been for nothing. The two surviving sons of Dyssinendoth had managed to rejoin their army and were directing the attack with their customary skill. One by one the People were dying, and still the Peryth advanced, their numbers without end like the grains of sand on the seashore.

'Bring Grugyn to me,' commanded Llew.

'Now, lord?' they questioned in surprise, for this was an ill time to call the leader of the warband from the fray.

'Now,' he said. 'Before the dark.'

Worried they waded across the river. The sun had set, but the slow twilight of the northern summer was still upon them, and it would be a long while till full night. He was going, his strength failing with the dying of the light, and with him went their hopes of defeating the Peryth.

They found Grugyn and brought him back. He stood with his head bowed, shamefaced and ill at ease as he looked down on the ruined remnants of the golden lord he had betrayed.

'They tricked me, Lord,' he said miserably.

'They could not have tricked you unless you willed it.' Llew's voice was cold. 'Come closer, Grugyn.'

Grugyn bent over the blood drenched form. 'Dark,' whispered Llew. 'So dark. I cannot see. Where are you?'

His hand fumbled in the air. Grugyn reached out and clasped it in his own.

'Forgive me, Lord,' he murmured.

Llew blinked, gripped Grugyn's hand with something of his old strength. 'Make amends,' he said, so softly the other had to strain to hear above the clash and clatter of the fighting across the river.

'How, Lord?'

'Take my sword and strike off my head.'

The other stiffened, made to protest.

'Do it. Else all is lost. Do it now.'

Grugyn swallowed, glanced nervously at Llew's loyal companions gathered around him. They met his eyes, contempt in their gazes, and one by one they nodded, almost imperceptibly.

'Hurry!' breathed Llew.

Grugyn straightened, took the sword still stained with the blood of Gall, and swung once at the white space between the golden circlets that girded the neck. The blade jarred against the ground. The head sprang off and rolled along the grassy bank, came to rest facing its executioner.

The familiar lips curved in a smile. Grugyn felt his heart's blood freeze within him as the head spoke.

'Now my father will come,' said Llew, and the eyelids drooped shut.

Regin struck an ominous chord upon the harp. 'In Dun Dewed, far to the north, the Crow Lord stirred and woke from his sleep.'

The crows leapt from the trees, shouting and crying. A great wind sprang up, blowing from the north, scouring the land with the summer dust. The warriors of the People who still lived were driven to their knees, coughing and choking. Those of them who could wrapped pieces of cloth around their faces and began to shuffle or crawl towards the river and the place where they had last seen their lord. Around them they could hear the two surviving sons of Dyssinendoth moving among the Peryth, bellowing orders and chanting spells against the storm.

Grugyn the Strong shrouded himself in his cloak and looked to the north whence the gale came. The dusk was in the sky, but in the north the heavens were blacker than night, a shining darkness that grew even as he watched.

'What do you see?' asked the head of Llew.

'Storm clouds gathering, though they are like no clouds I have ever seen before,' Grugyn answered calmly, for he had gone beyond fear. 'A thousand black specks rise from the ground and join the clouds, which thus swell with every passing moment. The clouds have an angry light of their own, and where they pass the trees bend.'

'The clouds are the dark birds of my father, flocking for their feasting. The black specks are the crows and ravens of the land climbing to join them. The light is the light of their eyes, and the gale is the beat of their wings. They will be on us soon. Tell our people to lie flat on the earth and beg the Lady for her protection.'

Grugyn did as the head bade him, though he himself remained standing, staring into the north, watching the doom coming upon them. Behind the black clouds was another shape: a mountainous, half-hidden wraith in the form of a gigantic man. He strained to see, oblivious of the People huddled around him begging the Lady for aid, oblivious of the screaming chants from the far shore of the river, where the sons of Dyssinendoth fought to hold the storm at bay.

'Lie down!' commanded the head in a voice which could not be disobeyed. 'Lie down. He is here!'

Grugyn roused as from a dream and flung himself to the earth. The wind whine rose to a ghastly howl, and the full majesty of the storm burst upon them.

Trees and rocks flew through the air, crashed and rebounded across the river. The ground shook and trembled. Men and horses screamed. Everywhere was the mournful, monotonous croaking of the crows and ravens. Grugyn struggled to breathe: the air seemed to be sucked away from him. A great hand pushed him flat, pressing so hard he thought his ribs would burst, then a second hand sought to pry him loose from his precarious hold. He scrabbled, clung with his fingernails, and through his head ran a mindless plea: Lady, Lady, Lady. His eyes, which had been tight shut, opened, and he saw the soil under his nose being drawn grain by grain into a long line which suddenly funnelled away into the sky. He dug deeper, feeling his clothes shred as the wind-driven dust flayed them from his body, knowing his flesh must surely follow.

The storm stopped. At first Grugyn did not dare look. Slowly he raised his head from the earth. All around him his comrades were doing likewise, expressions of frozen wonder on their faces. He sat up and looked behind him, across the river to where the Peryth had been.

They were gone, and all trace of the battle had gone with them. The land had been scoured clean.

Gathering his rags about him, Grugyn stood on shaky legs. He crossed to the place where he had struck the blow. The flattened grass was stained with the lord's blood, black in the twilight, but of neither Llew's body nor head was there any sign. For a long time he stayed staring down at the marks, while the night seeped from the hills and the air grew damp and chill.

At last he turned. The People were waiting, gathered in a patient ring around him.

'What should we do now, Lord?' they asked.

Grugyn drew a deep breath. Their eyes were on him, trusting in the starlight.

'Home,' he said, and started to walk.

'Their freedom was bought for them,' said Regin, 'at the price of the young son.'

He stilled the harp strings.

'So Grugyn achieved his desire?' said Seradwen.

Regin smiled thinly. 'After a fashion. He became Lord of Eidin, bred strong heirs who rule there to this day. But the payment was high. They say Llew came to him in his dreams, every night for the remainder of his life, and that he never found rest again.'

' "They say," ' she mocked. 'Do you believe that? It sounds like a late moral, tacked onto the end of the tale.'

He shrugged. 'Perhaps. But it cannot have been easy to rule a land named after the one you had betrayed. Llewthiniawn, the Land of Llew's Fort, that country has been called ever since.'

CHAPTER EIGHT

The Convent of St Helena was so utterly changed that for a moment Bedwyr wondered whether he had come to the wrong place. As he recalled, the nuns had been housed in an old villa, originally the family home of the convent's founder. The villa had been constructed in what Bedwyr thought of as the classic style: an open space framed on three sides by a single building. Even in its latter-day incarnation as a convent, it had been a civilized house, with glazed windows, painted and plastered walls, mosaic and concrete floors.

Now it had gone. Only the shell remained, the lowered walls serving as supports for storage sheds and stables. A new structure had been erected on what had been the central court. A timber hall three storeys high, it looked out of place in its rural surroundings, as if it had been bodily transplanted from the middle of a town.

The pony picked a path through the mud of the yard while Bedwyr gazed about him. A robin sat singing wistfully on one of the old walls. At the sound of his approach it cocked its head and regarded him hopefully. The instant the pony was clear of the mud Bedwyr dismounted, beating his gloved hands together to restore the feeling. The sudden movement made the bird take flight in a series of short hops, weaving between the thatched barns until it came to rest on the gable of the new building.

Bedwyr stretched and stared. The Convent had always been a wealthy foundation. The abbess in Arthur's time had been skilled at playing on the rivalry between the city of Lindinis and the imperial court at Caer Cadwy: the announcement of a gift from one had usually spurred a larger gift from the other. He could still remember the sweet tones in which the woman (head to one side, like the robin) had often remarked how *fortunate* the convent was to have *two* such generous groups of patrons.

As Bedwyr stood there gaping, a man came out of the hall and walked towards him.

'You wished to speak with someone?' the man demanded briskly while he was still some distance away.

'Yes. I am in search of the Lady Celemon.' He did not bother to mention Gwenhwyvar, knowing the man would deny all knowledge of her whereabouts.

'The Lady Celemon?' The man frowned. 'I do not think I can help you.'

'Indeed? Then perhaps I might speak with the Abbess.'

'The Abbess is extremely busy.'

Bedwyr eyed the man. 'How long has the present Abbess held her office?'

'Three years, thereabouts. Why?'

'And how long has she been a member of this community?'

The man shrugged. 'I have been here six years, and she was no newcomer when I arrived. At least twice that time, I should think.'

'Then if you will be so kind, tell her that the man who donated the wooden reliquary carved with the image of the Magdalene wiping the feet of Christ craves an audience with her.'

The man sniffed, considered him carefully, thought better of whatever he was about to say. 'Very well. I can try.' He glanced about him, raised his voice. 'Boy! Come, take this gentleman's horse.'

He led the way towards the new building. 'You can leave your weapons in the antechamber with one of the porters. You understand, we have to be careful these days. A place like this, outside the city walls, is vulnerable to gangs of thieves.'

'Have you had much trouble?'

The man shook his head. 'Petty theft, a bit of pilfering from the kitchens. This is a charitable house, and we do not deny alms to beggars. Unfortunately they do not always repay kindness with kindness.'

'Nothing more serious?'

'Not yet,' the man said darkly. 'But a house of women is vulnerable, for all we keep a large staff of able-bodied men to work the land. I expect you rode through the estate on your approach – you did come from Lindinis?'

'Not directly,' said Bedwyr as they entered the building. 'I had business elsewhere first.'

His guide glanced at him curiously before turning into a small chamber just inside the doorway, where a heavy set man was sitting on a stool by a brazier, paring his nails with a knife.

'Daniel, we have a gentleman here who requests an audience with the Abbess. Take care of him while I see if she is able to receive him.'

The porter grunted, intent on his task. Bedwyr waited, watching the knife probe around the cuticles, wincing in sympathy when the tip drew a bead of blood. The first man's footsteps receded along the corridor. The fire crackled softly to itself.

'Your sword.'

Bedwyr blinked. 'Are you speaking to me?'

'Your sword. Leave it in the corner.' The porter spat onto the rim of the brazier. 'Any other weapons as well.'

The spittle sizzled and shrank. Bedwyr stared at the porter and the porter studied his nails.

'If you please,' the man said without looking up.

Bedwyr unfastened his baldric, propped the sword and scabbard against the wall, drew the little eating knife from its sheath at his belt and laid it on the floor beside the sword.

'Good,' said the porter, shifting his weight on the stool.

They waited in silence. The sounds of the community drifted faintly through the building: women's voices, practising the psalms; the clatter of a loom; the firm tread of somebody pacing the floor above; feet descending a staircase and hastening through a door that banged behind them.

'Be a while,' said the porter. 'Why do you want the Abbess?'

'I am in search of an old friend.'

'A woman?' The porter put his knife away. 'Obviously,' he added, answering his own question.

'Your name is Daniel?'

'It is. And this is my den.' Unsmiling, he waved an arm to indicate the cramped chamber.

'I seek word of Celemon daughter of Cei.'

Daniel tipped back his stool, balancing it on two legs, laced his fingers behind his head. 'What makes you think she is to be found here?'

'She told me this was where she would come.'

The porter twitched his nose, examined him appraisingly while rocking back and forth on the stool. 'Who might you be then?'

'An old friend of her father.'

'I have been porter here for longer than I care to remember, and I must have heard that story a hundred times.' Daniel's face twisted in contempt and he let the stool fall forward with a crash. 'Scroungers, the lot of you – though I will say you look better than most, even if you have been living rough lately. Fallen on bad times, have you? Thought you'd look up an old acquaintance. What are you after? A square meal? You're a bit old to be taken on for work.'

Bedwyr let his eyes wander to the sword in the corner. The other followed his gaze.

'Sell it,' Daniel said harshly. 'You know what the Book says. "Them that live by the sword will die by the sword." Anyway, even if she is here, what makes you think she'll want to see you?'

'I do not know that she will. I can only ask.'

'Oh, very humble,' sneered the porter. 'Tell me your name.'

He found himself seized by a curious reluctance to say the words aloud.

'Come, don't be shy!'

'I am Bedwyr mab Petroc.'

Daniel burst into laughter, rocking back and forth on the stool. 'Another one!' he exclaimed, and raised his voice to call through the doorway: 'Paul, come and meet our visitor!'

After a moment a second man entered the room, his presence in the confined space forcing Bedwyr back against the wall.

'What?'

'Your honour, may I present to you the famed hero Bedwyr mab Petroc, formerly of Arthur's Court, now of nowhere in particular.'

The newcomer was a large man with an intimidating manner. He glowered at Bedwyr, then he too examined him from head to foot, taking in the patched cloak and the darned tunic.

'Odd,' he said to Daniel. 'Hasn't he been here before?'

'Aye. Funny how he can't keep away.'

'They say he is skilled at disguise.'

'Must be,' said Daniel. 'He was a lot bigger before. And he has managed to re-grow his hand since we saw him last.'

'Enough!' said Bedwyr, and struck the door with his fist.

There was an instant's silence before both men began to speak at once, less sure of themselves now.

'Not the first to claim to be Bedwyr,' said Daniel. 'Happened three or four times.'

'One thing about Bedwyr is that he lacked a hand,' grumbled Paul. 'Everybody knows that.'

'What is this?' demanded a third voice from the corridor.

The porters started guiltily, swung to face the door. A woman stood there, clad in a long dark dress, her hair concealed under a plain headscarf that cast her face into shadow.

'I have warned you before about being courteous to our visitors,' she said coldly.

Daniel swallowed, lumbered to his feet. 'He claims to be Bedwyr mab Petroc.'

She was not a tall woman, yet she dominated the space. Her eyes gleamed in the light from the brazier as she subjected Bedwyr to a deep scrutiny. He met her gaze forthrightly, returning look for look, trying to penetrate the darkness that hid her features.

'It might be,' she said at last, slowly. 'Sir, will you do me the kindness of removing your gloves?'

He peeled off his gauntlets, held up his left hand to reveal the scar running across its back, and waggled the fingers to demonstrate that they moved stiffly, all as one.

The woman drew breath. 'I do believe you might be telling the truth,' she murmured.

'I am,' he said.

She motioned impatiently to Paul. 'You have work elsewhere.' The big man touched his forehead and sidled past her without a word.

'Forgive our suspicion,' she said to Bedwyr. 'In these sad days there are many poor folk wandering the countryside who are deluded in their wits, and some who are outright rogues. We have dealt with many impostors over the years. Can you prove that you are indeed who you claim to be?'

'Celemon would know me, if she is still here. And you, you seemed to recognize me.' He frowned, still unable to discern any details of her face. 'Come into the light so I may see you properly.'

'That would establish nothing,' she said coolly, 'other than that you were once at Caer Cadwy – which I am prepared to accept, given you know enough to remember Bedwyr had not lost the left hand itself, only the use of it.'

He laughed. 'Of all things, it never occurred to me I might need to prove I am who I say I am. A woman recognized me in Isca from a glimpse she had had years before as a child.' He shook his head. 'Is Celemon still here? Tell me that much at least.'

He waited until it was clear she had no intention of answering him.

'You are cautious. Do you fear me?'

'Members of our community have been assaulted before. Some who come here in search of alms claiming to be members of Arthur's warband do not like to be contradicted.'

'Are they all impostors?'

'Or deluded, half crazed with hunger.' She made a small gesture. 'Yes. Most of their claims are absurd and easily dismissed; a few are harder to judge. We have had some pretending to be Gwalchmei or great Cei himself: blatant nonsense. Bedwyr mab Petroc is also a popular choice for men lacking a hand or even an arm. You are the first, so far as I know, to possess a full set of limbs.'

'Surely the matter is easily resolved. There must be somebody who remembers me. As I recall, several of the Companions' women planned to take refuge here if matters went ill at Camlann.'

'*The Companions' women* is not a term for which I have any liking,' she snapped, eyes glittering. She paused, gathering her thoughts, reached a decision. 'Very well. Come with me.'

She led him out of the close heat of the porter's chamber and into the draughty chill of the corridor. It was scrupulously clean, without a trace of grime or cobwebs, smelling of fresh beeswax polish and stale incense. Shafts of light came through the windows high in one wall, striping the floor with gold. The woman walked rapidly in front of him, so he still could not see her face, her feet tapping on the wooden boards.

'The Convent seems to be thriving,' remarked Bedwyr.

'Thriving?' she flung over her shoulder. 'Oh, you mean the rebuilding. It was necessary. The old house was falling apart.'

'I imagine the refugees from Caer Cadwy did not come empty-handed.'

The woman stopped in a patch of winter sunshine, her back very stiff, swung round. 'What are you insinuating? That St Helena's did well out of Arthur's fall?'

A purple birthmark sprawled across one cheek, merged with the beak of the nose. Her eyes were hard under a single dark brow, flecked with grey.

'Am I?' he said, struggling to keep his voice steady and not to stare. 'I think . . . I think what I am saying is that you owe something to his memory.'

Her face was flushed, the birthmark livid. She was trembling with rage. 'We owe *nothing* to the past.'

For a long moment she held his gaze, then spun on her heel and continued along the passage.

'Do you know me now?' she demanded over her shoulder.

He dredged the name from the depths of his memory. 'You are Morfudd daughter of Gwaredur Bow-back.'

'I am.' Her feet beat upon the boards as she stamped along the passage. 'And do you remember what happened to Gwaredur Bow-back?'

'I do. He followed Medraut to Camlann.'

'And died there, for his sins, leaving his family to live with the shame.' She wrenched open a door and ushered him through.

'It was not your fault,' Bedwyr said gently. 'Nor even his. Medraut was a persuasive man.'

The room was larger than he had expected, with plain white walls that made it seem even bigger. Two chairs and a low table occupied one corner under a small square window. Although spotlessly clean like the corridor, it had the feel of a place that was not used very often. The sickly-sweet smell of incense was stronger here.

'Sit if you wish.' She waved him to a chair, waited until he was settled.

'I accept that you are Bedwyr. You have his arrogance.'

'I have?'

Her smile had no warmth. 'Always an answer to everything. Listen to me, Bedwyr mab Petroc. Give me a reason why I should disturb Celemon in her life of contemplation.'

He thought hard and fast. Having himself lived as a monk for a number of years, he was not unsympathetic to what she was saying. When one put aside earthly cares, entered deep into communion with the living God, it was no light thing to be dragged back to the mundane world one had left behind. Yet his need was urgent. Although he had lost his pursuers for the present, sooner or later they would realize they had been fooled and rediscover his trail. Already he had wasted too much time working through the layers of protection that guarded Celemon.

Morfudd was expecting a reply.

'Tell her it is time.'

'*It is time*?' The woman enunciated the words with exaggerated care. 'Is that all?'

'She will understand.'

Morfudd peered at him doubtfully, shrugged. 'As you wish. If she refuses to see you, you will have no second chance.'

He lifted his damaged hand in acceptance of her terms, and after a final mistrustful glance – as if she suspected him of some trick – she left the room.

Far away he could hear singing: presumably the same voices he had heard earlier, all female and thus to his ears lacking the power and depth of a male choir. But then, he supposed, it was a matter of what one was accustomed to, and during the years in Lesser Britain he had grown used to the sound of men and boys singing in harmony. He closed his eyes and listened to the faint murmur of several voices joined in prayer in the next room. A handbell rang to signal the end of one period of duty and the start of another. The voices stopped, and he could feel the movement throughout the building as the nuns went quickly and quietly to their assigned places. That was what he missed, that sense of belonging, of being part of a greater whole.

The latch clicked. The woman who entered had to duck beneath the lintel. He stood, his tongue thick in his mouth, stepped forward, nearly stumbling over the table. She stretched out a hand to steady him, striding across the space between them.

'Celemon?' he said uncertainly.

'Bedwyr,' she said, and enveloped him in a bear hug worthy of her father, not releasing him until his ribs were bending under the strain.

'I was not sure. The Holy Mother insisted it was you.' She turned and smiled over her shoulder at Morfudd who had followed her into the room and stood watching them suspiciously. 'There have been so many. In the first few years we had a dozen at least, all claiming they had ridden with Arthur and expecting to be fed and housed for nothing. Those were bad days.'

She held his arm in hers and escorted him to the chairs, helped him sit. 'Have you come far? I thought you were in Brittany.'

He shook his head. 'I left Brittany three, nearly four years ago.'

'Did you?' She raised her eyebrows, and he saw in this middle-aged woman's face the child he had once known, expressing its wonder at some new marvel: a pebble shaped like a horse, a four-leafed clover, sunlight on running water. 'Why? Did you enter a monastery as you planned?'

'Yes, yes I did.'

'You must tell me all.' She hesitated. 'You look tired. Perhaps . . . I wonder whether the kitchens might be willing . . .'

'Stay where you are,' said Morfudd. 'I shall see what can be done.'

'A kind woman,' said Celemon as the door closed behind the Abbess. 'A little over-protective at times, but there is no harm in that where the younger sisters are concerned.'

He leant back in the chair, allowing himself to relax. A feeling of warmth rushed through him. Celemon had always been a favourite of his, both as a child and an adult, and the sight of her after all these years was more moving than he had expected. She was thin to the point of being gaunt and looked a great deal more than a decade older. Her skin was lined and pale, and her hair had gone completely grey, all trace of the magnificent tawny colour that had been her crowning glory now lost. Yet despite the changes he would have known her anywhere.

'I thought they would have made you the Abbess by now,' he said aloud.

'Me?' Celemon stifled her amusement. 'No. I would not accept even if it was offered. Too much like the old life: hard work and responsibility, no privacy. Besides, it was good for Morfudd. You recognized her?'

'Her face is memorable,' he said carefully. 'Of course, I never really knew her.'

'After Camlann she felt we – the newcomers to the Convent and many of the older sisters – would reject her because of what her father had done. Electing her Abbess proved that we value her for herself.'

'Laudable,' he said. The mole beside her upper lip twitched as again she suppressed a smile.

'Practical. Morfudd is the best person for the post, and she takes her duties seriously. A house of women is always vulnerable to rumours, and our survival depends upon the goodwill of the City Council.'

'Of Lindinis, you mean?'

She nodded. 'Because so many of us have, or had, associations with Caer Cadwy, the Convent is not always popular with the townsfolk – which is another reason why I would not have made a good Abbess. Morfudd was never of the court in quite the same way, and she has worked hard to keep us both in favour and independent. You will remember,' Celemon continued, warming to her task, 'the old hostility between the city and the caer. The City Fathers considered Caer Cadwy a dangerous rival, stealing their best craftsmen, diverting wealth and trade away from the city.'

'The country people loved us.'

'Oh yes. For them the caer was a blessing. A second market for their produce, an entire army and its followers to be equipped and fed. But from the point of view of the townsfolk, the existence of Caer Cadwy did much to hasten the decline of Lindinis.'

'Yet now Caer Cadwy is once more deserted –'

She shook her head. 'The craftsmen did not return to Lindinis. They had acquired a taste for royal courts and the attendant glamour. They would not be satisfied with a crumbling city falling inexorably into ruin. Lindinis is dying, Bedwyr, slowly but surely, and its inhabitants blame Arthur and his Companions. With some justification, one might add.'

He passed a hand below his chin, forgetting he no longer had a beard to tug. 'What of the Church? Surely the Church itself would keep you safe?'

'Oh my dear!' she exclaimed in an unmistakable flash of her old self. 'Where have you been these last few years?'

'Living as a hermit.'

'I might have guessed.' She laughed, twisted a lock of hair around a finger in a familiar gesture. 'The Church is not the power it used to be, not in these parts at least. With Arthur's death and the subsequent chaos, communication with Gaul and the Mediterranean has lessened, almost failed. The traders no longer put in to the mouth of the Severn, and the Narrow Sea is infested with Saeson pirates – but you must know that if you came home from Brittany within the last few years.'

He nodded, remembering the precautions the sailors had taken during the crossing: how they had pulled far into the west before running north, lengthening the voyage but reducing the chances of meeting a raider.

'Our Church is sundered from the heart of civilization, no longer receives nourishment from abroad. At the same time the true religion has always been strongest in the towns, in places like Lindinis – do we not call the country dwellers *Pagans*? As the towns decline, so too does the authority of the Church.' She shrugged. 'The reverberations of Arthur's fall have not yet ended.'

'I know. That is why I am here,' he said quietly.

163

She looked at him sadly, her eyes sparkling with moisture. 'Oh, Bedwyr. I could wish you had come upon another errand, or better still, no errand at all. After all these years it would be pleasant to meet simply as old friends, without some other motive. You were always my favourite uncle when I was a child.'

'Flatterer!' he said, trying to make her smile.

'You did not come to see me, did you?'

He hesitated, and was saved by the return of the Abbess, bearing a tray. Celemon leapt to her feet, startled, and Bedwyr followed suit, stepping forward to relieve the woman of her burden.

'You should not be carrying this yourself,' scolded Celemon.

'This is an honour,' said Bedwyr. 'To be waited upon by the Abbess herself!'

His light-hearted courtesy fell flat. Morfudd refused to relinquish the tray, insisted upon placing on the table herself. When she straightened she was frowning.

'Nothing special,' she said, indicating the tray. 'Cold meats, bread, dried figs, a little wine.'

'You are very kind.'

She considered a moment, the birthmark glowing in the light that came streaming through the high window. 'Not really. I would provide as much for any beggar who came knocking on our door, and you are Celemon's guest.'

'Sit, eat,' urged Celemon.

They refused to share with him, saying their own suppers would be waiting for them later. Celemon watched him with a proprietorial pride, like a mother feeding her son on his return from a long journey, or – he realized with a stab of discomfort – like a conscientious niece caring for an elderly and slightly infirm uncle.

'You have lost weight,' she remarked after a time, confirming his suspicions. 'Living as a hermit must have been hard.'

'The monastery was good training,' he said around a mouthful of fish. 'The first few months I was permanently hungry.'

She laughed aloud, and even the Abbess managed a quick twitch of the lips. 'I too,' said Celemon, 'I too. Those last years at Caer Cadwy I fell into the habit of overeating.'

'Caer Cadwy –' he began.

'I will leave you,' interrupted the Abbess.

'There is no need,' said Celemon.

'I think there is,' replied Morfudd. 'You have things you must discuss which are nothing to do with me.' She rubbed at the birthmark on her cheek. 'Besides, Bedwyr would prefer to speak to you alone.'

Celemon glanced quickly at her visitor, sighed in resignation. 'Very well. You are right, as usual.'

The Abbess nodded curtly to Bedwyr and departed.

'Is it me or is it all men?' he asked, pushing the final few morsels of food around the bowl on his lap.

'All men, I think. Apart from some priests and the Bishop. She finds it hard to forgive the way they stare and shudder at the birthmark. I think life at Caer Cadwy was doubly difficult for her: first the disfigurement set her aside from the other girls, and then her father – who in any case had no high opinion of her since she was not considered marriage material – joined Medraut's party. Ludicrous, really. She would have made an excellent wife to some minor lord with an estate to run, far better than half the simpering maids that were snatched up as soon as they were of age. And she is very loyal.'

'She is not content here?'

Celemon flushed, realizing she was herself on the verge of being disloyal. 'Let us say she is not a natural nun.'

'Whereas you are?'

'I am now, though it has not always been easy. I have charted a rocky sea to reach this safe haven.' As she spoke her gaze wandered, fixed upon the floor, upon the wall, anywhere except upon him. 'And you? How did you find being both monk and hermit? Did you make your peace with God? Presumably not, else you would not be here now. Did you realize the reason the Abbess came to find you? It was because at first I refused to see you.'

'I guessed,' he said, and there was silence between them, a silence that hung thick and heavy in the room while he waited with dread to hear what she would say next.

'I dreamt sometimes of your coming – especially after *she* went.'

He did not have to ask who *she* was.

'The same dream, every time. A man riding across a brown plain with a bloodied sword in his hand, and at his back a flock of gore-crows eager for food. Cities burned in his wake, and swollen-bellied children begged for crumbs, beseeching aid with arms brittle as sticks.'

'An ill dream,' he said softly. 'Sometimes there is power in dreams.' He shivered, for the room was not warm, having no heating of its own. 'Other times, I think they portray nothing more than our own fears and desires, perhaps not fully realized in our waking minds, but present all the same.'

She was not listening. Her eyelids were bruised with tiredness, and her white skin looked somehow thin, as if it would injure easily. Her attention appeared fixed upon the bowl in his lap, yet he had the feeling she did not see it. Her lips pursed, opened, pursed again.

'Go on, ask me,' she cried suddenly. 'Ask me the question you have come all this way to ask.'

He put the bowl on the table and rose, reaching out for her in her distress. She shrank aside, avoiding his touch, breathing quickly, her pale face flushed. Nonplussed, he stilled, unsure what to do next, caught at an awkward angle between the chair and table.

'What is it? Did you quarrel with her?'

Waving him to his seat, she pulled back the second chair and perched on its edge.

'I discovered God.'

The words were almost defiant. He paused, waiting for her to elaborate. He had heard others make similar statements in the past, and all of the speakers had meant something different.

'My one regret,' she said, 'is that I wasted so many years of my life.'

'Wasted? I would never have described your life as wasted.'

'All those years as a dutiful daughter, as a loving friend. Too much of my life was spent pleasing other people, not enough pleasing God.'

'Ah, well,' he floundered, playing for time while he thought what to say. He looked up and met her eyes, intent upon him.

'You are about to be condescending: to make some remark about living in a house of women, the way in which enthusiasms can sweep through small and contained communities; something about unhealthy influences.'

'I was not,' he said mildly. 'You forget, I myself lived in a monastery.'

'I have become zealous in my love of the Lord,' she continued as if he had not spoken. 'I see now where we went so wrong, why we failed. It is as Bishop Enoch told us long ago – you bristle at the mention of his name, but he was a righteous man, Bedwyr.'

'Self-righteous perhaps,' he muttered.

'A brave man, who fearlessly bore witness to the truth like a prophet of old . . .'

'Jeremiah,' he said.

'You mock him, as you always did, but can you not see he was right? Yes, compare him to Jeremiah if you wish, for like the Israelites in the days of Nebuchadnezzar, the Britons have done evil in the eyes of the Lord. We have rebelled against lawful authority, denied the word of the Lord, committed sacrilege and even set up false gods.'

'As I recollect,' Bedwyr said slowly, 'Jeremiah blamed the then king for many of the ills that fell upon the Israelites.'

'Yes,' she said eagerly. 'King Zedekiah, who saw the Babylonians despoil Jerusalem, his people carried into captivity, the slaughter of his sons and family.'

'Before he was blinded.' Bedwyr tugged at an earlobe, frowned. 'So what are you suggesting? That Arthur was our Zedekiah?'

'He saw his sons die and the Saesons fall upon us like a plague from God . . .'

'Oh nonsense!' The anger suddenly rose within him. 'If anything, it is the other way about. The Princes of Britain rebelled against Arthur, actively or otherwise. While he lived he protected the Church – a fact the likes of Enoch often conveniently forgot. And I would remind you that Jeremiah faced real perils, whereas if Enoch angered Arthur, the worst that was likely to happen to him was banishment from Caer Cadwy – which should have been no great hardship to him, since in his own words the place was a sewer of corruption.'

'You do not deny that the Saesons, and the Picts before them, are a judgement sent by God?'

He sighed wearily, the anger gone as swiftly as it had come. 'Celemon, I do not know. It is a question I have often pondered. All I can say is, if the evils that have befallen this land are indeed God's judgement, it falls hardest upon those least able to bear it, upon the peasants and the poor. They are the ones who die like flies when contagion strikes; they are the ones who are raped and slaughtered when an army sacks a town. The rich usually have some means of escape.'

'We sought to stem the tide with swords and spears,' she continued, ignoring his doubts. 'We would have done better to rely upon the prayers of holy men and women, upon the intercession of our priests. Everything we attempted came to naught.'

'Celemon, Celemon,' he protested, but she overrode him.

'Worst of all, we – and I include myself among the sinners – turned to pagan magic. Look what it brought us! The death of Arthur's heir at my father's hands! If Morfudd feels guilt because her father supported Medraut, think how much worse it is for me! Yet Gwenhwyvar was my friend.'

He struck the table with the flat of his crippled hand. She jumped at the noise, stared at him anew with large round eyes.

'This sounds like self-pity. Your father did only what was necessary, what any of us would have done, which is why both Arthur and Gwenhwyvar remained his friends and yours.'

'Until I came to God,' she murmured so softly he did not quite catch what she said. 'It was such a waste, Bedwyr, such a waste of all those lives. Think of them, gone before their time: my father Cei, my brother, your friends Cynon and Moried – a host of them. And worst of all, poor Lleminawg.'

'Why was Lleminawg's death worse than the others?' he asked, falling into the trap.

'Because he died the most futile of deaths. He died to win that accursed chalice, the very snare of the devil, perished at the hands of the pagan woman who was your lover while it suited her.' Her voice was full of venom and there was a fanatical gleam in her eyes. The words came faster and faster. 'What did it bring us but a trail of more death? It blighted what should have been the perfect years, the years following the victory of Badon Hill, the years of peace and rebuilding. Because of the chalice we marched to war in the north, in Gododdin, and Llacheu died. Because of the chalice all our work was undone. Because of the chalice Gwenhwyvar was seduced into blasphemy.'

'Seduced into blasphemy? What are you talking about?' he demanded, aghast, finding it hard to believe anybody who had known Gwenhwyvar could accuse her of blasphemy. Perhaps Celemon was referring to some form of heresy: questioning the need for priests as intermediaries between Man and God, like the Pelagians; or Augustine of Hippo's horrifying and absurd suggestion that new-born babes were damned unless they received grace through the sacrament of baptism.

'Do you not remember what she tried to do outside Eidin?'

He shook his head, not understanding her vehemence. 'That was the act of a grief-stricken mother.'

'What could be more revealing of her true thoughts? She did

not turn to God in her hour of need, but to the demonic powers of the heathen. You yourself were no better. You also treated with pagan deities and symbols as if they had inherent power of their own. Such things – the chalice most of all – come from the Devil not from God.' She licked her lips nervously; a gesture so unlike the Celemon he had known it was even more disturbing than the fanatical words spewing from her mouth. 'I tell you this for your own good, Bedwyr. It is not too late. Your soul may yet be saved.'

'Celemon, think!' he said, trying to reason with her before she had them both praying on their knees. 'Think about the Gwenhwyvar you knew. Think about Arthur. Think about your own father, for Heaven's sake!'

'For Heaven's sake indeed!' she said sternly. 'We laugh at the Saesons or the heathen Scotti for praying to stones or stocks of wood, yet we ourselves venerated a bowl steeped in darkness. Even now she clings to it, you know, refusing to give it up. I tried to persuade her it would be better destroyed, cast into a furnace and purified in fire blessed by the Holy Church, but she would not listen, preferring to cling to her sinful pride.'

'Where is she?' he asked.

The question seemed to steady her. 'Gone. In those early years after Camlann she travelled much, seeking out old friends and supporters. We agreed that would be safer than remaining in one place where her enemies might find her. Always she returned here to rest, often staying most of the winter.' Her face twisted. 'Then I came at last to God, submitting to the summons I had so long denied. We quarrelled. In my zeal – the fervour of a convert – I drove her away. I failed her, Bedwyr.'

'The game is not yet ended,' he said, and she smiled a little.

'That sounds like one of those remarks you used to make. Cryptic on the surface, but at bottom empty. The game ended at Camlann, where our world was sundered.'

'I think not.' He stood, manoeuvred between the table and chairs, began to pace the room. 'I was followed from Isca to Caer Cadwy. I lost them in the empty country towards Camlann. Tell me, if the game *is* ended, why should anyone bother to follow me?'

Her interest quickened, and for a moment she was the old Celemon, the woman he had expected to find. 'Who were they?'

'Their leaders were tattooed.'

'Children of Menestyr. Gwenhwyvar always said they would

reappear one day.' She frowned, touched the mole by her lip. 'Why now? What has changed?'

'I came home.'

She pulled her gown tighter round her body. 'Through you they hope to find her. Why did you come back?'

'Signs and portents. Dreams. A fear of dying in a land not my own.' He shrugged, paced faster. 'I don't know. It was a compulsion. I was drawn home, even as in my youth I was drawn to seek out Arthur, offer him my sword and my life.'

'You said you had been in Britain for three or four years, living as a hermit. Why did they not come hunting you sooner?'

'They did not discover me until last summer. Then they lost me for a while.'

She turned in her chair so she could watch his pacing. 'Bedwyr.'

He stopped, aware something had altered.

'Has it occurred to you that all you and Gwenhwyvar are doing is trying to recapture your youth?' Her voice was calmer now she was not discussing her faith. 'This smacks of the tales you used to tell me when I was a child. If these creatures truly want the chalice, why not give it to them?'

'It runs deeper than that. There is a blood feud between us. I avenged your father upon the body of their leader.'

'That is exactly what I mean.' She sighed in exasperation. 'Listen to yourself. You sound like a hero out of one of the old songs: some hairy barbarian with a bloodstained sword. "I came home," you say, and therefore the old feud begins again.'

He raised an eyebrow. 'Why, Celemon, that is the very point. That is the kind of world in which we live now. A few pockets may still cling to the old ways of civilization, like this Convent and for all I know the city of Lindinis, but out there –' he waved a hand at the walls '– the rules have changed.' He glanced at the window, measuring the amount of remaining daylight. 'Besides, the Children of Menestyr are not fit guardians of the chalice.'

'Bedwyr, you are an old man.' She was almost pleading with him. 'I have been watching you, sitting in that chair, pacing round the room. You are not the man you were ten years ago. How could you be? If you ride away from here with a head full of wild dreams the Sons of Menestyr will kill you.'

'What do you suggest? Years ago I swore an oath, to serve Arthur for as long as I lived . . .'

'Arthur is dead!' she shouted. 'Dead, dead, dead! Will neither of you grasp that? It is over, finished! The chalice is unimportant! Go and live your few remaining years in peace and contemplation, as you were supposed to do.'

'I cannot,' he said simply. 'I tried, but it did not work. Last summer Gwalchmei came to me in a dream. He told me prayers were not enough.'

She stiffened, made the sign of the cross.

'Hear me out. God made me a warrior. That is how I should serve him, with my sword. Others are better fitted to prayer.'

'Like me, you mean? Bedwyr, I beseech you: *listen to yourself*. Do you not hear what you are saying? Even if you were in your prime I would not – could not – agree with you.' She leant forward passionately. 'We tried your method. It failed, just as it has failed on every occasion it has been used this last hundred years. Look at Vortigern and his son Vortimer! They too died by violence, and all their work came to naught, exactly like Arthur and Llacheu. "Put up your sword into its sheath," Christ said to Peter in the garden, and I say the same to you now, for it will avail you nothing.'

Bedwyr studied his hands, the slightly swollen knuckles and the scar which had been part of him for so long he could barely remember a time when it had not been there. Perhaps she was right. All their years of fighting had come to nothing at the end. In his mind he could see Arthur taking that final terrible blow to the head at Camlann, the long sword sliding from nowhere to smite the Emperor from the saddle. He could see Cei's body, still and pale on its long bier when they brought him back from the place where he had fallen. He could see Gwenhwyvar's face, suddenly old and lined as she mourned for Llacheu her son, cut down in the fullness of his youth. And he could see the ruins of Caer Cadwy, where once they had planned to build a new Albion.

Slowly he raised his head and began to speak, making the words into an incantation.

'The Clearwater, the Blackwater. The River Bassas and the Caledonian Forest. Fort Guinnon and the City of the Legion. The Speckled Shore and the Mountains of Agned. Badon Hill. Nine battles and one man the victor in them all.'

'And what good did it do? What difference will it have made in a hundred years time?' she cried in exasperation.

'Why, this. That once men cared enough to risk their lives in the pursuit of what they believed was right.'

She laughed scornfully, the sound echoing around the room. 'Old man, you are a dreamer.'

He waited until she was quiet again. 'Where is Gwenhwyvar?'

Celemon shrugged expressively. 'I do not know.'

'You must have some idea.'

'None.' Her lips curved, and he stared at her as if at a stranger. 'Even I did know, I am not sure that I would tell you. As I recollect, Gwenhwyvar said that she would summon you when the time was right.'

'She is in danger.' He ran a hand through the hair over his temple. 'I scryed for her, but –'

'No,' she interrupted. 'I do not wish to hear of your heathen magics. They corrupt your soul, Bedwyr.'

'There is nothing heathen about scrying,' he protested.

'Oh, foulness!' exclaimed the Abbess from the doorway. 'Such a statement, and you a former monk!'

Morfudd came into the room, mouth taut, white with rage save for the ugly stain on her cheek. 'Shame on you, old man, shame on you! It is no wonder that God turned his back upon Arthur and the Companions. I would have expected you to have learned from the experience.'

She put an arm around Celemon. 'You have discharged your duty towards him?'

Celemon nodded. 'As best I can. But I have failed with him, even as I failed with Gwenhwyvar.'

'All that matters is that you tried.' She squeezed Celemon's shoulder, glared defiantly at Bedwyr. 'We do not know what has happened to the woman who was once the Empress of Albion. Nor, frankly, do we care. Now, I think your business here is concluded.'

Celemon rose and the Abbess shepherded her towards the doorway.

'Wait,' he said. 'Wait. Celemon, you were Cei's daughter. How can you be content with this?' The sweep of his arm included the Abbess and the enclosing walls alike.

She halted, hand upon the door jamb. 'I am happy, as I have never been happy before. I advise you to seek the same solace, that of giving yourself over utterly to the Lord.'

Then she stooped beneath the lintel and was gone.

Afterwards, riding through the dusk on his way to Lindinis and a bed for the night, he thought of all the things he might have said.

He could have spoken of a hierarchy of powers, with God and His angels at the top, men and beasts at the bottom. In between lay other things, the spirits of the land, older than Christianity but still part of God's Creation, like mankind neither good nor evil of themselves though possessing the capacity for both. For example, the power of the Sanctuary Wood at Porthyle was to his mind neutral, a kindly force the ancestors had worshipped as gods; that had been wrong, but the error lay with the ancestors, not the force. One might as well argue – and in this increasingly irrational age many people did – that the sea or the stars were of themselves good or bad.

The same was true of the chalice. Like the Sanctuary, it was connected with the guardianship of the land, but whereas the power of the Wood was limited to a small area around the Porthyle estuary, the chalice affected the entire island of Britain. He did not pretend to understand how or why: the answers to those questions were lost in the deeps of time. It was sufficient that it was so.

What mattered was that the chalice should not fall into the wrong hands. There had been an inevitability about the manner in which it had become Arthur's, a rightness to it, as if everything else had been leading to that moment: the years of learning the art of warfare as a youth, the mastery of the army after the death of Ambrosius, the nine searing victories against the enemies of the realm. In retrospect Arthur's progression from a junior officer to Emperor of Albion seemed preordained.

Bedwyr crossed the bridge and passed through the ruined gate of Lindinis, nodding to the bored guards as they prepared to barricade the road for the night.

What he should have said to Celemon was that nothing lasts forever, that all human endeavours are by their very nature ephemeral. A family comes through the gloom of the forest. They clear a patch of ground, build a home and plant a field of corn. For a while they live happily, then the children become adults and leave. The parents grow old and frail. Weeds grow in the field; the house tumbles down. The trees return, the darkness closes in once more, and soon it is as if the family had never been.

Yet whatever may happen in the future, nothing can ever alter the fact that for a few brief years there was a sunlit clearing in the forest.

CHAPTER NINE

'Will you show me the estate?' asked Regin in his deep bass voice.

Startled, Seradwen turned from the scroll she was studying. He was standing by the door, staring at her. 'Now?' she said.

He smiled, stepped forward into the room. His teeth were white and very even, and he was freshly shaved, the skin of his jaw still pink and stretched.

'You read? A dying art, except among the clergy, and even then it is no longer so common as in our grandparents' time.' He peered over her shoulder at the text. 'I noticed the scrolls yesterday evening, and wondered whether they might be yours. Obviously you understand Latin.'

'They were my husband's. Mainly practical treatises: Varro's book on farming; Pelagonius on the veterinary art; Virgil's Georgics.'

'You find them useful?'

His breath tickled her neck. She shifted slightly in her seat. 'Oh yes. Full of good advice. My Latin is not good, so often I have to puzzle out certain sections, and of course the farming parts were written for warmer climes, but it is helpful to find somebody else who faced the same problems hundreds of years ago and see what solutions they tried. This is Virgil on horsebreaking,' she added, tipping the scroll so he could read more easily.

'Was it not Virgil who said "Believe the man with experience"?'

'Did he? It sounds sensible.'

Regin laughed. 'What does he say about breaking in horses?'

'He recommends starting the three-year-old in the ring, school-ing him so he steps harmoniously and with limber stride. "Until you break them their hearts are too high flown," he says.'

'And you agree?'

'Entirely,' she said. 'Let them be familiar with people from an early age, but one should not begin schooling until they are three. Any younger and they are too young.'

'Fascinating. I had not thought of the poet in terms of horse-breaking.'

'A man of many skills,' she said, and fell silent, unsure what to say next.

Regin moved away, humming gently under his breath, poked at the scrolls on the shelf. 'Well, will you?'

She jumped. 'Will I what?'

'Show me around the estate.' His voice was impatient.

'Of course.' Seradwen rolled up the Virgil and reached past him to replaced it on the shelf. Her arm brushed against his waist. She felt the colour rising to flood her cheeks, and turned away, embarrassed, wondering what was wrong with her.

'I suppose you must need to keep good records,' he remarked as they crossed the inner courtyard.

'That was why I learned to read and write,' she said. 'We have to know which mare mated with which stallion, with what result.'

'And to do that you must learn Latin.'

She laughed, and the women working in the yard turned to see what had amused their mistress. 'Yes, though the records are kept in the form of notes and numbers, and hardly require any knowledge of the Roman tongue.'

'You could learn Ogham,' he suggested lightly.

'Scratches on a piece of wood. I, sir, write upon clay tablets, like a civilized person.'

'Ah, but the advantage of Ogham is that one can signal in secret across a crowded room.' He held the door to the outer yard open for her. She hesitated on the threshold, looked at him. They were almost the same height, though he had a habit of peering down his hooked nose which made him seem taller.

'How?'

'Why, by using the nose. Have you never heard of Sron-ogham?'

She shook her head, not sure if he was teasing.

'Ogham is a series of straight strokes seen against an edge, agreed?' He bent and drew a long line in the dirt of the courtyard. 'So, there is our edge. Now, here is the letter H, here the letter D.' He made one stroke for the H, two strokes for the D, both to the left of the line. 'And so on up to five, which gives us five letters, one for each finger. B to N are formed in the same fashion, but to the right of the line. The five vowels cross the line horizontally, and the remaining letters, M to R, cross at an angle. You see? Simple.'

Bemused, she stared at the ground. 'What about nose-ogham?'

'Sron-ogham? Like this.' He straightened and laid his fingers against the hook of his nose. 'Have you never heard the riddle "why is the nose ridged?" The answer is "to make easy the sending of messages".'

Seradwen burst out laughing. 'But you look ridiculous. How do you signal in secret?'

'Why, you leave out the vowels, keep the message short, send it slowly.'

'And pretend you have an itchy nose?'

He was laughing too. 'Well, perhaps you could vary the method. You could use Cos-ogham, where the shin serves as the line.'

'You would be twitching like a man with a bad dose of fleas.'

He shrugged, grinning. 'Anything will do as an edge.' His fingers fluttered rapidly across his jaw and nose. 'See?'

'What did you say?' she demanded suspiciously.

'Nothing important,' he said airily.

'Tell me?'

'Learn the letters and you may read it for yourself.'

'I want to know.'

He glanced up at the sky. 'We had better move. It is going to rain soon.'

'Tell me.'

He started across the yard. 'It's a secret. That's the whole point.'

Seradwen followed, taking long strides to catch up, and was about to pummel his back when she suddenly remembered that she barely knew this man. She stopped, lowered her fists and looked about her, remembering the workforce. Two youngsters engaged in mucking out one of the stables stood frozen, gaping open-mouthed at the mistress behaving like a young girl, their dung-laden forks steaming in the cold air. A man grooming a stallion stared as he combed the same patch over and over again, while a woman carrying a bucket cursed and hopped as she allowed the contents to spill over her foot. Pulling the cloak tight around her, she called: 'Where shall we begin?' Even to her own ears her voice sounded false.

He turned, a smile playing at the corners of his mouth. 'Where do you usually begin?'

She could feel herself blushing. 'The stallions, I suppose.'

'Then lead on.'

'We have five,' she said, moving towards the stables. 'Some experts, like Varro, recommend one stallion to every ten mares, but we find about one to eight is better. Do you know anything of horsebreeding?'

He pursed his lips and shook his head. 'Nothing.'

'With sheep or cattle one breeds for quantity. With horses one looks for quality.'

'And what constitutes quality?'

'Most of our horses are bred for the local lord, Gereint.' She was into the rhythm of her speech now, her earlier confusion forgotten as the familiar words came forth. 'Some are even acquired by Custennin himself. The majority are used by his warriors, though a few serve as ordinary riding hacks or carriage horses.'

'So you breed for aggression?'

'Not at all. That is a myth.' She eyed him dubiously. 'You must have seen cavalry mounts at work, even if you are a bard.'

He spread his arms wide. 'Naturally. But as a bard my mind was on the overall effect, not the petty details of the horses.'

'Liar,' she said good-naturedly. 'I believe you know all this already.'

'Explain it to me again. Remember what Virgil said about the man with experience.' His eyes gleamed with mischief. 'Or woman.'

She did not rise to this, instead leaning over the stable door to examine the bay stallion which was her favourite.

'Aggression, timidity, high spirits or laziness – none of these are any good. A warhorse has to work with others of his kind, to be keenly obedient. Anything less, and too much of the rider's time and attention are taken up with his mount.'

'I understand,' said Regin. 'I had a horse once – good runner, plenty of speed and endurance, but he had a nasty habit of trying to break your leg on a gate-post or tree. He always made it seem like an accident, as if he just happened to have misjudged the width of the opening. You know that look of innocent apology they get?'

Seradwen chuckled. 'All too well. As I said, obedience is what matters, obedience and endurance, coupled with gentleness, willingness, and a steadfast nature.'

'And courage, I assume. What about speed?'

'Reasonable speed, yes, but we are not breeding racers.'

Regin nodded. 'Yes. I imagine a mount that outdistances his fellows in the charge could be a liability.'

'Quite,' she said drily. 'He might go through a great many owners in a brief space of time.'

'Ah, but think of the glory they would win! Like poor Aulus Atticus at Mons Graupius, the ardour of whose horse carried him deep among the Caledonian foe, where he was slain.'

Seradwen frowned politely.

'You are not familiar with Tacitus?' he said, seeing her expression.

'I fear not.'

'Perhaps one day . . .' He let the words trail away.

She moved to the next stall, where Whitey glowered at her, wrinkling his teeth and rolling an eyeball.

'Now here we have the exception to all I have said. Whitey is one of the most vicious beasts I have come across, himself quite unfitted for use, yet for some reason he produces good offspring. And if I understood why, I could make this the prime stud in all Dumnonia.'

'Or all Prydein,' said Regin, snatching back his arm as the stallion snapped at his sleeve with worn yellow teeth.

Seradwen surveyed the yard. The hands had returned to work and were studiously ignoring their mistress and the bard. It was spitting with rain, and the sky was dark with the promise of more to follow.

'What do you do on wet nights when you are between halls?' she asked.

'Find a hedge or some kind of shelter. Dumnonia is easy. This is a kindly land, compared with parts of my home.'

'Try the moors above us.' She jerked her thumb in the direction of the high ground. 'They can be wild enough, in summer as well as in winter.'

'No doubt, if I were so foolish. But in Dumnonia one can travel gently from settlement to settlement and rarely need to sleep out of doors. This land is much more heavily populated than Dyfed.'

'What made you leave? I mean, you do not seem the type to be wandering the country.'

'Do I not?' he said with mock indignation. 'And what type do I seem?'

'Well born.' She half shut her eyes and squinted thoughtfully. 'You are well read, well educated. The horse you described, the one that tried to brush your legs against the posts, sounds far too high-mettled for a common bard. And you do not judge your audiences with the skill I would expect in one who lives by entertaining others.'

'Indeed?' He had gone very still.

'No. You offended the garrison at Penhyle, and you came close to causing a riot last night. Odd behaviour for one who depends upon pleasing his listeners.'

He sighed. 'I confess. I am new to my trade.'

'And before?'

'You guessed right. Minor Dyfed nobility, a younger son who quarrelled with his father . . . A sordid and commonplace tale. Shall we walk?'

Regin offered her his arm, and they stepped out into the rain, moving cautiously across the glistening cobbles. She could see Eudaf the smith watching them from the shadows of his bothy. The smith realized he had been noticed and waved his hammer in greeting before returning to his labours.

'Although I keep records of which stallion mated with which mare, with what consequence,' Seradwen said rather breathlessly, 'the truth is that Bodgath holds it all in his head. Sometimes we disagree, and nearly always he is right and I have misread my notes.'

'Bodgath?'

'The little man who was with me last night. The one of whom I spoke, who was my husband's horsemaster.'

'Of course.' Regin's lack of interest was obvious.

'He is the heart of the farm,' she said, more sharply than she had intended.

'Such people often are,' he said casually as they passed through the outer gate. 'Have you had trouble here?'

'Trouble?' He must have noticed the awkwardness between her

179

and her husband's cousins. For a moment she came close to unburdening herself.

'The platform above the gate. It is clearly newer than the wall.'

'Yes, yes we have, though not recently. Bands of dispossessed men and women, from the cities or the countryside to the east, driven from their homes by plague or famine. There is a word for them . . .'

'*Bacaudae*, they called them in Gaul. Peasants living by brigandage. But I would not have thought they would bother you here.'

'Not lately, not in my time. But there was trouble after the fall of Arthur, just as they say there was trouble before his rise.'

He nodded. 'Famine played a large part in it.' They strolled across the fields towards the meadows beside the river. The rain was blowing through the valley in writhing sheets, and though the hills and woods sheltered them from the worst effects of the wind, she pulled the hood of her cloak more firmly around her head.

'You know,' he said slowly, 'I sometimes think the land does not produce as much or as easily as in the past.'

'What do you mean?'

'I have travelled a lot lately, been to places of which I had only read or heard.' His face was suddenly sad. 'I have seen the desolation of Caer Cadwy and its abandoned hall, which my father saw when new. I have walked the ruins of the older sections of Verulamium near the shrine of St Alban. I have crossed Calchwinyth and seen her fields lying empty, untilled, her soil blowing into dust. I believe the land is not so fertile as in former times, when those parts of the island were renowned for being rich beyond measure.'

'Here the land is still good.'

He smiled at her loyalty. 'It seems so, yes.'

The rain was running off her woollen cloak, but his clothes, heavily patched and faded to a uniform brown, were fast becoming soaked. She could see them darkening even as she watched.

'Come, we need shelter,' she said, and grabbing his hand led them at a trot through the fields to the river and its line of trees. Her hood blew back and she felt the rain dampening her hair; his was plastered flat to his skull, and the water was trickling down his face. A small stand of holly grew beside the bank, and she pushed her way ruthlessly through the spiky leaves, dragging him in her wake.

'Mercy!' he cried. 'I think I prefer the rain.' He paused to disentangle his sleeve from a branch.

'What was the message in Ogham?' she demanded, threatening to pull him deeper into the foliage.

'Nothing.'

They stared at each other, laughing. Gradually his eyes sobered and his gaze became more intense. 'The lady is fair,' he said softly, his voice almost drowned by the patter of the rain on the leaves.

Seradwen could feel herself blushing. His fingers fluttered against his nose, and she giggled.

'It looks ridiculous.'

'Yes, but it is true.'

He bent forward and kissed her, tasting her lips and mouth.

'You are afraid,' he murmured. 'What is it? Your family?'

She retreated into the cover of the hollies. 'Yes.'

'Tell me.'

So she did, aware she was behaving like a dizzy girl with her first lover but unable to stop, pouring it all out while he listened and nodded or made small sounds of encouragement. She told him everything: how she had made the decision to marry the safe farmer Mordav rather than the unreliable warrior Nai, and had only come to love her husband after the wedding; how Mordav had died, leaving her alone at the mercy of his kinsmen; how she had hoped Nai might come in search of her but had not (and why should he when one thought about it?); how narrow and dull her life had become, and how much she hated the thought of growing old like this, childless and alone.

And all the time the rain beat down upon them, making the leaves crackle, filling the river so it rushed and gurgled where it parted around a boulder. When, much later, she looked back upon that morning, at what seemed in retrospect like midwinter madness, what she recalled of her confession was not so much the actual things said as the surroundings in which it was made: the dank and dripping holly, the background of running water breaking around the mossy boulder, the rain blotting out the farm and fields so they were alone in their covert, the pair of them standing close together with the moisture streaming from their hair and faces.

'You still feel something for this Nai?' he said gently.

'A daydream mixed with a touch of guilt. We were lovers once, years ago, and I left him. He was badly hurt shortly afterwards – a spear in the throat and the wound went bad.'

'He is fortunate to be alive. I gathered from Addonwy that he had been wounded again.'

' "Those who live by the sword shall die by the sword." '

'You do not approve?'

Her fingers toyed with the brooch that held her cloak, sliding the pin back and forth through the wool. 'Like anywhere else, we on this farm have had our difficulties. Bodgath tells tales – exaggerated no doubt – of standing off bands of marauders in the depths of winter. Without the warriors like Nai it would be worse, I suppose.'

'To live a decent life we need order,' he agreed solemnly. 'And order can only be imposed from above.'

'But by whom?' she said sharply.

'By those with power.'

'Yet it must be legitimate.'

He lifted an eyebrow. 'Custennin, then?'

She laughed bitterly. 'Custennin is merely the descendant of some glib-tongued landowner and magistrate who persuaded the local garrison to support him in his bid to rule the old civitas of Dumnonia.'

'You are cynical,' he said with amusement. 'Custennin claims an ancestry stretching back into the distant past, long before the coming of Rome. Does he not claim to be the rightful heir of the hero Cadwy?'

Seradwen made a rude noise. 'Of course he does, and no doubt it fools the peasants and those who know no better.'

'And you do know better?' he said, watching her from hooded eyes.

'Mordav's family have farmed here for generations. This was a great estate once, though we have abandoned much of the land or allowed it to be swallowed by others. The family were deacons and magistrates. One of them even sat on Vortigern's council – though his descendants do not care to be reminded of the fact, since that council helped open the door to the Saesons. The family kept records, and to them the Marcus who was the ancestor of Kynfawr and Custennin was nothing more than another noble-man, one among many.'

'Very well. So you have a low opinion of Custennin.' Regin flicked a holly branch, watched the droplets shower to the ground. 'Yet you seemed last night to feel differently about Arthur.'

'I was a child when Arthur died. I had not even met Nai.' She paused, frowned. 'In Arthur's day the land was settled, safe. We were secure. We could concern ourselves with the business of living without worrying somebody was waiting to take everything away. A farm, a horseherd, are very fragile things. A dozen determined men prepared to kill could destroy all you have seen. What laws we have can be manipulated by a greedy lordling with a warband behind him.'

'Was it not ever thus?'

'Not under Arthur. Now there is no certain rule of law, no redress against those more powerful than oneself.'

He raised an eyebrow, peered at her doubtfully down the hook of his nose. 'What redress can there be against a band of raiders from the ocean, or even the dispossessed from the east, whose lives are already so miserable that the taking of them is a mercy?'

'True enough, but what protection do we have against Custennin if he decides to seize our lands and goods? He is the law.'

'Surely he cannot go too far?'

'Far enough if he chooses his targets with care. I have heard stories . . .' She blinked angrily, tears of frustration pricking at her eyes. 'At times it all seems so futile.'

'Is the estate in danger then?'

She shook her head. 'Not while Gereint holds the Portion of Erbin. But he will not live forever, and who knows what might happen afterwards?'

'Everywhere life is hard,' he said sententiously.

'Of course it is!' she exclaimed crossly. 'But that is no reason for our supposed rulers to make it harder!'

He was standing so close that she could smell him: wet cloth and leather (not unpleasant), underlain with the familiar scent of the soap they made on the farm from lye and fat.

'So, my original question,' he said. 'What made Arthur legitimate? After all, he was from a minor branch of the old Roman nobility. He made his reputation as a soldier. What difference was there between him and the rest?'

She looked at him aghast. 'Don't you see? Don't you remember how it was? He made himself legitimate. He stood for us all, one land and one people, whatever our origins. He was like Rome herself come again. Why, when so many of our people fled over the sea to Lesser Britain, to what used be Armorica, they weren't going to a strange place, but merely moving within the Empire, as

183

I might move from here to the far side of Isca. In Arthur's day I could have gone to Gwynedd or Rheged and known I was still within the bounds of Albion; now, only ten years later, they are foreign lands with their own tyrants and their own customs.'

The words gushed out of her, and she was aware she was not saying what she meant, that Regin was watching her with a cynical lift to his eyebrow (curious that he had accused her of cynicism), that she would never convince him in a hundred years.

'How do you mean, he made himself legitimate?' asked Regin when she stumbled to a halt.

'I cannot explain. He just did. It was the reason they all followed him, the best of Prydein, the warriors like Cei, Bedwyr and Gwalchmei, the judges like Cengan and Dunawt; the reason why his court at Caer Cadwy or Kelliwig was filled with talent like none before or since, a glittering array of men and women . . .'

She gazed at the river. The boulder had vanished, swallowed by the dark water. While she watched a long white log raced down on the current, checked for a brief instant on the place where the rock must lie beneath the surface, bobbed and twisted free.

She turned back to Regin, beseeching him to understand. 'They recognized the majesty within him.'

'Medraut?' he said, with the same quirk of an eyebrow. 'Iddawg?'

'The selfish and the greedy are always with us. Like Grugyn in your story.'

'My story? Not mine.' He began to spread his hands wide, remembered the holly leaves. 'I think time has lent enchantment. I wonder whether you would feel the same if Arthur still lived, or if he had left an heir.'

'Do not doubt it,' she said.

He studied her features, then nodded slowly. 'Lady, on this matter at least I see we must agree to differ.'

'But on others?'

He grinned, and became again the man with whom she had run through the field, the man to whom she had opened her heart.

'On others we may agree.'

Catching her in the circuit of his arms, he spoke with a sudden urgency: 'Come with me when I leave.'

'What?'

'I mean it.'

She could feel herself blushing. 'I cannot. I have responsibilities . . . The farm, the horses . . .'

To grow old alone and unloved, waiting for something which would never happen.

'Come with me. For a month, two months.' His eyes were shining. 'Wander east with me. See the land. See the ruins of Caer Cadwy. We could even visit the Saesons beyond the Sallow Wood.'

'Is it safe?'

'Safe?' He flung back his head and roared with laughter. 'No, of course it's not safe. To leave your comfortable home, in the dead of winter, to wander the roads with a man you barely know, to travel to the territory of the barbarian outlanders where the very speech sounds like the barking of dogs . . . No, it is not all safe, and you must be mad to contemplate it.'

'I –' She remembered when her father had told her that Mordav had asked for her hand in marriage, she had walked the cliffs near Din Erbin, watching the sunlight on the sea, staring at the beds of weed hidden below the surface, brown and yellow and green, all the while thinking, wondering. Accept him, and be safe, the rest of your life preordained, as predictable as the course of a training march for young warriors where the specific incidents along the way may be unknown, but the route and destination are planned and thus dictate the kind of thing which will happen. Marry a farmer, produce children and grandchildren; struggle against the elements and the diseases to which both livestock and crops are prone, all the while aware that jealous eyes are watching, and that if you succeed you will not be allowed to enjoy the full fruit of your labours, but that some bully with a band of armed retainers will decide he has a right to take a larger share.

Yet she had chosen this, rather than drift on as she was, waiting for Nai to ask so she could live the precarious life of a warrior's woman. (She knew why he had not asked: he was a man of no family, save by adoption, no lands or wealth save what he might woo from Gereint his lord, no prospects save what he might win by the sword, and that at a time when the land was largely at peace and the chances of winning either reputation or great spoils seemed slender.)

She had made her choice – and she had loved Mordav, she had – but a part of her had always wondered what she had missed by choosing as she did. And now she was being given another chance . . .

Regin's voice, deep and persuasive, echoed her thoughts. 'What I offer is adventure. If you come to loathe the life, or come to loathe me, you can always return.'

He waited, an artful pause though his expression seemed sincere.

'I think I could love you,' he said softly. 'I am not saying I do, for we have hardly met, yet I feel I have known you all my life, been searching for you all my life without ever knowing that something was missing. I believed myself content until I rode into your yard and saw you striding towards me with that slight frown upon your face. With you I feel complete, and if I leave here alone you will haunt my dreams till I behold you again.'

The rain was still falling relentlessly. She looked down at her hands, the slightly swollen knuckles, the broken nails, turned them over and examined the calloused palms. Closing her eyes she thought of his long fingers caressing her body, and laughed aloud.

'No,' she said. 'You flatter me, but it would not work.'

She opened her eyes just in time to catch the flash of anger disappearing from his face: anger, and something else she could not identify.

'Shall we make our way to the villa?' he said after a moment. 'I see no purpose in remaining here to be drowned.'

Startled, Seradwen agreed. She had been expecting him to remonstrate with her further, to make more protestations of undying love, not to accept her refusal as easily as a gambler accepts the failure of a wager against long odds.

They walked briskly across the meadows, Regin a pace ahead of her. Studying the set of his back, she wondered whether the entire performance (and it had been a performance – now she had descended from the giddy heights she was sure of it) had been an elaborate prelude to a simple seduction, whether he would have shared her bed that night and have been gone in the morning, all promises forgotten.

Bodgath was waiting for them by the outer gate. At the sight of him, small, brown, and irredeemably shifty, a great wave of relief went through her. He was leaning on his stick and fiddling crossly with his cap, scowling at the grass by his feet. Regin strode past him as if he did not exist and vanished through the gate.

'Upset him, have you?' growled the little man. 'Shame.'

Suddenly weary, she stifled a yawn.

'Kept you up late, did he? You need be careful with these hedge bards. Rogues, most of them.'

'Is something wrong?' She could tell his heart was not in the banter.

He shuffled his feet. 'Not exactly wrong.'

'What then?'

'We are being watched,' Bodgath announced quickly. 'From the hills above the river. Saw their tracks yesterday, thought nothing of it, saw them again today.'

'Did you see the watchers themselves?' demanded Regin, reappearing from the yard, where he must have been waiting for Seradwen to join him.

'No.' Bodgath shook his head, his eyes fixed on a point above Seradwen's left shoulder. 'Prints and broken twigs was all.'

'How many?' she asked.

The little man scowled. 'Hard to tell. Perhaps a dozen.'

'Are you sure?' said Regin.

They ignored him. Bodgath's gaze wandered towards the fields and the horses grazing there. 'Had their own mounts,' he murmured.

'We had better put a guard on the herd,' said Seradwen. 'Bring in as many as we can overnight.'

'You think they are horse thieves?' Regin seemed startled.

'What else, this time of year?' she said impatiently. 'Honest men would have come down to the house.'

'Perhaps they don't like music and are waiting for him to leave,' Bodgath suggested slyly.

'I shall start organizing space in the stables. Regin, could you find Hoewgi and ask him to meet me there?'

He stared at her for a moment then bowed his head. 'Of course, Lady.'

Bodgath watched the bard cross the outer court, making certain he had gone this time before speaking. 'Funny they should come while he is here.'

Seradwen, her mind already full of the changes that would need to be made in order to bring the greater part of the herd within the walls, shrugged dismissively.

'Pure chance,' she said. 'Pure chance.'

CHAPTER TEN

Nai was so tired he felt as if he were peering sideways from his own body. He had not slept properly since leaving Penhyle. The journey to Seradwen's farm would normally take half a day: he had taken two, and he was not there yet.

Two days of using every bit of cover the land afforded: moving from wood to wood, from valley to valley, avoiding the hilltops and the open ground, sometimes going miles out of his way. Two days without sleep or decent food, pausing for rest only when it became too dark to continue in safety, half dozing with a part of him constantly on the alert for his pursuers.

They were close. Twice he had caught glimpses of them, dark men accompanied by one of Custennin's warriors, ostentatiously scouring the landscape for some sign of his passing. Both times he had waited, let the hunt move on without him, hoping that he was outside the ring of searchers. Hoping, but fearing the worst.

He was fairly sure they knew where he was: not exactly where, not that he was standing here beside the river in the dusk watching the mist rise from the water, but that he was within a few miles of this point. He was almost certain they had known all along, that he had never been far from their sight, that they had been playing a game with him, allowing him to make his slow circuitous progress while they watched, amused, superior, waiting for him to break cover.

Nai scowled. The river was swollen and fierce after all the recent rain, the water smooth with power where it pulled around the boulders. He could not cross. If he remembered correctly – and he had never visited the farm, only heard it described – the villa lay about half a mile upstream. In effect, he had trapped himself, committed himself to continuing along the river bank until he reached the farm. He could try breaking away, but he had the feeling that if he did so the hunters would stop him.

Coal snorted beside him. He looked down at his hands, saw they were quivering, and thrust them under his arms to still them. The ground was soft from the rain. This had been a meadow once, though now it was reverting to marsh. Behind him the mist was thickening to hide the hills. Ahead of him the river flowed from a wood, and he could see a path winding under the trees. In the failing light the wood was full of shadows, so that as his gaze passed across it he saw figures everywhere, crouching in the undergrowth or hiding behind the trunks.

Reluctantly he led Coal forward.

The soil was sandy under the trees, scattered with rocks and boulders like a dry riverbed. Roots waited to catch an unwary foot, and in places the flood had scoured miniature ravines into which he staggered while Coal floundered in his wake, hooves scraping loudly on stone. Once he came to a black pit of silent water, and seeing no way round without retracing his steps – not easy, with Coal's bulk behind him – he waded gingerly across, using a spear as a sounding rod, balancing on stones wherever possible, fearing to slip and wrench an ankle. The horse followed with a great splashing and ringing of rock. To Nai's relief, the ground abruptly opened out. On his right was the river, a dark line of trees and bushes with an occasional glint of water below them. To his left was a steep hill or ridge, sparsely clad in ancient oaks and thin whitethorn. The path suddenly seemed more like a path and less like a dry watercourse, though here too he could tell from the neatly swept look of the piles of dead leaves and sand that the river had recently burst its banks.

He was close now, very close, and he began to think about what he would say. Although he had never seen the farm he had a definite picture of how it would be: a long low building of stone with a thatched roof, surrounded by outbuildings and a complex of round houses for the workers on the estate. If he were honest, he had to admit he had never paid much attention when others had described the farm: having lost, largely through his own stupidity, the fight for Seradwen's affections to a man he had never met, pride had prevented him from listening when others had detailed her good fortune.

But he had listened long enough to discover it was a happy marriage, and at the time he had believed he was pleased for her. After she had gone, when he had been healing from the great gash Eremon's spear had torn his throat and he had for a while lost the power of speech as the wound turned foul, he had come to understand what he had lost by his failure to speak when he had had the chance.

He had not known her husband was dead until Addonwy had told him during one of his visits to Sanctuary Wood. And if he had known sooner, would it have made any difference? He would still have owed a duty to Gereint, the lord to whose service he was sworn, to Gorthyn, his foster brother and comrade, to the people of Dumnonia.

It was an odd thought that Coal had been born and bred on Seradwen's farm. Perhaps she had presided over his birth – his mind conjured images of stables, lanterns and a mare struggling to bring forth a foal, of a long-legged woman with her hair bound up in a scarf murmuring soft words of encouragement.

A gust of wind rustled the ivy in the trees. It was fully dark now. He stopped and closed his eyes, listening intently. Over the past few days he had come to rely as much upon the pony's senses as upon his own, and he leaned back into Coal, aware of the heat of the horse's body, the tickle of breath on his neck.

He reached up blindly and caught the horse's muzzle, opened his eyes and quartered the wood.

'Do you feel it?' His voice was soft, pitched for the pony's ears alone.

They stood in a bowl of sound, defined by the roar of the river on one side and the rustle of the wind along the ridge on the other. As he listened, he was able to tease out the strands, as one might tease out different voices from a crowd: there the squeak of branch on branch, there the whispy rub of leaf on leaf, there the scurry of rat or hedgepig in the brambles. The sounds fitted, belonged to the night.

He waited, the spear firm in his free hand. He was not alone, and knew it, but could not find whatever had alerted him to the presence of someone else.

'Where?'

Coal's ears twitched back and forth. Above them the moon

fought through the clouds, briefly illuminated the black surface of the river. What Nai had taken for the far bank was in fact a narrow island with a tree at either end. That flank seemed safe, and he did not believe there was anybody ahead of him, though he would have been hard put to explain why.

Which left the slope of the ridge and the path behind him. He dropped Coal's reins and squeezed past the horse, unbuckled his shield from its place on the crupper. The plain covering of hide rendered it almost invisible in the darkness, and he slipped it onto his arm with a sense of relief.

Then he drew the horse away from the path and around the spiky black branches of a thorn thicket, fending off the twigs with the rim of his shield. Behind the thorns was a fallen oak, the trunk slowly rotting under a tent of brambles and the root ball a mass of earth and grass towering higher than a man. Beyond that was a deep hollow, thick with dead leaves, and here he left Coal. Already he was wondering if this was wise, if it would not be better to keep moving, but the desire to know whether there was truly anybody on his trail drove him onward.

Nai scrambled out of the hollow and squatted beside the tree trunk, the spear buried in the detritus around him so its head would not catch the light. He arranged the cloak and shield to soften and disguise his shape, to make himself seem like an outcropping of the tree, covering his hands and pulling a fold of the cloak across his face to mask the skin. For a long while nothing happened. The river gurgled and roared, the wind rustled in the trees. An insect crawled across his forehead, but he schooled himself to remain still and ignore the tickle. An owl hooted, somewhere toward the edge of the wood. A second replied from nearby with a quavering, bubbling cry, and the two conducted a duet until the first took flight, and the hoots changed to a sharper call: *kiwack*, *kiwack*. Behind him he heard Coal shifting restlessly from hoof to hoof, and he listened in case something had disturbed him, but after a moment the pony was still again.

The moon shone down through a tunnel of cloud. He glanced up at the sudden brightness even though he knew it was a mistake, drawn by the sight of the abyss in the heavens, and when he looked back at the path a flicker around a tree trunk snagged his attention.

He strained his moon-dazzled eyes, staring into the shadows, sweeping his gaze from side to side, hoping to catch a repeat movement. It occurred to him that he was perhaps being stalked by somebody with greater woodcraft than his own, and for an instant he considered breaking for his horse. But in this light, over this terrain, a man afoot could move as fast if not faster than a horse, and besides, the advantage should always lie with the one who remains motionless.

His eyes ached and his legs were cramped. His pursuers must know that he was lying in wait, otherwise they would have passed him long since. And if they knew, then did he still hold the advantage by staying motionless? In their position, he would have circled away from the path and outflanked himself along the rim of the ridge. If Gorthyn had been with him they would have divided, one circling, the other going straight down the path as a decoy.

He drew the war-knife from its sheath, keeping it hidden under the cloak. The sword he had left on the saddlebow, thinking it would be more hindrance than help. The javelin he let lie, knowing that in this light and with so many trailing branches there was small chance of hitting the target.

A dark shape detached itself from the bole of the tree he had been watching, flowed from shadow to shadow along the path, moving without sound, seeming to flicker in and out of existence as it touched upon the moonlight then merged again with the darkness. A second shape followed, clumsier than the first, with a gleam of metal in its hand. This one turned his head as he crossed a pool of pale light. Nai saw the glimmer of eyes in an oddly ridged face, and shuddered with revulsion. The ridges were the scars caused by the Clan Menestyr's method of tattooing, and in the cold moon glow they became more pronounced.

They had not seen him, and the second man was going to pass very close to his hiding place. Nai readied himself, prepared to fling back his cloak and leap to his feet; the first man hesitated, froze into the thin trunk of an alder with a soft hiss of breath.

Coal shifted, sensing the presence of strangers, hooves rustling the dead leaves.

Nai uncoiled, striking hard into the stomach of the nearest man and using his momentum to drag the knife upwards and out again. The man screamed in shock and pain, staggered and began to fall. Nai shoved him into the path of the other, a vague shape rushing forward through the shadows, and followed, hurdling the dying man and swinging the war-knife like a cleaver.

The blade jarred against bone and he felt an impact against his shield as he spun to the left, crossing his opponent, light on his feet and fearful of tree roots but not daring look down, caught a flash of steel driving for his groin, had no time to block with his shield so parried with his knife, pushing the blade aside, countering with a strike for where the wrist must be and finding only empty air, slammed the shield home against some part of his opponent's body and twisted free, off balance as he did indeed stumble on a root . . .

The man was gone. Nai could hear the faint patter of footsteps receding into the distance, and then silence.

In the end he rode to the edge of the wood, though it took him three attempts to mount. All the strength had left his body, and he could not stop shaking. He crouched low on Coal's back, praying with a fervour he had not known he possessed, thanking God for his deliverance as he ducked beneath the branches, ignoring the reins and allowing the pony to pick his own route at his own pace.

He had killed another of the Picts. If they had hated him before, now they must loathe him utterly, and although they might be more wary, he did not think he had taught them to fear him. The trouble with feuds – God, he was tired and needed to sleep – was that the harder you fought to protect yourself, the deeper the danger into which you fell. Civilized men did not behave in this fashion – though he and Gorthyn had come close in their hatred of Eremon mab Cairbre. (But that was different. Eremon was a turncoat and traitor who had tortured and raped and burnt his way through the lands he should have helped protect.) The Picts, the Children of Menestyr or whatever you wanted to call them, had attacked him without warning while he was going about his business. If forced to it, he would have been prepared to pay compensation for their deaths – or, more exactly, since he had few personal possessions and no living kin, he would have asked his lord, Gereint, to pay it for him.

But he did not believe a few head of cattle or a handful of arm-rings would satisfy the Children of Menestyr. They wanted his death, he was sure of it, even though they might not want it until they had wrung from him the information they needed to find

Bedwyr. The more of them he slew to protect himself, the stronger that desire would become. They were not civilized, not heirs to the great traditions of Rome as were the people of Dumnonia. They were like the Saesons, savages from beyond the bounds of the old Empire, creatures with whom one could not reason.

Coal came to a halt beside a holly tree above a small stream. Nai could see a glimmer of light across the open ground before them, twinkling in the damp air. Then it started to rain and the light was blotted out as a squall swept across the meadows.

All around him the wood came to life, crackling and popping as the rain fell and dripped on leaf and branch. He flung back his head and listened, trembling slightly, one hand on his war-knife. It sounded as if an army was advancing towards him, and he pressed into the holly as though it might somehow save him from their attack.

The rain stopped as suddenly as it had begun, but the noise continued. Coal fidgeted nervously, snorting and blowing. There was nobody there, and Nai knew it with the same certainty as that with which he had earlier sensed the presence of the two Picts, but his courage seemed to have deserted him. He could not move, only sit in the saddle and listen to the dank dripping through the trees and bushes, the sharp holly pricking his exposed neck and head.

Gradually the clatter softened and died away. He unstrapped the shield from his arm and hung it over his back, drew a deep breath and urged the pony out from the safety of the tree. His stomach rumbled and gurgled. He was tired and hungry, needed the sight of friendly faces and a place where he could sleep properly without the constant fear of being wakened by an enemy standing over him.

They splashed across the stream and up into the meadow, Coal's hooves squelching through the grass, the light burning like a beacon ahead of them. A fence blocked their way, post and rail, well made and well tended, dividing the meadow from what looked in the moonlight to be good pasture, and he turned Coal's head to the left towards the gate.

Coal's pace suddenly quickened. He whinnied softly in greeting. Nai heard the drumming of hooves, then three ponies appeared, gleaming in the silver light, nickering in their turn.

'You're coming home, old friend,' he muttered and patted his mount's neck, wishing that the same was true of him.

'Who's there?' challenged a voice from the darkness. 'Get off, you devils, or I'll have the lads on you.' A faint quaver robbed the words of their menace.

Nai straightened, pulled Coal to a halt while the ponies crowded curious along the fence, eager for him to open the gate.

'I mean no harm,' he called in reply.

'It croaks like a crow,' the voice muttered to itself, adding more loudly: 'Who are you, and what do you want?'

'I am Nai mab Nwython, and I serve Gereint mab Cadwy. I seek the Lady Seradwen.'

'Do you, old crow? You choose an odd time to come calling.'

Nai spread his arms wide to show he was not holding a weapon. 'I had trouble on the road.'

'So has many a man, but most wait till daylight before they go trampling across other people's land.'

'I lost my way.'

'You left your road, for sure. Creature of the woods, are you?'

Nai managed a humourless laugh, thinking of the last two days. 'Sometimes I wonder.'

'I too,' said the voice. The ponies moved suddenly, revealing a small figure with a spear levelled in Nai's direction.

'Out of the woods you come in the dark of the night, bearing the arms of a fighting man. Are you for peace or for war, old crow?'

'Peace.' Nai slid wearily from the saddle. 'I have had my fill of war for this night. And I am very tired.'

The little man grunted. 'So is old Bodgath, keeping guard every night against the painted strangers in the hills and a day's work to be done on the morrow.' He kept the spear pointing at Nai, even though the fence separated them. 'How did you pass their watchmen?'

'I killed one and frightened the other away.'

'Ha!' exclaimed Bodgath. 'Why should I believe you?'

'Because my face is not tattooed. Because I speak like a Dumnonian, not a man of the north. Because if you are a friend of Seradwen, she will have mentioned me.' He paused, too tired to think of a fourth reason.

'Anybody could say what you say,' the little man growled obstinately. 'And why should Bodgath know of the Lady's friends from before her marriage to the Master Mordav?'

'If I wished you harm I would not waste my time talking in the moonlight,' retorted Nai. 'And had I known you would not believe me, I would have brought you the Pict's head.'

'Go and fetch it then.'

Nai glanced at the woods, a thick black shadow louring beyond the meadow, and shivered. He could feel the menace from where he stood, and knew that if he returned inside he would never come out alive again. 'No thank you.'

The little man cackled. 'Come then,' he said, lowering the spear. 'That horse you're leaning on is good enough for me. One of ours, by Breichir of the long forelegs out of a moorland mare, I reckon. How old is he now, and what do you call him?'

Nai flung back his head and laughed. 'Coal. I call him Coal, and he is in his seventh year.'

'That would be about right,' said Bodgath, unfastening the gate. 'Come, sweetling.' He clucked his tongue and Coal went forward trustingly, nuzzling the little man's tunic in quest of a titbit.

Bodgath led the way across the fields, using the spear as a staff. Now and then he called out to alert other guards to their presence. 'Not usually like this,' he explained. 'We don't trust the Painted Men. Don't trust any strangers much, but them least of all. After our horses, I dare say.'

'You are wise,' said Nai. 'How long have they been here?'

Bodgath sniffed. 'Been lurking a while. Spotted them two nights ago, sneaking around the woods and the hills, thinking nobody saw them.' He tapped the side of his nose. 'Bodgath saw them, though. Then today they grew careless, once the bard had gone, showed themselves more.'

'The bard?'

'That's what he said he was. Never seen a bard carry a sword on his saddle before.' The little man cleared his throat noisily. 'They let him out, though they tried to stop you coming in. Makes you think.'

The buildings were close. The gate was open, and what had been a single glow had fractured into a dozen or more lights scattered around a courtyard. 'You are a friend of the Lady's, yes?'

'I was,' said Nai. 'I hope I am still.'

'She has not been happy here since Mordav died. His cousins inherited the farm, and they are not easy.' Bodgath's tone was serious. 'Will you make matters worse, coming out of her past?'

Nai shrugged. The little man grunted and led him toward the

gate, through which he could see an inner wall with more torches flaring behind it.

They feel safer in the light, he thought, but aloud he said: 'Where was the bard from?'

'Dyfed, he claimed.' Bodgath paused on the threshold. 'May have been telling the truth. Talked funny enough.'

'A bard from Dyfed,' said Nai, thinking furiously. A Dyfed bard had visited Penhyle, sung a poem about Arthur and Cei which had infuriated Cadlew.

'He performed here on his first night.' Bodgath's eyes gleamed in the torch light. 'A hateful song, about Gwenhwyvar being unfaithful to Arthur. We hissed him down. There would have been a riot had the Lady not calmed us.'

'Seradwen?'

'Who else? He took a fancy to her afterwards,' Bodgath added slyly.

'I doubt he was the first,' Nai said calmly. The little man sniggered.

A pair of youths stood guard upon the gate, peering anxiously into the darkness beyond the ring of light cast by their torches.

'Visitor,' Bodgath said laconically, jerking a thumb at Nai. The men eased slightly, though the appearance of a well-armed warrior seemed to worry rather than reassure them.

'Hoewgi's idea,' muttered Bodgath as they passed through to the courtyard. 'Thinks the light will frighten off the bogeymen.'

'Makes good targets.' Nai surveyed the yard, noting the far wall with its door and gate, both firmly closed, the stable blocks and the great barn which he guessed had once been a bathhouse. Depending upon what lay beyond the wall the place was defensible, given the right men and the right commander.

Bodgath nudged him. 'There's Hoewgi in his finery. Mordav's cousin. And one of his brothers.'

A richly dressed figure was talking with another man near one of the stables. Neither looked up at the approach of the new-comers, and as they drew nearer Nai realized the pair were arguing.

'We have no proof they intend us any harm,' he heard one say. A lantern hung from a hook over the stable door, and both men seemed flushed, though it might have been a trick of the light.

'By the time we have proof it will be too late,' hissed the other, swinging round at the clatter of Coal's hooves on the cobbles. His face lit with hope.

'What's this? By the Trinity, thrice welcome if you are what I think you are!'

'Gereint's man,' said Bodgath. 'Friend of the Lady Seradwen.'

Nai was watching the well dressed man and saw him frown at the mention of Seradwen's name.

'I am Meirion, Mordav's heir. This is my brother Hoewgi. You are come in good time, warrior!' Meirion was expansive, relief writ large in every gesture. 'We were discussing these Picts camped upon our doorstep. My brother insists they mean no harm, but I have my doubts – and I know good Bodgath feels much the same,' he added condescendingly.

'You have seen them?' asked Nai. Both men started at the harsh sound of his voice, though Hoewgi hid it better than his brother.

'Not myself, no,' said Meirion. 'Bodgath has seen them. A frightening crew, from what I gather, their features distorted with scars and paint.'

Hoewgi snorted. 'Much exaggerated to my mind, if they exist at all, and being used as an excuse to ignore my orders. Bodgath, you may have been Mordav's herdmaster, but you take too much upon yourself.'

'Bodgath protects the herd,' the little man said sullenly, his gaze fixed on the ground. 'Does what needs to be done.'

'The warrior can advise us,' Meirion intervened smoothly. 'Bodgath is a valued member of our community, and after all, doubling the watch on the horses is not so great a hardship.'

'It is if it stops the men working the next day!' Hoewgi exclaimed, his temper rising once more.

'You are wise to guard the horses, whatever the cost,' said Nai. 'The Picts will steal them if they can. And the Picts are there all right, make no mistake about that. I killed one on my way here.'

Hoewgi blanched. 'Was that wise? Will they not seek vengeance?'

'Probably.' Nai gave him a cold smile and watched him recoil. 'Since he was trying to kill me at the time I feel no great guilt. If they are prepared to attack one of Gereint's household warriors going about his lawful business, you can take it they are prepared to attack this farm.' He paused, glanced around ostentatiously. 'It seems prosperous.'

'This is ridiculous!' The words burst from Hoewgi in a wail of frustration. 'Picts, in Heaven's name! They belong in the fireside tales of our grandfathers. No Picts have raided this land since the days of Ambrosius the Elder!'

'They are here now,' said Meirion. 'What do you advise, warrior?'

'Bring the horses and men inside the compound. If that cannot be done –'

'It cannot,' said Bodgath. 'Too many.'

'– then bring them as close as you can. Douse the torches and shut the gates. Let the men's eyes adapt to the night. Your sentinels in the fields are good, but make sure they are within range of one another. Pairs work better than individuals. Gather your main force here or in the house, somewhere from which they can respond quickly. They can sleep or rest until they are needed. Is the house itself defensible?'

'Yes,' said Meirion.

'No,' said Bodgath. 'Not without trained warriors.'

'Wait!' said Hoewgi, holding up a hand. 'Who are you?'

Nai turned. 'I am Nai mab Nwython, sometimes called Nai the Silent. As I have said, I serve Gereint mab Cadwy, Lord of the Portion of Erbin, of which this estate is a part.'

Hoewgi seemed flustered, unsure of himself. 'I see,' he said slowly. 'I have heard of you.' He glanced at his brother, found no help there. 'Forgive me, Nai. I am a farmer, not a warrior, and all this is new to me.' He coughed. 'Make what arrangements you think best with Meirion. Perhaps he could show you the villa.'

And a place to sleep, thought Nai, feeling himself sag. Whatever its faults, the farmstead was safe. Here he could relax secure in the knowledge that somebody would wake him if danger threatened.

'Of course,' said Meirion, laying a hand on Nai's shield arm. 'Bodgath, look after the warrior's horse.'

The little man bared his teeth and took Coal's reins. 'Good rub and mash, my pretty, that's what we'll give you.'

Nai watched him lead the pony away into one of the stables. The brothers clearly did not like Bodgath and made little effort to hide the fact, which struck Nai as foolish. Hoewgi had said that Bodgath had been his predecessor's herdmaster. To be master of the horse herd was to hold a position of enormous importance, almost sacred in its responsibility even in these nominally Christian times. Carnon, the great-hoofed one, was not yet forgotten, and it was still common in rural areas to find effigies of him in his horse shape discreetly hidden beside a spring or under a tree. If Nai had inherited this farm the one person he would have wanted as helper would have been Bodgath.

'He will do him proud,' said Meirion, misinterpreting Nai's gaze. 'Bodgath may be a funny little fellow, and he may not be capable of meeting your eye when talking, which I agree gives him a shifty look, but the man knows his horses. And he is as honest as one can reasonably expect, given that he was our late lamented cousin's choice as herdmaster.'

He led Nai towards the door in the wall, talking all the while.

'You must forgive my brother. The men are frightened – and I fear old Bodgath has made matters worse with his talk of what he has seen lurking around the perimeters of the property. We have had much chatter of demons, of wood spirits and the like. You know how superstitious the peasants can be. Hoewgi worries, even when things are going well.' Meirion cleared his throat nervously. 'And to be perfectly frank, Seradwen is not always an easy person. She resents our presence, very understandably. Who would not? But Mordav is dead, and there you are, God's will be done.'

'Where is Seradwen?'

The sound of Nai's voice silenced Meirion.

'Resting in her room. She said she would take the second watch. After all, the horse herd does belong to her.'

The door was not locked. They passed through to the inner yard, Meirion tugging at Nai's arm when he would have halted to take in the sight.

'Impressive, is it not? The place must have been quite something in the days of its glory. Now, as you can see, we patch and mend as best we can.'

Drawing closer, Nai realized what the man meant. The portico tiles, a soft pink in the lamplight, were cracked and broken. The walls needed new mortar, and the thatched roof off to his left seemed to be sagging badly.

'How old?' he asked.

Meirion shrugged. 'Nobody knows. My family claims to have lived here for generations.'

'Is it open on the inside?' From the corner of an eye Nai saw the other frown uncomprehendingly. He flogged his tired mind to make his meaning clearer. 'Is it all one space? Or is it divided by walls?'

'Oh, divided, divided horizontally and vertically. We are several families, besides the household servants.'

Nai paused at the foot of the portico steps, stared up at the row of windows above the pink tiles. The right wing was a blank wall, apart from a couple of doorways, but the left was studded with openings, some shuttered, others gaping blankly to the night or golden with the soft glow of lamps. One or two were still glazed.

'Are there windows on the far side?'

'Very few, and those both barred and shuttered,' said Meirion. He peered anxiously at Nai. 'You are exhausted, warrior. Would it not be wise to sleep, lest we need your services later? I will set sentries to warn us if anybody tries to break in.'

'Good,' said Nai, who was suddenly having difficulty keeping his eyes open. He slipped the shield from his shoulders, stretched and followed Meirion into the house.

The room he was given was a cell with a couch and a single chair. A tiny window high in the wall faced out onto the portico, and as he lay waiting for sleep – he had reached that stage of tiredness at which sleep will not come – he heard footsteps moving urgently back and forth along the verandah. He dozed, started awake with a shock that ran right through his body as he remembered he had left the sword and his javelins with Coal. It was not important, he thought as he settled again, he still had both knife and shield, the door was bolted, and he trusted Bodgath.

He did not trust either Meirion or his brother Hoewgi. Meirion was too glib. Hoewgi – well, he could understand Hoewgi, faced with something new and not knowing how to react, but the man's welcome had not been effusive. Neither brother had offered him food or drink, and even allowing for the fact that he was obviously exhausted, they had hustled him out of sight with indecent haste.

Nai came up out of a deep and dreamless sleep, confused. Somebody was tapping on the door of the hut, the bed had moved, and there seemed to be a hole high in the wall through which he could see a paler darkness.

'Who?' he croaked, his throat dry and painful.

'Seradwen,' called a voice, and memory came to him.

He swung himself from the couch, moved stiffly across the room, bumping into the chair, and found the door. He pulled the bolt with his left hand, war-knife in the other, standing well clear in case the door was suddenly kicked open.

She was alone, carrying a shuttered lantern.

The knife suddenly felt very large in his hand. He tried to sheath it, remembered he had removed his war-belt before lying down and hid the blade behind his back instead, gesturing awkwardly that she should enter.

'I am pleased to see you as well,' she said as she swept into the room. 'Do keep the knife in view if it makes you more comfortable. I know people can be funny about being separated from the tools of their trade.' She smiled sweetly.

'Harpers?'

Seradwen hung the lamp from a hook, released the shutters. Nai blinked as light filled the space, illuminating the patina of dirt and the cobwebs in the corners.

'They could have given you a better room.' She blew the dust from the back of the chair, seated herself. 'Did you say something about harps? I am sorry your voice is damaged. Bodgath did warn me you sounded like an old crow, and for once he was right.'

'For once?'

'Bodgath does not approve of me speaking with other men. I assumed from what you said that he had told you about our recent guest. The answer to your question is that Regin showed no signs of distress when separated from his harp. I have, however, no idea whether he clung to his instrument when asleep.'

Nai laughed. 'I have missed you.'

She assessed him carefully. 'And I you, on the whole. Put the knife away and sit down. Tell me what brings you here, and what threat these tattooed men pose to my horse herd.'

He cleared his throat, feeling the weakness in his limbs. 'May I have something to eat and drink?'

Her eyes narrowed and she glanced around the room. 'Did they not give you anything when you arrived?'

'They brought me straight here.'

'How ill mannered.' One foot tapped impatiently, and he remembered that she had always been quick tempered.

'I was very tired,' he said in mitigation.

'No excuse.' She ran a hand through her hair. 'This is no longer my house. My husband's heirs do not always behave with the courtesy I would wish. Can you wait a while longer? I would speak with you in private.'

He nodded, sat on the edge of the bed.

'So patient,' she said softly, and he could not tell whether she was teasing him or not. 'Why are you here?'

The directness of the question caught him off guard.

'I thought I was being clever,' he said after a moment. 'I needed a place to hide.'

'To hide? From these tattooed men?'

Nai inclined his head. The candle flickered in the lantern and the shadows fled across her face. 'Why?' she said. 'I mean . . .' She stopped. 'They are here for you? They were waiting for you.'

'They have followed me from Penhyle. Driven me, like beaters driving game for the hunter.' He rose to his feet, swayed slightly before he caught his balance. 'I think something has changed. They did not press me until I arrived here, but two tried to take me by the river.'

'To take you?'

'To kill me.'

Seradwen closed her eyes and shook her head. 'What have you done to them?'

'Until yesterday I would have said they wanted information they believe I alone possess. Now, I fear they have already found their answer.'

'So they do not need you any longer?'

'Not alive.'

She stared at him. 'What made you come here?'

He smiled ruefully. 'I wanted a friend.'

Her laugh was short and bitter.

Meirion found them in the kitchen, where Nai was wolfing a hunk of bread and cheese while Seradwen watched in silence.

The portly man's hair was tousled and his clothes were untidy. He clung to the door jamb, panting for breath, announced without ceremony: 'The Picts are at the outer gate. They have driven in our sentries, rounded them up like a flock of sheep with the butts of their spears. Now they demand we surrender you to them.'

'Anybody hurt?' Nai demanded around a mouthful.

'No, nobody was harmed.' Meirion hesitated, looked from one to the other. 'The Picts say —'

'Yes?' prompted Nai.

'They say you are an outlaw,' blurted the farmer, his face pale. 'They describe you precisely, even down to the scar at your throat and your manner of speaking. They say the High Lord Custennin has declared you a murderer!'

'I see.' Nai swallowed, drank from the beaker of mare's milk. 'And if you do not hand me over?'

'They will treat us as rebels against our lawful master. They will burn the farm, kill those who resist and sell the rest into slavery!'

Nai placed the beaker deliberately on the table. 'How many?'

'Five at the gate. They say the farm is surrounded.'

'All Picts?'

Meirion nodded, gulping frantically. 'I have a wife and children. Our people are farmers, not warriors. They will slaughter us!'

'What proof do we have they come from Custennin?'

The portly man frowned. 'I am not sure.'

Nai glanced at Seradwen, his face expressionless, then at the blackness of the window. 'How long was I asleep?'

'Dawn is not far off.' Meirion collapsed onto a stool, shivering. 'They want our answer, now!'

His face was pleading, and Nai felt pity for him, caught unprepared by events of which he had no experience.

'It will be all right,' he said inadequately, and patted the fleshy shoulder.

'The laws of hospitality —' Meirion gestured helplessly. 'If were not for the children . . . And they say the High Lord Custennin . . .' His voice trailed away, returned with new strength. 'We should not abandon you. The laws of God and Man demand we protect our guest.'

'Not beyond all reason,' Nai said as gently as he was able.

Seradwen snorted, stepped forward. 'Outside the gate, you say? Let us go and speak with them.'

She strode from the room and Nai followed, trying to imbue his walk with confidence, glad of the shield slung over his back and the war-knife in its sheath at his side. Meirion brought up the rear, scurrying to keep pace, his lantern waving wildly and casting strange shadows along the passage.

The house was silent. Even at this hour of the night Nai would have expected some noise, and he wondered whether the inhabitants were hiding in their rooms, waiting until the worst was over and he had been delivered up as the sacrifice for their safety.

Seradwen paused on the portico and Meirion pushed ahead of her. A man with a spear patrolled around the inner courtyard, scanning the roof line, while a second sentry sat at the bottom of the steps. The lamps had been extinguished or allowed to burn out, and the moon had long since set, so the only light came from the stars in the sky, sailing above the clouds. Meirion muttered a word of apology and closed his lantern to avoid ruining the men's night vision.

The sentry leapt to his feet as he sensed their presence. He grabbed Meirion's cloak as the portly man brushed past him.

'Did he agree?'

Embarrassed, Meirion jerked his head at Nai. The sentry's eyes were large and liquid in the dark. He released the cloak and held his hands out to Nai in supplication.

'I have a woman and daughter, warrior. Bodgath says the painted ones are mortal men, but I have never seen mortal men who look like that.'

'Be easy,' growled Nai. 'They will not harm you.'

The man flinched at the sound of Nai's voice, backed away with a bow. 'Lord be praised,' he muttered, resuming his post at the foot of the steps, and Nai wondered which Lord he meant.

The second sentry was of a different mettle. He halted at their approach, gave them a rough salute. 'No sign of the heathen. If they come over the roofs or the wall I shall be ready for them.' He grounded his spear, spoke directly to Nai. 'I used to deliver the young colts to Din Erbin for Mordav. I remember you, Chieftain, and the big man you rode with, Gorthyn mab Erfai. Good fortune go with you.'

Nai inclined his head in thanks.

The door in the wall was now heavily locked and barred. The spearman ushered them through and locked it again. The sound of the beam dropping into position behind them had a finality about it.

'It will not stop a determined attack, but it comforts the people,' said Meirion. He shuffled awkwardly. 'Some of them are willing to fight. Most though are like the first man: scared, both for their own sake and their families'.'

Nai felt he should say something, but could find no words. He doubted whether the Picts had any real designs upon the farm: he was the one they wanted, and if they could make him come out alone so much the better. He suspected they were bluffing about their numbers. They were certainly more than the five who had shown themselves, but not the twenty or thirty they would need to storm the place now it was on its guard.

Seradwen took his arm. 'I do not like this,' she said softly. 'And not just because you are an old friend.' There was the tiniest hesitation before the last word.

The outer yard was busy. Here the torches had been kept burning, though Nai was pleased to see someone had taken his advice and there were none around the gate. A group of men armed with a mixture of spears, knives and axes were gathered by one of the barns. Hoewgi seemed to be hectoring them, though most were squatting against the side of the building in a manner which suggested a distinct lack of enthusiasm for his speech.

Others were moving between the barns, carrying brooms, pitchforks, buckets and blankets in and out of the horse stalls. Bodgath was leaning on a stick supervising this activity. Nai moved in his direction, drawing Seradwen with him, although Meirion would clearly have preferred them to go directly to Hoewgi.

'Always start this early?' said Nai by way of greeting.

The little man grinned at a point somewhere behind his right shoulder. 'Bodgath thought might as well start work since all up and about anyway. Sentries covered themselves in glory. Lucky not to have their throats slit.' He spat neatly onto the cobbles. 'Alarums and excursions. Himself is proper mithered,' he added, jerking his head at Hoewgi.

'Picts still by the gate?'

Bodgath nodded. 'Sitting cross-legged in a half circle. One seems to be chanting gibberish to himself and pointing a stick at the farm. Hard to tell if he is possessed by demons, or a magic man.'

'He could well be.'

'Ah.' Bodgath's intake of breath was expressive. 'You know something of these strangers. Thought you must when they demanded you by name. Were they waiting for you?'

'I think so.'

The little man's head bobbed up and down as he considered this. 'Why?'

Seradwen's grip tightened on Nai's arm.

'At first because they believed I could tell them the where-abouts of a friend of mine. But I think something has changed. I fear they may have found him already.'

'And now?'

'If I am right they no longer need me.' Nai shrugged. 'They are a vengeful people, and I have killed a few of them.'

Hoewgi finished his lecture and walked across, nodding curtly at Seradwen, his face furrowed with concern. Bodgath opened his mouth to speak then closed it again at the sight of the farmer, whose finery – stained with wear now – looked ridiculous against the bustle of activity in the yard. Nai guessed the man had not slept, and that the night had been a long one.

Seradwen squeezed his arm and slipped away into the stables.

'Tell me,' said Hoewgi, ignoring her departure, 'is it true you are an outlaw?'

'No,' answered Nai, telling his only direct untruth since his arrival at the farm. (And even then, he was not certain it was an untruth.) 'Think upon it, Hoewgi. If Custennin wanted me, he would send his own men to fetch me, not these barbarians from the far north. They lie.' Under his breath he sent up a prayer that the Picts did not have Isgofan or another of Custennin's warriors with them.

'The laws of hospitality constrain me,' Hoewgi said, rubbing at his cheeks and eyes. 'I do not know what I should do.' He removed his hand and stared at Nai, hoping he would make the decision for him.

Nai smiled thinly. 'Let me speak with them.'

The farmer heaved an ill concealed sigh of relief. 'Of course,' he said, gesturing towards the walkway above the gate. 'That is what you should do.'

The platform was wooden, and more recent than the wall: a rickety staging constructed as a lookout when the times grew ever more uncertain. The farm might not be capable of resisting a determined band of warriors, but no doubt it had over the years seen off lesser assaults by parties of wanderers from the east, the dispossessed who came to beg and stayed to loot if the pickings seemed easy.

Nai let his vision adapt to the night, then clambered up the ladder and cautiously poked his head over the wall. The Picts were sitting in a semicircle, exactly as Bodgath had said. Four were unmoving, mere shadows in the darkness. The fifth, in the centre, was weaving backwards and forwards, holding something in his hands, droning softly to himself.

'The grass is wet for sitting in idleness,' he called down to them.

'Not so wet as the blood of our kinsmen.' He could not see which of them had spoken, but the drone continued unbroken.

'What do you want?'

'You, Nai mab Nwython. Three times you have killed, and three times the shades of our kinsmen have cried out to us for vengeance.'

'Come down!' cried another. 'Come down to us!'

The words were taken up in a chorus. It seemed to him that there were many more than four voices raised against him, chanting 'Come down. Come! Come! Come!' with a rhythm that made him think of blood, drumming through his head till he thought it would burst. And that was not the worst part. Underlying the chorus he could still hear the drone, circling, circling all the while, pulling the soul from his body, drawing him down into the dark.

His hands gripped the coping stone along the top of the wall. His fingers slipped under the ledge, whitened, the rough mortar cutting into his skin. The stone shifted under his grasp, and for a moment he was tempted to tear it loose and cast it down upon their heads.

'Steady, old crow,' said Bodgath.

Startled, Nai released his grip and drew a deep breath.

'Thought you were going to topple over the wall.' The little man stood beside him and peered into the night. 'Where are they then? I can hear them right enough, but blessed if I can see them.'

The Picts had moved while Nai's attention was distracted. The place where they had been was full of shadow and the faint gleam of dew in the starlight, and he could see by the darker patches in the grass where they had sat and walked, but of the men themselves there was no sign. The chorus of voices sounded more distant, as if they had retreated out into the meadows, well away from the cluster of buildings, yet the drone was if anything closer at hand.

'You can hear them?'

Bodgath snorted. 'I may be old but I'm not deaf. Of course I can hear them. "Come, come, come!"' he squeaked in falsetto.

'And the drone? Can you hear that?'

It rang through Nai's head, burrowed into his ears and buzzed there like a trapped fly; vibrated through his flesh and bone, set his teeth on edge and his muscles trembling.

The little man frowned. 'Drone?'

Nai imitated the sound and at once wished he had not, for it made his head ache and pulled him deeper into the madness, made him think of jumping from the wall and running out into the darkness with his arms outstretched to greet whatever awaited him.

'No,' said Bodgath. 'I cannot hear anything like that. Only those rogues in the meadow, sounding like a parcel of children about one of their games.' He peered at Nai's chest. 'It bothers you?'

'Yes.'

He scratched his jaw, sniffed. 'Dirty outlanders. I don't hold with coming to another man's land and stirring things up. They're frightening the horses.'

Nai could feel the sweat trickling down his forehead as he fought the compulsion to leap over the wall. The drone wound around him, sucking him down as a river might suck down a leaf floating on its surface.

'Old Bodgath has the mending of this,' said the little man, reaching into a pouch on his belt. 'Duck below the wall.'

'What is it?'

Bodgath grinned, a flash of teeth in the dark. One hand pushed Nai down below the level of the coping, urged him to sit. The other fiddled with what appeared to be a piece of wood or bone and a length of cord, carefully shaking out the coils in the string.

'Ready?' he said. 'Haven't done this since Mordav died.'

He began to whirl it about his head, gently paying out the cord. 'Got a bigger one at home,' he said, which was the climax of an ancient joke, and cackled wildly at his own wit.

Faster and faster he went, and as the slat of wood whirled through the air it made a roaring, whizzing sound, like the rush of wind which accompanies a sudden downpour.

'Come to my land, would they, and raise up their magics against our guest?' Bodgath screamed against the increasing noise. 'This is my place, as it was my father's before me and his father's before that, all the way back to the beginning when we all lived in the forest and Belin's Hound taught us how to speak to the horses. I'll not have it, I say, I'll not have it.'

The little man lumbered around the platform, a slow heavy dance that involved much shuffling and stamping, lifting first one leg then the other, bringing them down hard on the boards. The whole structure shook and trembled. Nai clamped his hands over his ears and pressed back against the wall, wondering whether he would be able to jump clear if the staging collapsed.

He could see Hoewgi and his brother standing open mouthed in the torch glow, gaping up at the whirlwind of sound the little man had created. The farmworkers were pointing, their faces avid with delight, and a few were imitating Bodgath's clumsy dance, shifting slowly from one foot to the other.

Seradwen moved alone, swimming in and out of the shadows, long hair loose around her shoulders, hands and arms describing complicated patterns in the air. She danced with her whole body, with every bit of her being, and the sight of her made Nai's heart glad.

Deafened, Nai could feel the laughter rising within him. In the east faint hints heralded the dawn, while in the north clouds were gathering. He could smell the rain on the air, taste it on his tongue even as the noise battered at his body. All thought of the Children of Menestyr and their summoning drone was gone, blown away by the roar of the storm Bodgath was calling down upon them.

He wanted to ride, to be with Coal galloping along the crests of the hills, the wind in their faces and the rain at their heels. He wanted to shout and laugh and dance, to hurl his defiance at his foes. He believed that if he were to cast himself from the wall this very moment waves of sound would bear him up like the waves of the sea, and he would fly across the woods and fields like an eagle searching for its prey, floating and spiralling on the currents of the air, and when he found them he would stoop down upon them and drive them forth, harrying them from hidey-hole to hidey-hole, and when he had done with them they would trouble him no more, not now or ever.

Gradually Bodgath drew in the cord and slowed the whirling slat of wood. As the sound lessened Nai heard the horses in the meadows, whinnying and neighing, the thunder of their hooves as they ran round and round the pastures. Below him in the stables the mares were calling back and forth, trumpeting their challenges and kicking at the stalls.

'Stirred them up,' Bodgath said with satisfaction. 'Will rain soon. Look!'

He pointed. The dawn was coming much faster than Nai had expected. The wood beyond the fields was already visible, the brown trees tossing in a wind which did not reach as far as the villa. Nai shivered, suddenly cold, looked above him at the sky, at the gathering clouds and the fading stars. His sense of time was oddly distorted, for it seemed to take forever to roll his head back upon his neck, his gaze sliding slowly from the horizon up into the endless vault of the heavens. His shoulders and the base of his neck ached as if he had sat unmoving through the whole night. The sky was lightening with every passing moment and the birds were singing sweet and insistent all around him.

'What falls as rain here will be snow on the higher ground.' Bodgath's voice came from far away. 'It is time for you to go out into the wilderness of the world, old crow.'

'Who are you?'

'Nobody.' The little man's lips twitched in a smile. 'I am less than nothing, a man who loves horses and the land of his forebears.'

'What are you?'

It was day now, true day. The clouds were black, the sun a watery ring with no strength. It was bitterly cold, the first few drops of rain falling fat and heavy on Nai's upturned face. The horses had calmed, and those in the pastures had returned to their grazing. He could see the tracks where they had galloped the circuits of the fields, following the neat lines of the fences as if marking their own boundaries, churning the soft ground to mud with their sharp hooves. He could also see a line of dark bruises leading away from the farm. A gash of white showed where a clumsy body had broken a rail while crossing a fence. The trail continued across the meadow, swerved at one point as if those who made it had met something that frightened them, then ended in the shadows under the trees.

'What are you?' repeated Nai.

The spell seemed to break and the world leapt back into its normal state. Bodgath was coiling the cord of his weather-maker around his hand, muttering to himself. Rain was falling on the wood in writhing wind-blown sheets, though they themselves were on the very edge of the storm and threatened by nothing more than a few drops.

'What am I?' said Bodgath in surprise. 'Why, one who would not have you fall into the hands of your enemies.' He scratched his scalp with his free hand, stowed the bundle of string and wood in his pouch, pulled a cap from somewhere within his tunic and stuck it on his head. 'That's better. Now, where's my stick?'

'You remind me of a friend,' Nai said as he gave it to him.

'The one those devils want?' Bodgath nodded towards the wood where the storm raged.

'Yes.'

The little man cackled. 'He is no doubt a great lord, accustomed to living in a fine hall with good food and plenty of drink. Not like poor old Bodgath, who has outlived two masters and does not care for the third; poor Bodgath who often goes hungry at night.'

He stilled, and his eyes drifted across Nai's face, settled on a point behind the warrior's left ear. 'You should find him, old crow. It is hard to be alone among enemies.'

'Yes.'

'Look in the east,' Bodgath said dreamily, his gaze focused on the activity in the yard. 'Not far. Out of my lands, but not far. Find him, and fetch the Lady home again, that is what you must do.'

'The Lady?' Nai spoke softly, afraid to break the little man's reverie.

Bodgath made no reply. He turned and started down the ladder, crooning an old lament to himself:

'High the hills, chill the wind,
Thin the cloak around my shanks,
Poor the pasture, hard my bed.
My Master's hall is dark tonight.
Roofless, lampless; no candle light.
Brambles twine where the hearth fires burned.'

Frowning, Nai made to follow him. As he waited for the shapeless cap to clear the way, a great gibbering and wailing arose from under the trees. Nai froze, one foot already stretched for an upper rung. It was the sound of a hunt cheated of their prey.

'They want you very badly,' said Bodgath, peering up past Nai.

Unable to speak he nodded, swallowed hard, moved across the platform and gripped the wall. Behind him he heard Bodgath hauling himself up onto the platform again, cursing softly.

The rain had stopped but the storm still blew across the wood.

The boughs of the trees waved in the gale, swinging wildly back and forth, flashing white, brown, ivy-green against the grey sky. Nai could see further into the wood now, into the flattened and trampled undergrowth, the swirls of dead leaves whipped and dropped by the wind. Figures moved against the gold and umber background: men and horses flickering in a line that broke and reformed among the trunks.

Most were retreating deeper into the wood, but one split away from the others, urged his mount towards the edge of the trees. He crossed the stream and rode out into the open, arms spread wide in an attitude of prayer.

'Nai mab Nwython!' he shouted. 'Nai mab Nwython! I am Peythan mab Menestyr, and Fferog was my son. Are you listening, you who are a dead man walking?'

His horse reared and plunged. Behind him the tempest scoured the trees with renewed force, sent sticks and leaves whirling into the air.

'Do you hear me, Nai?'

His voice was powerful enough to raise echoes above the storm. Nai leaned forward, hands white on the top of the wall. 'I am listening,' he called.

The dun pony wheeled in a tight arc, bucking and twisting. Peythan kept control with his legs alone, not once lowering his arms.

'I will drink your blood, Nai mab Nwython. I will drink your blood, however far and however long you run. My curse is upon you, Nai mab Nwython.'

He held the pose a moment longer, a crucified rider staring at the farm. Nai could sense the power of his gaze even across the meadows that separated them, the eyes burning into him, memorizing his shape and stance. Then the arms dropped to the reins and the horse sprang away into the wood, scattering sods of earth from under its hooves.

Bodgath shook his stick, mumbled below his breath. Nai's hair prickled. His skin crawled and his throat tightened. His sight blurred. He wiped his face, panting, and as his vision returned he saw hail was falling on the fields in a shower of hard whiteness that swept across the grass towards the wood.

'You should leave now while they are busy,' Bodgath said calmly. 'There is a side gate between the buildings. The outer barns will hide you from them.'

'What of you?' Nai gestured at the farm. 'Will they not return?'

'I think not, once you are gone. And if they do . . .' The little man shrugged. 'The Lord's will be done.'

'Thank you,' Nai said solemnly. 'From the bottom of my heart, I thank you.'

The little man shuffled his feet, stared at the sky. 'Find your companion and make an end, old crow. That will be all the thanks old Bodgath needs.'

CHAPTER ELEVEN

Lindinis had changed since Bedwyr had known it first. In those days – over forty years ago – the place had been half deserted, dying a slow death as wind and frost did their work. A handful of new buildings had been erected around the old market place in the centre of the city, but for the most part the inhabitants had huddled in their ancient houses, patching as best they could, making do with what they had.

Towards the end of Arthur's reign the citizens had embarked upon a determined schedule of reconstruction. They had demolished many of the more dangerous ruins, redesigned the market place, attended to the sewerage system, done much to improve the town. Lindinis would never be Bedwyr's favourite city, yet even he had to admit it was a far pleasanter place than it had been twenty or thirty years earlier. Large areas were still half empty and badly neglected, but the core of the town looked fit to survive a while longer.

The outer section, the area abutting the old wall, was now given over almost entirely to fields and vegetable gardens. Huts and houses straggled along the line of the road, and as Bedwyr rode between them he passed the occupants returning home from work. Some gave him a nod of greeting, but most dropped their eyes and hurried on, eager to be behind closed doors before darkness fell.

Bedwyr reined in on a slight knoll and looked about him. The night before last he had paid for lodgings in the middle of the town, not caring if he left a trail for his enemies to follow. Tonight was different. By this time the Sons of Menestyr would have realized he was not going to Camlann (he smiled at the thought of them lurking around the battle site, waiting for him to put in an appearance) and if one was travelling openly, without the need for concealment, there was no great distance between Camlann and Lindinis. It did not seem wise to spend the night in a public place.

To his right were the fields and huts; to his left was a rubbish-strewn expanse of waste ground, pocked with pools of water and bits of old masonry. He shivered in the failing light, wishing he had paid more attention to his surroundings the other day. The changes made it hard to judge exactly where he was in relation to the city he remembered. Somewhere near here there had been a block of rich men's houses, any of which would suit his purpose admirably if they were still standing, and, more importantly, untenanted.

He continued into the town proper, ignoring the curious stares he received from passers-by. The road, which had once run straight, now twisted and turned to avoid the new edifices: the solid surface made an excellent foundation, and the builders had not hesitated to take advantage of the fact. He turned into an alley where older tenements loomed so far above him that he seemed to be riding into darkness. There were not so many people now, and those he met pulled aside into doorways, waiting until he was safely past before resuming their journeys. Gradually their number dwindled, till at last he was alone, with only the scrape of the pony's hooves for company.

The alley debouched onto a broader thoroughfare. He hesitated, uncertain, staring at the street – milky where the light of the rising moon struck it, striped with long shadows cast by the blank walls and roofs. He pushed back his cloak and touched the hilt of his sword, then ventured out into the open, watching warily for signs of life, the horse's hooves louder than ever in the stillness.

Far away he could hear the sounds of revelry: raucous laughter and drunken shouting. A solitary lamp burned behind a barred window high on his left. Somewhere a child was crying. The air felt heavy, as if it might rain at any moment. He drew in to the side of the street, keeping to the shadows while the moon flitted from cloud to cloud.

In his experience city dwellers tended to cling together like sheep. The few who chose to live out here, in what had once been one of the most prosperous sections of the town, were the misfits and oddities, those with a hatred of their fellow human beings, or with secrets real and imaginary. At this very moment there would be eyes assessing whether he was dangerous, whether he was worth attacking for his possessions.

He should have wrapped the pony's hooves to reduce the noise on the cobbles.

The first door he reached was of oak studded with iron, and looked as if it were used on a regular basis. Then came an alcove the size of a small room, stinking of urine, and beyond it another door hanging on broken hinges. Dismounting, he peered into the darkness, saw the glimmer of white rubble lying in the hallway, marked it in his mind as a possible if he did not find something better, and moved on along the street.

More alcoves, all empty, their floors covered with grit and debris from the street. Once these would have been lockup shops, probably selling luxury goods since this had been a wealthy part of the town and rents would have been high. Another stretch of blank wall, the render crumbling and falling to expose the wood and stone beneath. A third door, less impressive than the first, the steps outside covered with grime as if nobody had passed this way in a long while.

He halted, glanced about him while the rain began to fall. The street was still deserted. He tried the latch, pushing against resistance. The hinges groaned, startling the pony.

Moonlight shone through the opening in the atrium roof. He led the pony inside and shut the door behind them. The great wooden bar was propped against the jamb as if someone had just slipped out for a few moments. He lifted it into place and immediately began to feel a little more secure.

He waited, sniffing the damp air, sure the house was empty. Listening, he heard the creak of timbers, the steady drip of rain from the atrium. He dropped the reins over the pony's head so it would stay by the door, drew his sword and began a cautious investigation of his new quarters.

The tiny rooms around the entrance had at some stage been occupied by squatters, but they were long gone, leaving behind them a collection of empty wine skins and dirt-encrusted blankets. A cracked jug sat incongruously in a wall niche designed to hold a marble bust. A broken brazier sagged under the weight of old ashes, reminding him that he was cold and would need a fire.

The house was the urban equivalent of the original villa at St Helena's, which was what had made him think of it as a refuge. It too had been built in the classic style: an inward looking house, lit by light wells and internal courtyards, isolated from the outside world. First came the hollow space of the atrium, which served as the main reception room, with the other public rooms arranged around it, so all their light and air came from the opening in the atrium roof. Beyond the atrium and reached by a side corridor were the family rooms, laid out in a similar fashion around the much larger garden courtyard of the peristyle.

Bedwyr had always had a hankering for a house of this kind. He had been raised in a rustic version of a villa, and had spent most of his life living in native houses that were part of a larger complex, as at Caer Cadwy. The classic Roman town house with its many variants had for years seemed to him the height of sophistication, the epitome of all that was best about the old civilization. At Caer Cadwy, one slept and sometimes ate in one's house, but daily life was lived elsewhere, in the Great Hall or in the open air. The attraction of a Roman town house was that it formed a self-contained unit: once inside, there was no need to leave for weeks or even months on end.

But those luxurious days were long past. Here there were no slaves to prepare food and tend the furnace that fed the under-floor heating in the best rooms. The house was cold and damp. The plaster was peeling from the walls, and several of the ceilings had either collapsed altogether or else were sagging so badly he did not care to stay under them for any longer than it took to ensure the rooms were empty. The ornamental trees and bushes in the peristyle had run riot, choking the space even at this time of year, blocking the gutters with dead leaves so the ground was soft underfoot. Bedwyr forced a path through the tangle of branches to what he assumed was the rear wall, only to discover yet another door concealed behind the pillars of the colonnade.

The iron catch was stiff with rust. He forced it open, knowing he must be the first to do so in a long time. A watery gleam of moonlight showed him the branches of an apple tree. Stepping forward in surprise, he found himself in what must once have been a fruit and vegetable garden. He could still see the shape of the beds in the grassy hummocks; broken trellising and withered brambles clung to the high walls. The rain was easing and the garden smelled good, making him realize how quickly he had become accustomed to the stench of the city and its mouldering houses.

A short while later Bedwyr was seated in front of a roaring applewood fire in the old kitchen off the atrium, while the pony grazed contentedly in the garden. He had discovered two more exits from the house: one from the peristyle and one from the vegetable garden. Both led into a side street running along the right-hand boundary of the property, and both were firmly barred. He was as safe as he was likely to be in Lindinis, and he had found himself a headquarters from which to operate.

By the clear light of morning the house did not seem so attractive. He woke shivering, wrapped in his cloak on the cold floor beside the ashes of the fire, and the first thing he saw was the greasy black stain under the tiny window, marking the place where generations of cooks had plied their trade. The room was festooned with cobwebs, and he could see his own trail in the thick dust on the floor.

Elsewhere was worse. The atrium had been decorated with marble floor tiles: these were cracked and gouged where somebody had dragged a heavy object across them. The white columns of the peristyle were green with mould. The corridors echoed to the sound of his footsteps, and the rooms, empty of all furniture, had the hollow feeling of somewhere long abandoned. The house was dead – more dead in its way than the Great Hall at Caer Cadwy, because the culture to which it belonged was gone as well. For him the sadness of it was that the house would never be replaced by anything comparable, only by crude peasant huts like those he had seen along the roadside.

Bedwyr prowled the house angrily, inspecting it with the fury of an owner who has returned home after a long absence to find his trusted steward has neglected his charge. When he stood in the courtyards he could hear the sounds of the city drifting over the rooftops, reminding him he had more important things to do, but he told himself it was vital he became familiar with every part of his lair before venturing out.

It seemed to him likely that the Children of Menestyr would by this time have realized he had no intention of visiting the field of Camlann. Presumably they would backtrack to Caer Cadwy, and thence Lindinis, hoping to rediscover his trail. There was always a chance they might try St Helena: it was after all common knowledge that some of the Companions' widows had sought sanctuary at the Convent after the last battle. If they did, they should receive short shrift. The Abbess had smiled meaningfully at him when he had warned her of the danger, and remarked that it took many men to maintain a place this size, men accustomed to dealing with unwanted visitors. Although he did not like her, he had faith in her cold competence.

The pony was grazing peacefully in the garden. He drew fresh water from the well – the rope and bucket so fragile with age he feared they would disintegrate before the task was finished – and propped open the door to the colonnade so the horse could find shelter in the house if the rain began again.

Then he returned to the kitchen. His belongings lay where he had dropped them the night before. He sorted through the pile until he found his spare cloak and a leather cap, which he hoped would change his appearance enough to prevent his hunters from recognizing him straight away. As he put on the cap he heard Celemon laughing scornfully, saying: 'Of course, a disguise! Hide the grey locks, old man: hide the grey locks and regain your youth!'

The sense of her presence was so strong that he paused and glanced about him, half expecting her to walk forth from the shadows.

Her words had bitten more deeply than she had known. Buckling on his sword, he hefted the weight of the blade in his broken hand, lifted the sheath on its straps and let it fall again. 'You are an old man,' he heard her say again. 'The Sons of Menestyr will kill you.'

She had made it sound inevitable, the conclusion any dispassionate observer would reach given the facts.

The long blade slid slowly from the scabbard, pale grey in the dim light. He moved, stepping carefully around the scatter of his possessions, working the sword to loosen his wrists and arms, gently at first, then with increasing speed and power.

In his mind the floor was covered with a fisherman's net, stretched taut so every rope was straight. The mesh was made of equal sided triangles joined by blue knots, and his feet were shifting from knot to knot, always at the perfect distance to keep his body in balance. He twisted and turned as he performed an intricate dance, forwards, backwards, sideways, his feet moving from one imaginary node to another, and his sword described circles in the air, flowing unendingly from one position to another, constantly in motion. Sometimes he took a half pace to break the rhythm, and the net miraculously reformed itself around him, guiding his movements so all he had to do was reach out to the next blue mark, like a man crossing a stream on stepping stones.

Faster and faster he went, parrying a blow by meeting force with greater force, sweeping the blade round so the counter attack surged from the defence, *was* the defence, the two becoming indistinguishable parts of a whole, and he danced around a pillar in the peristyle without any conscious memory of passing through the rest of the house, retreating now before a host of enemies, using the stained columns to cover his flanks, and the nodes were no longer blue but red, the colour of blood, and his legs and arms were tiring, his vision blurring and the sweat dripping down into his eyes, but they were upon him, the Sons of Menestyr, and he was Bedwyr Bedrydant, and he had never been beaten in combat.

Afterwards he sat upon the steps under the colonnade, waiting for his breathing to calm, chuckling at his own vanity. He might be old, but he was still good, and while it might not be true that he had never been beaten – though he had never lost in single combat – he had not slowed as much as one would have expected.

When his heart had stopped pounding and his legs had steadied, he rose and went out into the city in search of his prey.

CHAPTER TWELVE

'I will put you on your road,' she repeated.

'You will not,' Nai growled. 'It is dangerous, woman!' His knuckles were white on Coal's reins. 'Besides, you do not know where I am bound.'

'Small choice of roads from here,' she said sweetly.

She swung into the saddle, saw Bodgath watching her from the foot of the ladder by the gate. The little man raised an arm in salute, then looked away as Hoewgi hurried across the yard, shouldering through the crowd.

'Seradwen! What do you think you are doing?'

She glared down at him. 'Why so worried, cousin? I am leaving. Is that not what you wanted?'

Hoewgi flushed. 'Do not be foolish!' Even in his present disarray he still managed to sound pompous. 'You cannot possibly leave, not with those creatures out there, and certainly not with him.' He gestured harshly at Nai, who lifted an eyebrow.

'Oh but I can.' She was enjoying herself. The wind was cold on her face and the pony was eager beneath her.

'Leave?' said Nai, his voice cool and his eyes like flint. 'You said you were showing me the road.'

'So I am,' she said airily. 'It is a fine morning for a ride.'

Nai pulled his cloak tighter across his shoulders. 'Seradwen, it is bitter cold and about to hail again. Nobody but a fool would go riding on a day like this.'

'We are well matched then,' she called, urging the pony towards the side gate.

'You cannot take her,' Hoewgi said accusingly. 'I forbid it.'

She heard Nai laugh without humour. 'You stop her.'

He passed her with a thunder of hooves, his face set and grim. The door swung back, they ducked beneath the arch, and then they were out in the open, hidden from the Picts by the bulk of the farm buildings.

'Left,' she shouted, and led them at a gallop around the side of the barns.

The air was wet despite the cold, so that everything was slightly damp to the touch and even the leather reins were sticky between her fingers.

'I do not care for your cousin Hoewgi,' said Nai when they slowed at the end of the buildings.

'Mordav's cousin, not mine.'

'This is not wise.'

She grinned and held the pony to a fast trot as they took the track to the river. Nai twisted and looked behind them, but the farm blocked any view of the woods.

'I thought they fled.'

Nai grunted in reply.

'Do you think they are still there?' she persisted.

He brought Coal up so they rode knee to knee. 'They withdrew,' he said. There was an intensity about him that she found uncomfortable. 'A withdrawal is not flight.'

'We need high ground,' she said, and indicated the hills. 'The quickest route is beside the river.'

'For this I required a guide?' he snapped, but there was a hint of warmth in his eyes.

'You will later,' she said and set the pony's head for the path by the river as the clouds closed in and hail swept across the valley.

To begin with they went beside the water, climbing gently past rain swollen cataracts where the fish had run that autumn and she had gone out with Bodgath to watch their leaping glory, climbing towards the summer grazing grounds of the lower moors, climbing through drifts of trees, birch and ash and pine, through rocky defiles where the boulders were blurred with moss, the ponies' hooves sometimes scraping on the stone, through tiny meadows of harsh green grass that quaked underfoot, and all the while they went in silence until they reached a place where the river valley became too narrow and too rough for horses. Here they paused.

'I should have made you go back at once.' Nai stretched in the saddle, stared down at the farm below. 'Too late now.'

She followed the direction of his gaze and saw the tiny figures venturing out from the wood. They rode in a body to the farm gate, ten or twelve of them, and halted.

'Will the farm be all right?' she asked hesitantly.

'The Picts have tried threats; now they will try blandishments.'

She looked at him and realized he was a stranger, that the youth she had known was long gone, swallowed by time even as Mordav had been swallowed.

'I think –' He shaded his eyes. 'Can you see?'

'Somebody on the platform. Hoewgi, I expect. He's waving his arms towards the river.'

Nai lowered his hand. 'They will have guessed that much for themselves.' His tone was dry.

'He can hardly tell them anything else,' she said, driven to defend the man despite her dislike. 'He does not know anything else.'

'No more he does.' Nai sounded amused. 'Ah! See, they follow. Your friends and kinsfolk are safe.'

'They are not my kin.'

At first the Picts rode slowly, spread in a line to hunt for tracks, obviously not trusting what they had been told. Then, just before they vanished from sight under the shadow of the hills, they broke into a canter.

'Marriage kin,' said Nai. 'Come, guide, we should move. Where now?'

She urged her pony forward. 'This way. Over the water and along the ridge.'

They forded the river where it raced fast and shallow at the mouth of the gully, splashing through the peaty water, and passed beneath the overhanging trees to find not so much a track as the memory of a track, a fading hollow that in spring would be buried beneath the bracken. At this time of year they could just make out its course, twisting and winding through the trees and brambles, following the ridge for a while then suddenly plunging down the slope into the neighbouring valley.

She noticed how warily Nai rode, his right hand never far from the quiver of spears hanging at his saddle, his eyes constantly scanning their surroundings. When she made to speak, he motioned her to silence.

As they neared the moor the land became steadily wilder, the trees smaller and more gnarled, carved by the wind into strange shapes. Twice they startled deer, and once they saw the traces of a bear, paw-prints and a scattering of dung, though thankfully not the creature itself. The weather worsened, growing colder and wetter. Mist hung between the trees, distorting the misshapen forms still further, so that several times Seradwen saw what she thought was a figure watching them, only to discover a twisted oak when she came closer. Once her pony, Mischief, nickered as if in greeting, but there was nobody there.

'We are close to the open ground,' she said after a while. 'Now you must choose. We can stay under the cover of the trees and skirt around to the east until we reach the headwaters of the River Oak.' She paused, trying to assess his reaction, but he gave her no clue. 'Or we can cross the wasteland.'

'Which would you do?'

'With pursuers?' She thought for a moment. 'Cross the moor. If we move fast enough we can be hidden before they reach the tree line.'

'Bodgath promised snow.' There was the faintest question in his voice.

'Then it will snow,' she said firmly.

Nai grinned. 'I thought as much. The moor then.' He reached behind him and removed a sword and scabbard from the saddle, looped the baldric over his head and shoulder, adjusting the position until the weapon hung to his satisfaction.

Seradwen stared. 'I did not know you had a sword.'

She had seen his war-knife earlier, and the javelins were obvious. A sword was different. A sword was the weapon of the well-born, worth as much if not more than a good stallion; an object designed expressly for the purpose of killing people. She had not expected Nai to be carrying a sword.

'It was Gorthyn's,' he said curtly.

The mist lifted as they left the trees behind and ventured into the open at a hand gallop, Seradwen in the lead and setting the pace, carefully watching the ground under the heather roots, detouring around the places where the recent storms had left the black peat gashed and broken. Ahead of them towered a great tor, a single rock atop a green mound. Around its base lay a mass of clitter, small stones and large scattered arbitrarily across the short cropped grass. The horses were panting by the time they struggled up the last of the slope, and Seradwen slowed Mischief to a walk once they were over the brow of the hill.

Nai dropped the reins and slid from the saddle. 'Wait,' he said.

The tor fell neatly into two halves, divided by a patch of muddy grass which was a continuation of the green mound, running right into the heart of the stone. Seradwen watched Nai scramble up the spit of grass, then snorted and followed him, keeping low. He glanced back angrily, his boots sliding on the mud, and shook his head in exasperation.

The space at the top was like a fortress, a hollow between two rearing walls of stone. Nai removed his shield and propped it against the stone, then flung himself up the nearest wall in a burst of energy. Seradwen paused to study the rock face, saw it was old and weathered, full of crevices and fissures, chose her route and reached the top at much the same time. The two of them flattened themselves against the summit and looked back the way they had come.

The woods were blue with mist. As they watched a flock of crows flapped into the air, circled in a desultory fashion and settled again.

Seradwen felt Nai shudder beside her.

'What is it?'

'That is how it began. A disturbance of crows.' He rolled onto his side, examined her face. 'You should not be here. Why are you here?'

'You could have prevented me had you wished.'

He frowned. 'You are a grown woman. You make your own choices. But the Sons of Menestyr are dangerous men. And they seem to have the support of Custennin himself.'

She scraped at a growth of lichen. 'What do they want?'

'They seek a man called Bedwyr, and through him – though they may not realize it yet – the Lady Gwenhwyvar.'

'Gwenhwyvar? Arthur's Gwenhwyvar?'

He nodded. The lichen unpeeled from the stone in a furry white patch.

'What has this to do with you?' The Nai she had known had been a very ordinary young man, one among many of Gereint's warriors, with no close kin except his foster family. Bedwyr and Gwenhwyvar were the stuff of legends. If they still lived and wanted help, they would surely seek it from one of the royal houses of Prydein, not from a landless warrior with no kinsmen of any renown.

Nai's smile was crooked. 'Erfai was my foster father. But that is not why.'

She blushed that he had followed her thoughts so easily. 'Of course,' she said. 'Erfai was Bedwyr's nephew. I suppose that makes you a foster great-nephew?' She peered at him doubtfully, not sure the relationship had any meaning.

'I am probably the closest thing to a kinsman he has left. But that is not why I am here.'

He turned onto his belly and stared intently at the tree line.

'Why then?' she hissed, but he laid a hand on her arm to quiet her.

A shape moved under the dark trees, resolved into a man leading a pony. Even at this distance Seradwen could see the sweat matting the animal's coat; it had been ridden hard, and looked blown. The man squatted to examine the ground, straightened and gazed towards the tor. Although Seradwen knew he could not possibly see them, he half raised a hand in a mocking semblance of greeting before retiring back into the trees.

'Peythan.' Nai pushed himself away from the rim of the rock, let his feet dangle over the drop to the inner hollow.

'Who?'

'The one who shouted the challenge after Bodgath's storm.'

'What does he want?' Seradwen slithered down the face of the stone until she stood on solid earth again.

'Me. I killed his son.' Nai's voice was matter of fact. 'I would imagine he has come on ahead to find our trail before the snow hides it.'

Seradwen swallowed. 'What do we do now?'

'Mount and ride.' Nai took the slope at a run, used the horns to haul himself up into the saddle. 'You are the guide. Choose a direction.'

Before them the hills and valleys rose in great brown and yellow sweeps to where the massive clouds piled the sky above them. Shafts of sunlight shifted from granite tor to granite tor as shadows fled hurriedly across the landscape. The weather was changing fast and the most northerly clouds were ominously hard and grey. Seradwen could smell Bodgath's promised snow on the wind.

'This way,' she said, and led them deeper into the moor.

They talked as they rode, talked of many things: of Bedwyr and Arthur and the mysterious chalice sought by the Sons of Menestyr; of Gorthyn mab Erfai, Nai's friend and foster brother, and Eremon mab Cairbre, their old foe, slain by Nai on a moonlit beach; of horse-breeding and the growing of crops; of the unsettled state of Dumnonia and the summer's attempted ousting of Custennin by the leader of his warband; of Bodgath and the dislike felt for him by Hoewgi and the brothers, who were jealous of his knowledge.

'Mordav?' Nai's voice was gentle.

'It was a good marriage. I grew to love him.' She gestured helplessly, said again: 'It was a good marriage.'

He nodded slowly. 'You never regretted the freedom of your youth?'

She curled her lip. 'I grew up, Nai. People do. The old life began to bore me. I needed what Mordav could give me: a sense of purpose, a sense of belonging. We cannot all live our lives like you warriors, with no thought for the morrow, safe in the knowledge that someone else will provide.'

'Ah well,' he said a little thickly, 'at least we do not see as many morrows as most of you farmers.'

They continued in silence, descending a long slope to the clear brown waters of a stream. Here they dismounted and moved carefully along the bank, looking for a point where they could cross easily. The cutting was deep and the stream bed rocky, and by the time they came to a suitable place it had begun to snow, in small hard lumps that stung their exposed faces.

For a while they kept to the far bank of the stream, until the ground grew marshy and they were forced to climb out of the valley and onto a featureless pale brown plain. The snow thickened, the flakes falling fatter and softer; already a thin sprinkling lay on the hills.

The wind had dropped. A sense of silence and utter loneliness swept over Seradwen. In the distance long ridges rode in dusky waves against the horizon, but in the foreground the landscape was fast becoming as grey and dreary as the sky above. She climbed into the saddle, gesturing to Nai that he should do likewise, and arranged her cloak about her, pulling the hood over her hair.

'We could lose them now,' she said, her voice loud in the stillness. 'Before the snow settles and leaves fresh tracks.'

This open land was nothing like so open as it seemed. The ground was a mass of hollows and declivities, of ridges and false crests. The mist was closing in and visibility was shrinking rapidly: even as she waited for Nai's response the far hills were swallowed by the greyness.

'Where do you want to go when we have lost them?' she demanded when he made no answer.

'East.'

She tried to remember the shape of the moors. The south and its soft farmland lay behind them. If they went east, they should strike somewhere along the headwaters of the River Oak, which ran through a tree-clad valley that would shelter them from the storm. To go west or north was dangerous, for nothing except the bleak high ground lay in those directions. They had seen no signs of life since reaching the moor, not even the wild ponies who ranged freely summer and winter, which suggested the animals knew bad weather was coming and had fled to the lowlands. Only a fool would ride out into the worst of the moor at this time of year.

'We must go east,' Nai said heavily. 'I do not think we can survive a blizzard on the high moors.'

'Which way would you go if you were alone?'

He thrust back his hood and glared at her. 'I am not alone.' Flakes settled and melted on his dark hair.

'They will find us in the river valley.'

'Perhaps.' He shrugged, let his hand brush the butts of the javelins waiting in their quiver.

'They do not need to hound our trail when they know where we are going,' she said, thinking aloud. 'And you cannot fight them all, however good you may be with your spears.'

Nai shifted in the saddle impatiently. 'No,' he snapped. 'No, I will not take you out into the wasteland to die there.'

'Yet you would choose that route if you were alone.'

She swung Mischief's head to the north and kicked him into a trot, ignoring Nai's protests.

The touch on his face was soft, melting into the bristle of his young beard. The flakes caressed as they fell, lay on the ground like the silver scales of a trout's flanks, shrank and vanished from moment to moment.

The ponies had long since slowed to a walk. Nai patted Coal's neck as the animal plodded up the long hill, grunting to himself. Nai huddled deeper into his cloak, flexed numb fingers within their leather gloves. Seradwen was ahead of him, a shapeless bundle swaying in rhythm with her horse's motion. He suspected she was asleep.

On the far side of the crest the land fell away. The sky was huge, a hard slate-grey, and the wind was strengthening again. The top of the hill was strewn with boulders of all shapes and sizes, black and green with moss or lichen, and the ponies picked their way cautiously, for the stones were buried deep in the heather roots and not easy to see.

Nai's face was icy with the chill of the wind. He wrapped a fold of his cloak around his nose and mouth, and closed his eyes to rest them briefly.

He came to with a start as the unwisdom of dozing while following a sleeping guide occurred to him.

Seradwen and Mischief were no longer ahead of him.

His heart leapt within him and he was abruptly wide awake. The ground at the foot of the hill was rent into fissures of dark swampy soil running in every direction, so that Coal had been steering a path from tussock to tussock of moor grass or heather root, choosing his own route without reference to the other horse. Even as Nai realized what had happened Coal came to a halt.

Nai shouted and slipped from the saddle. His feet hit the earth like two unfeeling blocks of wood, so he would have fallen had he not clung to the pony. When he stamped up and down to restore some life, the ground squelched ominously under his boots. The snow was still falling, fat wet flakes that melted as they landed.

'Seradwen!' he bellowed. His breath hung in the air until it was caught by the wind and blown away.

He seemed to be standing in a marshy plateau on what felt like the top of the world, though mist was all around so he could not see the horizon. He turned his face to the sky and sniffed the wind, wished he had not. The flakes were suddenly falling thick and fast, and the wind smelled of the north, of ice and blizzards.

'Seradwen!' His voice was hoarse and feeble amid the muffling snow.

'Here!'

The reply was faint. Nai peered into the mist, seeing shapes everywhere. He took a step forward and the earth quaked beneath his feet. Coal refused to move. The horse's hooves were sinking into the peat where he stood, but though Coal quivered and twitched he would not come on.

Nai soothed him, tried again. His own feet were sinking now, and he could feel himself beginning to panic.

'Beware!' Seradwen's voice came from over to his right. 'Bog!'

'I know!' he growled, and struggled to turn the pony. Coal was obdurate. The snow stuck to Nai's lashes, blinding him. Angrily he dashed a hand across his face, and the pony flinched.

'Come on!' he screamed.

The world narrowed to a white blur. The wind whined across the peat bog. Flurries of snow stung his face as he sought to make the horse back up, shoving with his shoulder against the muscular chest. His hands were freezing even through the leather gloves. Ice was forming on his cloak, in his hair. Coal stood foursquare against the storm, patient with misery, the veins on his muzzle thick cords, tail drooping. The flakes were still melting on his body, but he too had ice tangled in his mane, crystal pebbles glistening in the coarse hair.

Nai drew a deep breath. Everything was swirling black and white. 'You must move,' he said. 'You move or you die.' He was pleading now, the anger gone. 'Come,' he said, taking the reins loosely in one hand and walking slowly around Coal's body, using the tussocks as stepping stones, not looking behind him to see if the pony would follow.

He was aware of the slack being taken up, the reins pulling taut, then with a sucking sound the horse lumbered in his wake, guiding him from behind by baulking when Nai chose a route he did not approve.

'Where are you?' Her voice was faint. It sounded farther away than earlier.

'Stay still!' he shouted. 'Keep calling. I will come to you.'

He lost all sense of time. There was only the wind and the cold kiss of the snow, the tug of the reins in his left hand, the next few paces of ground, the dark green hummocks fast being buried under the blizzard, the bright patches where black water lurked, the borders of the pools marked by soft rushes poking above the white drifts. And through it all, Seradwen's voice, singing an old antiphonal song about two brothers who loved the same girl and went hunting together, and only one of them returned alive.

Like a thread her song drew him, so it seemed to him that even as he was leading Coal so her singing was leading him, pulling him out of the quagmire to the solid earth. He raised his eyes to the whirling storm, half hoping to see her form loom out of the mist, but there was nothing, just the tiny white specks floating against the black, or the black floating against the white.

Siren song, he thought, and wondered whether he had not gone astray, whether the song had any existence outside his own head. The cold, coming on top of the last few days with their lack of decent food, was sapping his strength. The snow, where it had settled in drifts against the hollows, looked soft and inviting. One could imagine wrapping oneself in a white mantle and wait out the worst of it. He had food in the saddlebags and Coal might be persuaded to lie as a windbreak.

Arms caught him as he stood contemplating a snowdrift.

'Nai!'

He blinked and the world sprang into focus.

'I thought I had lost you.' Seradwen's face was anxious, the lines around her mouth deeper than he recalled, the flesh ridged into sharp little creases.

'Not so easy,' he murmured.

'This place,' she said. 'It eats the will.'

'Yes.' He shook his head, stared into the whirling greyness. 'Something old. Powerful, callous.'

He could almost see it delineated in the storm: massive, solid as the moorland boulders, wearing the shape of a man wrapped in a cloak the colour of dead bracken. The hair would be the green of the rushes that grew around the black pools, the beard deep and springy as moss. The face would be grey, cleft and cracked like the granite tors, and those parts of the skin which were not hidden by hair and beard would be covered with strange markings, dark and pale patches tinged with yellow like the lichens that encrusted certain stones.

In his mind he heard Bedwyr describing the woodland sanctuary at Porthyle: 'A place where our ancestors talked to the land. Some say it answered them.'

'The spirit of the place,' he said aloud.

Seradwen's grip tightened on his arm. 'Bodgath would say we should not have crossed the moor without making an offering.'

The howl of the wind tore away her words so he did not hear more than half of what she said, but her meaning was clear.

A wise man riding into new land made an offering to the spirit of the place to show he meant no harm, intended no disrespect.

For a small spirit one might make a small offering: a few drops of wine or mead, a morsel of bread and cheese, a mere token delivered with a casual flick of the wrist. For a power like this, presiding over the moors in all their bleak hostility and already roused to anger, something much greater would be necessary.

Nai slumped against the pony's chest, feeling the twitch of the muscles under the coarse-haired skin. Not Coal. They would both die here before he would sacrifice his horse. Not Gorthyn's sword, the next most valuable object he owned. The sword was his last link with his friend and foster brother. Not his war-knife or shield. Not his spears – it would have to be all of them, and that was too much. Food seemed too paltry, and though honey cakes and the like might coax a house or a woodland spirit into helpful behaviour, he doubted whether such titbits would have much effect on what confronted them now.

'We need treasure,' shouted Seradwen.

'Treasure,' he repeated dully. She was right. They needed gold or bronze or copper, good bright sunlit metals to be eaten by the dark soil.

Memory came to him just as a gust caught him and sucked all the air from his lungs, the searing cold like ice in his chest. Staggering, he clung to Coal's coarse mane, the frozen pellets beading the hair hard to the touch even through the thick leather of his gloves. The pony tossed his head and Nai fell, landed on his knees in the wet snow.

Seradwen called his name. The wind shrieked and the horse lurched, his hooves dragging through the snow and narrowly missing his master where he lay huddled on the ground.

Nai grabbed the girth and hauled himself upright, crooning under his breath to calm the pony as he reached for the bag he wanted. The buckle was awkward. The leather jammed on the metal, refused to budge. For a moment it all seemed far too much effort. His eyes were tired, but closing them made no difference to the constant weave of black and white.

The glove was in his teeth, choking him, the leather wet and slick. He tugged, spat the gauntlet away. His hand was numb, yet the metal of the buckle still burned as he forced his bare fingers to fiddle the strap through the loop.

Cloth. A lump, and another lump, wrapped deep inside his spare tunic. His hand tunnelled through the folds. The outlines of the brooches and pins he had taken from his attackers at

Sanctuary Wood were clear to the touch, yet he could not reach them.

In a sudden flash of rage he ripped the tunic from the bag, shook it wildly, the wind nearly tearing it from his grasp. They flew through the air, impossibly bright against the grey the world had become, and plummeted into a snow bank where they lay in a neat half circle.

'For you!' he bellowed as he swayed with the gale, leaning into Coal's reassuring bulk. The tunic flapped and Coal shifted nervously, almost spilling him to the ground again.

Seradwen caught and steadied him. 'See!' she mouthed.

He stuffed the tunic into the bag, bent to rescue the glove before the wind took it, turned to look at his offering. The pieces had begun to sink into the drift – or perhaps they were merely being buried by the continual fall of fresh flakes. The pins had already vanished and the brooches were fast disappearing, leaving only the impression of a circle crossed by a thin bar.

He imagined them slipping deeper and deeper, floating down through the snow to the black earth beneath, and then the earth itself opening up so they went on sinking, very slowly, down down down through the peat to where eager hands with fingers like gnarled heather roots awaited them . . .

'Let us go free,' he muttered to the storm. 'Let us go free.'

They started to walk, slamming their feet hard into the snow to keep themselves awake, reins looped in the crooks of their arms. The ponies followed obediently, keeping pace so there was no pressure on the reins, and all around them the wind whined and the snow flew in flurries, some from the sky, some flung anew from the ground.

For a long while they continued walking, occasionally nudging the other to make sure he or she was still awake. Seradwen appeared to know where she was going, though it seemed to Nai it did not much matter where they went provided they left the heart of the moor behind them. He drove himself on, aware he was close to the end, marvelling at the stamina of the woman beside him, his head and shoulders bowed under the weight of the storm. The cold bit into his bones and the snow came thick and fast, while the grey mist pressed ever closer.

Perhaps the pins and brooches had not been enough. Perhaps the spirit wanted more.

If they froze to death up here it could be months before

anybody found them – assuming they found them at all. Neither the Children of Menestyr nor their friends would ever know what had happened to them. They would become a mystery, their tale trotted out around the fireside to while away a dull winter evening: Seradwen verch – he had forgotten her father's name – and Nai mab Nwython, who rode in search of Bedwyr and Gwenhwyvar and were never seen again by mortal man.

He was desperately tired. Seradwen nudged him, poked him harder with her fingers. Something had changed. He raised his head, but his lashes seemed to have frozen together so the world was a grey-white blur.

The wind had dropped. The snow was still falling, in silence now, and it was not so cold. His ears ached.

'Not much farther,' said Seradwen. 'We must bear a little to the right now.'

Even after Nai removed a glove and carefully wiped his eyes he could not see more than a few paces ahead. The dizzying swirl of the snow was constant, and he floundered blindly through the drifts, sometimes finding himself thigh deep as he broke the crust hiding a hollow.

The flutter of the flakes parted for a moment and he saw a shadow waiting for him, taller than a man, looming grey and motionless in the mist. A wave of pure terror washed over him and he felt the blood freeze within his veins. He swallowed, mouth dry, took another step and tasted despair, bitter at the back of his throat.

'Can you run?' he asked.

'No,' she said, stopping beside him. 'What is it? Not a man, surely; not out here.'

Amid the tumbling snow Nai could not make out any detail, but he did not need to. He already knew how the figure would look: grim and gaunt, the grey skin marked with black and white blotches of lichen, the hair the green of the pithy soft rushes, the beard a tangle of moss. It was angry, and it had come to claim its own.

His legs managed a few more paces before they failed him. He halted and stood with bent head in acceptance of defeat, the last of his strength draining away. He was aware of Coal brushing past without breaking stride, ignoring him, and he let the reins fall free to allow the pony to go. Coal plodded towards the figure, seemingly unafraid, while Nai waited for the end. Behind him he could hear Seradwen saying the *pater noster* over and over to herself.

He shifted uncomfortably, wondering why he was not dead, then looked up cautiously, expecting to see the grey shape towering above him. If anything the figure was farther away than he had thought. The horses were standing slightly beyond it, tails tucked between their legs like dogs, quartering the ground for the few blades of grass that poked through the snow where the covering had been thinned by the wind. Nai frowned, not understanding.

'Well, come on then!' he croaked. Coal started, peered at him curiously before resuming the search for food.

The shape was oddly slender and unnaturally still. Nai limped the last few paces with Coal watching warily, and flung his arms around the figure in a plea for mercy or a quick ending, for some kind of resolution.

The granite was rough under his frozen cheek, and very cold. At first he could do nothing but clasp the pillar, shaking in every limb, while his eyes slowly traced its outline. It was a boundary stone, nearly twice his height, erected by the giants who had owned this land before the coming of true men.

'Did you see it too?' he demanded of Seradwen as she joined him.

She nodded, unable to speak.

The snow fall was lessening, dying away to a few dry specks floating slowly through the dull air. Nai hauled himself upright, still clinging to the pillar. He guessed it had been placed here to mark the division between the safe summer grazing lands and the black peat bogs of the bleak high moor.

The mist was lifting, and somewhere a bird was singing. He could hear running water in the distance, see how the ground folded away into a narrow valley not far from where they stood.

'We are safe,' he said in wonder. 'We are safe.'

Seradwen glanced anxiously at Nai as they followed an animal track along the side of the valley. He was exhausted: his face grey, his movements slow and tentative, like those of an old man.

Here, on the lee side of the cleave, the snow lay thinly, the white clumps of dead grass that had stayed unburied dirty against the dazzle of the dimpled fall. On the other slope the snow was heavier, sculpted into smooth mounds that hid rocks and bushes.

At the bottom of the valley was a black stream running fast and furious over dark boulders, its banks fringed with ice.

'Let me help you into the saddle,' she called above the rush of the water.

Nai paused, one hand clutching Coal for support, and nodded wearily with a shadow of a smile.

With some difficulty she pushed him onto the pony's back, then herself mounted Mischief and led the way. The animal track had begun well, but it quickly dropped towards the dark and uninviting stream. She kept to the higher ground, meandering back and forth to avoid the worst of the slope, with one eye always on Nai.

'My legs are dead,' he croaked before they had gone very far. 'Locked under the saddle horns.' He laughed softly, but it was a laughter that was very close to tears. 'There is a dignity about dying on high moors while engaged on a perilous quest. There is none at all about being trapped in your own saddle.'

Seradwen frowned. Although she was not lost, in the sense that she knew which direction would carry them down from the moor, she did not know exactly where they were in relation to the places where they might find food and shelter, which was what Nai needed. Her original goal – once the decision to cross the moor had been made – had been a farmstead on the banks of the Whitewater. She and Mordav had traded sheep and cattle with the owners in bygone years, and she was sure of a welcome there. But the storm had driven them off course, and although she suspected the dark stream below them was a tributary of the Whitewater, she could not be certain. There were other farms scattered along the borders of the moor, and any of them would do at a pinch, if she could find one.

'Happens to boys,' murmured Nai. 'Not trained warriors.'

She looked back at him. He was slumped awkwardly in the saddle. From time to time his entire body was seized with shivers, great twitching shudders that ran right through him.

The cleave broadened and the first trees appeared: alders and willows growing along the line of the stream, gnarled and bent by the winds so they seemed to be leaning over to admire their own reflections. A fox dashed from bush to snow-clad bush, rolled in a drift with legs waving wildly, suddenly took note of the horses and riders across the stream. For a moment it stared, coat still caked with soft white, then it shook itself and was gone, scuffing the snow in a single line of prints as it set its hind paws exactly in the traces of its fore feet, vanishing over the rim of the valley in a flash of pale russet.

She felt a surge of joy as the fox disappeared. They were alive. They had beaten the storm, the moor and its guardian. Nai might be exhausted, but she did not think there was anything seriously wrong with him that hot food and a warm couch would not cure, provided she found them soon.

The cleave merged with a larger valley and she tried to remember if she had ever come this way before. Everything looked different in the snow. A path angled to the left and passed through a stand of silver birch. The sound of running water grew ever louder. Along one slope the ground looked ragged and broken, even under the snow, and she guessed these were old delvings left by those men of a former age who had scoured the moor for tin or copper. She could smell wood smoke on the air, very faint, and she hesitated, trying to picture which farm was near.

'Go on!' growled Nai.

Frowning, she signalled at him to be silent. It could not be a farmstead. They were still too close to the high moors. She turned to him to seek his advice, but he seemed to have fallen asleep. Unless some other traveller was loose upon the moors in winter, the smoke could only come from one place. If Nai were fit, he would probably prefer to continue. But Nai was not fit and the decision was hers. Gnawing her lower lip, she eased Mischief forward.

From the corner of one eye she glimpsed movement, black against the darkness of the stream, flickering across the shadows of the valley bottom, and her heart leapt for fear that their pursuers had somehow, impossibly, reached here before them.

It was a cow, a shaggy black barrel of a beast with wicked horns. As she progressed around the curve more cattle came into view, their faces mild beneath the savage horns, peering short-sightedly from under their fringes at the newcomers.

Mischief trod delicately, picking his way around the snow the cattle had churned into ridges with their hooves, keeping a wary watch on the splayed horns. Nai was still unconscious, but his pony plodded patiently in Mischief's wake.

Then there was the scent of wood smoke on the still air, seasoned birch and green alder mixed with oak, and under the wood smoke the smell of cooking: mutton and burnt fat.

The light was amber in the afternoon sun. They rounded the final curve of the valley, and there were the buildings swimming honey-pale against the white background, suddenly springing into focus. Even the surrounding granite wall, high enough to keep animals from the enclosure, was more gold than grey.

On either side of the gate were a pair of tall wooden crosses, their outstretched arms limned with snow. The enclosure was dominated by an oblong thatched hall that stood by itself in the middle of the space, another cross towering from its gable. Over in one corner was a second building only slightly smaller than the first, half hidden by a group of huts. More huts were scattered around the area; some looked very new, though it was hard to tell under their covering of snow.

The ponies quickened their pace unbidden. Their hooves rang on stone as they came to a definite track leading to the gate, and a man wearing a shapeless woollen hat appeared from one of the huts, staring in surprise.

'Peace be upon this place,' called Seradwen.

The man took a moment to answer. 'And upon you, lady, and your companion.' He dragged open the wattle barrier, grunting with the effort of breaking the grip of the ice that had sealed it to the ground. 'Where have you come from? Not across the high moor, surely?'

She worked Mischief through the gap and brought him to a standstill. 'We have,' she said. 'And we would beg a night's shelter in consequence. My companion has been too long upon the road. He has need of food and warmth.'

The man blinked, eyed the second pony and its burden dubiously. 'No need to beg, lady. God's welcome is upon you, and upon your steeds, who must be both brave and strong to have brought you safe over the hills. Can your friend dismount?'

Seradwen leant back and nudged Nai. His eyes opened, squinting against the light. 'Where are we?' he growled. 'Who are you?'

The man flinched at the rasp of the broken voice. 'At the monastery of St Martin.'

'St Martin.' Nai closed his eyes with a contented smile.

'Can you dismount?' the man asked anxiously.

'No,' said Nai, still with his eyes shut.

'No,' said the man, 'I do not suppose you can.' He turned and shouted a wordless summons over his shoulder. 'Let me lead you towards the hall. Many of my brothers and sisters are in Chapel, but we should find some help.'

He pushed the gate shut, stuck a finger under his hat and scratched at his head. 'Over the high moor, eh?' he muttered to himself, adding aloud to Seradwen: 'We do not receive many visitors even in summer, but I think you will find our hospitality acceptable. We are not an austere order, you understand, despite our isolation, not the kind who refuse meat, wine and mead, insist on harnessing themselves to the plough and performing work better suited to the beasts which the Good Lord has provided for that very purpose.'

The man led Coal towards the lesser building, talking all the while. Seradwen let the sound of the voice wash over her. The one certainty about monasteries, she thought with relief, was that they were havens of peace and civilization – unless of course they were in parts of the country vulnerable to attack by the Scotti or Saesons. Kings and sub-kings might quarrel, lords might raid their neighbours' cattle, but since the days of the Emperor Arthur only the very rash had interfered with a Christian community. Those who did were cursed by the Church in all its majesty, and vengeance usually fell upon them swiftly.

'Why, I have heard of this young fellow Samson on Piro's Isle off the Dyfed coast,' the guide was saying. Seradwen pricked up her ears at the mention of Dyfed. 'You know about Piro? A most holy man, of good family – his father was one of old Agricola's loyal supporters. When Agricola died and his son Vortepor took control of Dyfed – a great many years ago now, back in the days of the Emperor Arthur – Piro, who was then quite youthful himself, decided upon the contemplative life. Safer, probably, than being at Vortepor's court: Vortepor is famed for his rages. Piro studied at holy Illtud's school, then founded his own community on the isle which will forever bear his name, and over the years gained a reputation for learning and scholarship.'

The man seemed able to talk without the need to draw breath. The story came out in a seamless babble.

'This youngster Samson also studied with holy Illtud, but of course by that time the saint was a very old man. Samson was a bit of a zealot – you know the type, always keen to do more than their neighbour – and Illtud's nephews worried that when God gathered their uncle to him, Samson was likely to succeed Illtud as head of the school, thus depriving them of their birthright. Samson himself was unhappy – Illtud's regime was not harsh enough for him. More than once the aged saint was obliged to rebuke his young pupil for excessive fasting.'

The man stopped and regarded Seradwen. Feeling some response was required, she nodded encouragingly.

'Anyway,' he continued, 'Illtud arranged for Samson to join the community on Piro's Isle, which had a reputation for being austere. It was isolated by the ocean, you see, away from the temptations of the flesh. Young Samson soon impressed the monks with his zeal, and they made him steward of the monastery, a most important post and one which I myself have the honour of holding in our own little community.'

He smiled up at her and gave a modest bow.

'Poor old Piro overindulged one evening. He woke in the middle of the night with a thick head and a full bladder, wandered outside in search of the latrine, missed his way and fell down the well-shaft. You may smile, my lady' – he wagged a finger – 'and indeed the story does have its amusing side, though it was not funny for Piro. The monks pulled the poor old chap out and put him to bed, but he was never the same. Shock, I imagine. He died quite quickly afterwards: a great loss to British learning.

'Then, Lord preserve us, the monks decided to elect young Samson as Piro's successor. Perhaps they felt the rule had become a little lax: the dinners too ample, the mead too free flowing. It did not take them long to regret their choice. Eighteen months was all Samson lasted as abbot of Piro's Isle. A mere eighteen months, and then they parted by mutual agreement, the monks wishing him on his way with gifts and prayers, the abbot eager for the solitude of the desert.'

'What happened to him?' asked Seradwen, interested despite herself.

'Oh, he went off to Ierne,' the steward said dismissively.

'To Ierne?'

'A group of Irish monks who had heard of his piety stopped to see him on their way back from Rome and persuaded him to go with them.' The man shrugged. 'I do not suppose we will hear any more of him. People who go to Ierne rarely return. Apart from Holy Patrick himself, of course,' he added hastily. 'And even he took six years to get home.'

Roaring with laughter at his own joke the steward brought Coal to a halt outside the building.

'Teilo! Will you talk till sunset?' barked a voice. 'Our guests require assistance.'

Nai opened his eyes to the sight of the steward bobbing from foot to foot. 'Yes, Father, yes,' Teilo muttered, staring about him ineffectually.

An old man in a plain brown robe came out of the refectory. He was bareheaded, almost bald with only a few wisps of white hair behind his ears. His eyes were a piercing blue, and his face was the most austere and lined Nai had ever seen, a mass of seams and wrinkles. He gave no sign of noticing the cold.

Seradwen stepped forward. 'Forgive us disturbing your solitude, Father.' Nai could tell that she was nervous. 'My friend's muscles have stiffened. I do not think he can dismount.'

The old man's smile transfigured his face. Nai saw that some of the age lines were in fact old scars, healed to a thin whiteness against the dark tan of the skin. 'Thighs locked in the horns of the saddle, eh? It happened to me in my younger days. Once the muscles are taut one needs to be lifted free.' He gestured with his right hand at the steward, the sleeve riding up his forearm. It too was creased with old wounds, pale and puckered against the brown. 'Teilo, fetch help from the hall. Wethenoc and Lasrian are within, both strong men.'

They waited while the steward bustled inside, the Abbot smiling benignly, his calm blue gaze sweeping across and beyond them.

'We came across the high moor in the snowstorm,' Seradwen volunteered uneasily.

'A strange thing to do, but no doubt you had your reasons.'

This time the voice was cool, the tone polite but verging on disinterest. The Abbot reminded Nai of Bedwyr in his guise as hermit: the same certainty, the same inner strength and stillness, the same ability to concentrate absolutely on the matter in hand to the exclusion of all else.

A pair of burly monks appeared and with much puffing and groaning lifted Nai clear of the saddle. His legs refused to support him so they held him in the air, one on either side, looking to the Abbot for instructions while Teilo led the horses away, promising to look after them as if they were his own. At the Abbot's bidding the monks carried Nai into the hall and put him down on a bench beside the central hearth, where a fire blazed.

One monk knelt and chafed Nai's legs with hard fingers, kneading the muscles to release their tension.

'It will hurt,' warned the Abbot.

The massage would have been sensual if performed by a woman. Performed by a man there was something vaguely repulsive about it. The monk had tonsured the crown of his head in the Gallic fashion, but the hair was beginning to grow again in an uneven stubbly bristle. On the edge of the shaven patch was a large black mole: Nai wondered if the man knew how ugly it looked.

The hall was hot. He let his eyes slip shut again. The sweat was prickling all over his body. He reached out and took Seradwen's hand, squeezed it gently, felt the answering pressure.

In the background people were reading or reciting, the words weaving together like the humming of bees: '*Habentes zelum dei, sed non secundum scientiam, ignorantes dei iustitiam et suam quaerentes statuere . . .*' The flames of the fire burned yellow and gold against his eyelids, flared red as a log collapsed in upon itself.

'Catch him, Lasrian,' said the Abbot's voice from far away, and Nai felt a strong arm around his shoulders, preventing him from slipping sideways on the bench.

Suddenly he came wide awake with a gasp as the pain jolted through his legs.

'I warned you,' said the Abbot, amused.

The monk ceased the massage and rose to his feet with a gap-toothed grin. 'It will pass,' he said. 'Only a form of cramps.'

Nai gritted his teeth and beat slowly upon the bench with one fist. He did not know whether to move the limbs or try to keep them absolutely rigid. The slightest effort sent agony flowing through his thighs, but not to move seemed worse, and to be postponing the inevitable.

'Try walking,' advised the Abbot. 'Sometimes it helps.'

The gap-toothed monk offered his arm. The other, Lasrian, stood back beside the Abbot with a watchful stance, reminding Nai of a warrior guarding his lord.

'You are Nai mab Nwython,' the Abbot said as Nai staggered around the hearth, the life slowly returning to his legs. 'A much sought-after man.'

The shock burned through Nai. He could barely stand, let alone resist, and Seradwen was still seated on the bench, too far away for him to protect her in his present state. Both monks were heavyset, powerful men, and the Abbot looked formidable for all his age. The gap-toothed monk's grip tightened on Nai's arm; having already felt the strength of those fingers, Nai had no doubt the man could crush the bone if he so desired.

The voices droned in the background: '*Nox praecessit, dies autem appropinquavit. Abiciamus ergo opera . . .*'

' "The night is far gone and the day approaches. Let us therefore cast aside the works of darkness and put on the armour of light," ' quoted the Abbot.

Nai waited, legs trembling, ignoring the man holding his arm. Lasrian shifted uneasily beside his master. Seradwen twisted in her seat to watch, sensing the incipient violence around her, her face bewildered.

'Romans, Chapter thirteen, verse twelve,' said the Abbot. 'The passage continues with the exhortation that we should turn to Jesus Christ Our Saviour. Are you a Christian, Nai? Or do you follow the pagan practices of so many of our countryman?'

'I am a Christian,' said Nai, uncertain where this was leading. The longer he could keep them talking the more time his legs would have to recover.

'Of course. You were raised as part of Gereint mab Cadwy's household. Erfai mab Amren was your foster father. Your own parents died in the plague when you were yet a small child.'

'You know much about me.'

The Abbot stared at him consideringly. 'You interest me. Last summer you slew the renegade Eremon mac Cairbre. Most people reckoned Eremon a skilled swordsman, whereas your own reputation was always as a javelin fighter. Yet you killed him at close quarters, fighting hand-to-hand.'

He gestured to the gap-toothed man. 'Let him go, Wethenoc.' Again the sleeve slipped and Nai saw the scarring on the arm.

'You yourself were a swordsman?' Nai took an unsteady step towards the Abbot. Lasrian tensed.

'I was,' said the Abbot. 'I am.' He smiled. 'You have a great many choices ahead of you, of which this is the first. You may choose to trust me, or you may choose not to trust me. But I give you my word that neither I nor any of these about me are servants to the Children of Menestyr.'

'And Vortepor of Dyfed?'

The Abbot's eyes narrowed and he studied Nai appraisingly. 'So, you reckon him still a player in this game, do you?'

Nai was aware of Seradwen on his right, waiting for some sign from him. He took another step, swayed and nearly fell.

'You may be correct,' the Abbot continued when Nai had regained his balance. 'I can say only that to the best of my knowledge there are none of his servants in this room.'

'Who are you?' demanded Nai.

'You do not know?' Surprise flickered across the Abbot's face. 'I assumed you had come here deliberately. Surely it was not chance that brought you here?'

'We needed shelter,' said Seradwen. 'The decision was mine.'

He turned to her as if he had forgotten her presence, studied her carefully. She flushed, met his eyes forthrightly, defying him to look at her face instead of her body.

The Abbot let his gaze return to Nai as if there had never been a contest. 'I am Angus of the Eoganacht Maigi Dergind in Albae, Angus of the lands of the Children of Eogan in the Plain of the River Oak in Albion.'

'Eremon's kin,' said Nai.

Angus raised a hand. 'And Lleminawg's. That connection is one of which I am much prouder.'

'You were the leader of Custennin's warband,' said Seradwen.

'For many years.' His face darkened. 'Now, I am as you see.' He gestured to indicate the hall, the white faces watching from the far end of the room. Nai noticed for the first time that some of the monks were women.

'You can walk now?' Without waiting for an answer, Angus nodded at the gap-toothed monk. 'Wethenoc will show you to our guest quarters. I fear they are very simple, for we are a new foundation, as perhaps you already know. Once again you have a choice. We have another visitor. The two of you may share with each other, or Nai may share with the visitor.'

'I will go with Nai,' Seradwen said quickly.

'Very well.' The Abbot's tone changed. 'There is one simple rule it is my duty to explain to you. We are a mixed community, men and women living and working together in praise of God's holy name. To avoid scandal we segregate our sleeping quarters. The men have their cells here, hard by the refectory. The women sleep on the far side of the chapel – you may have observed their huts on the way in. Nai, you are welcome to wander wherever you wish within our enclosure, except in the direction of the nuns' cells. The chapel is of course open to you at any hour of the day or night, but if you wish to visit it after dark – which will be soon, judging by the sky – then please request one of the monks to accompany you to avoid any complications. Seradwen, you we will trust to avoid the monks' huts. Of necessity you must pass them to reach the refectory.'

He smiled thinly. 'Forgive me, but we have found it best if this simple rule is made clear at the outset. I will arrange for food to be brought to you this evening, and we shall not expect you to dine with us in the hall this night.'

They were dismissed.

'Did you know?' demanded Nai.

Even in the golden lamplight he still seemed grey and strained, though the platter of food served to them by Teilo the steward had done much to restore his strength.

'About Angus?' She shrugged, shifted on her stool. 'I guessed. I had heard there was a monastery somewhere on the moor, and I knew the smoke I smelled was not from a farm. I would not have brought you here had I not thought it necessary.'

His face relaxed a little and he swung his bare feet up out of the draught coming under the door.

'Besides, this is a monastery, Nai. A place devoted to God.'

'Angus does not strike me as a natural monk,' Nai said drily.

'A natural monk!' she scoffed. 'What is a natural monk when it is at home?'

'I do not know,' he said seriously. 'But there are people who are happier when they have renounced the pleasures of the body, and I do not think our Abbot is among them. People like that Samson the steward was talking about.'

'You were awake? I thought you slept.'

'Barely awake. It seemed wise to appear weaker than I was.'

'Could you have dismounted?' she asked in surprise.

He grinned. 'No, that was not feigned. I am sorry, Seradwen. I think it was lack of food that caused it. I should have insisted we eat during the day, but I was afraid of our pursuers.'

'For my sake,' she said softly, and shuddered at the memory of Peythan emerging from the shadow of the trees.

'For both our sakes.'

She turned away, knowing that he lied. Shadows danced around the room as the light flickered in the draught. The highly-polished bronze lamp gleamed with a fiery glow where it reflected the flame. It was held from the wall by a crescent-shaped spacer, and her eye idly traced the chains from which it was suspended: three short lengths fastened to the bowl, joined at a ring which in turn dangled from a longer length that hung from a beam in the ceiling. The lamp was a curiously ornate piece of work to find in a monastic cell, which was the kindest way of describing the room.

'We should rest,' said Nai, leaning back on the sprawl of rugs and blankets that was the sole bed.

'Yes,' she said, her mouth dry.

'I saw Angus look at you. I understand why you did not wish to spend the night alone.'

'It was not being alone that I feared.'

'Quite,' he said, and patted the couch beside him. 'Come. We are old friends, you and I, and you are perfectly able to fight me off if the need arises. If you wish I will fetch my sword and we can sleep with it between us, as men say Flur and Caradoc once did.'

She shook her head, remembering that this was Nai and not some rough-voiced stranger. 'No. I am sorry. You will think me foolish. It is simply that I did love my husband.'

The wind had risen while they were talking. Seradwen could hear it howling around the building, sifting through the thick fern thatch. The draught from under the ill-fitting door made the lamp leap wildly. Something clattered outside, scraped and thudded against the wall, was torn free with a crash and sent tumbling into the distance. Voices called, half stifled by the gale; heavy feet pounded past and somebody laughed.

'Lash it down!' said a man from the other side of the door.

'Hush, you will wake them,' said a woman's voice.

'What a night!' exclaimed someone else. 'Come on, quickly, or the wind will take the rest of it.'

The feet and voices receded. Nai was flat on his back with his eyes closed, the blanket and the sheepskin cover tangled around his waist. She could see the scar on his throat, livid in the lamplight, and she wondered that he could speak at all.

The wind raised puffs of dust on the floor. The hut seemed to be breathing around her, in and out, inhaling through the door-way and exhaling through the thatch. The lamp flame was pale yellow with an inner tinge of blue, curving with the draught. She stood and blew it out.

Nai fell into a fitful sleep filled with ragged nightmares through which the wind wailed and moaned like a living thing.

He was on the high moor again, approaching the standing stone that stood like a guardian at the edge of the habitable land, and this time as he came near the stone turned to meet him. He kept his gaze fixed upon the ground. The snow had gone and the yellow grass was dry and brittle beneath his boots. There was a pool of dark water where the pillar had stood, and he could see the surface shake and tremble as the guardian moved towards him.

A grey hand reached down to his chin, held it in a rough grasp, the fingers cold and hard. The pressure increased, and as he tilted his head in response he was very aware of how easily the grip could have crushed the bones of his jaw.

He had been wrong about the hair. The guardian was bald apart from the white wisps above its ears. But about the face he had not been wrong: it was cracked and scarred like the stones of the moor, and the eyes were a penetrating blue that looked deep into his soul and found him wanting.

'It is all right,' Seradwen said beside him, and he was aware he must still be dreaming, since Seradwen had left him long ago to marry her farmer; and even if she had not, he would never have brought her across the wasteland in the dead of winter, when the days were so short it seemed God stinted the light. It was a pleasant dream though, unlike the other, and he reached out to stroke her hair – russet under the cloak of darkness – feeling the warmth of her body against him.

'What of the sword?' she murmured; and later, as if denying some betrayal: 'Remember, I did love Mordav.'

CHAPTER THIRTEEN

Lindinis was small enough for the citizens to know each other by sight if not by name, yet large enough that it still – despite what Celemon had said – drew traders and travellers to shelter within its walls. There was a thriving open-air market in the shell of the old bathhouse, and this was where Bedwyr began his search, thinking that any stranger would be drawn by the noise and activity here at the heart of the city.

His head was hot under the cap. He had never cared for hats, preferring the looseness of a hood in bad weather. Helmets he disliked intensely, hating the feeling of constriction, the sensation of something jammed upon his scalp, the loss of sight and hearing. It was a prejudice he had shared with Arthur and Cei, and as a consequence it had become unfashionable to wear a helmet among the Companions – if Arthur had been wearing a helmet at Camlann, he would not have fallen to a head blow.

Bedwyr tugged the cap down over his skull, shutting out the thought.

The walls of the bath complex had been lowered to make them safe, leaving a rectangular shell over forty paces in length, open to the sky. The space was crowded with stalls and barrows, all overflowing higgledy-piggledy into the aisles, so the potential customers were obliged to clamber over the merchandise. At first glance the stalls seemed to offer every conceivable type of goods, from food, drink and fuel through clothing and footwear to metalwork and jewellery. Bedwyr halted on the worn cobbles near the entrance and drew a deep breath.

'Confusing, isn't it?' said a cheerful young man with a pair of new shoes under his arm.

Bedwyr nodded.

'There is a pattern. The vendors tend to stick together. Potters in one group, cobblers in another, bone and ivory merchants in a third. You just have to plunge!' the man added with a grin, stepping around a beggar blocking the entrance.

Taking his advice Bedwyr hurled himself into the crowd. At first he was pushed and jostled, continually obliged to step aside to allow someone to pass. Then, suddenly, he found himself moving differently, moving as he had in the days when he had been one of the most powerful men in the island of Prydein, choosing a course and not deviating from it regardless of who was in his way, forcing them to turn aside.

Around him the stallholders shouted their wares, using a mixture of Latin and British depending upon whose attention they were trying to attract (though Latin was more common), their cries merging into an unintelligible whole. Negotiations between purchasers and sellers tended to be loud and fierce, and payment made in whatever came to hand: scraps of old coins, lumps of metal, other goods.

There were some, he judged, who probably made their livelihood by running from stall to stall, bartering object for object until they reckoned they had made a clear profit and could begin again. One section of the market was given over to antiquities, remnants of the Roman past: statues large and small, brooches, medallions, tiles, lamps and crockery; even, to his astonishment, architectural features. One man was trying to sell a collection of decorated columns and massive black beams, extolling their virtues to the passers-by: 'Lasted a hundred years, last a hundred more – from the house of the famous courtesan Livia, beloved of Magnus Maximus and the Emperor Constantine himself.' He noticed Bedwyr watching and winked. 'We deliver, my masters, we deliver to the site of your choosing. The poet Juvenal sat under these timbers. Agricola planned his campaigns against the painted men of the North in their shadow. If only they could talk, eh, if only they could talk?'

Lindinis is alive, thought Bedwyr, remembering the dying city he had known a generation earlier. Celemon, shut away in her nunnery, had been wrong. This place was thriving. He could feel the vitality, see the zest in the faces of the people.

'Perhaps you, sir, might be interested? In view of the connection with Agricola? Not that I could deliver to your home.'

For a moment Bedwyr thought the man was talking to him. Then he saw the flicker of long dark hair above a colourless cloak, over on the far side of the timbers. At once he pretended to be engrossed in a collection of Samian ware on a nearby barrow (the unchipped bowls a glowing, glossy red although he knew they must be well over two hundred years old, and they made him think of Gwenhwyvar, who had flung herself into making bowls and vases after Llacheu died as if this would somehow assuage her grief), while his eyes scanned the throng around him, searching for the Pict's companions.

It was the one with the unruly bay horse, he was almost sure. The way the Picts dressed and wore their hair made it hard for him to tell them apart – though he would not soon forget the one who had offered him the yellow cap in Isca – but this fellow seemed younger and less certain of himself than the others. The man was about the same errand as himself, surveying the crowd for a sign of his quarry, trying to shake off the attentions of the stallholder, who was growing louder and more extravagant in his promises, relishing the embarrassment he was causing the stranger.

'Take some culture back north with you, my master! A fine carved pillar – look at this craftsmanship around the top!'

The Pict scowled, pushed the stallholder aside. Bedwyr watched him walk briskly away, the crowd parting around him as if they sensed the danger latent within him.

'Are you buying or loitering?' snapped the woman who owned the barrow.

'Loitering,' said Bedwyr, smiling sweetly, and stepped across to the stallholder, who was clutching one shoulder with an aggrieved expression on his face.

'Did you see that? All he had to do was say no.' The stall holder shook his head sadly. 'These foreigners have no manners.'

'How do you know he's a northerner?'

The man tapped the side of his nose with a finger. 'Ah, well. I could say it was the result of years of experience, dealing with all shapes and manner of men, but you wouldn't believe me, would you?'

'No.'

'Or I could say it was his accent that gave him away.'

'Since he did not speak, I doubt it.'

'Then I might say I had heard him speak earlier.'

'You might.'

'But would you believe me, there's the question?' The stall-holder turned his head on one side, examined his interrogator shrewdly. 'There again, would I care?'

Bedwyr felt in the pouch at his belt, pulled out an old coin. 'I would care,' he said, and tossed the coin to the man, who caught it smoothly in mid air.

'I know they are Picts because they are staying at my brother's inn, the old mansio. They were here before, a couple of days ago, looking for a man.'

'Really? What sort of man?'

'An elderly man, with grey hair that might be long or short, or hidden under a hat.' He stared pointedly at Bedwyr's cap. 'He might have a beard or he might not. He would be of normal height, neither especially short nor especially tall, wiry, fit for his age, and one hand –' his eyes dropped to Bedwyr's hands '– would be so badly scarred by an old wound it was almost useless.'

'How many of them?'

'Seven. One has a face he keeps concealed all the time. My brother caught a glimpse, but I did not see it for myself.' The stall holder sounded regretful. 'Hideous it was. All scars, blue and green, like circles. That's why they call them Painted Men, see?'

'I know,' said Bedwyr, watching the crowd.

'They are meeting someone today,' the man said suddenly. 'They told my brother because of the extra mouth to feed. One of Custennin's warriors.'

Although he was not aware of it, Bedwyr must have betrayed his astonishment.

'*That* surprised you,' the stallholder said in satisfaction. 'Surprised me too. Picts and Custennin of Dumnonia. Hard to imagine what they would have in common.'

'Did they say what they wanted with the old man?'

'No.' The stallholder licked his lips. 'It reminds me of a story my father used to tell, about one of Arthur's Companions fighting Picts here in Lindinis, years ago before I was born. Bedwyr mab Petroc was his name.'

'Your father?'

The stall holder grinned. 'No, the Companion.'

'The last of the Companions died at Camlann. And if Bedwyr had somehow survived, he would be a very old man indeed by now.'

'I suppose,' said the stall holder. He shrugged, sighed. 'Yes, you are right. It is just –' He waved his hands in the air, floundered for words. 'Bedwyr was a legend. I would like to have seen him once, so I could tell my children.'

'And if you did see him, what would you say to him?'

'I would say –' The man stopped, thought for a moment. 'I would say: Take care! The wolves are running.'

Bedwyr felt a shiver pass down his spine. The same phrase had gone through his mind the night before last.

'Tell me,' he said aloud, 'is there anywhere I can find a locksmith?'

The stall holder frowned. 'There used to be one off the Forum, but he gave up or died.' His face brightened. 'I know. Over in the far corner of the market with the metalworkers. Little fellow, doesn't say much. Deals in old locks made new again.'

'My thanks.' Bedwyr started in the direction the man was pointing, hesitated and returned. 'One last question.'

The man nodded.

'Do you ever sell any of these things?'

The man glanced around him at the balks of timber, the ornate columns. 'Yes,' he said. 'Yes, I do. Not that it matters to me. I work for the City Fathers.'

Bedwyr stopped at a food stall and bought himself a platter of bread, cheese and onions, which he ate standing at the counter. The crowds were thinning, perhaps because the sky had darkened with the threat of rain. Around him the traders were struggling with canvas awnings, fighting against the rising wind. One or two shook their heads dubiously, began to pack their goods.

A pair of hard-faced men strolled past him, picking their way along the aisles between the stalls, their eyes constantly surveying the crowd for signs of trouble.

'City Guard,' said the woman behind the counter, who had followed his gaze. 'Saesons, mostly. Gallows-bait, the lot of them!' She spat expressively.

He nodded, remembering, as the cold rain began to fall, another day in Lindinis nearly thirty years before, when he had fought with Painted Men from the North and Saesons from the City Guard. At the time he had thought he was protecting Vortepor of Dyfed, and if he had known then what he knew now he would not have lifted a finger in the man's defence.

'This will drive the marks away,' the woman said sourly, glaring at the sky.

She was right. Already he was becoming conspicuous, standing alone in the rain with his food.

'You have somewhere to shelter?' she demanded abruptly. 'It's turning to sleet.'

'Yes, I thank you.' He laid the platter on the counter and smiled.

'They are tough on people without a place to go, the City Guard.' She shook the crumbs from the dish. 'You don't mind me asking, do you? Us old ones have got to watch out for each other, and you look a bit weary.'

He had not really been defending Vortepor on that night thirty years ago. He had been fighting for Teleri, though he had not yet met her: Teleri who was to become his lover.

'Are you all right?' said the woman.

'Yes.' He shook himself. 'Yes, I am all right. You are kind.'

He waved farewell and moved swiftly towards the area where he had been told he would find the locksmith. More and more of the traders were packing their booths, wheeling away their barrows. Those who remained stamped their feet and flogged their arms against the cold. The sleet rattled on the awnings, gathered in the gutters, stung exposed flesh. The wind moaned around the walls and between the stalls, whirled the market debris into the sky and flung it down again.

The locksmith was on the point of departure. When he realized Bedwyr was a genuine customer he spread his wares across the plank that served as a counter, silently demonstrating how easily the padlocks snapped shut, how quickly the key fastened and unfastened them.

'And a hasp?' said Bedwyr.

The man grunted, produced several. 'Weakest part,' he said. 'This one folds on itself to hide the nail holes.' He shrugged. 'Win you time, is all.'

'Time is all I need.'

'For a door?'

Bedwyr nodded.

'How thick?'

Bedwyr held up his fingers to demonstrate. The man sniffed, rummaged through a bag under the counter, spread a set of iron spikes across the counter.

'Use these. Too long, see, so they will stick through the far side. You bend the tips back over. Won't hold for ever, but can't be ripped out easily.'

'Good.'

They dickered for a while though neither's heart was in it. The locksmith kept glancing at the sky and shivering, and Bedwyr was impatient to return to the house, which he had of necessity left open. At the end the man wrapped the purchases in an old rag and tied the ends to make a bag.

'Fortune be with you,' he said as he handed it over. 'These are not secure times, unless you have a tail of armed men to keep you safe.' He opened his mouth in a soundless laugh and returned to his packing.

The sleet changed again to cold rain as Bedwyr walked through the streets to the house. He passed two more of the City Guard sheltering beneath a portico: big men, wearing mail-shirts under their woolen cloaks, carrying sword-bladed spears. They stared at him as he strode by them, marking him as a stranger (though perhaps that was no more than his sense of guilt, since he planned to break their laws). He felt the weight of their eyes upon him down the length of the road until he was able to turn into an alley.

The house was damp and chilly. He bolted the door behind him and moved through the building, checking for signs of intruders. His belongings lay as he had left them in the old kitchen, and so far as he could tell nobody had entered the house in his absence. The pony had moved into the shelter of the peristyle and nickered hopefully at the sight of him. He spent a few moments fussing the creature, then found himself a good solid piece of stone which would serve as a hammer.

It was odd, he thought as he began to fix the padlock to the door between the house and the garden, to realize that for the vast majority of people life continued exactly as before, unaffected by the upheavals following Arthur's death. What had – for him, for Celemon, for Gwenhwyvar – been an event so important that Celemon could in all seriousness say their world had been sundered at Camlann, had for the citizens of Lindinis been a minor disruption in their daily lives; a tragedy or a triumph depending on their point of view, but not something that freed them from the necessity of finding their daily bread. He doubted if it had even interrupted their schedule of rebuilding.

And if that were true of Lindinis, the city which lay closest to Caer Cadwy and the centre of Arthur's rule, how much more true it must be for those further afield, in the far west or north.

He drove the first pair of spikes through the door frame and stepped through the opening to hammer the points flat against the wood. Perhaps Celemon was right, and it had all been for nothing. *What difference will it have made in a hundred years' time?* she had demanded. If you asked one of the traders in the market, they would probably stare at you blankly, not understanding the question. Even the more sophisticated citizens would look puzzled, or would smile at your naivety. 'None at all,' they would say if they deigned to answer. 'Arthur spent his life on the borders, fighting Saesons and Scotti raiders, dealing with recalcitrant barbarians in the north. Nothing to do with us – except that we paid for it with our taxes. Relief that he has gone, really.'

Bedwyr closed the door and measured the position for the rest of the hasp. He wondered how long he could remain in this house without being detected. Driving in the great nails was a noisy process, louder on the door itself than the frame: every blow echoed flatly around the garden and presumably the neighbourhood. If the City Council were engaged in selling what they could salvage from demolished buildings, they must lay some claim to abandoned houses like this, keeping out squatters and other undesirables, or the houses would be torn apart by those in search of an easy reward. Sooner or later there would be a knock at the door and a bailiff with a demand for rent standing on the doorstep, or a squad of guardsmen come to evict him.

The prospect made him smile. Bedwyr mab Petroc, once the greatest warrior of the age, driven from his refuge by something as mundane as a bailiff. There was a time when he could have commandeered this house and a dozen like it, in any town in Britain, and none would have dared gainsay him. Now he was reduced to fitting his own locks.

He picked up the padlock, pushed it shut, fiddled with the small brass key, then opened it again. Under the oil the mechanism was old and worn, but it seemed to work well enough. Tossing the stone aside, he stood contemplating his handiwork. It would not stop a determined assault, but then neither would the internal bars on the doors. With luck, the lock would only need to keep people out of the house for a single day.

Darkness was coming early. The wind was whining around the peristyle and its pillars. The branches of the ornamental trees tossed and squeaked under its force, shivered under a brief shower of hail. Bedwyr propped the door open for the pony and retreated to the kitchen, where he relighted the fire and stretched out on the bed he had made from his spare clothing. Tonight he did not feel so secure, and he found himself waiting for the sound of hobnailed boots in the street outside.

He slept for a time and woke, as he usually did, during the watches of the night, lay listening to the sleet or hail rattling on the roof of the atrium, the moisture dripping into the courtyard. The fire had burned low. He roused himself to toss on another log, then, since he was now wide awake, took his sword and a whetstone from his pack, sat cross-legged honing the edge of the blade.

The Sons of Menestyr were meeting one of Custennin's warriors. Once Custennin had been ambitious, eager to fill the empty place left by Arthur's fall. But lately Custennin's grip upon Dumnonia had loosened. There were rumours that he thought of abandoning everything and becoming a monk, that he had been worn down by the constant struggle to keep and wield his power. A ruler without his warband was nothing, and according to what Bedwyr had heard in Isca, Custennin had nearly lost control of his during the summer.

It might therefore be to Custennin's advantage to treat with the Children of Menestyr. Even if he no longer desired to be the next Amherawdyr of Albion – a title which was now meaningless – he probably believed that possession of the Chalice would help him strengthen his grip upon Dumnonia. Even better, in some ways, would be the presence of Gwenhwyvar herself. Bedwyr could imagine some kind of bargain between Custennin and the Sons of Menestyr: in return for allowing them to range freely through Dumnonia on their quest, Custennin would be in some way associated with the recovered Cup of Sovereignty that had once belonged to Arthur. Or perhaps the key was Gwenhwyvar. Perhaps the Children of Menestyr had deduced that they could not find the Chalice without also finding Arthur's Queen, and had therefore agreed to hand her over to Custennin in exchange for being permitted to depart with the Cup.

Bedwyr frowned and shook his head. It was possible, but it did not ring true. There were too many chances for deceit. Custennin might decide to keep both Chalice and Queen; the Children of Menestyr might kill or abandon her and run for safety with the Chalice rather than risk being cheated.

Gwenhwyvar. Like a fool he had thought that once he discovered Celemon (and he had not expected finding her would be so easy) he would also discover Gwenhwyvar. It had never occurred to him that the two women might have changed, that their long and seemingly unbreakable friendship might at last have come to an end. And yet, why not? Everything they had shared had gone, from the town of Caer Cadwy where they had made their home to the ideal of Albion to which they had devoted their lives.

So where was Gwenhwyvar? He had assumed, because Dumnonia was safer than most parts of Britain, because Gwenhwyvar had been born in what were nowadays considered its eastern extremities – for any number of reasons, not least his own prejudices – that she would remain in the area. But thinking about it now, once she had severed relations with Celemon and St Helena's there was nothing to keep her here. In fact, since almost any part of eastern Dumnonia would be filled with reminders of the past, it was much more likely that she would have gone elsewhere. Perhaps she had fled to Lesser Britain, just as he had done, or some obscure district of Gaul.

He laid the sword aside and replaced the whetstone in his pack. The pony was moving around the peristyle, crashing through the bushes; he heard one of its hooves scrape on stone. The wind had dropped and the night was suddenly very still. An owl called in the distance. A dog barked briefly and was abruptly silent. Bedwyr walked out into the atrium and sniffed the air under the light well. Frost glittered along the eaves, and it seemed to him it might snow before dawn, which would make what he had to do on the morrow more difficult.

He yawned, returned to the old kitchen and the fire. Buried deep within his saddlebag was a small wooden bowl. He took it out, filled it with water from his leather flask, and placed it on the floor beside the fire.

Teleri had taught him this, Teleri whom he had first encountered in this very city – though he had not then realized she was a woman, had not even really registered her presence, had simply accepted her as another of Vortepor's followers. He could see her strong-boned face before him now. To his eyes she had been beautiful, though many had found her ugly. She had been brave and talented, generous with her knowledge.

(*To a point*, said a small voice in the back of his mind. *She did not share everything with you.*)

Teleri had shown him how to scry, how to focus his attention on a reflective surface – water, polished metal, a mirror – and see within what was and what had been, and sometimes what might be, and to distinguish between them.

Strictly, as a former monk, he should not practise magic. Yet he and many others of his faith believed that power came from God, and to ignore it was to risk offending Him. Whenever he had doubts, he remembered the parable of the Talents, the rebuke delivered to the servant who buried his gift in the ground and made no use of it – and though he feared many in the Church would have replied this was mere sophistry, a twisting of Christ's words to suit his own pleasure, it was a comfort to him.

If he *were* damned, it would be for the other things he had done in his life, the slaughter in which he had gloried, the love of killing against which he had struggled so unsuccessfully (*so half-heartedly*, said the voice) since he was a boy.

The fire was burning well, with a good flame and little smoke. The water was clear in the bowl, so clear he could see the grain of the wood, see the tiny ripples in the surface reflected as shadows on the bottom, see the flame dancing across the face of the deeps, and there was Gwenhwyvar's face as she bent over him in Erfai's tent, her hair silver and her face white as bone, and the flame was red and gold, yellow where it touched the rim, wheeling and blurring as he emptied his mind of everything save her name, her image, calling her to him as the hunter calls the deer, as the lover calls the beloved.

Moonlight in the Great Hall at Caer Cadwy. The white owl sat on a rafter, preening its breast. Bedwyr could see every feather, every vane on every feather, could even see the black cobwebs hanging from the beam on which it perched.

The owl raised its head, the round eyes staring, the rays around them giving it a look of surprise. Bedwyr's viewpoint shifted to the direction of the owl's gaze.

The door of the hall opened and a figure blocked the light. For a moment he thought it was himself, that he was witnessing his own arrival in the hall two days earlier, then he saw the newcomer was much larger and bulkier, filling the doorway.

The man limped the length of the hall, skirting the firepits, his face in shadow.

'Please,' muttered Bedwyr, not daring to hope. 'Please.'

The owl burst from the beam in a flutter of white wings, spiralled to the man's arm, which lifted to meet it. The two froze in that position, then the owl sidled down the arm to the shoulder and began to nibble the man's ear.

The man moved, his limp less pronounced. He brought the owl to the doorway and stepped outside, and Bedwyr's viewpoint followed him. His face was hidden behind the white bird, but Bedwyr could see his hair, which was auburn streaked with grey around the temples.

'Arthur,' he whispered.

The man looked up as if he had heard and smiled. He lifted his arm again, and the owl shuffled from his shoulder to his wrist, where it waited like a falcon about to be unleashed.

Suddenly the man tossed it into the air.

The white bird circled the hall, wings beating against the night, spiralled into the winter sky, reaching higher and higher, a speck of brightness in the great dark.

'We are not quite done,' said a voice.

CHAPTER FOURTEEN

Nai and Seradwen broke their fast in the refectory, leaving the hut – which the night before they had thought a miserable little place – with some regret.

Lasrian came to find them as they were finishing their meal, and glanced knowingly from one to the other.

'The Abbot asks if you would care to join him,' was all he said aloud.

They nodded their acquiescence, and he led them out into the compound. The snow had gone, but frost clung to the edges of the puddles it had left behind, and the sun was weak and watery behind the clouds. Some of the monks and nuns moved between the buildings, greeting them gravely as they passed, and Nai began to see the possibilities of such a life: the sense of belonging, the freedom from worry about the next day's food or shelter.

'No,' whispered Seradwen. 'You would not make a good monk.'

Lasrian brought them to the second of the great halls they had seen as they approached the monastery. Like the refectory, it was built of timber, a much more permanent affair than the huts that surrounded it. The walls were formed from well-seasoned oak planks, and Nai wondered at the labour involved in fetching such materials to this desolate place.

'What is this?' he asked Lasrian as the monk laid his hand upon the latches of the double doors.

'See for yourself!' Lasrian flung open the doors and gestured for them to enter.

Peat fires smouldered at either end of the long space, their smoke drifting through the thatch. Lamps and torches hung from the walls and the twin rows of posts dividing the space into nave and aisles; not all were lit, so that the corners of the hall were filled with shadows.

In the middle of the space, directly in front of them, two half-naked men circled each other, carrying long blades that gleamed in the torchlight. The Abbot watched critically from the shelter of a pillar. The blades met with a clang: one man staggered while the other whirled and struck hard for the ribs, pulling the blow at the last moment.

'Distance, distance, distance,' shouted the Abbot. 'Keep moving, Isag. It is not enough to block. You must attack, attack, always attack.'

The men rushed together, blades moving so fast that even Nai was hard put to follow what was happening. Iron rang dully on iron, the impacts coming so rapidly the sounds merged into a single note that echoed around the rafters.

'Break!' called the Abbot.

The men fell apart, panting heavily. One, Isag, leant upon his sword and stared at the ground. Nai could see a great red blotch spreading across his side where the flat of the blade had struck him.

'Distance,' repeated the Abbot. 'Isag, you are allowing him to dictate the distance. If you do that you have lost, because he is better at close quarters than you. Open a space between you. Keep him guessing. Make him work for his victory.'

Isag raised his head and nodded wearily. His face and torso were streaked with sweat.

'Very well,' said the Abbot. 'Enough for the present.' He stepped away from the pillar, raised his voice. 'Wooden blades and shields. Practise your forms.'

There was a rustle of movement and a dozen or more men stepped away from the walls where they had been hidden by the shadows. Some wore the plain brown robes favoured by many of the monks; others wore ordinary tunics or went bare-chested like Isag and his opponent. They paired off, raised their shields and went at each other with their wooden swords, till the hall was filled with the rhythmic clatter of strike and counter strike.

Angus watched until he was satisfied his pupils could be left, then strolled across to Nai and Seradwen.

'What do you think?' he asked. The pride in his voice was obvious.

'They are dancing!' exclaimed Seradwen, and indeed they were, shifting from foot to foot, weaving from side to side in a series of preordained movements that reflected the actions of their hands and arms.

'Lleminawg,' said Nai.

The Abbot nodded, his eyes reflecting faint amusement. 'That was why he was called the Dancer. Or one of the reasons, anyway.'

'Eremon did not fight like this,' began Nai, then suddenly recalled he was talking to Eremon's kinsmen.

'Eremon was of a lesser generation,' said Angus. 'Otherwise you would not have killed him. How well do you think you would do against one of these?'

Nai shifted uncomfortably. 'The sword is not my weapon.'

The Abbot smiled coldly. 'Perhaps you would like a practice bout later. Your fellow guest seems keen to try his hand.'

Before Nai could ask about this other guest, Seradwen spoke, intent upon steering the conversation away from Eremon and the Abbot's challenge.

'This seems a strange occupation for a man of God.'

Angus laughed. 'This too is done for the greater glory of God, the Lord God of Hosts. Some serve Him with the prayers of their mouths, or by copying and disseminating His Scriptures. Some labour in the fields, dedicating to Him the fruits thereof. My harvest is of a different kind, but it is no less His.'

He pointed to the stools around the peat fire at one end of the hall. 'Let us sit. There are things we must talk about.' Beside the stools were a jug of red wine and some beakers. The Abbot filled three and passed them around. Seradwen tasted hers cautiously then raised her eyebrows.

'Gaul?'

Angus shook his head. 'Southern Italy.' He stretched on the stool, seeming in no hurry to begin their discussion.

The wooden staves clattered in the background. Nai looked around him. Last night they had slept in what was essentially a peasant's hut, a rough dwelling that could be raised in a single day. This hall, like the refectory, was the product of far more work. The walls were panelled and smelled of beeswax polish. The pillars had been sanded until they were perfectly smooth. The floor was of beaten earth rather than boards, but given the use to which the hall was being put that made sense. 'You are a wealthy foundation?'

The Abbot smiled at him. 'In some respects. I myself was not a poor man in my previous life. Some of my brethren prefer a simple existence, and I have no objection, provided they do not carry matters too far. Excessive zeal is as much an error as ostentatious wealth. There are those who eat dry bread by the measure – then boast about it beyond measure; or drink water, but from the cup of hatred not of love; or refuse to travel in carriages or on horseback, and thus regard themselves as superior to other people. Of these, it is written most truly: "death has entered through the window of their pride." I am a tolerant man, but I will not tolerate intolerance in others.'

'How did you come to be their abbot?' asked Seradwen. 'It is not so long ago you took holy orders.'

From the body of the hall came a low murmur of conversation as the men finished their exercise. A few laid their weapons aside and departed, but most remained, gathering around the second fire at far end of the hall.

The Abbot watched them fondly. 'How could it be otherwise? Some of us are called by God to high estate, others to a lower. I was leader of the warband of Dumnonia, a man accustomed to command.' He sighed. 'Custennin grew to fear me, for he was aware of his own failings. He is not a man who inspires love in others. I had trained the very warriors upon whom his power depended: their first loyalty was to me, their master. Therefore he bruited it about that I plotted rebellion, had me seized and bound along with those others of his kindred whose influence he feared.'

'He had some loyal followers then,' interjected Seradwen.

Angus scowled. 'There are always those who can be bought with gold,' he said harshly. 'Their time will come. One of his brothers he executed on some pretext. The rest of us he dared not harm and instead sent into exile. This monastery was founded to hold me. Some of its inmates are no doubt his spies, with orders to prevent me from leaving. Fortunately I do not wish to leave. Where would I go? Thanks to Eremon's foolishness, my kindred no longer hold their lands along the River Oak.'

He refilled his beaker and offered more to Nai, who held up a hand in polite refusal.

'Thus I am a monk because of Custennin, who himself desires

to be a monk – or sometimes thinks he does. So we torture others with our own worst nightmares, just as we attribute to others the failings found in ourselves, calling this one rash and this one selfish.'

Seradwen frowned, not following, but the Abbot ignored her.

'When I was a warrior, I was determined to be among the best. If in my old age I must be a monk, then I resolved to bring to my new calling the same energy I had brought to being a warrior. I am not a man for book learning, though I would not deny its importance. Nor am I a farmer, or a beekeeper, or a mead-maker, or any of the other occupations considered suitable for a monk. I am a weapons' master, and a leader of men and women.'

His eyes flickered across them both, discarded Seradwen and fixed upon Nai. Somebody laughed at the far end of the hall, the sound hollow under the high roof. A pair of men stepped out into the nave and began to practise with war-knife and shield, their movements slow and sinuous, stopping often to repeat a sequence until both had perfected it.

'A monastery is a kingdom in miniature,' Angus said quietly. 'A community, with its own economy and society. We are not yet self-sufficient, and we rely upon others for luxuries like this wine we are drinking – but the same could be said of Dumnonia, or even Albion under Arthur. Without trade we would wither away and die, even as the diocese of Britannia died after the fall of Rome, when we were cut off from the rest of the world.'

'Surely Albion is Britannia!' objected Seradwen.

'Is it? Or more accurately, was it?' The Abbot lifted an eyebrow. 'I think not. Albion was something new, something created on the foundations of Britannia, but no more Britannia reborn than a timber hall raised upon the ruins of a stone fort is the same building as its predecessor. The two may have coincided in space – though arguably Arthur's Albion extended much further north – and they may have shared certain elements of their past and certain customs of their inhabitants – but they were not the same.'

'Both are gone,' rasped Nai.

'True,' acknowledged the Abbot. 'That much they have in common. But whereas it would not be desirable, let alone possible, to restore Britannia – none of us would wish to be ruled from Rome – the restoration of Albion is a different matter.'

Nai sipped his wine. The men with the war-knives were moving faster now. Both had small circular shields covered in red leather, with protruding iron bosses that rose to a rounded point. These they manoeuvred rapidly, trying to catch their opponent's blows on the metal boss rather than the wooden boards, at the same time striking around the other's shield, aiming high for the head and shoulders or low for the leg. The blades were blunt, but even so Nai winced as he saw one hit the other's outstretched knife arm under the elbow: the struck man gasped and faltered, leapt back out of range, nursing his arm.

'They are good, yes?' said Angus. 'All my life has been spent in the pursuit of the best. The best swordsman, the best warband.' He picked up the wine jug and offered to refill Nai's beaker.

Nai shook his head. The Abbot topped his own beaker, belatedly waved the jug at Seradwen. She also refused.

'The best swordsman?' said Nai.

Angus drank deeply. 'In my time I have seen them all perform, both at practice and in battle. My own cousin Lleminawg, and the other great swordsmen of Arthur's Court: Cei, Gwalchmei, and Bedwyr. Of that older generation, I would rate Lleminawg the master, with Cei a close second by virtue of his strength. A single blow from Cei was worth three from any other man. But for technique, for grace, for sheer beauty in action, none could match Lleminawg.'

'What of Bedwyr?'

Nai waited for an answer. The sound of feet beating back and forth across the earthen floor grew louder as the combat grew more furious. Both men were grunting with effort now, their breath coming in pants. One of the watchers shouted some encouragement, then was silent as a quick flurry of blows rang against the shield boss of his chosen man.

'Bedwyr,' the Abbot said reflectively. 'Bedwyr. Of course, I did not know him when he was young, only when he was already well into middle age. He was one of those upon whom Fortuna smiles: even when he wanted to die, fate kept him alive.'

'Then from his point of view she did not smile,' said Seradwen.

A blunt forefinger traced the line of a scar from cheekbone to chin. 'He was good, certainly, but to my mind he enjoyed it too much, allowed his love of killing to cloud his judgement. Cei and Lleminawg fought for the pleasure of fighting, which is as it should be. Bedwyr relished inflicting pain. There are men like that, and they are best avoided. There is no art in them.'

Nai opened his mouth then closed it again. The cold blue eyes raked across him, softened slightly.

'For his sake they hunt you. He is not worth it.'

'How much do you know?' asked Nai. Seradwen kicked his ankle on the side hidden from the Abbot.

Angus nodded slowly. 'I still have friends in Custennin's warband. Isgofan, who leads the search for Bedwyr, was once my pupil; and though I am no longer either his captain or his master, he yet seeks my advice when he is near.'

'Have they found him?'

'In Lindinis.'

'So they no longer need me.'

The Abbot bowed his head. 'No.'

'I can go home?' he asked disingenuously.

Angus laughed. 'We none of us can go home. The world moves around us, Nai. We cannot go back. Have you not discovered that yet?'

Nai glanced at Seradwen, who frowned. 'The Children of Menestyr,' he began.

'You have killed some of their number,' the Abbot said quickly. 'They will not forgive you easily, if at all. You are safe while you remain here, of course, but who knows what might happen when you leave?'

'Perhaps you should become a monk,' suggested Seradwen.

'You would be welcome,' the Abbot said smoothly. 'Most welcome.'

'This Isgofan,' Nai said tentatively.

The Abbot drained his beaker and stood. He looked down at Nai, then gazed the length of the hall at the two fighters, who were locked in a tight embrace, struggling to throw each other but hampered by their shields.

'A very dangerous man. A swordsman to match the best of Arthur's Companions. I doubt Bedwyr could have taken him even in his prime.'

'Your pupil?'

'My achievement.'

It was a statement of simple pride. The austere face swung towards Nai, challenged him to comment.

'In our day Isgofan is an unrivalled swordsman. A generation ago he would have served the Emperor: of necessity, since the best is worthy only of the best. But we have no Emperor, Nai mab

267

Nwython. There is no worthy master for a man of Isgofan's talents. Worse, there is no cause in which he may exercise them.'

'Like Eremon,' murmured Nai, remembering how the renegade had said, near the end, that if Arthur had still lived he might have become one of the Amherawdyr's Companions.

'Perhaps. Though I think Isgofan is the better man. He is loyal to his lord, and a true friend to his friends.'

The door opened and a monk peered cautiously through the gap. The Abbot sighed wearily. 'I must be about my duties. The weather is not good. I would suggest you stay another night.'

'We would be grateful,' Seradwen said promptly.

'Thank you,' said Nai.

Angus inclined his head. 'That is settled then. Now, if you will excuse me, I must away to the chapel.' He lifted a hand to keep Nai on his stool. 'You will no doubt wish to make your devotions at some stage, but there is no need to do so now. Remain here and finish the wine.'

They watched him stride down the hall. His followers snuffed most of the lights and fell into place behind him. When the door had closed behind the last of them Nai bent for the jug and topped the beakers.

'What do you think?'

Seradwen sniffed. 'He does not like women – or at least, he does not like the conversation of women – and he does not like your friend Bedwyr.'

'Warlord or monk?'

She tapped her teeth with the rim of the beaker. 'On today's showing, warlord.' She considered a moment, shrugged. 'Perhaps that is unfair. The monks and nuns seem content, and we have not seen him at worship. What do you make of him?'

Nai rubbed at his cheek, freshly shaved that morning. 'A monastery would be a good place to raise a fighting force in secret.'

'He said himself the place was probably full of Custennin's spies.'

'True. It was just a thought.' He spun the beaker between his palms, watched the wine swirl against the thin pottery. 'He is a man who likes to show off his knowledge. He went to some pains to tell me who I was when we arrived yesterday.'

Seradwen stifled a smile. 'The state you were in, he probably thought you needed reminding. He knew my name as well, without being told.'

268

'Did he?' Nai frowned. 'I missed that. I assumed you had given it to the steward.'

She shook her head. 'I never had a chance. The man would not stop talking.' She let the wine fill her cheeks, savouring the taste. 'What was all that about the best swordsman?'

Nai made a face. 'Nonsense, mostly. Oh, there is some truth in it. I have seen Bedwyr fight, and I know he is so much my superior that any comparison between us would be absurd. I suppose there may be people in the world who are more skilled than Bedwyr, and this Isgofan is obviously in his prime. But even the greatest swordsman in the world can be killed by a novice, by somebody who knows no better than to do something utterly unpredictable. Being skilled does not make you invulnerable.'

Seradwen closed her eyes and leant against his shoulder. 'Some people love making lists. Hoewgi is like that. *This* is the best stallion, *this* the best mare.'

'Exactly.' He ran his fingers through her hair. 'Tell me, why did you kick me? And why did you agree to stay another night?'

'I kicked you as a warning that the Abbot was not to be trusted. And I agreed to stay partly because you need the rest, and partly because he did not want us to leave. If we tried to go now, I think there would be some very good reason why we should not.'

'We could always fight our way out,' he said with a flash of teeth.

'You can if you like. I shall wait here and make the preparations for laying out your body when they bring you back.'

They sat in silence for a while, enjoying the wine and the warmth of the fire. The extinguished lamps ticked quietly as they cooled. The shadows thickened as the surviving torches burned low.

'Is it true, what he said of Bedwyr?' Seradwen asked quietly.

Nai grimaced, shifted uncomfortably on his stool. 'There is some truth in it.'

She waited until it was obvious he would say no more, then murmured: 'Yet your loyalty is given to him?'

'Yes.' He lifted her head from his shoulder so he could see her expression. 'But there is no need for you to give him yours. You should go home, my love. I have less to offer you now than the first time. Then I was merely impoverished; now I may well be an outlaw as well.'

She chuckled. 'Did you not hear the Abbot? We cannot go back, any of us. Not you, not me. Not your friend Bedwyr.'

'I suppose . . .' He stopped. 'No. That is true for Bedwyr, who has no home. It is true to a lesser extent for me. Of those I played with as a child, only Addonwy and Cadlew are still alive. The rest have fallen in battle, or died in accidents or of sickness. But Gereint is still my lord, and one can always make new friends. I cannot return to the Din Erbin I knew as a young man, but I can return to a place where I shall be welcome.'

'I cannot,' she said simply. 'Nor can you, if you are an outlaw.'

'Bodgath and the others on the farm? Surely they need you? And the horse herd?'

She shook her head. 'For as long as I remained there was conflict between the old way of doing things, which was Mordav's way, and the new way of the cousins. Without me they will be forced to work together. One day I can go back, but not for a while,' she added with a note of satisfaction in her voice.

'So you abandon security, possessions, position? To wander in the middle of winter with a landless vagabond?'

'Yes,' she said happily. 'Such a relief, to have no responsibilities.'

'It is like two communities living side by side,' said Seradwen as they readied themselves for the evening. 'The monks and nuns on the one hand, and the warriors on the other.'

'Yet some of the warriors seem as devout as the monks.' Nai rummaged among the bedding for his cloak brooch. 'Did you see the expression on their faces as they left the chapel? A kind of ecstasy.'

She grinned at him mischievously.

'What?'

'Nai the Silent,' she said mockingly. 'I think you used the wound to your throat as an excuse not to talk.'

'Perhaps. Most people make a lot of noise without saying anything.'

Seradwen pulled the thick folds of her robe closer about her. The lamp was turned low, the flame casting little light and large shadows across the room. She shivered, though it was not particularly cold in the hut.

'The two parts seem to mix together well.' Nai pulled on his boots and tightened the thongs.

'That is what makes me wonder whether I am wrong to mistrust the Abbot. At first I thought Angus was using the community to hide his warriors, but the people here are so clearly content and at ease with each other that I do not see how that can be true.'

As they crossed the yard to the refectory, Seradwen thought that they had been wise to stay a second night at the monastery – even if the choice had not been entirely theirs.

She shrugged herself deeper into her cloak, stiffened her muscles against the bite of the wind. It was freezing already. The ice had reformed on the puddles with the coming of the dark, and it crunched under her boots. Other figures, wrapped in heavy robes, were converging on the hall. A light mist, a frost smoke, clung to the hollows between the huts, so the figures seemed to appear from nowhere, striding purposefully for the beacon of soft light that was the refectory.

She touched Nai's arm. 'How did Angus know they had found Bedwyr?'

'I wondered that. The messenger must have broken his journey here.'

'You think Peythan's band were summoned to join the others in Lindinis?'

'I do.' Nai held back to allow a pair of nuns to enter the hall; they glanced at him curiously from under their hoods, and one smiled at Seradwen.

'Are you not afraid for him?'

'Yes,' said Nai, and held open the door.

Wethenoc greeted them with a gap-toothed grin. He took their cloaks and hung them on a row of pegs, then held out a hand.

'Your war-knife, friend. You will not need it here.'

Seradwen felt Nai's body tense. For a moment she thought he would refuse to surrender the knife, then suddenly he relaxed and unbuckled the sheath.

'I had forgotten I had it,' he said lazily.

Wethenoc indicated the far end of the room. 'The Abbot awaits you.'

The trestle tables had been rearranged, so the refectory resembled a lord's hall, with one table at right angles to the rest. The monks and nuns were for the most part already seated, though there were a few gaps in the benches. They conversed in whispers or sat primly in silence, waiting to be served. Others were carrying in great cauldrons of stew and setting them down in the middle of each table. A shaven-headed man stood behind a lectern near the central hearth, his long skull glistening with sweat, reading in a low drone from what Seradwen assumed was a bible; from his expression, this was a punishment rather than a privilege.

The high table was a different matter. As they approached Seradwen heard a buzz of conversation and the ring of laughter. The people here were much more brightly dressed; the Abbot himself wore a yellow tunic open to show his grizzled chest hair. At the sight of them he straightened in his chair.

'Come,' he cried. 'Find yourselves a place!'

They squeezed through the company. The high table had been served before the body of the hall, and some of the diners had already begun to eat. Platters of beef and mutton were being passed among the company, followed by jugs of wine and beer. The Abbot was drinking mead, Seradwen observed.

She abandoned the struggle along the row and plumped herself down in the first vacancy. Teilo the steward turned to her, his chin shiny with grease.

'My lady! What a pleasure!' He pounded the table. 'Meat here, meat I say, meat for our guest!'

'A contrast between high and low,' remarked Seradwen as he loaded her place with food.

'Eh? Oh, you mean the fare.' Teilo smiled. 'Our Abbot allows each of us to choose for him or herself. Some of us prefer a simple diet; others feel it our duty to feed the body as well as possible. Even Samson did not forbid his monks wine, you know, and as I said yesterday, he was an austere youth.' He tapped the side of his nose. 'Too much zeal is as bad as too little.'

He launched into another of his long and complicated tales, concerning two rivals for a bishopric in Gaul and the feasts they had given to win supporters to their cause.

Seradwen glanced around the table. Nai had found a seat by the Abbot and was busy eating, nodding occasionally in response to some remark from Angus. Beside him was a heavily-built man in travel stained clothes, who was so ostentatiously engrossed in conversation with his other table partner that she had the feeling he was deliberately ignoring Nai. She herself had Teilo on one side and an elderly nun with a dissatisfied expression on the other; to the best of her knowledge the woman did not utter a word all evening.

More dishes came and went, and Teilo continued with his interminable anecdotes. She had half hoped that as steward he would be responsible for overseeing the servers, but either they were very well trained or someone else behind the scenes was in charge. When Teilo began to tell the familiar tale of St Martin, the former soldier who became a bishop and founded one of the great monastic schools with a scriptorium devoted to preserving works both sacred and profane, she allowed her gaze to wander among the rest of the company.

There was a man sitting at the end of the board whose face she could not see clearly, for his head was bowed over his food. He seemed to be suffering from a cold. Every few moments he rubbed his nose or wiped the sweat from his brow. She glanced back along the row of diners and saw the Abbot holding his glass of mead to the light, apparently lost in contemplation of its depths.

'Of course,' said Teilo, 'it was one of Martin's pupils, Amator of Auxerre, who ordained Holy Patrick.'

Angus put down his glass, ran his fingers along the thin scars on his face, massaged his jaw and yawned widely. The man with the cold had raised his head and was looking around the table with an abstracted expression, as if lost in thought.

'Regin!' she exclaimed.

'Regin?' said Teilo. 'Ah yes, the bard. He has promised to entertain us later.'

'He is the other guest the Abbot mentioned? I thought he was bound for Din Erbin.'

Teilo shrugged. 'Bards travel where they will. One can no more control their passage than the flight of birds.'

'And who is the man sitting beside Nai?' she asked, seizing the opportunity to divert him from the subject of St Martin.

The steward coloured slightly. 'A former pupil of our Abbot. His name is Eri mab Ynyr.'

'One of Custennin's warriors?' She toyed with her goblet of wine. 'He appears to have ridden far.'

'From Lindinis, I believe.' Teilo coughed, filled his mouth with bread and chewed rapidly.

'Yet he seeks Abbot Angus rather than Custennin his lord? How curious.'

Teilo was saved from the necessity of a response by the Abbot, who rose to his feet and clapped his hands for silence.

'Tonight we are most fortunate, for we have among us one who is gifted in the telling of old tales, the kind which held our ancestors enthralled long before the coming of Rome.'

The elderly nun beside Seradwen sniffed loudly and gathered her things. A sound like the wind in the trees came from around the hall as others did likewise.

'As is our custom, those who wish to leave may do so now,' the Abbot said smoothly.

A bench scraped. At least half the company shuffled to the door, where Lasrian and Wethenoc waited to help them find their cloaks.

'Regin is from Dyfed, across the Severn Sea, but this night he has promised us a story from further north, from the land of Gododdin, where I myself once ventured as a young man. It is a tale replete with tragedy, with fate and foreboding, for it is a death tale, which my ancestors called an *Oitte*, and not without meaning for our own day.' The Abbot's voice dropped, and his listeners leaned forward to hear his words. 'There was magic in old times, and it may linger yet.'

The bard rose from his seat and moved into the middle of the hall by the central hearth, carrying his harp. He strummed a few notes, adjusted the tuning pegs, glanced up and smiled at Seradwen.

'In the beginning of the world the People lived in scattered communities under the trees of the great forest that stretched between the mountains and the sea,' he said, and the music of the harp reared among the pillars and rafters of the hall, so that it seemed to those present that they sat beneath the branches of tall trees, under a canopy of leaves.

'Have you heard this tale before?' The Abbot's breath, redolent of mead, fluttered against Nai's cheek.

'Yes. Not in this form.'

Regin sang of the young Son, how he came across the waves from Dun Dewed in the bright light of morning, to be the saviour of his people.

'He is good,' whispered the Abbot as the harp evoked the lap of the waves upon the shore. 'Not great, but good.'

'He is the bard who was at Seradwen's farm?' murmured Nai.

Angus smiled to himself. 'You should be grateful to him. Without Regin to prepare the way, I doubt Seradwen would have left her home.'

Nai grunted. The man beside him, who had not addressed a word to him throughout the meal, turned and scowled.

'At Custennin's court it is customary to keep a still tongue when a bard performs.'

'The fault is mine,' said Angus, leaning across Nai. 'Forgive me, Eri.'

'Of course.' The man inclined his head in the Abbot's direction, but his eyes remained locked on Nai. After a time he bared his teeth and looked away.

The tale came to an end with the audience shivering at the thought of the disembodied head issuing instructions even as it lay upon the bank, and of the great storm scouring the land of its enemies.

'So tell me,' said Angus as the last strains of the harp died away among the rafters, 'did Grugyn profit by his treachery?'

'Who can tell?' rasped Nai. He cleared his throat with a drink of ale. 'Does it profit a man to hold the rule? That depends upon the man.'

'The problem facing the People, you will note, was similar to that facing Albion after Camlann.' The Abbot rubbed at the creases and scars on his face. 'They of course had Grugyn. We had no one.'

'Because Medraut had also fallen in the battle?' Nai refilled his goblet. 'Was that not the futility of it? If Medraut had been patient –'

'You think so?' Angus regarded him impatiently. 'If Arthur had intended Medraut to be his heir, he would have adopted him, as he himself was adopted by Ambrosius the Younger. No, Arthur never meant Medraut to succeed him.'

'Who then?' demanded Nai.

'I think Arthur was waiting for someone.' Angus drummed his fingers on the table top. 'You must remember there was a deeply mystical side to the Amherawdyr. He believed himself chosen, by God, by fate, whatever, and I think he expected his successor to arrive in the same way – simply to appear at the court one day and make his qualities manifest.'

'Who?' repeated Nai.

'We shall never know now,' the Abbot shrugged. He fixed Nai with his cold blue eyes. 'You, perhaps?'

'I am not a leader of men,' Nai said quickly, then saw that he was being teased.

Regin struck a chord in the middle of the hall and stilled the murmur of conversation. He shifted away from the hearth, mopping his brow, and raised a laugh from his audience.

'Warm work,' he said. 'At this point it is customary to give you some lighter fare, a rollicking yarn filled with humour to aid the digestion of the first piece. But I know that here within this monastery you are serious folk, dedicated people, learned scholars all. And it has often seemed to me that the tale I have just told, the tale of Llew the Young Son and the treachery of Grugyn the Strong, has a more recent counterpart – a companion piece, if you like. This too is a death tale, this too is set within Gododdin, and this too tells how a young son was brought down by treachery.'

His audience stilled, and Nai noticed that a few of them cast uncertain glances at Angus.

'As your Abbot told you, I am from Dyfed. To say that Dyfed is not Dumnonia is to state the obvious. Our traditions and outlook are different. We are divided from the rest of Prydein by the mountains that march along the spine of our country, so that we were never so heavily influenced by Rome as those of you who live in gentler lands. We, like you, suffered much at the hands of Scotti raiders – even now that menace is not entirely gone – yet we and they share the same blood. Many of our ancestors came out of Ierne, and in their day they also were great reivers.'

'Come to the point!' snarled Eri. Nai suddenly remembered where he had heard his name before.

'Our hearts were never given to the Amherawdyr as firmly as yours: not because we were not loyal –' Regin raised a hand to forestall criticism and the man beside Nai snorted loudly '– but because we were more distanced from the centre of things than you in Dumnonia. That distance lends detachment, and perhaps helps us to see more clearly than you. Listen, and judge for yourselves.'

Without pausing he went directly into his tale. He sang of Arthur and a realm at peace upon the surface, of great warriors with no wars to fight, of jealousies and resentments, of slights real and imagined. The old hatreds finally came to a head in the far north, and Arthur's son was sent to prove himself under the guidance of Cei. But Cei, ageing and half blind, was envious of the other's youth and prowess, and did all he could to make Arthur's son seem a fool.

The Abbot's fist crashed into the table top, making Nai jump. Regin faltered to a halt.

Angus stood. His voice was soft in the silence of the hall. 'No. It was not like that.'

Regin glanced around as if seeking support, turned back to Angus. 'Is that not what I was saying? We see things from a different point of view. What is dead ground to you is –'

'No,' repeated Angus. The skin was tight around his mouth and nostrils, mottled on his cheekbones. 'Sit down, bard.'

Regin made to protest but the Abbot overrode him. 'You travel this land singing your songs, telling us of an Arthur we do not know. Were you not my guest I would say you lied, and I would say you lied for some purpose of your own. Do you seek to reduce Arthur in our estimation so that some lesser mortal may seem fit to take his place? Is that it? Are you preparing the way for Vortepor of Dyfed to seize the rule of Albion?'

The bard stared at him incredulously, spread his hands in appeal. 'Like a latter-day John the Baptist, you mean?' If it was an attempt to lighten the atmosphere it failed.

'Be careful. I am a tolerant man, but I will not tolerate blasphemy.'

Angus was quivering with rage, and Nai wondered that his anger should have sprung full formed so quickly. Regin lifted the harp, seemingly still unaware of the passion he had aroused, and the Abbot's voice cracked like a whip. 'I bade you sit!'

Regin stared open-mouthed, his face white. After a moment he shook his head in studied disbelief and shuffled to his place at the table.

The Abbot took a deep breath and glared around the company, as if seeking another target for his rage.

'Master,' Eri said soothingly, leaning across Nai. 'Will you not tell us yourself what happened? It is a tale of which I have heard many versions, but never your own.'

'Mine?' Angus wiped his forehead with his sleeve. 'Mine? No, it was too long ago, and brings back memories I prefer to forget.'

'Persuade him, you fool,' Eri snarled in Nai's ear. 'He was there, saw it all. You are his guest; he will talk if you ask.'

Amused at the blatant way in which he was being manipulated, Nai sat up and touched the Abbot's tunic.

'Please,' he said. 'For if those who know the truth do not speak out, the lies of others will prevail.'

Angus frowned. 'I wonder whether the bard is right,' he mused. 'It is a strange place, Dun Eidin.' He shook himself, turned to Eri. 'Did you call me master? I am no longer your master. I am the Abbot of St Martin's.'

'You will always be my master,' Eri said with a crooked grin.

'It is a long tale, and in parts complicated,' Angus said to Nai. 'More than one night in the telling, I think.' He seemed suddenly uncertain, as if his rage had drained him of his strength. 'Do you understand why Eri calls me his master?'

'You trained him,' said Nai.

Angus nodded, his eyes unfocused. 'My cousin Lleminawg went to Arthur's Court and made a name for himself. I was younger, little more than a boy, and I knew that if I followed him I would always walk in his shadow. Not only was I younger, but I also belonged to a junior branch of the family.'

The Abbot stretched, the sleeves of his robe slipping up to bare his scarred forearms. 'So I chose a different direction. We had been tutored in arms by the same people, and they said that I was close to being Lleminawg's equal. Rather than follow him to Arthur's Court, I remained with Kynfawr, Custennin's father. I served him for many years, fighting the Scotti raiders on our northern shores. Sometimes Arthur's men joined with us, but more often we fought alone, Kynfawr's warband. I rose high in Kynfawr's counsels, a man with a reputation of my own. The fact I was Lleminawg's cousin mattered less and less with each passing day. In time I became Kynfawr's master at arms. I taught them all, the men who are now Custennin's warband.'

'I know,' said Nai.

'Of course you do,' murmured the Abbot. 'Of course you do.' He swayed slightly, caught the table edge and steadied himself. 'But I did not spend my whole life in Kynfawr's service. For three years, three magnificent years, I was one of the Companions. I rode with Arthur, and there are not many men now living who can claim that honour.'

He filled his glass and pushed back his chair. Nai, who had feared he was drunk and about to become maudlin, suddenly saw that he was nothing of the kind. He pushed between the diners and strode out into the open space where Regin had stood.

'Come, listen,' he cried, his voice waking echoes in the rafters, 'and I will tell you how Llacheu died, Arthur's son, fruit of the White Queen's womb and repository of all their hopes.'

CHAPTER FIFTEEN

Again the old bathhouse was crowded. The threat of snow still hung in the air and the grey sky, and had brought many people out to do their marketing before the weather closed in. As Bedwyr moved among them he heard muttering about what a long winter it would be if snow fell before the shortest day. Most looked harried, and those who could afford it were trying to lay in supplies, knowing that the farmers from outside the city walls would not return until the weather improved.

He pushed his way between them, picking a path around the stands and barrows, searching the crowd for some sign of the men who had been pursuing him for so long. The cap was pulled down firmly on his head, disguising his hair, and his sword was belted close to his side, concealed under his cloak. Behind him someone was playing a pipe, the music thin and plaintive, almost lost in the noise as the stallholders shouted their wares or bargained with their customers.

Hunter and hunted, Bedwyr twisted through the throng with the sound of the pipe threading after him, and he found himself moving to its rhythm without knowing why, using it to guide himself around the people and the trestles with their spillage of goods sprawled across the aisles, slipping past the blockages as a branch caught in the current of a river might slip around the rocks in midstream. Long after the music was lost behind him he continued to weave through the crowd, his eyes testing every face, and when he saw the group at the far end of the market in the shadow of the old wall he did not break step but glided on among the stalls, keeping the passers-by between him and his enemies.

There were four of them: short and stocky men, standing with their backs to the wall, surveying the crowds in the manner of men who did not expect to find what they were seeking. He paused beside a broad-hipped woman who was examining great rounds of cheese on a barrow, using her body to shield him from the Picts. She glanced at him suspiciously, one hand checking the wallet at her girdle; he smiled gently, and craned around her bulk as her attention returned to the cheeses.

The four were joined by a fifth man, tall and lithe with fair hair. The group conferred, one of the Picts waving his arms in remonstrance; the tall man laughed and patted him on the shoulder, then turned and surveyed the crowd. Bedwyr drew back into the shadow of the woman, his movements calm and unhurried so as not to attract attention. The woman shifted uncomfortably, glared; he touched his cap as if she had just given him an instruction and walked away, keeping his head low and not looking behind him at the watchers.

He lost himself in the flow of the crowd, going where they went, halting when they halted, letting them carry him away from the Picts and the tall man. Now he walked in step with a mother and child so an onlooker might think he belonged with them, now he became one of a party of middle-aged men strolling among the clothiers' stalls. When they stopped to feel the quality of some woollen cloaks – nodding knowingly as they rubbed the material between finger and thumb – he stopped with them, and casually glanced back as if searching for an acquaintance.

The Picts had not followed.

Laughing among themselves, the middle-aged men had begun to bargain with the stallholder for the cloak. Bedwyr squeezed between them and made for the side of the market. Two small boys sat on top of the wall, which was lower here in the middle than at either end, their bare legs dangling as they chewed on wrinkled apples. They watched him approach with interest, obviously wondering if he was going to order them down off the wall – as he came close he could see them preparing reasons why they should remain.

'A fine viewpoint you have there, young masters,' he called.

The larger of the two gave him a gap-toothed grin. 'We can see everything without being trampled,' he said proudly.

'Everything? Surely not everything.'

'Everything,' echoed the smaller boy.

Bedwyr pretended to consider for a moment. 'Very well. Can you see four men standing together in the far corner?'

'No,' said the first boy. 'I can see five, though,' he added. 'The northerners who talk funny and the man from Custennin.'

'My father says Custennin is a –' began his friend, stopping suddenly when the first boy kicked him on the shin. 'Ow, what did you do that for?' he wailed indignantly. The first boy ignored him, watched Bedwyr with a tense expression on his face.

'On the whole I am inclined to agree with your father,' Bedwyr said smoothly. The larger boy relaxed. 'You seem well informed for a pair of urchins.'

'Uncle Math works at the inn.'

'Does he now?' Bedwyr pursed his lips, considered both children. 'I agreed to meet one of the northerners here in the market, but I cannot remember where.'

'Why don't you ask the others?' said the smaller boy. His friend bent and whispered in his ear, and his eyes widened. He stared at Bedwyr, glanced uncertainly at his friend, wriggled awkwardly on the wall.

'So what I was wondering, young masters, is whether you from your elevated position can see a single northerner standing by himself, or looking as if he is searching for someone.'

'By the cobblers' stalls,' the smaller boy said obligingly. 'He was here yesterday as well.'

'I thought they were all looking for you,' said the first boy.

'Did you?' said Bedwyr. 'Tell me, how long does the market last?'

The boys were taken aback at his ignorance. 'Till dusk, or bad weather, or till all the customers are gone.'

'No, I meant how many days.'

'There is always somebody here,' said the larger boy. 'Except in the dead of winter.'

'And in the spring the traders come from Gaul,' the other said enthusiastically, 'with whole cart loads of big pots full of wine and oil. Then the market livens up.' He stared around at the crowds. 'Today is quiet. Nothing ever happens here once the ships stop coming.'

'Thank you, young masters. Over by the shoemakers' stalls, you say.'

'Yes, he's still there by himself. I think one of the cobblers is trying to sell him a pair of shoes.'

Bedwyr grinned and sketched a farewell. The Picts had obviously let their purpose be widely known. He suspected it was only a matter of time before somebody remarked that a stranger was staying in one of the abandoned houses and deduced this might be the man the Picts were seeking.

He hastened through the crowd in the direction the boys had indicated, making no effort to be unobtrusive now. As he went he pulled the heavy gloves from his hands and tucked them in his belt, hitched back his cloak to reveal the hilt of his sword. People glanced at his face and stepped aside to let him pass; mothers pulled their children in tight to their sides and held onto them even after he had gone by.

The Pict was loitering beside a display of cheap shoes, trying simultaneously to avoid the attentions of the stallholder and keep an eye on his surroundings. Bedwyr barged past him, catching him on the shoulder and reaching out with his scarred left hand to steady him.

'Your pardon,' he muttered from the corner of his mouth, and strode on down the aisle, turning at its end to look behind him with what he hoped was an expression of consternation, as if he had belatedly realized whose shoulder he had brushed.

The man was staring after him with mingled horror and surprise. Their eyes met, and the man seemed to gather himself. He assumed a nonchalant air, as if Bedwyr were nothing more than a clumsy stranger and it was pure chance that sent him strolling in his wake.

Bedwyr walked briskly to the entrance, feet slapping on the cobbles, determined to give the man no pause in which to summon his companions. A small group were exchanging pleasantries by the gap in the wall where the doors to the bathhouse would once have been; he wove between them, moving faster now, but not so fast his follower would lose him.

At the corner of the street he risked a quick glance behind him. The Pict was about ten paces back, looking worried. Bedwyr guessed that the man was unused to cities, and had no idea how to track his quarry without being seen.

Bedwyr's original plan had been to lead the man a dance through the city before arriving at the house. But it seemed to him now that the man would lose him if he complicated matters, so he abandoned that idea. Instead he went by the most direct route, staying on the main thoroughfares. His one dread was that they might encounter a patrol of the City Guard: the Picts had been so open about their purpose in Lindinis that they must have some official standing, and the man might be able to request or command the Guards to arrest him – which would prove awkward.

He could feel his shoulder blades prickling. The hardest part was pretending he did not know the man was immediately behind him: every instinct was telling him to turn and fight, to seize the Pict *now* and drag him into an alleyway, while he still held the advantage, before the man decided to launch his own strike. An alley gaped before him and he turned into it without thinking, skirting the beggar lying in its mouth, his footsteps echoing from the blank walls, the smell of rotting garbage strong in his nostrils. He could sense rather than hear the Pict keeping his distance, beginning to understand the rules of the game they were playing, and he hitched his cloak on his shoulders, paused to tap a foot as if to dislodge a stone from his boot.

Children were playing somewhere beyond the high walls, shrieking with delight. The air was suddenly full of woodsmoke as a down draught eddied into the mouth of the alley. Someone was stewing mutton in one of the nearby houses. The walls were grey and grimy with the accumulated soot of the years – centuries probably. This was the sort of place where one might be set upon by thieves even in daylight – and if that happened now, he wondered, would the Pict flee or dash forward to his aid?

He left the alley, coming out onto a street of timber houses. The sky was like beaten pewter. The beasts carved on the eaves of some of the buildings seemed to be crouched against the coming storm. He moved faster, not daring look back, almost trotting in his eagerness to be home and have done with this.

Three more turns and he was approaching the house. To a casual glance, or to someone unfamiliar with the design of Roman town houses, it was not obvious that the scattered doors in the walls all gave access to the same building. The shop alcoves, most of them the size of a small room, made it appear that several properties, rather than a single house, lay behind the wall. A native of Lindinis would not have been fooled for a moment, but a Pict from the far north, unaccustomed to cities, might believe that a man who disappeared through one door would remain inside until he came out by the same door.

Bedwyr closed the garden gate behind him, dropped the bolt into place, and broke into a run. He sprinted across the garden, fumbling with the padlock key, and hurled himself into the house as the latch sprang open. He raced through the peristyle, startling the pony, skidded across the atrium to the main entry, and heaved the great bar out of its sockets.

Two ragged old men were huddled on the steps of the house opposite. They gave no sign of having noticed him as he moved cautiously to the corner. The Pict was standing beside the garden gate, irresolute, one hand outstretched to the latch. Bedwyr saw him tense his body against the strength of the bolts, frown and step back, contemplating the wall. For a moment Bedwyr thought he was going to hurl himself at the coping and haul himself over. Instead the man shook his head and ran his fingers through his hair. He glanced around and Bedwyr flattened himself against the corner, but the man seemed to have no sense of being watched.

The Pict took a few paces towards him, halted and turned, stood studying the position of the gate. Then he started walking again, his attention on the buildings around him, oblivious to what lay before him. Bedwyr stepped out into his path and struck hard, once, straight to the stomach.

The Pict groaned and doubled over. Bedwyr seized him by the shoulders and half walked, half ran him into the house, tripping him as they entered so the man went sprawling across the stone floor in a tangle of arms and legs while Bedwyr barred the door.

'Now,' he said aloud, and even to his own ears his voice sounded cruel.

He did not have much time. He needed to break the man quickly, with a minimum of noise.

The Pict moaned, tried to sit up. Bedwyr clouted him over the ear, leant down and pulled the knife from the man's belt.

'Talk,' he said.

The man gaped at him, unbelieving. Bedwyr wove the knife before the dark face, the tip almost scoring the flesh, reversed direction and broke the Pict's nose with the hilt.

'Talk,' he said again.

The man coughed and spluttered, choking on his own blood, eyes wide with pain and shock.

'Listen to me,' said Bedwyr. 'There is something you should know. I enjoy hurting people. Do you understand?'

He darted forward with the knife and sliced the man's cheek.

'A long time ago I killed one of your kinsmen. I did it slowly, taking my time.'

'Gwydawg,' gasped the man. His hands waved feebly.

'Yes. I will serve you the same way unless you tell me what I want to know. Forget any dreams of being a hero. There will be no glory in your dying. When I have finished your friends will not recognize your corpse.' He slashed again, and another trickle of blood joined the smears on the man's face.

Inside he felt a sick excitement and knew he was close to losing control.

'Talk to me,' he growled.

The man swallowed, adam's apple bobbing, began to speak, the words coming in a torrent. His accent was thick, and Bedwyr had to listen hard to make sense of what he was saying.

'Wait, no more, no more. The lady sent me, the old one, riding with the others. They want you alive for the sake of the chalice – then they will kill you – but she sent me with them to keep you safe. I am with you, not against you. That is why I did not fetch any of the others when I saw you in the market. Believe me, you must believe me, not cut any more. Teleri verch Afallach, Teleri daughter of Afallach, the old woman whose power is waning now, all used up, she sent me.'

'Teleri?' Bedwyr said in wonder, and drew back a little, the bloodied knife loose in his hand.

'Yes!' The man was on the verge of weeping. 'The others, her kinsmen, say she is too old, not right anyway a woman should have the rule, but she has led us since you killed the last of Pedrylaw Menestyr's sons, Gwydawg.'

Long ago, in vengeance for Cei's death. And if the killing of Cei was no better than murder, so too was what he did to Gwydawg, toying with him as a cat toys with its prey, forcing the man to pick up his sword and continue fighting long after he should have given him a clean death. It was one of the few acts in his life of which he was utterly ashamed.

'So much killing,' he said aloud.

'To prevent more she sent me,' the Pict said eagerly. 'She bids you find your lady, Arthur's Queen, unmake the Cup of Sovereignty, so save our people from themselves. They are eaten up with the need for it, live only for the days when they were its guardians. But that time is done now.'

Bedwyr laughed humourlessly. 'Find Gwenhwyvar? Easier said than done. And why should I care what happens to your people?'

The man summoned what dignity he could manage with his broken nose and blood smeared face. 'You did wrong when you slew Gwydawg. You owe us life.'

'Why should I trust you?'

The man's voice changed, became huskier. ' "I will cling to you as the ivy clings to the tree." '

Bedwyr stared at him. It might have been Teleri speaking: an older Teleri, her voice roughened with age, no longer honey-sweet, yet still Teleri. The words were certainly hers. He could remember how she had looked up from the tablet on which she was sketching the shape of an island (pale freckles floating on the dark tan of her skin) to speak, to reassure him that he would not lose her.

But he had.

'Very well,' he said. 'I believe you.' He glanced at the knife with disgust and flung it clattering across the passage. 'What else can you tell me?'

'Custennin of Dumnonia allows us to search his lands for some sign of you or Gwenhwyvar.' The Pict winced as he tried to straighten his nose between his fingers. 'A condition is that we keep some of his men with us.'

'And what does Custennin gain from this?'

The Pict shrugged. 'Nobody told me. Perhaps he hopes to seize the chalice for himself? We do not care. Dirmyg who leads us now the lady is gone has plans to avoid Custennin's men if we succeed.'

'What do you mean, now the lady is gone?'

'Teleri left our homeland before we did. All through my childhood she ruled us, like her father before her, but today Dirmyg and his followers are our rulers, and she is gone into exile.'

The man was calmer now Bedwyr had tossed the knife aside, his speech easier to understand. 'Always she has come and gone as it pleased her. But then she had much power. Today her magic is used up, and men follow Dirmyg.'

Bedwyr frowned. 'This Dirmyg is here, you say?'

'Here in the city, yes. We divided our strength to speed the search. One group went to the holy wood where rumour said you had been living; the other to Isca.'

'Where you found me.' Bedwyr rubbed his chin.

'We did not know it was you, not for certain. Not until you led us to the ruined caer. Nor do we – they – know whether you have the chalice or if it stayed with the woman.'

'Gwenhwyvar,' Bedwyr said with a hint of menace.

The man flinched and bowed his head, accepting the correction. 'The Lady Gwenhwyvar. You were the only trace we had. Dirmyg cast the bones, studied the entrails of the beasts he offered to the gods, read the flights of the birds in the heavens. He chose to lead the party that went to Isca, and he was right. The gods favour him.'

'Yet you are still loyal to Teleri?' said Bedwyr, curious.

The Pict spat on the hem of his cloak and wiped some of the blood from his face. 'I am,' he said simply. 'The other group were not fortunate. Isgofan, who is Custennin's man, brought word of what befell them.' He glanced slyly around the cloak.

'And?' Bedwyr demanded impatiently.

'They met the one who had taken your place at the wood. They sought to take him alive, thinking he might know where you had gone. Three of them are dead and more are hurt. They will join us when they have finished him.'

Bedwyr drew a deep breath. 'Nai.'

'That was the name Isgofan gave him. He was a friend of yours?'

'Was?'

The Pict shrugged. 'Now they know we have found your trail, they do not need him alive. If he is not already dead, he will be soon.'

Bedwyr leant forward and hauled the man to his feet. 'There is water in the garden,' he said, indicating the way through the house. 'Wash your face. None of the cuts are deep.'

The man paused, his expression unreadable under the mask of blood. 'I might run.'

'You might,' Bedwyr agreed levelly. 'It does not greatly concern me.'

He turned aside into the kitchen and gathered his possessions, carried them out into the garden. The horse came to his whistle and he set about saddling it while the Pict bathed his face in the bucket.

'I have never seen that before,' the man said after a while. 'A horse coming to a whistle, like a dog.'

'He is bored,' Bedwyr said. 'It does not work every time.'

'If they catch you,' the man said hesitantly.

'Yes?'

'They will hurt you much more than you have hurt me.'

Bedwyr slipped the bit into the pony's mouth, tightened the harness. 'Your kinsmen have no reason to love me. Nor I them.'

'But my kinswoman?'

The man's voice was soft, insinuating. Bedwyr rounded on him so rapidly the horse shied and the man stepped back, narrowly avoiding the bucket.

'The game is almost played to its end,' snarled Bedwyr. 'I cannot tell them what I do not know, however badly they hurt me.'

The Pict stared at him blandly, the cuts on his face oozing fresh blood that trickled down to mingle with the pink froth on his beard. 'She never took another man.'

'How noble.' Bedwyr tugged the girth, adjusted the breaching and breastcollar. 'I however am not a noble man, as you may have gathered.'

He strode into the house to check that he had not forgotten anything. The Pict trailed behind him.

'Tell your friends,' Bedwyr said over his shoulder, 'that I do not know where Gwenhwyvar has gone. Nor do I know what has become of the chalice. Admittedly, even if I did know I would not tell them, but what I say is true all the same. Tell them also,' he added with rising anger, 'that if a hair of Nai's head is harmed I will wreak such a vengeance upon them that it will make what happened to Gwydawg seem like a peaceful death.'

The sound rolled through the empty house like thunder. They stared at each other, caught in a moment of complicity despite the damage Bedwyr had done to the man with fist and knife.

'Tell them yourself,' the Pict said, his voice oddly flat.

Bedwyr broke into a run as a second great blow shook the main door. A chip of wood leapt across the corridor. A plank cracked with a loud report as a third blow boomed through the house, and suddenly the strikes were coming in a swift and unrelenting rhythm. Another splinter flew across the passage, and Bedwyr saw the grey of an axe-head peer blindly into the house before it was wrenched away.

'Run,' the Pict said without emotion.

'I am tired of running.'

The man shrugged and shrank back against the wall, wrapped himself carefully in his cloak as if shutting himself off from the world. 'They say this Isgofan is a master swordsman,' he remarked inconsequentially, and pulled the hood over his head.

Bedwyr glanced at the Pict in disbelief and drew his sword. The door shuddered and burst slowly apart in a cloud of dust. A man leapt through the gap, long knife in his hand, saw Bedwyr and paused.

'What do you want?' said Bedwyr.

Teeth gleamed in the shadowed face. The man loped forward, knife raised: Bedwyr stepped to meet him, slashed the sword across his chest, and shoved him back into the doorway.

For a long moment nothing happened. Then the wounded man began to scream, writhing in the wreckage of the door. Three Picts flung themselves through the gap in quick succession, hurdling their comrade and rebounding from the walls, blades whirling.

'I thought you wanted me alive,' laughed Bedwyr, the joy of combat bubbling within him, and took the first's legs from under him.

The remaining pair watched him, moving more warily now they had seen him act, covering each other as they advanced along the passage.

He retreated before them, smiling, beckoning them on with his damaged hand, then lunged, catching one off-guard with a quick strike to the right wrist, and found himself committed to continuing forward against the other.

The light was bad and he could not see clearly, was aware only of dark shadows leaping all around him. He felt something snag momentarily on his jerkin, spun and put out a foot to avoid colliding with the wall, used the momentum to shove himself toward the atrium, abandoning the corridor. Somebody was sobbing behind him. He dropped a shoulder and let a spear slide past his head, struck upwards with the sword and found an obstruction. A shape reeled backwards, shouting, and then he was out into the light of the atrium, panting for breath and his legs weak beneath him.

Two were dead, or so badly hurt they would not trouble him again. At least two more were wounded, one of whom would not be using his right hand for a while. Together with his informant that made five of the original seven.

His breathing steadied. He could hear voices, see movement in the dimness of the passage. He shivered, bent his legs to keep them supple, felt the cold prickle of sweat drying on his body.

'Come on then!' he shouted impatiently, and tapped the flat of his blade against the marble floor tiles.

They were thinking now rather than charging straight at him. Two men appeared in the mouth of the corridor, carrying spears and small targes. They edged towards him, holding the spears underarm to take full advantage of their length, supporting them with their forearms so they could be used to parry his sword. The men separated as they entered the atrium, keeping the spears pointed at him, moving out to either wall, herding him back. If he had had a shield he might have risked an attack. Without one it seemed wiser to retreat.

Behind the spearmen came the tattooed man bearing an axe, and at his side one of the wounded, right wrist swathed in a bloodstained bandage, face pale in the daylight.

'Which of you is Dirmyg?' Bedwyr asked mockingly, for the name meant 'scorn' in the tongue of Prydein.

'I am,' said the tattooed man, 'and scorn upon you indeed, Bedwyr mab Petroc, that have tortured and murdered a well born young man this day.'

'Murdered?' said Bedwyr, stepping carefully back to the door leading to the peristyle, his eyes never leaving the spearmen. 'He was alive when your ruffians broke into the house.'

'Shame upon me that I came too late,' Dirmyg said as if he had not spoken. 'A grief it is to me that I dallied in the market place, did not heed my kinsmen's urgings. An impetuous youth he was, and one who admired you — mistakenly as it proved. Why, old man, he believed your legend, for all we told him it was a lie.'

'You killed him, did you? Stabbed him as he sat in the hallway. He must have known you would.' He flung himself forward, suddenly angry at the manner of his informant's death, the way the youth had accepted it as inevitable, the fact that he himself had hurt him needlessly. He drove the nearest spearman back in a flurry of blows, beating on the shield and the shaft of the spear, laughing at the terror in his opponent's eyes; side-stepped the counter attack from the other man, who had come rushing over,

291

and took advantage of their disarray to slip into the corner where the passage led deeper into the house.

'It is not we who have done the killing here,' Dirmyg shouted after him.

'Not for lack of trying,' he called in reply.

The door here had been left open too long and had rotted in the rain. It would not slow them for more than an instant, so he did not bother to close it, instead watching them from the cover of the corridor to see what they would do next.

The first spearman seemed to be in trouble. Bedwyr guessed he had been wounded earlier and was now in pain after his exertions. While he waited the man bowed his head and leant against the atrium wall, clutching his ribs.

'What do you want with me?'

At first he thought they would ignore him. Then Dirmyg stepped into the centre of the courtyard, hefting the axe in his hand.

'We want Arthur's widow. We want the chalice your friends stole from our fathers long ago.'

'An old argument, not worthy of an answer. And if you think I would give the Lady Gwenhwyvar up to the likes of you, you are even more deluded than I thought.'

He was enjoying himself. The four Picts posed no great threat unless he made a mistake, and his line of retreat to the pony was secure behind him. Later there would be time for regrets, for guilt at what he had done to the youth and the pleasure he had taken in causing pain, but for now there was only the weak winter sunshine on the cracked marble floor tiles, and these four fools trying to disable him.

'Like all Arthur's men, you kill wantonly and justify your murders with talk of the greater good,' cried Dirmyg. 'How many of those who have dared disagree with you over the years are still alive? The reckoning came for Arthur, but you somehow escaped. Not for much longer!'

He hurled the axe at Bedwyr's head.

Taken by surprise, Bedwyr ducked and flung up his blade to ward off the heavy missile. The impact nearly drove him from his feet. The wooden shaft swung round his sword and caught him on the ear. He swayed, gasping, sick with pain though he knew he was not seriously hurt and it would pass, it would pass if he could just hold on, and in that moment the Picts were upon him.

They had dropped their spears and drawn their war-knives. They pressed him close, the injured man apparently recovered – or else he had been shamming all the while. Bedwyr stopped thinking and let his body take control, battering the small shields, slicing his strokes so the blade did not catch in the wood and leather, his feet moving in a rapid dance that carried him away from his attackers, left them colliding with each other as he glided deeper into the passage.

He pulled open the door at the far end and felt the wind leap past him into the corridor. He glanced back and saw the four of them entangled in the gloom, a single outline against the light from the atrium.

As he looked they came after him, their anger overcoming their fear. They had regained their spears, and they came cautiously but with determination, trying once again to herd him into a corner. He allowed them to manoeuvre him away from the path running down the middle of the peristyle, and hurdled the brown briers which were all that remained of somebody's flower garden, his feet slipping in the slimy mulch that had gathered under the eaves. He clung to a pillar, chest heaving, sword heavy in his hand.

One of the spearmen saw his chance, lunged ahead of his fellows. Bedwyr watched the long blue spike slide toward him, aimed at his midriff; at the last moment he rolled around the pillar, sword swinging.

The other Picts were screaming a warning, but the man stood gaping as his target vanished, frozen in his thrust, unable to release the spear which was now on the wrong side of the column, neck neatly bared as if he were waiting for the blow as his target reappeared beside him.

The sword struck and blood fountained across the stained white of the pillar. The spear clattered on the paving stones.

'Go!' said Bedwyr into the silence that followed. 'Go!'

The three survivors stared at him, eyes wide with terror.

'Oh beautifully done!' said a new voice. 'Beautifully done!'

A man in a faded brown cloak stood by the entrance to the peristyle, hand raised in salute.

'It is true then. Dirmyg has succeeded where his betters have failed in driving the old fox from cover.'

The newcomer stepped forward. 'I confess, I had expected someone larger. Perhaps you have shrunk a little with age –

though now I think on it I remember my master saying you were never a big man. Bedwyr Bedrydant, was that it? Bedwyr of the perfect sinews. I am delighted to see you. My only regret is that we could not have met as equals. I would have liked to test myself against you in your prime.'

'Who are you?' demanded Bedwyr, easing away from the pillar.

'Ah, forgive me. I am, of course, Dirmyg's mentor, his guide in these strange lands – well, strange to him at least – Custennin's man – or do you prefer to call him Constantine in the old style?' White teeth flashed against tanned skin. 'I am Isgofan mab Banon, and you are Bedwyr mab Petroc, and my prisoner.'

The last was said so softly Bedwyr was not sure he had heard correctly.

'I am your what?'

'My prisoner,' Isgofan repeated, still smiling. His voice hardened. 'Please stop moving. There is nowhere for you to run. You merely delay the inevitable.'

Bedwyr raised his sword. The three Picts waited near the body of their comrade as if they had no further part to play in this. Dirmyg stared at him, his expression unreadable under the tattoos. Bedwyr frowned.

'You appear to be alone,' he said.

'Oh I am, I am.' Isgofan rubbed his chin and Bedwyr heard the rasp of stubble. 'Two of my escort are waiting by the front door, together with the rather smelly beggar who guided us here. We found the youngster's body, by the way. What made you kill him? Surely it was not necessary?'

'I did not. That was Dirmyg's work.'

Isgofan lifted an eyebrow, regarded him thoughtfully. 'Dirmyg? How unfortunate. I suppose he tortured him as well?' He paused, laughed. 'Not a very likely story, and hardly worthy of one of Arthur's Companions. But there, it is often the way, is it not? The reality rarely matches the legend.'

Bedwyr edged another five paces towards the door leading to the garden.

'Please stand still.' Isgofan tossed back his cloak and drew his sword. He raised his left hand to cover his throat, and Bedwyr saw the fingers were covered with rings of silver and black iron, like a partial gauntlet.

'I shall not tell you again,' Isgofan said conversationally. His sword lashed from side to side like the tail of angry cat, moving faster and faster as he warmed his muscles.

'I do not understand your part in this,' said Bedwyr.

'The penalty of age,' said Isgofan, strolling in his direction. 'The wits slow. The body rebels. Come!' He held out his left hand while the blade in his right wove about him. 'Give me the sword. Surrender yourself to me. I do not wish to hurt you.'

Bedwyr shook his head, retreated behind a pillar.

'Oh dear,' sighed Isgofan. 'You are even slower of wit than I had thought. Come, we are civilized men, you and I, the heirs of Rome.' He waved the beringed hand at the Picts as he bounded up the steps to the colonnade. 'We are not like these barbarians. There is no need for violence between us. Surely your blood lust has been sated by the bodies you have left lying through the house?'

'You are confident.' Bedwyr twisted around another column, his eyes never leaving Isgofan.

'Naturally. I am the best swordsman of my time – with, I suppose, the possible exception of my master – just as you were once the best of your time. That is why it would be a tragedy for us to fight – a tragedy with only one possible ending. For this, my friend, is my time, not yours.'

One moment the man was three pillars away, his smile mocking, his blade flickering endlessly through the heavy air. The next he was beside Bedwyr and their arms were locked together, the rings were squeezing Bedwyr's fingers on the hilt, and the sword was being wrenched from his grasp.

Isgofan laughed and danced away, a blade in either fist, both whirling through the first fat drops of rain.

'Can you manage now?' he shouted to the Picts.

They stirred from their daze, the three of them, and walked along the shelter of the colonnade, Dirmyg slightly in the lead. Bedwyr watched them come, unable to move. The tattooed man's features were twisted in an expression of triumph – this much he could read – and their hands were reaching out to seize him, to drag him away to their lair, and he had failed, failed utterly.

'Ah Celemon,' he groaned as his knees gave way beneath him and he toppled into Dirmyg's grasp, knocking the Pict off balance, and – whether by accident or design not even he could have said – his head lifted up into the Pict's face. The grip on his tunic was suddenly loose, and he was moving again, running for the door to the garden, and Isgofan was bellowing with rage, the slap of feet loud on the paving stones behind him. He burst through the door, slammed it, felt the crash of a body against it, reached for the padlock with slippery hands, praying that the key was still in place. The top of the door bulged as someone tried to force it open. All his strength was now going into holding it closed. The lock refused to fit into the hasp. His free hand was shaking so badly he could not steer the hoop through the eye. He could not hold much longer. The door shook under a renewed assault and his feet began to slide under him.

The padlock snapped shut and he turned the key.

Then he was running across the garden with the pony's reins looped over his wrist, pulling back the bolts of the gate and hauling himself into the saddle, while the garden echoed to the sounds of thunder and splintering wood and bellowing voices. The pony leapt beneath him and he was out in the glistening street without knowing how he had come there, reeling unbalanced in the saddle, black rain falling hard around him, white water frothing in the gutters, and the way ahead was clear and the angry voices were soon left far behind.

CHAPTER SIXTEEN

1

The Abbot's voice filled the hall:

'Come, listen, and I will tell you how Llacheu died, Arthur's son, fruit of the White Queen's womb and repository of all their hopes.'

That is how they begin this tale in the halls of the Saesons, and a fine tale it is, the way they tell it, filled with last stands and mighty heroes going to their deaths with grave dignity.

My version is different. This is not the polished fable the Saeson gleemen sing, where the warriors debate their dooms back and forth before they strike a blow. Nor is it the version our own bards sing, the long elegy for the best among all the youths of Albion, with its descriptions of sunlight glinting on a blade in a place of stone, the gulls wailing overhead, the sea glittering in the distance, the ravens waiting to be fed.

If I can I shall tell you the truth, the truth of how Llacheu came to die at the hands of his father's oldest friend.

And I know. I know because I was there.

But my tale is not only about Llacheu and Cei. It is also about a man called Angus mac Connor, a man in the fullness of his strength, twenty-five years ago when the world was young, a man skilled in the use of arms, a man eager for adventure; and it is about the friend he made, Wulfstan Swaerta's son, leader of the Gyrwe in Dewr.

I remember how the leaves of the beech trees were almost translucent in their newness as we rode out from Caer Cadwy on a fine morning at the peak of the year. We laughed and we talked as we rode on the first stage of our long journey, travelling free and easy with light hearts and minds, riding through the summer country towards what we now commonly call Caer Vadon, but in those days was still chiefly known by its Roman name, Aquae Sulis.

So much has changed.

At that time Arthur had been Amherawdyr of Albion for three years or more. The realm was at peace, and had been since the great battle of Badon Hill half a decade earlier. The Lords of Prydein might grumble about this usurping soldier who had declared himself their overlord, while the Saesons in the east might likewise lick old wounds and growl whenever we went near, but none in all the south dared give defiance.

Albion was at peace, and Albion was wealthy, as she had not been since the time of doomed Gworthigern, when our grand-fathers and great-grandfathers were children. The old trade routes were open once more, and ships from far off lands brought their fine wines and oils to our shores. For three years our harvests had been good, till our granaries groaned under the weight of the wheat stored within them, and our herds flourished on the plentiful grazing.

Looking back, it seems that the sun always shone by day and the rain fell solely at night, and then gently, enough to water the crops without ruining them. The people were happy, the wars and plagues which had troubled our country since the departure of the Romans were over at last. Our government was just, though resented by some – but then all government is resented by somebody, usually those of evil intent who hate the restrictions placed upon their wrongdoing.

It seemed to us then, and it seems to me now (and I am aware, I who have said I hate blasphemy, of both the blasphemy and the hubris) that we had come close to creating an earthly paradise. And yet a mere three years after Arthur became Amherawdyr and ushered in this new age, this golden age of plenty, the Army of Britain was on the march once more.

Have you ever seen an army on the march? Nowadays the

warbands walk or ride without true discipline, every man fending for himself, moving through the country like a biblical plague of locusts, leaving a trail of devastation in their wake. A horse needs five hours or more good grazing each day, or else you must carry hard rations with you to make up the amount, for while nobody expects the horses to return from a campaign in as good a condition as they left, without adequate food they soon become useless. The men also must be fed, and although in friendly territory you may be able to barter supplies, or may have them already prepared at special sites, the wise commander carries provisions with him which he will supplement as he may.

So when I say we rode forth light-heartedly from Caer Cadwy, do not imagine a rabble of warriors such as one might see today. By the same token do not picture to yourself a neat column of horsemen and horsemen alone, riding caparisoned for battle – though we were indeed entirely a cavalry force, for reasons which I will explain in a moment. Behind us came the supply wagons, the mules and pack horses carrying our belongings, and the spare mounts trailing along in the rear, each section with its own escort.

We were six hundred men, marching the length of Britain from Caer Cadwy in eastern Dumnonia to Dun Eidin in northern Gododdin, and we were marching to war.

I thought myself blessed to be among them. I was never high in the counsels of the Companions, like my kinsman Lleminawg, but I was privileged to be of their number.

I was a warrior, and the Army of Albion was the greatest band of warriors in all Prydein. Being admitted into their company was the highest accolade a fighting man could be given – and besides, their cause was just.

Nowadays I am a man of God. This change was not entirely of my own will, and certainly it was not easy to reach this haven of virtue, this place where daily I offer up prayers to the Lord that he may have mercy upon my sinful soul. A part of me knows that if it were not for the fact my body has aged, I would never have changed my ways. The salvation for which I hope will be more a consequence of old age and physical weakness than the product of a truly contrite heart.

'Ego occidam et ego vivere faciam; percutiam et ego sanabo, et non est qui manu mea possit eruere.'

'I shall kill and I shall make to live; I shall strike and I shall heal, and there is nobody who may deliver from my hand.'

These are the words of the Lord, spoken through his prophet, and I know that they are true. Once I was a great sinner, a prideful man, the servant of good though misguided masters. Now I am the servant of nobody except God, and that is better, though to my sorrow I am still a proud man – let me freely admit the fault.

I am proud of those I knew and loved. First and last is the one-time Lord of Dumnonia, Cunomorus or Kynfawr, who was twice my master, at the beginning and at the end. In between, for three years, I served great Arthur, Amherawdyr of Albion. I rode with men such as this world has never seen before or since: Cei, Gwalchmei and the like, the Companions of Arthur, immortals each and every one.

It is no wonder then that I am proud. On their behalf I dealt death to those they deemed worthy of death, showed mercy to those they deemed worthy of mercy, little knowing that such things are the prerogative of God, not of mortal men.

All through my boyhood I wanted to be a warrior, a master of the sword like my older cousin Lleminawg the Dancer, the Fated One, the light-footed hero of Arthur's warband. For me, the sword was always the ultimate weapon, the glamorous blade, as superior to its poorer relatives the war-knife and spear as my uncle Niall, who was Lleminawg's father, was superior to the peasants that tilled his fields.

As a boy I spent every free moment spying on the warriors at their exercises, then imitating them to the best of my ability. My father laughed when he caught me at my childish practice, but not unkindly. Since such things always come best when taught by a stranger, he arranged with my uncle Niall, who was the head of our family, that I should be fostered out to the Court of Kynfawr, Lord of Dumnonia, even as Lleminawg had been fostered before me.

There I learned not to despise the war-knife or even the simple spear, how to handle a shield, how to work combinations of weapons and how to oppose them. But my first love was the sword, the double-edged and pointed blade, the horseman's weapon, the nobleman's companion.

It is my fervent hope that God will forgive the eagerness with which I learned to wield a sword, the glee with which I used it against those Scotti pirates foolish enough to raid our shores. I wasted my youth and manhood, time which would have been better spent contemplating the wonders of God, in vainglorious activity. I grew haughty, counted the riches of this world above the riches of heaven.

Over the years I rose high in the counsels of Kynfawr. Often we rode with Arthur's warband, for even in the days when Arthur was no more than Master of the Armies of Prydein, Kynfawr was always loyal to him, and would send troops to help him when he could. When Arthur declared himself Amherawdyr, Kynfawr was among his keenest supporters, and it was at that time, being myself ambitious, I begged permission to offer my sword to the Emperor. Kynfawr agreed, albeit with some reluctance, for he valued my services.

Perhaps I flatter myself, but I believe Arthur would have accepted me on my own account, for I was very good with a sword. Still, it was never easy to join the Companions, and after Arthur became Amherawdyr the island was full of noble youths desperate to wear the red tunic which was the mark of Arthur's Household. I was fortunate, for my place was assured, in part because of Kynfawr, whose recommendation was worth more than most, and in part because of my cousin Lleminawg.

I was Lleminawg's kinsman, and it was through Lleminawg that Arthur had received the Sovereignty of Albion. At that time we knew only the bare bones of what had happened on the Island of Shadows in the far north-west, and those bare bones made little sense. But everybody was aware that Arthur owed Lleminawg a great debt: a debt now unpayable, since Lleminawg had perished out there on the islands in the trackless wastes of the ocean, beyond the bounds of Britain.

Certain things were common knowledge. Arthur had sailed with an army to put down the reiver Hueil, whose lair lay in the Iardomnan, the Western Isles. The destruction of the pirate fortress was not hard to accomplish, but at the last moment one of the wounded came to life and stabbed Arthur in the thigh.

To most of those present, this counter raid upon the raider Hueil had been the whole purpose of the voyage. Some might have wondered that Arthur chose to take with him so many of his greatest Companions: Cei, Bedwyr, Gwalchmei, Lleminawg and the like, men who had proved their worth a hundred times, when an expedition of this nature was more commonly used to blood untried troops. If any did wonder, they assumed it was merely because the days of war were so clearly drawing to a close, now that Arthur had defeated all his enemies, that this was probably the last chance for the older Companions to fight together on the same field.

But the truth was Arthur had always intended to go farther north, into the unknown isles, and essay the ancient test for the Sovereignty of Albion. It was said – and this may or may not be true – that when the Legions of Rome first conquered Britain, the symbol of Sovereignty was concealed in the far north, amongst that ancient people the Attecotti, the Old Ones, who claim to be descended from the original inhabitants of Britain. For over four hundred years the symbol of Sovereignty, a wonderfully worked chalice unlike any other in the world, was guarded by a single family, who thus called themselves the Clan Menestyr, the Children of the Cupbearer.

The candidate for Sovereignty had to pass a single test, easy to describe but hard to perform. He had to walk – or dance – a labyrinth, a single spiral path that curled around upon itself to a central darkness. And Arthur, with a spear wound in his leg which would have killed a lesser man, could not even stand upon his feet.

The Companions, Cei, Bedwyr and the rest, decided they must return south with all speed, delaying the test until Arthur was recovered. But after they set sail a great storm blew up, scattering their fleet. Most of the Army eventually limped home to civilization, and when the count was taken, it was discovered that among the missing vessels were two particular ships, the most important in the fleet. One was the galley carrying Cei and Gwalchmei. The other was a sturdy merchantman. On board were Bedwyr, Lleminawg and the wounded Arthur.

What happened next has never been widely known – not, I think, because it was ever intended to be a great secret, but simply because those who returned did not care to talk about it.

Seven survivors of the shipwrecks were washed ashore on the very island they would have sought had things been otherwise, and captured by the Children of Menestyr. Lleminawg the Leaper, the Dancing Man, the Fated One, undertook the test on Arthur's behalf. He won the Sovereignty for his lord, and the chalice came back to the south with Arthur. But Lleminawg did not return, and his burial place is unknown. For that reason

Arthur owed him much, and I was made welcome among the Companions.

There was another consequence of the trial, one which has some relevance for several now sitting in this hall. The Clan Menestyr had kept the chalice safe for over four hundred years. In all that time no claimant had come anywhere near success. Inevitably the clan had grown to look upon the chalice as their property, a private possession occasionally displayed to outsiders, a source of pride and prestige. I do not believe it had ever truly occurred to them that one day their guardianship might come to an end. When it did, they were bereft, the whole reason for their existence destroyed at a single stroke.

At a single stroke. Say rather, by two strokes, delivered during the final part of the ceremony. In those two strokes lies the nub of the matter, the deeds that marred Arthur's victory, though they were none of his doing. Lleminawg had danced eight parts of the maze, answering the riddles put to him. But the ninth and last gate was guarded by a masked warrior, who thrust at him with a wickedly-barbed spear. It seemed then that Lleminawg, unarmed, must soon fail, for not even he could hope to evade the spear for long within the confines of the hollow maze.

At that point by the Grace of God, Cei appeared on the rim above the labyrinth, Cei whom they had all thought drowned, and threw Lleminawg a sword. The Dancer struck, dashing aside the mask and dazing the warrior. What was intended as a ritual combat now became real. Bedwyr, standing on the rim with the other captives, uttered a great shout which stayed Lleminawg's hand before he could strike the killing blow.

Bedwyr had seen the masked warrior unmasked, and realized it was the woman Teleri, the woman he had loved, by whose wiles they had all been brought to this place. She in her turn was disorientated by that first blow. Not knowing where she was, seeing only a man trying to kill her, she lunged with her spear. And that was the first dolorous blow, and it was struck in error by one who was sworn to abstain from violence.

The second dolorous blow was dealt by Cei the Long Man: mighty Cei, best-hearted and most noble of Arthur's warriors; Cei who never did a cowardly deed in all his life; Cei whose conduct had always been beyond reproach.

Unlike the others he had come to shore from the shipwreck alone, in a strange land at the end of the world, a barren waste of sand and grass. He had hunted without success for his fellows, for Arthur whom he loved as he had never loved any other, and most men would have despaired to find themselves in such a pass.

Then Menw the magician, the half-druid, slipped free of his captors and went in search of Cei, for Menw, though quiet and unobtrusive, often overlooked among the boisterous Companions, was a man of strange powers, and it was no coincidence that he was among the survivors of the wreck.

Menw found Cei, brought him to the labyrinth in time, it seemed, to save Lleminawg from failure. The Long Man plunged through the Attecotti, brushing them aside as the bear brushes aside the importunate hounds who wake him from his winter sleep, and cast Lleminawg his sword, leaving himself unarmed. It was then that Pedrylaw Menestyr, seeing the ruin of all his dreams, flung himself upon Cei.

But Cei without a weapon was not one whit less deadly than Cei fully caparisoned for battle. The Long Man broke the Cupbearer's neck and flung the body into the pit of the labyrinth.

That was the second dolorous blow, the slaying of Pedrylaw Menestyr, who was the Lady Teleri's father.

The doom of Britain is that by her own action she will undo herself. Time and again we of Britain have broken faith with both man and God, with both our rightful rulers and with the holy mother church: time and again God has sent his scourges to bring us back into a righteous way of life. We have suffered under the depredations of the Picts and the Scotti from overseas, we have groaned beneath the yokes of the Saesons and our own unjust rulers.

Arthur sought to change all that, to create a new realm, the realm of Albion, here in the island of Prydein.

And yet from the very first the realm of Albion carried the seeds of its own destruction.

Those two acts, the accidental slaying of Lleminawg and the killing of Pedrylaw Menestyr, stained what should have been a bright enterprise with the indelible mark of blood, right from the very beginning. There are some who would say Pedrylaw Menestyr deserved his fate, being no more than a pagan priest, a false magician like those priests of Baal who once strove with Elijah, and I would say there is much truth in that. But the deed was ill timed, all the same, for the chalice signified birth, the antithesis of death.

In blood it was born, and in blood it would perish, the Empire of Albion.

This was one of the riddles the guardians asked Lleminawg as he danced the labyrinth: 'Seven possessions to a king.'

'Not hard to name,' he replied. 'A sword, a spear, a knife, a whetstone. A mantle of royalty, a game board for wooden wisdom. A chalice. And an eighth possession a king must have: an heir.'

3

So we rode north that early summer, not long after the leaves had reached their first full green, while they were still young and fresh with promise. The whole world was fresh with promise: the days were lengthening and the nights were growing shorter; the corn shoots were flourishing in the fields; the weather was fine and clear; the land was at last at peace.

Even the message from Cei at Eburacam, that the men of Gododdin had broken the Amherawdyr's truce and come south, raiding and burning deep into Dewr, did not disturb us overmuch.

All my life I have remembered that ride, forgetting the bad parts, the flies which must have pestered us every step of the way, the dust which must have caked our clothes and hair, the heat and stench of sweating men and horses.

What I remember are the good things. I remember the woods, how it was like being underwater, moving among dappled green shadows through which scurried birds and small animals, even as the trout twitch among the waving weeds of the river bottom. I remember Gwalchmei the Hawk reining in beside me to shade his eyes and watch the buzzards wheeling in the pure blue vault of the cloudless sky. I remember the streams of sweet water flowing through the valleys, the fields and meadows we passed, lush and well tended, the children running out after us, mouths agape, with no fear in them. I remember the ridges along which we rode, and the forests laid out beneath us, mile upon mile of fair country, and the breeze stirring through the trees so the leaves flashed their colours at us, no two shades the same.

It is rich land to the east, much richer than ours, and spring comes earlier. A child can work the soil, for the tilth is friable and easy to cultivate, fine soft earth begging for the plough. The corn grows high and strong, turning to a sunlit gold brighter than any metal as it ripens, so that our best fields here in Dumnonia seem mean and stunted by comparison.

Until I rode with Arthur's Men I had no idea the island of Britain was so wealthy. I am no farmer, but my heart was filled with envy for those who live in the lands of the east, in the low country of Britain.

Then there were the cities, prosperous and strong, beside which our own Isca is merely a large village: cities strung like jewels along the necklace of the great road which runs north and east across the island. After Aquae Sulis came Corinium, and I remember well the contrast between the sprawling ruins of the ancient town on the one hand, and the smart new buildings on the other, with their timber porticoes and balconies, cunningly crafted, lying snug within the walls of the old amphitheatre. There we were feasted, all six hundred of us, and when we departed in the morning the citizens lined the route and cheered us on our way.

We moved fast, as fast as our supply wagons would allow, following the road up to Lindum. In Lindum we had a day of what was by then much-needed rest. Most of my comrades sought out the painted women of the town, the strumpets who are to be found in any large city. Some however, even though they were not usually renowned for their piety, spent the time in prayer at the church in the market square: for here, it was said, Arthur himself had prayed for victory against the heathen Saesons the night before he had ridden forth to give battle at the Blackwater. All the world knows what success God granted him that day, and from that time to this the Saesons have not dared approach the walls of Lindum, save as humble supplicants.

There at Lindum word awaited us from Cei. He himself, as Arthur's regent in the North, had latterly been quartered at Eburacum, or Caer Ebrauc. Now Eburacum, as you may know, has long been famed for the quality of its foot soldiers, so that men speak of the steel spearmen of Caer Ebrauc in the same breath as they speak of the horsemen of eastern Dumnonia. Many of them were Saesons, or of Saeson descent, but over the years they had proven their loyalty to their adopted city.

Cei had taken the foot and marched north into Dewr, knowing the cavalry he had summoned from Arthur would catch up with him on the road. In this he acted as the Amherawdyr would have acted, moving at speed to take his enemies unaware, for they would expect him to await reinforcements before leaving the safety of the walled city.

From Cei's despatches we learned that the raiders were falling back into Gododdin, and that the men of Dewr were rallying to his standard as he marched. Gwalchmei, who was our Captain, decided we should make all haste to join with Cei, so on the morrow we set forth again, leaving the supply wagons to follow at their own pace.

As we travelled, the country changed. We passed through marshy valleys, skirted forests choked with brushwood and under-growth. The road, which had served us well till now, became rougher. White dust covered everything, inflamed and stung our eyes. The horses began to go lame. By the time we reached Catraeth we had lost perhaps a sixth part of our number.

Just outside the fort at Catraeth lie the remnants of the old amphitheatre. I was scouting ahead with a man named Matgan, the two of us out alone in advance of the host. In all our long march we had seen nothing which posed any threat. We were tired at the end of the day, and careless in the knowledge we were near the safety of the town.

The land thereabouts is flat, bounded by long low hills on the horizon, all of them heavily wooded. To my eyes, accustomed to the sudden steep valleys of Dumnonia, it was dull country, and I was more concerned with my horse's hooves as he picked his way across the gravel-strewn highway than with what lay ahead.

'Jesu Christ!' Matgan exclaimed. He reined in his mount and crossed himself.

I glanced up, trying to make sense of what I was seeing. Beside me Matgan was fumbling his warboard onto his arm, his horse dancing nervously beneath him.

A company of men awaited us before the bank of the am-phitheatre: well armed, with big wooden shields and heavy spears, wearing thick leather jerkins that would turn most blows, and matching leather caps that hid their hair. Their leader, who had obviously heard the sound of our horses' approach, stood a few paces in advance of the rest, his mailshirt gleaming in the rays of the dying sun. His face was concealed behind a great helm of the kind one rarely sees but often hears about: a boar-crested iron cap with long cheek pieces reaching almost to his chin, and a nasal bar that cast his eyes into shadow and made his expression unreadable.

That was bad enough, not knowing whether these were friends or foes. Worse was the area in which they stood. As I said, the old bank of the amphitheatre was behind them: smooth and grassy, rounded with age, a common enough sight outside most of our cities. But up against the bank was a series of structures, and it was these structures that confused my eye.

There was no pattern to them, no obvious plan one might grasp. Tiny thatched huts, barely the length and width of a man's body, were mingled with larger buildings standing atop their own mounds. Then there were other mounds, humps of gravelly soil in all shapes and sizes, some infested with ragged weeds, many still naked to the sky as if either more recent or else better tended.

Amid this muddle were a number of wooden posts like pillars, a few of them crowned with the bleached or yellowed skulls of deer and sheep, the antlers and horns still attached. Some of these posts had been crudely hacked with a knife into a vague semblance of a human being, while the rest were simple unadorned trunks with the bark still on them. Again they were not all of the same age, some being so old they were on the point of rotting into the ground.

Rags and ribbons were everywhere, fluttering noisily in the evening breeze. As we came nearer my pony began to sidle and prance, frightened by the sight and sounds, so that I closed the gap between us and the waiting men crabwise, in a manner most undignified.

To the best of our knowledge Catraeth, which at that time owed loyalty to the Lord of Elmet, was still in friendly hands. If it had been taken then we were in trouble indeed: firstly, because it would mean the entire country was in arms against us, and secondly because Cei and his foot soldiers would be isolated in the north, surrounded by enemies.

I confess a frisson of fear ran down my spine as I approached the waiting warriors: fear, and – God forgive me – anticipation, for I had never faced men like these in battle, and I was eager to meet the challenge of something new.

'Who are you?' shouted Matgan, a throwing spear in his hand.

'We are the Gyrwe of Dewr,' replied their leader, which meant nothing to me. 'Are you Arthur's men?'

His accent was so barbarous I had difficulty following his words.

'We are,' said Matgan.

'Then well met!' cried the leader, flinging back the boar's helm to reveal a bundled knot of straw coloured hair. 'I am Wulfstan Swaerta's son, left here by the great lord Cei to guide you on your way.'

I recognized the name, having heard it mentioned in the talk around the campfires on our march. This Wulfstan was a grandson of that Soemil who called himself king of Dewr, and ruled a small part of that region. The Saesons had been in Dewr for generations, though Soemil was the first of their kind to claim the rule, and Soemil's subjects were a mixed group of British and Saesons. Of course, by no means all the Saesons thereabouts acknowledged his authority, while many of the British of Dewr kept their old tribal name, Peryth, and loathed him and all his works; even so, it was possible that one day Soemil's kingdom would be a force in the northlands, and Wulfstan was rumoured to be favoured among his heirs.

Over the years Arthur and his advisers had taken trouble to forge strong links with men like Wulfstan, believing it better to bind them to us with friendship at an early age, rather than deal with them unknown when they came to power in later life.

Matgan relaxed, and I copied his example. 'Where is Cei?' he asked.

The Saesons grinned. 'Still far ahead of you. He marches fast and furious up the North Way, out beyond Caer Weir, and my good friend Llacheu scouts ahead of him with the horse.'

I frowned, displeased on several counts. The savage spoke of the Emperor's son as if they were equals, which was both a nonsense and impertinent. Also, Cei's action seemed rash to me. It was one thing to drive the raiders to the borders of friendly territory, but another to follow after them, alone and unsupported. I knew that Cei had a few cavalrymen with him, enough to form a screen between his army and the enemy, but they were not numerous. To allow the Amherawdyr's son to lead them out in advance of the main force struck me as incredibly dangerous.

One of the Saesons stared at me, then nudged his fellows and murmured something in their own tongue, which to any civilized man sounds like the barking of dogs. They laughed aloud.

'Your followers are amused?' I said coldly, hand on my sword hilt.

Wulfstan rubbed at his upper lip – he was clean-shaven, which surprised me – and I remember how the red light of the setting sun filled his eyes, so once again I could not read his expression.

'What did they say?' I demanded angrily, certain they were laughing at me.

'They wonder,' Wulfstan said carefully, 'they wonder whether you ride your horse crabwise in that curious fashion because there is a bad smell beneath your nose.'

Matgan snorted with laughter. I glanced at him angrily, my comrade who should have been supporting me, and the sight of my furious face roused him to further mirth. The Saesons grinned and slapped their legs.

There was a moment when things could have gone either way. I could feel it hanging between us, waiting for me to make my choice. Wulfstan was smiling lazily, one hand on the boar-crested helm, ready to slam it down over his face again, the other curled loosely about the hilt of the sword at his side. Behind him his followers watched us intently, their merriment abruptly ended, and I felt rather than saw Matgan beside me, suddenly sober, preparing to drive his horse across mine and prevent any bloodshed.

My lips were tight and unnatural. I forced them into a semblance of a smile, placed my right hand in full view against the rim of my shield.

'No, lad,' I said. 'It is an ancient custom among my people to approach those of royal blood slantwise. Health and a long life to you, Wulfstan of Dewr!'

Wulfstan shouted with laughter. He pulled the helmet altogether free of his head and tossed it underarm to one of his followers.

'We have food and drink prepared for you,' he said. 'Firewood in plenty for campfires, and a farrier, ready at his forge if your mounts need attention. These things the Lord Cei told us to do, and we have done them. One of you ride back to your hosting and bid them make all haste to join us. The other may come with us and inspect our preparations.'

I did not care for the manner in which he gave us orders, but what he said made sense. I looked at Matgan, who shrugged and wheeled his horse.

'Try not to start any fights, cousin,' he said.

I was surprised, for I had thought he would be the one to stay. Then I remembered that in his youth he had fought at the Blackwater, where Soemil had led the Saesons of Dewr in an attack upon the lands around Lindum. Perhaps he had good reason to avoid spending time in the company of Soemil's grandson.

'What is this place?' I asked as I descended from the saddle.

'This?' said Wulfstan. 'This is where we lay our dead to rest. Our people have lived here for a long while, as you can see.'

A sweep of his hand indicated some of the older mounds. Now that he had told me, I could see they were obviously graves.

'Here the gods watch over those who have gone before.' He pointed at the wooden posts. 'We are many peoples, so we have many gods. There is Fosite of the Frisians, Lord of the Pillar at the heart of the world. There is Niord, there are the great ladies Frig and Rheda. And there,' he added proudly, 'is Father Wotan, my own ancestor through the line of Baeldeg and Brand.'

To my eye the crude carvings were identical, though no doubt a devoted worshipper could tell the difference between them. I was not sure whether he believed that these stocks of wood, these graven images, housed the spirits of the demons he honoured, or whether they were simply intended as representations, mere portraits to remind the faithful that the gods were ever present. In fact, I suspected that to his unsophisticated mind the distinction would have been unclear.

'You too have many gods,' he said. 'But then you too are many people.'

For a moment I thought I had misheard him. His accent was still thick, though I was finding his speech easier to follow as my ears accustomed themselves to the way in which he mutilated our tongue. I stopped and stared up at him, for he was a tall man, even without that great helm on his head, and my legs were still a little bowed from the long hours in the saddle.

'We do not!' I began indignantly.

He smiled pityingly, like one who has often heard this argument and now prepares to demolish his opponent. 'You who follow the religion of Christ, you have three gods: the father, the son, the ghost – though whose ghost I have never understood. Then you visit the shrines of dead men, whom you admit to be mortal, Alban, Aaron, Julius, and lay offerings at those places, treating them even as we treat the shrines of the lesser spirits like Sceaf of the Corn. Your countryfolk worship such a multitude of gods that a simple man like myself cannot keep track: Carnon, Mabon, Llew, the Horse Lady and dozens of others. Your city dwellers, who claim to be so – superior? is that the word? – to the countryfolk, set up statues to gods so ancient none can now recall their names, set them up outside the walls of their towns and hie there when the priests of Christ are not looking.'

'You misunderstand!' I spluttered, and he cast his cold blue gaze upon me.

'Do I?' he said. 'Arthur himself has often said he rules over one land filled with many peoples. Yet you, his close companions, insist on behaving as if we, the Eingles who have served your rulers well for over a hundred years, were newcomers, invaders, barbarians not be trusted, something less than human. I was born in this island, and Arthur does not treat me thus. Nor does his son, Llacheu, who I am proud to call my friend. So why do you?'

Suddenly he was looming over me at close quarters, crowding me back into my horse, whose reins I still held. The rings of his mailshirt pressed into the bare flesh of my forearm, and I felt his weight pushing against the crook of my elbow.

'Answer me!' he demanded, and now his eyes were blazing in the glow of the setting sun.

Later, of course, I thought of many things I might have said. I might have spoken of the Saesons' inability to keep a treaty, of their endless treachery; of the fact that though some of his fellows might trace their ancestry back through several generations in this land, most were indeed newcomers; of their worship of strange and bloody gods, who constantly demand the sacrifice of livestock and even living men.

At the time I was speechless. The attack had come so quickly I was caught quite unprepared. One moment we had been idly discussing religion, the next I had become the target of all his pent-up resentments.

'If I have given you that impression, I apologize,' I said carefully. 'I value you as allies, as fellow subjects of the Emperor. I too am a friend of Llacheu.'

This last was not strictly true, but it seemed a useful thing to say.

After a long pause the weight on my arm lessened. 'I find your words hard to follow,' he said slowly, which I thought ironic, given his own. 'You have an accent unlike any I have heard before.'

(In those days there was much more of the Irish in my speech. It was a conscious affectation among my kinsmen to keep the memory of our origins in Ierne alive.)

'Yet I accept your apology. You are not a bad man, merely ignorant, like so many of your countrymen.'

Had we been alone I think this final piece of effrontery would have been too much. As it was, I obeyed Christ's precepts and turned the other cheek, and we made our way to the camp in some semblance of amity.

4

The upshot of this, as I should have known, was disaster.

During the evening I was summoned to Gwalchmei's tent, where I found the commander foregathered with the other senior officers of our army. The upstart Saeson princeling was standing in one corner with his arms folded across his chest, listening intently to the flow of orders coming from the commander.

At this time the Hawk was a little past middle age, a lean spare man of imposing presence. He spoke softly though firmly, and rarely needed to raise his voice. On his mother's side he was kin to Arthur, and those who were jealous of his success attributed his rapid rise to this connection, but those of us who served under him knew Gwalchmei would have reached a similar eminence even if he had been born a slave. There was a greatness within him, just as there was a greatness within Cei and Bedwyr, his only peers among the Companions.

(Years later, long after I had left the Companions and returned to the service of Kynfawr, I heard that Gwalchmei the Hawk was dead, cut down in a minor skirmish at Peryddon in Gwent. I remember I was fitting a new cover to a shield when somebody brought me the news, and I laid my work aside while the tears blurred my vision and trickled down my cheeks, and the youths to whom I was teaching swordplay fell silent in wonder at the sight of their hardbitten old master weeping like a child.)

'The very man!' he said as I entered the tent. 'We need somebody to ride with Wulfstan and his Gyrwe. Are you fit for the task?'

That was the thing about Gwalchmei, the reason men spoke of his golden tongue. He had the art of persuasion in his very bones. I had no desire, as he probably guessed, to have anything whatsoever to do with the Saesons. Yet I found myself agreeing, with feigned enthusiasm, to act as intermediary between our main force and these new auxiliaries.

I was reluctant for more than one reason. I did not care for Wulfstan and had no trust of his men, who seemed to me the usual gang of barbarians, like as not to cut my throat on the pretext of some imagined slight once we were clear of the camp. Also, I wanted to be with the main force, with my comrades, under the eyes of my commanders in the hope of winning glory or promotion.

The recent peace had made it hard for an ambitious man to gain advancement and I was hungry for success. Regrettably – and this is the hard truth about that kind of army – great deeds need to be witnessed by those who can make a difference. Fighting heroically with only the Saeson oafs to witness my heroism would do me no good at all.

'What are our orders?' I said aloud.

'You move out at first light and try to catch Cei before he finishes this fight by himself.'

My face must have expressed my surprise, for Gwalchmei smiled.

'Wulfstan and his men can ride, you know. The Saesons may fight on foot, but they are perfectly capable of using horses to transport themselves to the battlefield. Eh, Wulfstan?'

The Saeson princeling unfolded his arms and stepped forward. Even among those seasoned warriors, the veterans of Arthur's wars, he was a powerful figure, and the lesser officers stepped aside to give him room. Only Gwalchmei did not seem to be in awe of him.

'Our ponies are fresh, unlike your mounts. We can go far and fast, tell Cei you are close behind.' He turned to me, pushed his big face into mine. 'I asked for you, Angus mab Connor, because I have never met a man of the south-west before. I do not count Llacheu, because Llacheu is the son of Arthur and Gwenhwyvar, and therefore belongs to all this land, not just one corner. You seem like a warrior, and I know you can ride, if oddly.'

Gwalchmei quirked an eyebrow, his falcon's features amused. I guessed the Saeson had told him of my sideways arrival at the cemetery.

314

'I shall be honoured,' I said through clenched teeth.

So began my time with the Saesons of Gyrwe. Gyrwe, I later discovered, was simply their barbarian name for their own particular tribe, one of many among what they termed the 'Deir-Saetan', the dwellers in the land we call Dewr. This is one of the things we forget most easily about the savages: that the divisions among them are as deep and far-reaching as those among civilized men. In fact, those divisions are probably deeper. Whereas we share certain things in common – the memory of Rome, a love of cities, above all the certainty of Christ's sacrifice – which make our quarrels, however vicious, as it were family affairs, the Saesons lack that unifying culture. Indeed, by definition, being barbarians they have no culture, though some among us have pretended to find some semblance, some shadow, of shared custom and habit.

Nor do they possess true intelligence. They have cunning, cunning in plenty, and they are good at striking bargains. They prate of honour, by which they mean the ability to tell the biggest lie without being found out. They hedge their lives with strange rituals and superstitions, carry amulets they consult constantly for advice. Like sheep they hate being alone, have no real feel for animals or the countryside, for anything outside their herd. It is said their earliest ancestors sprang to life in the great pine forests of Germany, and this may be true, for they have both a dislike of open spaces and a deep-rooted fear of trees and woods.

From which you may gather I did not – do not – care for them.

Their ponies were the sorriest collection of jaded nags I had ever seen, and I am a man who is fond of horseflesh. The beasts were hammer-headed, narrow-chested, shallow in the girth – seemed to possess all those signs one normally looks for in order to avoid. If they had been bred for the purpose, one could not have found a worse selection of horses.

They were neglected as well. Nobody expects ponies out on campaign to be in the same condition as horses that have spent all summer being gently exercised, but these creatures were a mass of sores, of galls caused by ill-fitting equipment: simple failings that any half-competent rider should have dealt with himself.

We set off like a party of farmers returning home after an evening spent drinking the proceeds of a successful market day: in heavy headed and resentful silence. Half a mile up the road three of our number dropped out, cursing their beasts for going lame. A mile or so further along a man fell off, and lay snoring insensible at the roadside while his fellows ignored him.

'Will you leave him here?' I asked Wulfstan, incredulous. He shrugged indifferently. 'Why not? When he wakes he'll either follow or go home.'

I shook my head in disbelief, and cantered to the head of the cavalcade, to ride a while in solitude.

This was fertile land. I could imagine how it must have been before the raiders came south from Gododdin. One could still see the smoke-blackened ruins of the farmsteads in the valleys, and from the state of the grass on the high ground one knew that until recently it had been well grazed by sheep and cattle. Now the country seemed lifeless, apart from the wild things, the birds and foxes and deer.

In some fields the crops still flourished, growing towards a harvest that would never come. In others they had been trampled or burned, wanton destruction for its own sake. Occasionally we saw people in the distance, but they fled before we came near, and there was no purpose in chasing them. What could they tell us that we could not see for ourselves, that a great army had fallen upon them, cruel and brutal, harrowing the land as it had not been harrowed since the days of Vitolinus and Coel the Old.

Our nights we spent in the open, huddled around a campfire we lit more for reassurance than for warmth. Gradually the Saesons grew accustomed to my presence, thawed and began to treat me as one of themselves. Wulfstan was always a little apart from the rest of them, a little distant, conscious of his royal birth and breeding.

No. There I do him an injustice. He was ready enough to do his share of the work, and never baulked at dirtying his hands. Nor did he have the habit of some leaders I have known, of giving too many commands in order to assert his authority. I think it was the other way round, that the men were never entirely easy in his presence, never completely themselves, and therefore he kept himself apart that the others might relax.

One evening he told me of his upbringing. Like us, the Saesons (or at least, the Saesons of Dewr; I cannot speak for them all) sometimes foster their important children with other like-minded lords. Wulfstan was unusual in that he had been fostered with a lord of Bryneich, a Briton who was kin to the Kunwydyon, the lords of Gododdin, our present foe.

'They are a strange people,' he said, stretching lazily by the fire. 'Even odder than the rest of you Wealas. I suppose it stems from the fact they were never altogether conquered by the Romans.'

I had noticed, as I came to know him better, that his vocabulary had improved. He was capable of expressing quite complicated thoughts. At the time I was not sure what this proved about his intelligence: one can teach a horse to perform a series of intricate actions, to respond to certain signals, but at the end a horse is still a horse. Likewise with Wulfstan. Although he advanced ingenious arguments, I assumed they had been taught to him in the household of his foster father. How much he truly understood, deep down, of what he said, I was never certain.

He must have seen my expression, for he grinned at me. 'You are a southerner, and would not put it that way, I know.' He sat up and proceeded to lecture me on the past of my own land.

'The Romans never conquered the far north. Oh, they sent armies and boasted of their triumphs, laid waste strongholds and villages, burned crops and drove away livestock, slaughtered those who opposed them. But they did not conquer and hold the north as they did the south, and for that reason they built the two great walls to keep the natives penned within their territories. The northernmost wall, the one of turf, was soon given up, but the wall of stone they manned until the very end, and over the years a series of towns grew up along its length, a long thin settlement stretching from sea to sea.'

I listened, my mouth open in disbelief. The previous evening he had translated for me the gist of an argument between two of his men. One had insisted the Wall (the stone wall, the great wall which yet stands) was built by giants, the same giants who had raised the mighty pillars and columns one can still see in the cities. The other had replied this was nonsense, that these things had been raised by the wizards of Rome, raised in the space of a single night to awe the natives into submission.

Wulfstan had translated this without comment, and I had naturally taken it that, like the rest of his savage nation, he found the works of our ancestors with their mastery of stone a mystery, inexplicable except in terms of giants and wizards. Now he was giving me a third explanation, and one which sounded to me – bearing in mind I knew less of our past in those days than I do now – much like the truth.

'The wall divided the tribal lands of the Gododdin, so that

317

there were always strong links of birth and blood between those who lived north and south of the barrier. The presence of so many people, the soldiers in the garrisons and the civilians in the towns, made a demand for food and other supplies, like leather and wool. The wall brought wealth to those who lived nearby, gave them markets for their goods.'

I nodded, seeing it might be so.

'Although the region between the wall of stone and the wall of turf never became civilized in the sense that even the westernmost part of your own Dumnonia became civilized, its people tended to look south to the Roman province for the good things in life. They were outside the Empire, yet a part of it, bound to it by ties of trade and kinship. They were the frontier, the people living in the hinterland, and as the generations passed they became proud of their position and their heritage.'

He rubbed at his nose, ran his fingers along his upper lip. He had not shaved since we left Catraeth, and his face was showing a fine stubble which made him look older.

'Beyond the turf wall, beyond the hills of Bannog where the high mountains begin, was the wild country. There men and women still painted or tattooed their bodies, worshipped their gods, lived lives unchanged from those their forebears had lived since the dawn of time.'

He drank from a bottle proffered by one of his followers, passed it on to me.

'As Rome weakened, these Picts from beyond Bannog grew bolder. Their raids became more daring, better planned, and at first the brunt of those raids fell upon their closest neighbours, the people of Gododdin. The men of Gododdin fought back, formed friendships among themselves to resist the attackers, called upon the Romans to help them. For years they fought a series of bloody and thankless skirmishes against the raiders.'

The fire crackled. In the flames I saw what he described: men riding in the saddle day and night, too often in the wrong place at the wrong time, scurrying back and forth like ants. It was familiar stuff. I had done it myself along the coasts of Dumnonia, spent days fruitlessly patrolling against the Scotti raiders. More time is taken in hunting for the enemy than in fighting him, and if one does find him all that follows is a quick flurry of blows, to little effect and no great glory, while he pulls back to his waiting ships.

Wulfstan waited till I looked away from the fire before he

continued. 'Then, as the pattern of the days to come grew clearer on the weaver's loom, the lure of loot from the towns along the Wall grew stronger. The Gododdin lords began to ally themselves with their old foes the Picts, and to attack the soft lands to the south. A world which had been stable for a hundred years or more suddenly became an uncertain place.'

'True everywhere,' I said, 'if our grandsires are to be believed.'

He laughed aloud, so the others turned and peered at us through the dusk. For a moment I had forgotten I was talking to a Saeson, had taken him for one of our own, but the sight of those hard and alien faces turned in our direction quickly reminded me that I was among strangers, and far from home.

'My own grandfather spins a fine tale,' said Wulfstan. 'He came here on the ship Saefugl, Seabird in your tongue, her white wings wafting him across the ocean, and joined with the giant Hengist, mightiest of men. Many were the adventures that befell him!'

Before he could start on them I dragged the subject back to Gododdin.

'So Gododdin has a long tradition of raiding south?'

'It does. You must have heard of Cunedda, whose name is still spoken in these parts.'

'Of course. I count men of Gwynedd among my friends, and everyone knows that the Lords of Gwynedd are the heirs of Cunedda, who came from Manaw in Gododdin. For that very reason, the Lord Bedwyr is presently in Gwynedd, dissuading the Lords of Gwynedd from joining their kinsmen in rebellion.'

'Aye.' Wulfstan smiled grimly. 'Let us hope he succeeds.' His hand rasped across his chin and he spat into the fire. 'Before Cunedda went south-west to Gwynedd, he wrought great destruction on the cities of the Wall. In my foster father's hall they sing the song.'

He flung back his head and chanted the lines I had heard sung at Arthur's court on a winter's night. Then they had not made much impression upon me, but now, far from friends and close by the very country they described, they made the hairs bristle on the back of my neck. In Wulfstan's voice I could hear the surge of wild warfare, the thunder of horses' hooves as their riders swooped down on the ill-defended cities.

Men quake before the violent one, Cunedda.
The length of the wall the townsmen shake.
To the slaughter he leads the men of Bryneich;
Between the seas they raise a new wall of fire.

'As you know, Cunedda was from Manaw, which lies in the far
north of Gododdin, near the Sea of Iuddew. Yet in his day – a
hundred years ago or more – he came to dominate the whole
land.'

'Why then did he go south?' I asked, curious to see what
answer Wulfstan would give.

'Sometimes a man tires of his homeland,' he said. His eyes
gleamed in the firelight, then blinked shut. He sat motionless, and
his men, who had stirred when he had burst into Cunedda's song,
glanced across to see why he had fallen silent.

I waited. After a while he opened his eyes and said: 'It is not so
strange. In Gododdin he was one among many; in Gwynedd he
became Lord of all.'

There was a wistfulness in his voice I understood well. As I
have said, I was in those days an ambitious man, all too aware of
the way in which the years were passing with ever-increasing
rapidity. I knew I would never become lord of my kinfolk – there
were too many others with a stronger claim – and the days of
carving out one's own domain had passed, at least for my kind.
The best I could hope for was a position of influence at some
court, and the greatest of all courts, of course, was that of Arthur
the Emperor. But the older generation – Cei, Bedwyr, Gwalchmei
– held all the positions of authority, and they were not likely to
give them up for a long while yet. In other words, my way up the
ladder was blocked, and short of some well-witnessed act of
astounding heroism, seemed likely to remain blocked.

If this was true of me, it was also true of Wulfstan. He too was
a member of a large kindred. His grandfather had many sons, and
those sons likewise had many sons, by many wives. Our lords
maintain the Christian custom of having one wife at a time – in
public at least, though we all know most of them keep a dozen
mistresses tucked away for private pleasure. The Saesons being
barbarians have no such scruples, and shamelessly have as many
women as they can, breeding children by them without discri-
mination. Thus their numbers constantly increase, which is why
they are always in search of new land.

I digress. My point is that Wulfstan, though better educated than most Saesons, was merely one among many. Even if his father Swaerta took Soemil's place when the old man eventually died, that was no guarantee that Wulfstan would follow in his turn. In any case, he would have a long while to wait before the power he undoubtedly desired became his. Which is why he became wistful when he thought of Cunedda, and what Cunedda had achieved a century earlier.

'Gododdin is a land of many provinces, and within each province there are many strongholds,' he said suddenly, just when I thought he had forgotten me altogether, or had fallen asleep. 'Gododdin has no single ruler, nor even one family which might claim to be pre-eminent. Every province has its own lord, every stronghold its chieftain. The play of power shifts back and forth between them as the gods and fate decide. At the moment the lords of Eidin dominate the land. Theirs is the mountain court, far famed in song: Eidin ysgor, Eidin the stronghold on its rock; otherwise called Llech Llew Tuath, the Rock of Llew's People.'

His gaze met mine across the firelight. 'That is where we are bound, Weala. Llech Ysgor.'

I have never claimed the gift of prophecy or foresight. For the most part, I have found that those who do claim it are the kind who like to be wise after the event, the kind who will tell you with great sincerity, every word charged with meaning and emotion, of how they felt the premonition of evil at some crucial moment – yet neglected to mention it at the time for fear of worrying their companions.

I will say only this. When Wulfstan spoke of Llech Ysgor, I felt a grief come upon me, a grief such as I had never known. Tears sprang to my eyes and blurred my vision. My breathing became short and awkward. A sob escaped my throat. The strength left my body so I could not move, not even to hide my distress.

'What is it?' he demanded, not unkindly. 'Are you ill?'

The fit ended as abruptly as it had begun. I wiped my eyes, made light of my distress, pretended something I had eaten must have disagreed with me.

But later that night, as I lay curled on the ground waiting to sleep, it came upon me again.

*　　*　　*

In the morning all was well and I quickly forgot the incident, attributing it to the food or the water, which had looked none too wholesome.

Now we rode through thick woodland. Wulfstan told me that this had been farmland in former years, and as I looked about me I saw that what he said was probably true, however unlikely it might seem. Though the woods contained saplings and mature trees, there were no ancients, none of the mossy giants one would have expected. The ground too showed traces of terracing, where wind and rain had once shifted freshly-ploughed soil, and in places there were odd humps and mounds, half hidden among the undergrowth.

'Those were the houses of the people,' he said, and I believed him.

I noticed that his men clutched their charms of bone and horn as we passed these mounds, muttered to themselves and made signs to ward off evil.

'They are afraid of the old dwellers,' said Wulfstan. 'These woods are rich in ghosts. I have heard tell of men who hunted deer or boar among these trees. When they made the kill, the beasts cried out in human voices, some speaking in forgotten tongues, others using the speech of your folk.'

'And what did they say?' I asked.

He turned his fierce blue gaze upon me. 'They begged for mercy, Weala, as your people always do.'

His laughter gusted among the trees, sent the birds which rested there shrieking into the sky. His men joined him without knowing the cause of his mirth, finding it politic to laugh when their princeling laughed.

At last we came to signs of civilization. First, the pasture lands, where sheep and cattle grazed and the herders were grown men, heavily armed, who hailed us suspiciously until they discovered we were friends. The raiders from Gododdin had passed them by, seeking softer prey in the south, but for all that they still rode armed and ready to protect their herds. Then came the settled country, the small fields our people always use on the upland where the living is hard, and the crops ripening in their rows. Last was the city of the Wall, which was a miracle and wonder of a kind I had never seen before.

You could see the place had often been attacked, had withstood sieges more than once. The masonry was blackened where fires had caught hold, the stones chipped and broken where they had suffered the bombardment of rocks. The houses had been built, demolished and rebuilt so many times that you could no longer judge their age, and the level of the street kept changing, rising and falling, which the wise men tell me is a sure sign of great antiquity, for every generation builds atop the work of its predecessors.

After the silence of our ride, I found the bustle of the city overwhelming. The Saesons however looked neither to right nor left, did not allow themselves to be distracted by their surroundings. Grim faced, they pushed a path through the crowds, forcing the locals to make way for them.

'I hate these places,' Wulfstan murmured from the corner of his mouth as we passed through the market square, lined with wooden booths where one could buy every imaginable service. 'People like ants, and all of them want something.'

The town was fuller than usual because so many had fled to the safety of its walls and would not leave until Cei had settled with the Gododdin raiders. I say Cei, because I still thought in terms of the army being commanded by Cei, but in fact the name upon everybody's lips was Llacheu.

'Off to join the young Prince?' shouted an old beggar on a street corner.

A woman fetching water from a cistern stopped and stared at us. 'What makes you think Llacheu needs the likes of them?' she jeered.

Wulfstan bellowed with laughter and blew her a kiss. 'I'll be back to deal with you later!'

'Chance would be a fine thing,' she returned, waggling her hips. 'Watch out for the Painted Men – and their women, who have sharp knives.'

'I'll vow you're no painted woman but a fine fresh creature longing for the touch of a real man,' he called over his shoulder as we made one of those sharp turns which are the mark of a Roman city, and I thought it clever of him to have captured the double meaning of painted woman in a language not his own.

They say that Julius Caesar banned all wheeled vehicles from the streets of Rome during daylight hours. If this is true, then he was a wise man indeed. We found ourselves caught in a tangle of carriages and carts, hurling oaths and imprecations as we tried to fight our way through, the heat and stench worsening with every moment.

'Clear the road!' bellowed Wulfstan.

The ponies whinnied and danced, bucked and lashed out at the crowd. One of our men wailed and clung desperately to the saddle.

'By the hammer!' Wulfstan swore in frustration. 'Clear the road, you maggots!'

His anger made his accent more pronounced, provoking a chorus of jeers and whistles from the rougher elements of the crowd. We were trapped behind an ox-cart, the driver of which was studiously ignoring us, sitting at his ease while a pair of slaves struggled to unload his cargo of pots. A string of mules, their panniers bursting with vegetables, were trying to squeeze past, and a small coach drawn by two well bred horses sought to come toward us.

The noise and heat were making my head swim. Behind me our troop were on the verge of losing control of their mounts. I had visions of bolting ponies and trampled civilians, and wondered how I would explain to Gwalchmei that we had never actually reached Cei or the enemy, but had fallen apart while crossing a friendly city.

I urged my pony forward, lowered my spear and used my best parade-ground voice.

'In the name of the Emperor! We bear despatches for the lords Cei and Llacheu!'

The carter woke from his daydream and peered at us as if seeing us for the first time. His face creased into a gap-toothed smile.

'For the young Prince? Why did you not say so, my masters?'

He shook the reins and pulled the cart around a corner. The mules followed, and the coach driver, who a moment ago had been edging his horses forward into a non-existent gap, reined in and waved us through. As we drew level with the body of the coach a priest or monk leant out and called: 'God's blessing upon you, my heroes!'

I glanced at Wulfstan, whose face was impassive apart from a slight twitching around the lips. Our eyes met, and I realized he was controlling himself for my sake, to avoid giving offence.

'Well done,' he muttered, and I burst into laughter.

A small incident, yet it made a great impression on me at the time. A priest, blessing soldiers! A surly carter, shifting his wagon! He was loved, was Llacheu, loved as the hope of Prydein, the boon of Albion. His father's life, his mother's life, had long since passed the point of being public property and entered the realm of myth: the victorious warrior, the faithful beauty. Arthur and Gwenhwyvar as people, as individuals with needs and desires of their own, had been lost, buried under the weight of legend. They had become distant figures: the Emperor and his Empress, symbols that no man or woman expected to meet, unreachable and untouchable.

Llacheu was different. He was flesh and blood, a warm-hearted human being with golden hair and a handsome face. He was young, and he was known to be kind, with a friendly word for all about him. He was daring, as daring as his father had been, and men said he was the one who drove Cei and the host of Eburacum on along the North Road to punish those who had broken the Emperor's peace.

Some of us in Gwalchmei's force had muttered of the rashness of such a move, striking into hostile territory without adequate support or supplies. Yet it was just such a thing as his father might have done, and there is no doubt in my mind that by acting as he did he greatly reduced the damage done by the Gododdin raiders. Widely scattered, they were forced to withdraw quickly, without time for further looting. Much of what they had stolen they abandoned in their haste to reach safety. Their first attempt to regroup was a failure, for Cei and Llacheu were already upon them before they had completed their muster, and they finished by fleeing ignominiously all the way back to Dun Eidin.

Small wonder Llacheu was the people's darling!

I had scarcely known him. (I did eventually admit this to Wulfstan, with some trepidation, but by then we were friends, and he thought it a great joke.) The Army of Prydein was large, and Caer Cadwy a busy fortress city. I did not serve in the same cavalry wing as the young prince and our paths rarely crossed. He tended to mix with friends of his own age, naturally enough, or with men who had known him since birth. I was older, and a newcomer to the Companions, moving with a different crowd.

What little I saw of him I liked. As I said, he was a handsome man, with a face and figure to turn the girls even if he had not been the Emperor's presumed heir, with a pleasing disposition and a growing reputation for bravery in battle. He had helped Cei burn out a nest of devil-worshipping witches in the mountains of

Gwynedd, had ridden with Bedwyr into the fenland marshes and fought with the rebellious Wolfings, a tribe so wild they were shunned even by their fellow Saesons. On both occasions he behaved well, and I think that if he had not, if there had been some hidden failing his seniors had tried to conceal, word would have soon spread among the Companions, who were accustomed to judging a man on his merits rather than his birth.

In short, Llacheu was the perfect youth, everything one might have hoped for in one of his parentage.

Too perfect, you may say. Distance in time and an early death have perhaps lent a glamour to what was in reality a very ordinary young man. Others have suggested as much, not least among them Medraut and his brother Iddawg, who were of an age with Llacheu and knew him better than I. But then we all now know what Medraut's word was worth, and I do not recollect that I heard him criticize Llacheu at the time.

All I can say is that I never heard anyone speak ill of Llacheu in his lifetime, that the common people loved him, and that while he lived he gave hope to us all.

We left the city and the Wall behind, rode out into Bryneich, over the moors and wild lands. Now we were truly on our guard, expecting an ambush at any moment, but the country was empty. We passed the ruins of the old houses, forlorn walls naked to the sky, enclosures choked with weeds, and my mind turned to how different things must have been once, when it was considered safe to build beside the highway. These days, in that kind of country, we hide our homes in the dips and hollows, well away from the road where the raiding parties ride. Sometimes we saw smoke in the distance, and once or twice sheep grazing on the hills – those nights we ate mutton round the campfire, greasy fingers filling our bellies with scorched meat, lying back belching happily, arguing about whose turn it was to stand guard. Of people we saw none, yet we knew they were there, hiding in the heather or the shelter of the little woods in the valleys, watching and waiting, hoping we would pass them by, hoping a miracle would drive us from their land.

Cei and Llacheu had not harried Bryneich, as they might have done. They had passed through leaving the land almost untouched, intent upon driving the raiders all the way back to Eidin. Sometimes we passed signs of skirmishing along the road –

a dead horse, the fresh mound of a grave, broken shields – but for the most part the country was so peaceful the war seemed like a dream. Birds sang above and around us, woodpeckers rattled in the trees. Deer fled our coming. The sky was blue and empty of cloud, the sun fierce at our backs. A soft breeze kept the heat from stifling us. We talked and we laughed as we rode on this the last stage of our journey, talked of many things. Wulfstan began to teach me his harsh tongue, and I practised my few phrases on his followers. In return they taught me their obscenities, words not fit for the man of God I have now become, and they giggled helplessly when I unwittingly insulted Wulfstan. As I came to know them I realized how young these hard men were under their heavy beards, that some of them were only a year or two older than my own sons, who were still to my mind children.

I showed them how to care for their ponies, how to check their equipment fitted properly, how to treat minor sprains and injuries. Their poor beasts were hard pushed to keep pace with mine, and often I glanced over my shoulder, thinking that Gwalchmei and the Army of Prydein would soon be upon us, and all our solitary riding for nothing. But in fact, though I did not know it at the time, Gwalchmei was making a broad sweep through Bryneich, showing the power of Arthur to as wide an area as possible, and was still several days behind us.

While we travelled in pursuit of Cei, messengers had been passing back and forth between the two armies. (I discovered later that these messengers had sighted us on the road and given us a wide berth, unsure whether we were friends or foes, unwilling to run the risk of guessing wrong.)

The latest couriers from Cei had implied there was no longer any need for haste, that the Long Man now held the instigators of the revolt penned within the fortress of Eidin. All that remained was to punish the transgressors, and this Cei was in no hurry to do now the danger was past, rightly reckoning that a little anticipation would make the punishment more effective. Besides, he needed to rest his men, who had marched far and hard on his behalf.

(Llacheu, they said, hot-blooded and impetuous, was all for storming the citadel straight away, but Cei overruled him.)

Six hundred men Gwalchmei had brought nigh the length of Prydein, a feat worthy of Arthur himself. Yet at the end they became an irrelevance to the siege of Eidin, for that fight was fought by Cei and Llacheu with their original army, of which Wulfstan and his followers were a small part. Of all those six hundred who had ridden so boldly from Caer Cadwy on a spring morning, only one man took part in the storming of the invincible citadel, and I was that man.

5

The Abbot opened his eyes, which he had closed some time before in the throes of his storytelling. His bitter blue gaze swept across the company, fixed upon Nai.

'I am weary,' he said. 'I shall finish tomorrow.'

He signed to Lasrian, who stepped forward and helped him into his cloak. 'God keep you all through the night,' he said, and left the hall so rapidly the others scarcely had time to mutter a farewell.

Eri stirred in his seat beside Nai. 'Now there is a man,' he growled. 'An honest man, not afraid we might think less of him for admitting he was once ambitious. A hater of Saesons who made a Saeson his friend. A man who was loyal to the Amherawdyr while the Amherawdyr lived, but who does not cling to the past.'

Nai filled a goblet with wine, drained it at a swallow. 'Yet you follow Custennin, not Angus.'

'A man is loyal to his lord.' Eri's face darkened. 'And to his land.'

'Just so.' Nai rose, nodded, and made his way to Seradwen, who was waiting for him by the door.

Together they went out into the night. It was snowing again: small hard flakes fluttering on the wind, settling and vanishing on the frosted puddles. Nai took Seradwen's arm, paused a moment to let his eyes adapt to the darkness. The sound of chanting came to them in fitful snatches, mixed with the whine of the wind around the buildings.

'I do not see him as a praying man,' murmured Seradwen.

'His prayers would be demands,' said Nai, and she laughed as a flurry of snow crystals stung their faces.

'Somebody is devout,' she remarked as they passed by the chapel and the chanting became clearer.

Nai paused despite the cold, and listened to the voices, male and female alike, joined in the praise of God. The singing was frail against the roar of the wind, and from time to time one voice or another faltered or failed, for these were not trained singers but simple men and women at the end of a long day, yet the song endured, stronger than its parts, even as life itself endures regardless of the fate of the individual.

'Come,' said Seradwen, and drew him away.

CHAPTER SEVENTEEN

⁓

'Try a bout against Isag,' said the Abbot. 'Wooden swords, shields.'

Nai glanced around the training hall. The Abbot's pupils lounged against the walls. One bent to the man beside him and whispered something; the second man stifled a smile without taking his eyes off Nai. They were all watching him, weighing him, assessing his every move even now before he had so much as touched a weapon, and he began to feel unnaturally aware of his body, so that the very act of walking across the open space to where Isag waited with a pair of wooden blades and two small round shields became fraught with difficulty.

Isag was the man he had seen fighting yesterday with blunted iron blades. Once again Isag was stripped to the waist, and Nai could see the bruising across his torso. He seemed to carry himself stiffly, and Nai wondered whether some of his ribs had not been cracked. At all events, if Nai needed to finish the fight quickly (and whatever Angus might say about practice bouts he could tell from the eagerness of the onlookers that this was going to be a fight) a hard blow to the ribs should render the other helpless.

The wooden swords were a clever imitation of the real thing. He took the one Isag offered him, his fingers finding the four deep grooves carved in the hilt. The oval guard was just wide enough to protect his hand. The blade was the length of his arm, the edges rounded but, he thought, still capable of inflicting an injury.

'Shield,' said Isag. The man's crown was shaved in the Gallic style of tonsure, which made it hard to judge his age.

Nai slipped his left hand into the hole behind the shield boss and gripped the leather strap. He swung the wooden sword through the air, letting it whistle, accustoming himself to its lack of weight.

Isag grinned, and Nai saw the man was younger than he had guessed.

'Are you ready?' Isag stood with his feet apart, shield held out from the middle of his body, sword raised above his shoulder.

'A moment,' said Nai, trying the blade again. From the corner of his eye he could see Seradwen watching anxiously; he gave her what was intended to be a reassuring smile but probably looked more like a condemned man's farewell.

'Who will give me odds on Isag?' Eri's voice demanded loudly behind him.

'Hush, Eri. We are men of God,' the Abbot said in mock reproof.

'Half the priests of Prydein would wager a year's livelihood on the actions of two flies.' Eri's laughter boomed through the hall. 'You need not worry, Master. Your brethren are incorruptible – or at least, I have no takers. What about you, bard?'

Regin shook his head. 'I intend no disrespect to Nai, but I think not.'

'You too, eh?' said Eri. 'Of course, putting one of Gereint's provincials up against a man trained by Angus mab Connor . . .'

Nai stopped listening. He took his stance, left leg forward, shield out to give maximum protection to his torso, and acknowledged Isag's salute. The other was smiling over the rim of his shield, waiting for Nai to attack, perfectly balanced, ready to move in any direction.

'Always hold something back among strangers,' old Huw had told him, years ago when he was a lad learning how to fight. 'The man you are sparring with today may be trying to kill you tomorrow.'

He went forward warily, and Isag slipped aside so the wooden sword hissed through thin air.

'Come on!' shouted Eri.

He swung for Isag's shoulder: the sword cracked against the shield, jarring his wrist. Isag stepped around him, still not using his own blade, and Nai knew he would be dead if this were for real. He cut for the exposed right leg, but it was gone long before the sword reached the place it had been, and the other's blade was singing around him, rolling across his head to touch first one shoulder then the other, tapping his sword arm thrice in quick succession, then whistling away to drive up into his groin, and if he had not leapt high into the air it would not have stopped at his thigh.

'Enough,' said the Abbot. He rubbed his forehead, stared at Nai in bemused wonder. 'You killed Eremon?' he muttered, barely loud enough for Nai to catch the words.

Nai shrugged, laid the sword and shield on the ground, and walked back to Seradwen.

'May I try?' asked the bard.

'Why not?' said the Abbot. 'Lasrian, give him a bout.'

Regin picked up the sword and swung it a couple of times, testing it much as Nai had done. Then he raised it to head height and did something with his hand that made it seem to trickle down like water till the tip touched the floor, then up again as if it had a life of its own.

'Ah,' said the Abbot, and nothing more.

Lasrian relieved Isag of his weapons and took his place opposite Regin.

'Mind my fingers,' said the bard.

The monk laughed. 'I did not care for your harping.'

Regin frowned, and the two of them were suddenly moving, the wooden blades resounding against the shields.

'Most fights, as you know, are over in a matter of moments,' Angus remarked to Nai. 'Occasionally they last a little longer.'

The bard was in retreat, dancing backwards, weaving from side to side. Lasrian pressed him hard, raining blows on shield and sword alike, striking with tremendous force.

'It is good for my pupils to practise with strangers. They become too accustomed to each other's foibles. Best of all is to practise with someone trained in a different tradition.' The Abbot stretched lazily, added: 'I have always had a fondness for people from Dyfed. My first wife came from Dyfed.'

Regin shifted his stance, and now it was the monk who was trying to hold his ground but slowly being driven back if he was to avoid being struck.

'I think this is no common bard,' commented Angus, and Nai glanced at him sharply, for if what Seradwen had surmised was correct, then these two were better acquainted than either was prepared to admit.

'A man of many skills,' said Seradwen.

The Abbot turned his head with a slow, ironic smile. 'Indeed.'

Regin's sword spun in his hand, impossibly fast, and found the gap in Lasrian's defence. The impact echoed through the hall.

'You will stay one more night?' the Abbot said as if nothing had happened. 'The weather remains unsettled.'

'We would be honoured.' Nai sketched a bow. 'Provided we are not imposing on your hospitality, I have a strong desire to hear the end of your story.'

Lasrian lay on the floor, coughing and fighting for breath. The bard dropped his shield and knelt beside him.

'Eri has news of Bedwyr.' The Abbot's face was expressionless. 'Eri is Isgofan's comrade?'

'His back-to-back man. They are high in Custennin's counsels.' Angus twitched an eyebrow. 'You must miss Gorthyn.'

The bard helped Lasrian to his feet. The monk clutched his stomach where the wooden sword had hit him, limped to the wall where his friends awaited him.

'He will not be rude about Regin's playing again,' remarked Eri, drawing up a pair of stools. 'Shall we sit?'

Nai pulled a second pair of stools across for Seradwen and himself. There were times when he missed Gorthyn more than he could say, when he found himself turning to catch the big man's reaction to some event and was shocked afresh to remember that Gorthyn was dead. Gorthyn would have had no trouble dealing with a man like Eri: he would simply have sat and stared at him until the other dropped his gaze.

'They say you are a good javelin man,' Eri said condescendingly.

'He is,' snapped the Abbot. 'He has never claimed to be a swordsman. Do not underestimate Nai mab Nwython, Eri. You would be wise to make a friend of him, and it is for that reason I have brought the two of you here together.'

Eri had the grace to look abashed. 'Forgive me, Master. These past few days have been hard, and –'

The Abbot's voice cut across him. 'Do not apologize to me, but to Nai, who has not had an easy time himself. He was half dead with exhaustion when he arrived here, indeed, without the Lady Seradwen he would probably not have arrived at all. And when you have begged his pardon, tell him what Custennin told you when he first sent you out in the company of the Painted Men.'

'Very well.' The burly man extended his arm to Nai, said formally: 'I crave your pardon, warrior. May we pretend that we have not encountered each other before now, and that I regard all of Gereint's warband as paragons?'

There was a faint twinkle in his eyes, and for the first time Nai saw that it might be possible to like him.

'Of course,' he said, aware of the harshness of his own voice compared with the warm tones of the other.

'As you may know – I assume you spoke with Addonwy in Penhyle – the High Lord Custennin charged us with the task of guiding and protecting these Picts who call themselves the Children of Menestyr. The story we put about was that they were in search of a hermit who might cure their King's son of some disease. The truth of the matter was that they were in search of Bedwyr mab Petroc, or a man they believed to be Bedwyr.'

Eri looked up as the Abbot's pupils filed from the hall, the bard among them.

'Prayers,' said Angus. 'My deputy will take my place.' He shifted impatiently on the stool. 'Nai knows about Bedwyr and the Sons of Menestyr.'

'Nai knows more than I do,' Eri said with a wry smile. 'Forgive me if I belabour what is common knowledge to the rest of you. Custennin charged us with the task of keeping watch on the Picts. We were to give them what assistance they required, to establish their good faith with the lesser lords of Dumnonia, and also to prevent them from taking the law into their own hands.'

'You did not succeed,' said Nai.

'No, we did not,' acknowledged Eri. 'There were four of us. They divided their party. The smaller group went east to Isca and thence Lindinis. The larger remained in this area. At first we saw no need to accompany the smaller group into those regions where Custennin's writ has no real force; later Isgofan and I, thinking that group most likely to be successful, went in pursuit of them. Our comrades stayed behind.'

'Why then did the Picts come to Porthyle alone?' Nai demanded coldly.

'That was our mistake,' Eri said with great sincerity. 'We knew you were there, had taken the hermit's place. We thought they would simply ask you a few questions, then go. It seemed to us

334

there was no reason for you to be aware of the hermit's present whereabouts – if indeed the hermit of Porthyle was the one we sought. We gave three youngsters the task, and unfortunately events overtook us.' He shrugged. 'Once you had killed them, whatever the rights or wrongs of it, duty demanded we take you into custody.'

'And now?' asked Nai.

'Ah, now!' The burly man glanced at the Abbot. 'My former master has persuaded me that this is holy ground. Besides, I have no wish to quarrel with you. You see, we found Bedwyr, only to have him slip through our fingers.'

Nai stifled a smile.

'But,' Eri said firmly, 'and it saddens me that I must be the one to tell you this, Bedwyr is not the man you think him. Unless I have misjudged you badly, you will not approve of his actions any more than I do. I tell you, I am a hard man – one does not survive as a member of the High Lord Custennin's warband without being a hard man – but I was sick, sick to the stomach, when I entered that house and saw what he had done.'

'What are you talking about?' growled Nai. Seradwen put her hand on his leg.

'Lindinis,' said Eri. 'Lindinis, and what Bedwyr did to a youth who trusted him.'

'What did he do?' Nai's voice was raw in the silence. Seradwen dropped her hand.

'Easy, Nai, easy,' soothed the Abbot. 'This is as difficult for Eri to say as it is for you to hear. Not a pretty tale. I fear my old comrade has lost control at last.'

'What did he do?'

They flinched from his anger, Angus as well, and for an instant he felt ashamed. Angus was dressed as a man of God, and had been one of Arthur's Companions. Even if he did not altogether trust him, those were two good reasons why the Abbot was worthy of his respect.

'Bedwyr tortured and slew one of the Picts, a mere youth.' Eri's tones were measured, and Nai, who was watching his face intently for some sign of a lie, could not doubt the truth of what he was saying. 'Without consulting Isgofan and me, the Picts decided to send a boy to make contact with Bedwyr. They thought he would find it less menacing than dealing with a group. Until then, you see, he had fled every time we came close.'

335

Eri gestured with resignation. 'Bedwyr took the boy to the house in which he was staying, tortured him until he had wrung from him whatever information he wanted, then most cruelly killed him.'

The burly man leant back on his tool. His forehead was beaded with perspiration. He sighed and moistened his lips. 'Master, I think we would all be helped by a drink.'

Angus nodded and himself fetched the jug of wine and four beakers.

'This is not pleasant to recall, Nai.' Eri drank from the mug the Abbot gave him. 'The boy was hurt very badly before he died. I am not talking about slashing someone a few times with a knife, shouting at them, keeping them off balance, confused and frightened, so they will tell you what you want to know. I have done that. I am not proud of it, but I have done it when I deemed it necessary. The boy had been tortured long after he must have been incapable of speech.' Eri peered gloomily into beaker. 'Bedwyr had gone on inflicting pain for the sake of inflicting pain.'

'A bad business,' the Abbot said smoothly. 'Nai, I see by your face that although this is a shock, it is not entirely unexpected.'

Nai had lost all sense of others being present, so completely had his attention been concentrated on Eri. He roused himself and turned his attention to the Abbot, who was regarding him with an expression of kindly concern.

'Bedwyr —' His tongue clogged his mouth. He sipped the wine, let it wash against the back of his throat, hating the taste, hating the hall in which he sat, hating everything about this monastery and its reasonable, cultured Abbot forcing him to hear these things he had no wish to hear.

'He told me he had struggled all his life with the desire to hurt others,' he said, and the admission felt like a betrayal.

'Now that desire has overwhelmed him.' The Abbot steepled his fingers, shook his head sadly. 'A terrible tragedy, for he was a great man once, among the noblest of Arthur's Companions. But to fight one's true nature is not easy, especially as one grows older and one's powers begin to fail.'

'Isgofan disarmed him, and we thought we had him then,' said Eri. 'He was too quick for us, and escaped.'

'Isgofan disarmed him?' repeated Seradwen.

'Aye.' Eri's voice was bleak. 'But only after he had killed three of the Picts, and maimed two more.'

336

'A dangerous man indeed,' said Seradwen.

'You seem to take this very lightly,' Angus said reprovingly.

'Your pardon if I give that impression.' Seradwen placed her beaker carefully on the floor. 'It was not my intention. But I am a little puzzled. What do these Picts want with this man, and why is Custennin helping them?'

The Abbot smiled sadly. 'Why, there we come to the full tragedy of the matter. You see, these people are not Bedwyr's enemies, though he still perceives them as such. They are the followers of the Lady Teleri, Bedwyr's one-time lover, the woman who first set Arthur on the road to sovereignty. They mean him no harm.'

'Why then did they attack me at Porthyle?' demanded Nai.

Eri glanced uncertainly at the Abbot and, finding no help there, shrugged. 'This too is not easy to say.' He sucked his teeth. 'But is it not possible that was a misunderstanding? You are a frightening man, Nai, when your rage is upon you. If you caught them unawares –' He shrugged again. 'I can see how it might have happened. Once you had killed one of them: well, they are a fierce and bloody people from beyond the bounds of our civilized lands. Among them the blood feud still counts for much.'

'I see by your face this thought has occurred to you,' Angus said quietly.

Remembering what Addonwy had said in Porthyle, Nai stared blindly at the Abbot. Was it possible? The first man had been standing by the ponies when he had slithered down the embankment and shouted a greeting. The man had turned, reaching for a knife, and run at him.

'It was so quick,' he said aloud.

And the others. They had found him lying in wait for them. Their manner had not been gentle, but then if they were afraid . . . Fear makes men cruel.

He shook his head. 'Perhaps. I cannot tell.'

'What a world we live in,' Seradwen said after a moment, 'that our first reaction to a stranger is to attack him.'

'A sign that our world lacks strong governance,' Angus said gravely. 'In Bedwyr you may see the whole in miniature. While Arthur lived he was able to hold his passions in check. Now Arthur has gone, Bedwyr is at the mercy of his own failings, like a dismasted ship at the mercy of the elements, driven hither and thither without purpose.'

337

'So what do you suggest?' Nai asked wearily.

The Abbot fingered the thin scars on his cheek. 'At present, nothing. I will not ask you to betray the man into our hands – and I think you would feel it a betrayal, whatever the rights and wrongs of the matter. Nor will I ask you to withdraw. What I would ask is simply this: that if you are successful in your search for him, you tell him what we have discussed here today. Tell him it is not too late for redemption, that though the Children of Menestyr are a vengeful race, we of Dumnonia are his friends, and wish him no ill. Tell him it is time for the chalice of Sovereignty to go home, to be removed from our lands, to prevent lesser men quarrelling over who shall follow in Arthur's footsteps. Tell him – tell him it is time for an end.'

'What is wrong?'

Nai stood in the doorway of the hut staring out across the yard. The smell of rain was like a cold perfume. Water dripped from the thatch, trickled through the drainage ditches beside the paths. A few huddled shapes ran from shelter to shelter, splashed through puddles muttering what might have been curses had this not been a monastery.

'What is it?' Her voice was gentle behind him. 'Is it what they said about Bedwyr?'

He bit his lower lip hard enough to make himself wince.

'Shut the door and light the lamp.'

'In a moment,' he said, gazing into the dove-coloured rain, the air cool and wet against his skin. 'He is out there somewhere. Alone.'

'He has been alone a long while,' she answered, surprising him for he did not know he had spoken aloud.

He latched the door, shutting out the rain, and fiddled with flint and tinder, coaxing the flame into life. The glow filled the room, turned her hair to a shower of molten copper.

'Bedwyr was all I ever wanted to be,' he said. 'Wise and kindly, the greatest of warriors. At peace with God.' The lamp flickered in the draught from under the door. 'I never knew Nwython my father.'

'I know,' she murmured.

'Erfai raised me, loved me, but he was not and never pretended to be my blood father,' he continued as if he had not heard. 'I was always aware another man was my real father. Erfai and Gorthyn were big men, and sometimes I used to feel like the runt of the litter. I would pretend my real father had been like me, smaller and darker, and that one day he would come for me.'

She put her hand on his forearm, her face hidden beneath a mask of dancing shadows, her eyes liquid fire, and she seemed to him like a stranger.

'I grew up, forgot my childish imaginings, accepted my parents had died of the plague, would never return. Then I met Bedwyr. He was everything I had dreamed of. I liked him on sight.' Nai half smiled. 'One couldn't not like him.'

'And now?'

'And now I am not sure.' He raised his head, searched the shadows gathered in the curve of the wall. 'I knew him for a single summer day. He saved my life by coming back into danger when he could have escaped. The child Eurgain loved him.'

'All of which are points in his favour.' She nodded thoughtfully. 'Do you believe what Eri told you?'

He drew a deep breath. 'It had the ring of truth.'

'Which merely proves that Eri believed it – or that he is a skilled liar, which I agree does not seem probable. Angus yes; Eri, no.'

'Angus?' he said, momentarily distracted.

'Oh, I think so.' She spoke briskly, and he remembered afresh this was not the girl he had once known but a mature woman with a wealth of experience. 'Only in a rightful cause, of course. I have met men who were as honest and trustworthy as the day is long, until it came to the merits of their horses. Then they had no scruples.'

Nai bent and pulled off his boots, sat down on the bedding. 'What makes it more credible is that long ago Bedwyr killed Gwydawg mab Menestyr in similar fashion, toying with him when he could have ended the fight.' He weighed the boots in his hand, flung them aside. 'I fear he may be a man living in the past. He kills easily, by his own admission enjoys killing. I can imagine such a man turning rogue.'

'A while ago you told me he was a kindly man,' she said drily.

'Kindly to his friends; fierce to his enemies. Is that not the mark of a warrior? Do the bards not sing of the heroes of Arthur's Court, that they were like wolves in battle and like lambs in the presence of women?'

Seradwen's eyebrows leapt into copper curves; then she burst

339

into laughter. 'Nai, Nai. There are times when I wonder if we live in the same world. Bards lie for their living.'

'Yes, yes,' he said crossly. 'But the point stands, however exaggerated.'

'What worries you then? Are you afraid you are on the wrong side? The behaviour of these Picts has hardly been exemplary.'

'No,' he said hesitantly. 'If anybody now living can be said to represent Arthur's will it must be Bedwyr.' He tugged his hair, scowled and touched the scar at his throat, shook his head doubtfully. 'The crux is the chalice, the chalice of Sovereignty. It is the chalice the Sons of Menestyr want. Bedwyr is only a means to an end. And if it is indeed Teleri who controls them, then I do not understand why, having found Bedwyr, they did not simply reveal themselves to him.'

Seradwen frowned and made to reply, but before she could speak there was a tap at the door. She looked at Nai, who straightened and put a hand on the hilt of his knife, then released it when he noticed her expression.

'Either we are safe, as Angus promised, or else it would be of little use against his warriors,' she said reprovingly, and opened the door.

From where he sat Nai could see only silver sheets of rain. He could hear the gurgle of water rushing across the yard, could smell the damp air blowing through the doorway. He blinked, saw a colourless shape standing in the opening.

'Come in, quick,' said Seradwen.

Trailing a fringe of silver droplets the man entered the room, which at once felt cramped. Nai drew his legs up onto the bed to give the newcomer more space.

'What a day!' exclaimed Regin. He pulled off his cloak and shook it through the doorway, then tossed it aside on the floor. Seradwen shut the door, and the hut seemed smaller than ever.

'Forgive my intrusion,' said the bard, smiling and bowing.

'I thought you were going to Din Erbin.'

Nai glanced curiously at Seradwen. There was a distinct note of accusation in her voice.

Regin ran a hand through his hair. 'Ah yes, I was. But the woods around your villa seemed alive with watchers – I know now they were waiting for you, warrior – so I set a different course.'

'Did you come over the high moor?' asked Nai.

'No, no.' The bard shook his head hastily. 'I have not your daring, or your local knowledge. I came by an easier route. I confess,' he added with a bow on Seradwen's direction, 'that our conversation about a monastery in the wilderness had aroused my interest.'

'I see,' she said. 'It was a surprise to find you here.'

'As much a surprise for me. I thought you had resolved to remain at your farm.'

'Did you?' she said coolly, and Nai smiled to himself, recognizing the way her eyes had narrowed. 'An even greater surprise to me,' she continued, 'was that you already knew the Abbot.'

Regin seemed taken aback. 'Already knew him? Not until my arrival.' He cast around for a seat, realized there were only the bed and a single stool, sank to his haunches instead.

'You saw how I aroused his wrath last night.' He spread his hands in appeal. 'Did that strike you as the action of an old acquaintance?'

'Why do you persist in blackening Arthur's name?'

'It was a song about Cei and Llacheu,' he protested.

'Answer the question.'

He rubbed the back of his neck, tilted his head, tried and failed to peer down his nose at her as she stood over him. 'I have a contrary nature.'

Nai laughed. 'You do.'

'Look,' he said. 'I have come to beg a boon of you. Think carefully before you reply.'

'I am always careful with the granting of boons,' said Nai, the soft growl of his voice turning what might have been a joke into something more menacing.

'When you leave here you will go to find Bedwyr.'

'That is no secret.'

'Take me with you.'

Seradwen gasped. Nai saw her cheeks darken in the lamplight. He rubbed his throat, stared with wry amusement at the bard.

'Why should we? I have small reason to trust the men of Dyfed.'

The bard bowed his head in acknowledgement. 'Yes, I heard the High Lord Vortepor was involved in the raid upon Porthyle.'

'Involved?' Nai exclaimed. 'You have a pretty way with words, bard. He was its chief instigator!'

'I am not Vortepor,' Regin said with dignity. 'Nor am I his slave.'

'Then what do you want with Bedwyr?'

'I want . . .' Regin hesitated, then suddenly the words came tumbling from him. 'He was the greatest warrior of the previous age. And he is still alive, when all believed him dead. I want to talk with him, an eyewitness to the court of Arthur. I want to see him wield a sword, quickly, before it is too late. If any man is a hero, he is, and if I do not take this chance it will never come again.' He slowed, grinned ruefully at Nai. 'You do not trust me. I cannot blame you.'

'He travels best who travels alone.'

'There are two of you. And the Children of Menestyr are hunting you. My sword and your spears – we would make a good pair.'

'Have you not heard the news Eri brought? Isgofan disarmed Bedwyr in Lindinis, and Bedwyr tortured and murdered a young Pict. Do you still see him as a hero?'

Regin rocked back on his haunches. 'The Abbot said it would affect you. That Isgofan disarmed him – well, Isgofan must be more than thirty years younger. I would still like to see him fight. As for the other, I cannot see why you all take it so seriously.'

'Can you not?' said Nai.

'No. Murder!' he said scornfully. 'What does murder mean? The youth was aligned with his foes.'

'In Dumnonia, murder means killing someone who is unable to defend himself. I do not know how it is in Dyfed.'

Regin gave a bark of laughter. 'In Vortepor's Dyfed a wise man deals with his foes when they are at their greatest disadvantage and cannot defend themselves.'

'Here we abide by the law.'

'What law?' scoffed the bard. 'Why, Seradwen, you told me yourself that Custennin was only the upstart descendant of some glib landowner. What right then has he to impose rules upon the rest of you?'

'The right of sovereignty,' said Nai.

'Which is why you, having broken his laws, have promptly surrendered yourself to him,' Regin said slyly.

'The law is the reason Angus our host is still alive and not rotting on a gibbet. A lesser man than Custennin would have executed him.'

'I thought you did not like Custennin,' said Seradwen.

Nai turned to her. 'I do not,' he said gravely. 'He is a frightened man, unworthy of his father's office. But he is all we have. He is the lawful lord of Dumnonia, and if we overturn him because we do not like him, then we rock the foundations upon which our world is built. If we replace Custennin with Angus, then in a year's time some other lord may decide he does not like Angus. That way lie chaos and endless civil war.'

'So what are you saying?' mocked Regin. 'That Custennin is the lawful lord, therefore his laws are lawful? You argue in circles.'

'No. I am saying that sovereignty may be held by good men or bad men, but is greater than those who wield it. The sovereignty of the land is that which abides deep within it. Rulers may be corrupt, but sovereignty remains undefiled.' Nai shrugged, added lamely: 'I am not a bard, to be good with words.'

'And if tomorrow your own lord, Gereint, decides to move against Custennin? What then?'

Nai smiled sardonically. 'Then we shall see, bard.'

'You interest me,' said Regin. 'You are not the simple warrior I took you for. I would talk with you further, and I do not think that is possible in this place. The monks make many demands upon my time. Already I am late for a meeting with a pair of scribes who want my help in deciphering a scroll.'

'I cannot prevent you from coming with us.' Nai's hand forestalled Regin's reply. 'But if we find Bedwyr, I can make no promises concerning the welcome he may give you.'

'That is fairly spoken.' The bard rose to his feet, lifted his head and stared down at Nai on the bed. He made as if to speak, changed his mind, nodded abruptly to Seradwen. 'By your leave, my lady.'

After the door closed behind him there was silence apart from the patter and drip of the rain. Nai leant back and closed his eyes, aware of Seradwen moving around the hut. The hilt of his knife was digging into his ribs; he pulled at his belt to twist it around.

'I should keep it close,' she said sharply. 'You may need it soon. Tell me, was the Abbot's man as good as he seemed this afternoon?'

Nai opened an eye. Her face was flushed and her movements were short as she burrowed into her pack, pulling out scarves and holding them against herself before discarding them.

'He was. If anything, better.' He laughed without humour. 'In my vanity, I had planned to hold back. As it was, I gave my all to no effect.'

She paused with a length of green fabric stretched across her shoulders. 'Does it matter to you?'

'It would not,' he said carefully, 'if it were not for the fact that I must soon face them or men like them. I dislike feeling helpless.'

'Is that why you want Regin with us?'

'No.'

'Why then?' She began to fold the scarves and replace them in the pack.

'Because he has a fondness for you.'

She stilled, and her expression tore at his heart.

'Would it be better if I returned to the farm?'

He knew what it cost her to ask, and knew too that there was only one possible answer he could give.

'Yes; but if you go I shall follow after and fetch you back.'

'Tied across the cruppers of your mount?' she said with a flash of her old humour.

'If need be.'

'Hah!' She returned to her packing, folding and folding the scarves until they were tiny squares which gave no hint of their real size. 'It seems to me we are like two small children lost in a great forest full of hungry bears and wolves. I do not trust Regin. He lied about not knowing the Abbot. I think you can take it that he and Angus are in some sense in league, though they may not like each other. Regin is more than he appears: he is not as accustomed to performing in public as a bard of his age should be, and he handles a sword like a warrior born. As for the Abbot himself, he should be a powerless exile caged in this remote fastness, yet Eri has ridden out of his way to report to him rather than Custennin.'

'He led the warband once. Old loyalties die hard.'

'Yes,' she mused, tilting her head to one side so the lamplight washed her jaw a reddish gold. 'And I suppose it must be a formidable undertaking, to hunt the last of Arthur's Companions. No doubt Eri feels the need for the Abbot's moral support. Well enough for Eri to say they intend Bedwyr no harm; Bedwyr obviously regards them as enemies.'

'Do you think they will let us leave?' Nai asked suddenly.

344

'Now they have lost him again? Oh yes, and especially if we have Regin with us.'

'The bard may prove our safe conduct.'

'He might.' Seradwen nodded thoughtfully. 'You may have been wiser than I thought in allowing him to come with us.'

CHAPTER EIGHTEEN

1

I remember (*the Abbot said that evening, looking around the crowded hall*) the heat and the bustle and the dust, the constant coming and going as messengers rode back and forth. I remember the smell of the cooking fires, the pennants flapping on the breeze, the long lines of tents, the stench of the latrines. The noise was constant, the shouts in strange dialects, British, Latin and Saeson, the arguments between the different factions in the camp over food and water, while in the background the smiths' hammers beat on fresh weaponry, blades clashed in mock combat, javelins struck targets of wood or straw.

I remember Eleuther of Eburacum, red-faced and choleric, striding among his men as they whetted their steel spears, the long rasping sound echoing across the plain. I remember watching the spearmen march, moving as one man, seeing them wheel behind the cover of their shields at the blast of a horn, then form into column and wedge and square, and I remember thinking that if they could manoeuvre like this when they were facing a live opponent who was fighting back then they were dangerous indeed.

We had taken the place we were assigned, in the horse pastures between Eidin and the great mountain of Llew's Seat, not far from the river. Eidin's horses were ours now, those that had not been spirited away to the hills, for there was no space for them all in the citadel and they had perforce been abandoned to us. Wulfstan needed fresh mounts for his men, and I went with him to help him choose.

'Riding does not come easy to me,' he confessed as we made our way through the rows of leather tents. 'I feel safer with both feet firmly on the ground.'

'That is because your horses are no good.' I sought for an image to explain what I meant. 'It is like the difference between throwing an ill-made spear and one well crafted: the good spear will go where you put it, the bad one will fly off at a tangent.'

'Or good wine and bad,' said a voice behind me. 'A little of the bad wine will make you wish you were dead. But a good wine is a joy to drink.'

Wulfstan spun on his heel, roaring with delight, and gathered the newcomer to him in a bear-hug. In a moment the pair of them were wrestling up and down the alley, each struggling to throw the other, and I was skipping like a madman under the hot summer sun, hard put to keep from being knocked down. At last they tripped over a guy rope and crashed to the earth, where they rolled in the dust, first one and then the other on top.

Although they were friends, these two, and both were laughing, there was an edge to the tussle. As it continued we gathered a crowd, mostly of Llacheu's followers among the Companions, for we were in their section of the camp. Naturally enough they shouted for their leader, the Amherawdyr's son, and Wulfstan's face grew flushed with the effort of the struggle. It may have been no more than the heat – they were both running with sweat by now – but I was glad when both scrambled to their feet and stood regarding each other, chests heaving.

'Well met, Weala,' panted Wulfstan.

'Well met, Saeson,' said Llacheu, and they embraced.

Gradually the crowd dispersed so only the three of us were left standing there in the aisle between the leather tents.

'Who is your friend?' The young prince shaded his eyes and peered at me.

I came out from the shadows and bowed my head.

'Angus mab Connor!' he exclaimed before I had a chance to speak. 'How do you come to be with this rogue, this pirate's son?'

'Do not talk of pirates. Boats make me seasick,' Wulfstan said lugubriously, and I burst into laughter at the thought of this giant, this descendant of men whose name was a byword for seamanship, retching over the side at the first breath of wind.

'I asked for him,' Wulfstan said to Llacheu. 'Even though he is not a serious man, he shows signs of promise. And he can ride a horse sideways, which is a rare thing even among the Companions of Arthur.'

'True,' said Llacheu with a grin. 'Yet he has a reputation for seriousness among his own people. I myself would reckon him a good reliable man, a skilled fighter, steadfast in danger.'

'Perhaps,' said Wulfstan. 'But then your idea of steadfast is not mine. You are a flighty lot, you Wealas, all dash and glitter and no staying power.' He gestured in the direction of Dun Eidin, concealed by the tents. 'Look at the Men of Gododdin. We turn out to fight them and they all scurry back behind their walls.'

'Which will afford them no safety.' Llacheu's face changed, his light-heartedness vanishing. 'Tomorrow we will make our assault upon them.'

'We do not wait for Gwalchmei?' I said in surprise.

He looked at me properly for the first time, and I saw his father in him, the same strength and determination.

'No. Gwalchmei pacifies the rest of Gododdin. We shall do this alone, as proof to all Albion that the Emperor's reach is long and rapid.'

And proof that you are worthy of being his son and heir, I thought to myself, though I did not say anything.

'So,' he said, putting his arm around Wulfstan's shoulders. 'Where were you going?' They began to move between the tents, leaving me behind.

From a distance one might have taken them for brothers. They were of a height, and similar in build. Both were fair, though Wulfstan's hair was the colour of straw, while Llacheu's had the reddish highlights he had inherited from his father.

'Angus was going to pick me some horses.'

'Good.' Llacheu glanced back at me, his expression puzzled when he saw I was still standing in the alley. 'Are you coming, Angus?'

I hurried to join them.

The Men of Gododdin will tell you that in all the long years of its history Dun Eidin had never fallen, until Cei and Llacheu came there in their wrath.

In those days, as now, it was a place renowned for its richness and luxury. 'Mynyddog Mwynfawr', the poets sometimes call Dun Eidin: the mountain court of great wealth. They claimed its heroes dined every night in the great hall, reclining on fleece-lined couches, drinking fine wines or honey mead from vessels of glass and horn. Meat was always roasting in the kitchen, and the generosity of the welcome its lord gave to strangers was famous. Great pine logs crackled and snapped in the hearths, and it was never cold in that place, not even in the depths of winter. Every evening a bard sang to the warriors and their ladies, entertaining them with tales of love and war.

The men and women dressed in brightly-coloured gowns of cunningly woven wool or linen, covered themselves in jewellery of gold and silver, rings on their fingers and toes, brooches and necklaces on their breasts that sparkled in the firelight. The women – and sometimes the men – dyed their locks in different shades, then plaited their hair by interlacing the tresses, weaving the shades together. They bound the plaits with silver thread, or hung little globes of gold at the end of every tress, that jingled and shone as they moved.

The whole hall became a mass of whirling light and colour, sweetly perfumed with infusions of herbs sprinkled on the floor rushes, and the smell of pinewood burning on the fires. Dun Eidin rivalled the splendours of that greater gathering in the south at Caer Cadwy, where Gwenhwyvar and Arthur held court.

That is what the poets say. Whether or not it was true then, let alone now, I cannot tell you. By the time I myself entered Eidin matters were much changed.

It is a strange place, Eidin. Betimes the last bastion of the lowlands against the highlands, and betimes the first bastion of the highlands against the lowlands. Conquered by Rome, but not held for long. Always in the hinterland, a place between, neither one thing nor the other.

It is also a sacred place, sacred since the dawn of time and the coming of Prydein mab Aed and his hosts. Here, as you have heard, the Young Son first held court among the kingdoms of men, and from here he was betrayed to his death that his people might live. Here, some say, ruled the mountainous one, the wealthy one, whose name is often confused with the city, and his throne is still to be seen, half hidden among the clouds and mists that constantly swirled about it. Others say the throne belongs to Llew, and certainly Llew gave his name to the Rock and the surrounding countryside: Llewthiniawn, the Land of Llew's Fort.

There are dark tales too, tales one has heard before, told of other places and other times. Once there was a king in Dun Eidin whose wife died, leaving him with only a daughter, slim and graceful, called on that account Teneu, the slender one. A wise woman told the king that his daughter's child would cause his death, so he shut Teneu away in a tower, sealing the door with a knot so intricate that he would know if anybody other than himself had visited her. Yet somehow the life quickened within her, and fearing what her child might bring he cast her adrift in a small boat on the Sea of Iuddew. The currents took her and she was washed to the shore, where she was delivered of a boy. She named him Cunthigern, Hound Lord, and gave him over to the druids to be raised in the greenwood. In time he became a man, trained in the mysteries, and, knowing that the prophecy must be fulfilled, he returned to Dun Eidin where he had been conceived. There he slew the one who was both his father and grandfather, flinging him down from the top of the tower in which Teneu had been imprisoned, and took the rule of the place for himself, keeping it for many years until his own death came upon him.

We can none of us escape our fate.

The three of us examined the ponies in their pounds, and chose a handful for the use of Wulfstan's Saesons, picking those which seemed to us the sturdiest and least lively, the most suitable for inexperienced riders. At every point Llacheu conferred with me, and we must have been there a long while, discussing the merits and faults of each animal, for eventually Cei himself came to find us.

'Hardy but lightweight,' Llacheu was saying. 'Eidin was famous for its chariot ponies in days gone by, and you can still see the lines in their breeding.'

' "Long striding, well fed, swift are the horses of Eidin." ' Cei's deep growl took us by surprise. Llacheu started guiltily, and glanced at the position of the sun.

'Even so,' said Cei. 'It grows late. Our emissaries have returned from Dun Eidin and you were supposed to meet them.'

He peered at the pony we had been examining, caught its head and forced open its mouth, grunted dubiously. Then he stepped over the barricade and trapped the horse's near hindleg between his thighs, like a farrier, and scrutinized the hoof.

He was the biggest man I have ever seen, was Cei, much larger than either Llacheu or Wulfstan, neither of whom were small men. The pony recognized his enormous strength and confidence, stood quietly without struggling though a moment earlier it had been fretting nervously. It looked tiny beside him, more like a hound than a horse.

I had heard that Cei's sight was failing him, slowly but surely. Watching him now I could well believe it, for he bent his head so low his nose was almost touching the hoof, even as some monks, their eyes ruined by long hours poring over scrolls in gloomy scriptoriums, are forced to bend over their books before they can focus on the letters.

'Hoof fever,' he said, straightening and releasing the pony. 'The creature has been overworked and not allowed to cool properly.' He glared at Wulfstan, as if holding him responsible. 'What do you know about horse care, boy?'

It was the only time I saw Wulfstan abashed. He shifted from foot to foot, blushed scarlet. 'Not much, lord. I can learn.'

Cei held him with a steady gaze. 'See you do.' He turned to Llacheu. 'I assume you intend this Saeson to requisition a few remounts?' His voice was harsh.

'I do.' Llacheu swallowed, and I saw that he too was unsure of himself, though he had known Cei since birth.

'Very well. You will inform the Master of Horse and obtain his consent.'

'I have done so.'

The Long Man smiled coldly. 'Good. I am glad to discover you have not forgotten everything you were taught.'

Now it was Llacheu who blushed. 'I am sorry, uncle. I met my friend, and forgot my duties.'

'You did. Bad enough in any officer, worse in a commander.' He stared at Llacheu a moment longer, then suddenly seemed to relax. He ran a hand through his thinning blond hair, which was loose about his face, massaged his forehead.

'I am no better,' he said ruefully. 'I should not reprimand you in front of your comrades, not unless your crime is truly heinous. And I forget my manners. You are Angus mab Connor, poor Lleminawg's kinsman.'

He swung towards me with something of the speed which

made him so deadly in battle. It was an effort not to shrink away, and had the fence rail not been at my back I am not sure I would have managed it.

'I am, lord.'

'Then welcome. How was Caer Cadwy when you left?'

'Much as usual,' I said, uncertain how to answer. It was a curiously mundane question from such a legendary figure.

He screwed up his eyes and squinted at me, appeared satisfied with whatever he saw. 'Good,' he said, 'good.'

Cei had none of the natural ability to set people at their ease which both Llacheu and Arthur possessed in abundance. An awkward silence grew between us while he peered around, seeming to search for something suitable to say.

'Good,' he repeated.

He cleared his throat, grasped Llacheu by the arm, drew him a little aside. Wulfstan and I took this as a signal that Cei desired privacy, and we moved away along the fence rail.

The Long Man's voice was not made for whispering.

'As I said, Atlendor and Menw have returned from Dun Eidin,' he growled.

Llacheu's face quickened with interest. 'And?'

'They will not surrender.'

'No surprise in that.' Llacheu tapped his teeth with a forefinger, an odd gesture I had seen him make before when he was thinking hard. 'So we launch the assault tomorrow morning?'

Cei nodded. 'As we planned. An all-out attack by the foot. We have no space for subtlety.'

I glanced at Wulfstan, who was eavesdropping as shamelessly as I. Our eyes met, and he shrugged expressively, for we had both seen the defences we must face. At this late date I cannot be precise about the appearance of Eidin, for I never saw it clear, only veiled by the dust and smoke of Cei's army. As best I can recall, the rock on which the citadel is built rises steep and sheer to the north, towering above the meadows and marshes that run down to the Sea of Iuddew. To the east and south, looking towards the great hill of Llew's Seat, the slope is long and gentle, and there lay the main fortifications, the walls and ramparts behind which our enemies waited.

This was the way we would have to attack, up the long slope, fighting for every foot of ground. I had never taken part in an assault upon a fortified position, and neither had Wulfstan. To our inexperienced eyes the defences looked strong, and we knew the men of Gododdin would be desperate, with nowhere left for them to run.

'Did Atlendor and Menw see anything useful inside the walls?' asked Llacheu.

The older man tilted his head to the sky. 'Of the defences? Only what one would expect. Piles of slingshot by the gates, men practising their archery and spear-casting. A confident and plentiful garrison.'

He paused, and Llacheu watched him intently, waiting for him to speak again.

'There is more?' the prince prompted after a moment.

The big man sighed. 'Yes, and I am not certain what to make of it. The two of them were received within the hall. Gurfelling was there, the Lord of Eidin, sitting on his High Seat, surrounded by his lesser lords. He listened to what our men had to say, to our offer of honourable terms if Eidin surrendered, then looked around as if to test the feeling of the gathering.'

Cei's fingers drummed on his thigh. 'You know me, Llacheu. In my life I have seen some odd things, many of them connected with your father.'

Llacheu smiled at this, but the big man's expression remained troubled. He wiped the sweat from his brow, played idly with a strand of hair. Had he not been Cei, one might have thought he was nervous.

'I am not like Bedwyr who spent weeks closeted with that northern woman who cast a spell upon us all. I do not pretend to know anything of magic. My strength is in my body, in my endurance, and if other people choose to attribute my prowess in battle to strange powers, then that is their prerogative. But you know, and I know, it is not true. Most of what we call magic is simply the result of training, of anticipation, of coincidence. A man applies himself to learning the art of woodcraft, and people decide he must have sold his soul to the Devil because he can move through a forest in silence.'

Coming from Cei this seemed remarkable. I knew he was not a religious man – oh, he attended church regularly enough, made the right noises at the right time, paid lip-service to the priests, but he was not religious, in the sense that someone like Bedwyr was religious.

Yet by the same token Cei was not an ordinary man. He might

353

deny magic – whatever 'magic' may be, and I am not now thinking of sorcerers caked in the dried blood of their sacrifices reading spells from scrolls of human skin, though I do believe such magic exists and I also believe that those who practise it are forever condemned to the torments of Tartarus – Cei might deny magic, and yet he himself was, in some fashion I find hard to describe, of the very stuff of magic, in that at certain times a power would descend upon him and he would become clothed in a majesty no mortal could possess.

To my mind these transformations came from God, either directly, or indirectly through the intervention of an angelic power. My friend Wulfstan would probably have said they came from the spirits of the land, which is perhaps another way of expressing the same thing. The sceptics I have read since, the pagan authors of old Rome (in whose works Cei himself was well versed), would probably have said that we who witnessed such transformations were deluded, had allowed our fear or admiration of his massive size and strength to cloud our vision. They might have been right. I can only say that they never saw what I saw, there upon the heights of Dun Eidin, at sunset on the next day.

'This is not to be repeated,' growled Cei, glaring in our direction. I jumped, having forgotten that he must know we could overhear every word. He took a step towards us, menace in every line of his body. 'I will not have it bruited through the Army that our opponents are using magic.'

He paused, let the threat sink into our minds.

'I have been acquainted with Menw for many years, since long before you were born, but I know him no better now than I did the first time he rode into Arthur's camp near Fort Guinnion and offered us his services. Rumour has it he trained as a druid, and it may well be true.'

He moved still closer to us, drawing Llacheu with him. 'Menw often dresses his remarks in strange and portentous language, phrasing things in a manner I find infuriating. For all that, I trust his judgement.'

Llacheu's lips were parted and he was listening intently. The youth who had frolicked in the dust with Wulfstan had vanished, and in his place stood the leader of men, the Amherawdyr's son, the warrior captain who was more than a simple warrior.

'Menw tells me that from the moment he entered the hall he could sense something evil,' continued Cei. 'A feeling of oppres-

354

sion, which at first he attributed to the fact the Gododdin lords gathered there must be aware that they were doomed. They must either surrender, and thus be humiliated, or else fight and almost certainly die.'

(That was another thing about all of Arthur's Captains. They had become so accustomed to victory it never occurred to them they might fail in any undertaking, and perhaps as a consequence of this confidence they always succeeded in whatever enterprise they began. And that too was a form of magic.)

'When Gurfelling paused to take the mood of his followers, the sense of oppression grew stronger. Menw stood in the middle of the hall with only Atlendor for company, and the Gododdin lords who were gathered around the walls were staring at the pair of them with naked hatred, which is never comfortable. Being an envoy is always a chancy matter, since so much depends upon the temper of your host, and Menw says he had made up his mind they would not be leaving the hall alive.

'The silence deepened. Menw could feel Atlendor at his side, tensing his muscles. And then a man moved forward from the shadows behind the High Seat.'

Cei hesitated, and I could see the perplexity and pain in his reddened eyes. 'You will remember, Llacheu, and perhaps you also, Angus, that Atlendor and Menw were among those who saw Lleminawg walk the labyrinth.'

Wulfstan frowned and looked from one to the other of us, not appreciating the significance of this. Llacheu gestured impatiently for the Long Man to continue, as one might to a subordinate who was taking too long to reach the heart of the matter. He had, I think, momentarily forgotten that it was Cei who was speaking. An expression flashed across the Long Man's features, passing so quickly that I could not recognize it, could only register that it was familiar from some other context.

'At first Menw could not see much of the newcomer's features,' Cei continued. 'The man was silhouetted against the light, his face concealed. But Menw could see the outline of his hair, tousled and unkempt, and two plaits on either side of his face, which swung and danced in the air like snakes as the man came forward. The man shambled, moving in a jerky style that reminded Menw of somebody he had once known who had broken both legs yet lived and learned to walk again, though always awkwardly.

'The newcomer stopped a few paces short of where Menw and Atlendor waited. Now they could see his face. It was a mask of blue and green.'

'Menestyr!' exclaimed Llacheu, and exhaled softly.

Cei nodded. 'Exactly.'

'But here? In Gododdin?'

'As an honoured guest. No, more than an honoured guest,' Cei corrected himself. 'When the man spoke, it was clear he spoke for all within the hall. He told Menw that the time had come for a few debts to be paid, the first of many. The death of a father, the seduction of a sister, the theft of a chalice. We could bluster all we liked, but we were not now dealing with savages and barbarians, to be cowed by one man's overblown reputation.'

'Yours?' interrupted Wulfstan, puzzled.

Cei half-smiled. 'I think he meant Arthur. He said there would be, could be, no negotiation between us. We were slaves of a foreign power and a foreign god, the ghosts of the Roman invaders. The men of Gododdin were free men, who would stand or fall in the manner of their ancestors.'

'How did Menw reply?' asked Llacheu.

Cei leant against the railing. 'Not well, he told me, not with his customary eloquence. He said it was hard to describe the effect the man had upon his audience. Thinking about it afterwards he could not remember much of what the man actually said, yet at the time even he was beginning to have some sympathy for the other's point of view. Perhaps we were being unjust. After all, cattle raiding was a long and venerable tradition, something we had all indulged in at some stage. Perhaps we were taking a sledgehammer to crack a nut, and perhaps this was typical of Arthur's tyranny.'

Llacheu flushed angrily, and Cei held up a hand to forestall his comments. 'Menw told me he tried to refute the other's argument, but when you came down to it, there was little to refute, scarcely any substance to the other's oration. Yet the man had talked for a long time, and it did not seem to either Menw or Atlendor that he had repeated himself. Their own efforts were lame and halting in comparison, and besides, the mood of the hall was against them.'

'Does this mean then,' I said hesitantly, 'that these tattooed men have been behind the whole affair? Has Gododdin been manipulated into this war, that we in our turn might be lured here?'

Cei raised his head and studied me. 'That is the question I have been pondering since Menw's return. If this is a trap, the trap lies within Eidin itself. There is no other force within reach –'

'Are you sure?' Wulfstan demanded sharply. 'What of the sea? A hostile fleet could anchor in the Sea of Iuddew.'

'There is no force within reach,' Cei repeated. 'Believe me, I would know.'

The weight of his gaze fell upon Wulfstan, who opened his mouth to speak then closed it hastily as the implications of what Cei had said hit him. The Long Man had spoken firmly and confidently, without any hint of boasting, and I for one did not doubt what he said.

'We have a good idea of the strengths and weaknesses of the army within Eidin,' he added, rubbing a hand across his jaw. 'I cannot see any great surprises there.'

'No horde of Picts suddenly bursting out from behind the walls when we launch our attack?' said Llacheu.

'As the worms issue forth from the cracks in the rocks when the sun shines?' Cei grinned at the prince, like one sharing a private joke. 'I doubt it. I think we would be aware of them.'

'What then?' Llacheu drummed a fingernail against his teeth, lost in thought. 'Pure mischief? I find it hard to believe Gurfelling would let himself be persuaded to defy my father. I think this was a raid gone wrong, not part of some deep-laid plan to draw us here. I think Gurfelling's young men grew restless and he allowed them to ride down into Dewr to lift a few head of sheep and cattle. More men joined the war parties than he had expected, and matters quickly got out of hand. Now he cannot back down without great loss of prestige and honour.'

'Perhaps. And that may indeed be Gurfelling's view of how the affair began,' said Cei. He dropped his voice. 'I believe our tattooed friend would tell a different story.'

'Every man tells his own tale,' remarked Wulfstan, which sounded like a proverb.

'Exactly.' Cei shot him an approving glance, and now I recognized the expression which had earlier flashed across the Long Man's face. It was the look a master who is generous in spirit (and they are few, such masters, few and far between) might give a pupil who has performed some act which signifies he has learned all the master has to teach him, and thus henceforth they shall be equals.

357

'The tattooed man would say that by his powers he had driven a great wedge between Arthur and the North, perhaps even between Arthur and the Princes of Britain. If we take Eidin tomorrow, the North will see it as an act of aggression by a southern Emperor, whatever we may argue about provocation or the protection of our fellow countrymen. Once the other Princes of Britain have had time to reflect upon the consequences they will probably feel much the same, viewing our invasion of Gododdin as an interference in the internal affairs of one kingdom that bodes ill for the rest of them.'

I had never heard Cei speak in this manner. Because he was a giant of a man, because he was renowned for his massive strength and stamina, one tended to forget he was also highly intelligent, schooled in all the old Roman arts – Grammar, Rhetoric and the like. One tended to forget that Arthur had made him his Vicarius in the North not simply because he was larger and stronger than other men, but also because he was wiser than most.

Until he had spoken it had not occurred to me that the Lords of Prydein might see our actions as a threat to their own sovereignty. Nor, judging by Wulfstan's frown, had it occurred to him. Neither of us were versed in such matters: I myself, for all my pride, was in those days a simple warrior who took no thought beyond the immediate present, while Wulfstan was accustomed to his own people, who have never been renowned for their subtlety. The intricacies of men like Vortepor of Dyfed or Cadwallon of Gwynedd, men who weigh every word or action however trivial, testing it for meaning, were beyond our comprehension.

Llacheu grimaced, like one acknowledging an unpleasant truth. 'We have discussed this before, uncle. What choice do we have? If we do not act, if we do not punish Eidin and Gododdin, then they will all move against us and each other. The Amherawdyr's peace is a fragile thing, easily shattered. Albion is like a spider's web, a mass of finely-spun threads all pulling in different directions. Break one, and the fabric of the whole is weakened. Break two or three, and the web will collapse.'

Cei managed an abortive smile which merely deepened the furrows on his face. Looking at him as he stood there in the merciless sunlight, I realized with a shock that he was growing old, that his hair was more grey than blond, that his great frame was slumped with tiredness.

'So tomorrow we fight,' he said. 'But be warned, Llacheu, be warned. I fear the Children of Menestyr, and I fear their vengeance.'

2

Llacheu went early to his tent that night, which was wise. Wulfstan soon followed his example, wrapping himself in his cloak and lying down near his men.

I tried to sleep and failed. Do you know that feeling, when your body is tired and you want to sleep, but cannot because your mind is racing? The summer nights are shorter in the north and dawn comes early, and I tossed and turned, growing more and more desperate, angry and frustrated, all too aware it would soon be light and time to rise.

I was apprehensive, as one always is when one knows one must fight on the morrow. Apprehensive, but not afraid. What worried me was Cei's plan of attack – not that I considered myself a master strategist. My viewing of Dun Eidin had been confined to a single circuit of its defences on the morning we arrived. From what I had seen, the fortress was impregnable on three sides, where the rock rose sheer or almost sheer from the meadows; only to the south east was the slope gentle enough to be climbed.

If you have ever studied the camps our ancestors built before the coming of the Romans, you will have noticed how the banks and ditches always channel would-be attackers in certain directions, leaving them exposed to the defenders on the ramparts. The movements of the attackers are limited and controlled right from the very beginning, before a blow has been struck.

This seemed to me the same thing. We were going to assault Eidin in the obvious way, in the obvious style, by the obvious route. Unless our foes were fools or asleep, they could not fail to realize what we were going to do and prepare accordingly.

You must understand I had no better plan. If Bedwyr or Gwalchmei had been with us, they might have devised some clever scheme for climbing the sheer face and taking the defenders by surprise. Arthur would probably have somehow lured the Gododdin men out onto the plain and beaten them in open battle. All we had was Cei, bull-headed Cei, whose one idea was to charge straight at the enemy and overwhelm them by brute strength. It seemed to me a lot of people were going to be killed the next day, and I began to pray I would not be among them, or if I was, that I would be worthy of my death.

After a while I abandoned my attempt to find sleep and sat up. The moon was out, nearly full, riding high in the sky, casting a clear white light across the meadow. The Saesons were snoring all around me, dark shadows against the pale ground. I rose and tiptoed between them, careful not to wake them, and made my way towards the horse pastures.

Twice I was challenged by sentries, Eleuther's men, strangers to me. Each time I had to talk quickly to convince them I was one of Arthur's Companions, and in the end I think it was more my southern accent than anything I said which prevented them from arresting me. Their obvious nervousness did much to soothe my apprehension, for the knowledge that one is not alone is often a great comfort.

At length I came to the edge of the camp and stood looking out into the darkness, to the deep shadows under where Llew's Seat lay crouched like a lion waiting to spring. It was a warm night despite the clear sky, or perhaps it was merely I myself who was warm, for I remember that I was sweating under my cloak.

Tomorrow would be the day. Tomorrow would be my chance to prove myself, once and for all, to perform some act of valour which would make men mention my name in the same breath as that of my kinsman Lleminawg, as a worthy branch of the same tree.

I spread my arms wide to the heavens and prayed, muttering the words so the sound would not carry, imploring God to give me the courage, skill and opportunity to make my reputation. For a time I lost myself in my petition.

'You also,' said Llacheu from beside me.

I started, not knowing how long he had been standing there. He laid a hand upon my arm to steady me.

'Easy, cousin, easy.' His voice was soft and soothing. 'I too could not sleep.'

His face and hair were silver in the moonlight. People said he took after his father in appearance, and that was true, but with the night robbing him of his colouring I could see the resemblance to his mother, the same fine bones which had made her the fairest woman in all Prydein.

'I needed a few moments of peace,' he said. 'Tomorrow every eye will be upon me. If I falter, the army will falter with me.'

'You will lead the assault?'

'The second wave. Cei wanted to lead it himself, but his sight is worsening and I prevailed upon him to give me command. He will hold the reserves, with Atlendor to advise him of how the battle goes.'

He was talking too much, but I was one of the few he could trust not to betray any indiscretions. I was a Companion, and therefore loyal to the death, and I was not personally involved in arranging our dispositions, so would not take his comments as criticism.

'Menw will command our cavalry. He will form a ring around the northern side of Eidin, to prevent the defenders from escaping down the cliff.' His teeth gleamed briefly in the moonlight. 'Menw is supposed to have the power of going unseen. Interesting to see if it works the other way round.'

I laughed, then asked him the question I had been burning to ask since he appeared beside me. 'You are happy with Cei's plan?'

Llacheu shrugged. 'I see no alternative, short of starving them out.'

'It seems so predictable.'

'True,' he said. 'But I do not think that matters. We do not have time to lay grandiose schemes, and in case I doubt if attacking from any other angle is practical.'

He massaged his left biceps, flexed his arms. 'Many think of Cei as a simple man. It is an impression he likes to cultivate. When he was at Caer Cadwy, before my father became Emperor, he used to challenge new arrivals to wrestle him.'

'Yes,' I said drily. 'An action which endeared him to the common folk who love a spectacle, but was hardly the behaviour one expected from one of the Amherawdyr's intimates.'

'That was the point,' said Llacheu. 'My father's enemies always underestimate Cei. People see him as an amiable giant with no small talk who also happens to be a great warrior, unbeaten in hand-to-hand combat. Few see Cei as a soldier, as a general second only to Arthur himself. They think my father favours him because of their long friendship, that Cei was made Vicarious of the North as a reward for his faithful service. They think the post is a sinecure, that he is a figurehead advised and controlled by wiser men. They are wrong.'

I grunted ambiguously, not wishing to contradict the young prince. I did not doubt that Cei was Vicarius because of his ability. What I doubted was Llacheu's claim that Cei was a strategist.

He laughed aloud. 'I dare say you heard that it was I who drove this army on to Eidin? Not so, my friend, not so. It was Cei who decided our strategy, who pushed us on mile after weary mile into the enemy's heartland. "Don't react: act!" he kept saying, knowing that by marching on Eidin we would force the raiders to retreat far more effectively than by seeking them out and engaging them in Dewr.'

This did surprise me. Like everybody else, I had assumed the impetus for the march came from Llacheu.

'But you are worried about tomorrow,' he said. 'Where will you be yourself? With Menw and the other Companions?'

I shook my head. 'Gwalchmei ordered me to stay with Wulfstan.'

He grinned at me. 'Then we shall be together!'

There was a boyish enthusiasm about him which made it easy to understand why Cei had been unable to remain angry with him for long that afternoon. You would have thought we were old friends, not passing acquaintances, that the fact I would be near him in the battle line was important to him on some deep level. Perhaps it was. Though he would have his own bodyguard around him, perhaps he felt safer knowing another Companion would be close by.

I have said that I was ambitious, ambitious as only a man who is no longer in the first flush of youth can be ambitious. Another man would have played upon this new friendship with the Amherawdyr's son, used it to his advantage, and I confess the idea had crossed my mind several times during the day.

But I could not. I have done things before and since of which I am not proud, used and discarded people as seemed necessary. Llacheu was different. Even now I find it hard to say why he was different. I liked him, of course – it would have been difficult not to like him, with his youth, his puppy's naivety and enthusiasm. To have tried to use him, to have exploited his friendliness for one's own ends, would have been a betrayal – though that is not the answer, since betrayal comes easy to us all. Underlying Llacheu's youth was something else, the solid rock of the man he would become, the worthy successor to his father. Like

Arthur, he would never lose his ability to dream dreams and put them into practice, would never come, as the rest of us come, to accept that certain things are not possible. One could smell it on him, the greatness which would one day be his, when he grew into his full powers.

I think . . . I think the truth of the matter is that I loved him, though I barely knew him.

We chatted a while longer, then he left me to my solitude. The sky had changed while we talked. The stars were fading around the horizon, and overhead a long cloud had formed: a mackerel cloud, pale fish scales on either side of a black backbone. The moon moved slowly through the dark belly, and the long tail stretched into the distant south, dimpled as the foreshore when the tide is out. Far away the first bird sang.

I was happy, that last dawn.

3

The morning was chaos and confusion. I had snatched a brief sleep as the sky grew pink and was vaguely aware of men moving around me, feeding and arming themselves. One of Wulfstan's Gyrwe eventually shook me awake, murmuring in broken British that I was a cold one, colder than the depths of Helheim, which is their version of Tartarus, the abode of the unloved dead. I took it as a compliment.

My eyes were gritty with lack of rest, painful in the bright sun. I felt sluggish and slow. Wulfstan was being dressed by two helpers, who were holding a sheepskin jerkin and guiding his arms through the holes. He roared with laughter at the sight of me.

'I thought you would sleep through the day!' he bellowed.

'You have managed without me so far,' I said, and massaged my neck, which was stiff. 'I feel terrible.'

The helpers began to lace Wulfstan into his mail shirt. A third man approached, carrying the great boar-crested helm.

'What is happening?' I asked.

Wulfstan frowned as they pulled the cords too tight. 'Looser, looser!' he growled. 'I must wear the thing all day!'

Behind us I could hear men calling and screaming. Feet tramped past on the far side of the tents, shaking the earth, and I heard orders being shouted. In the distance a horn blew, hard and brassy, then another on a different note, high and shrieking.

'Cei had sent in his archers and slingers to cover the skirmishers,' Wulfstan said happily. 'The skirmishers are trying to clear the way for the spearmen.'

The Gododdin men had made the approach to the citadel as difficult as possible by digging ditches and filling them with sharpened stakes, by scattering boulders and tree trunks along the road. The idea was to break up any formation which tried to march upon the lower gate. Our skirmishers, our light troops, were trying to drag these obstacles out of the way, or use them to fill the ditches, so that the spearmen would be able to manoeuvre as a solid body. In the meantime the skirmishers were exposed to bombardment from the walls – which was no bad thing from the point of view of the rest of us, since it wasted the enemy's ammunition.

'What do you call those slings on a stick?'

I looked at him suspiciously, but he seemed serious.

'Fustibalus,' I said. 'A sling-staff.'

'Ah!' He returned my gaze solemnly. 'Good range they have. Must be nigh on two hundred paces.'

A corner of his mouth began to twitch.

'Sling on a stick!' I said in disgust, and he broke down in howls of laughter, slapping his knees and thighs.

'We shall go and see in a moment,' he said, wiping his eyes. The man with the helmet offered it to him and he waved it away impatiently. 'No. It will only make me a target.'

He spoke in British, absent-mindedly, but the man understood his meaning. Another brought him his shield, a heavy board of polished limewood, decorated with the badge of his family, a seagull in full flight.

'Come!' he said.

Well enough for you, I thought, encased in your mail, with a fine shield on your arm. Still, I had no intention of going within range of the ramparts, and I was eager to find out what was happening.

I followed him through the tents in the direction of the noise, watching him swagger ahead of me as if he owned the world, as if this army were his to command.

'You are ill-tempered this morning,' he called over his

shoulder. 'Perhaps you will cheer up when the fighting starts. Will you approach the enemy sideways this morning, or is that only for Saesons?'

He was not a man one could resent for long.

This early stage of the battle for Eidin was a matter of probe and counter probe. Our purpose was to weaken the defences before the main assault went in; theirs, to discourage us from coming too close. At times the air would be black with missiles, then there would be a lull while figures scurried back and forth scavenging what they could, and then it would begin again. It is a simple truth that in this kind of fighting a vast number of missiles are needed to put one man out of action. In those days I did not realize quite how many, but experience has taught me that during a lengthy engagement at least fifty to a hundred arrows are loosed for every man slain. Arrows are costly and time consuming to make; slingshot is less so, and common river pebbles, which at close range will serve as well, cost nothing save the effort of gathering them.

Which explains why Cei, Llacheu and Atlendor were standing on a knoll regarding the proceedings with expressions of satisfaction on their faces. Despite what Wulfstan had said about the archers being ordered forward, it was actually our slingers who were providing the covering barrage. They were using slingshot, by which I mean not the lead bullets one sometimes sees even nowadays, but pebbles baked in a casing of clay to bring them to the right size and weight. The clay cover shattered on impact, and the surviving stone was virtually useless to the enemy, who were thus unable to replenish their ammunition from our own misses.

An arrow, on the other hand, can often be used a second or even third time. Our men were busy scavenging whatever they could find from the field, taunting the archers on the walls. Every arrow loosed at this stage was one less to be loosed at our spearmen when they made their advance, and our commanders were pleased by the black rain which periodically swept across the open ground before the outer gate.

'No discipline!' I heard Cei growl as I donned my war-gear, fetched by one of the Gwyre. 'I had thought better of Gurfelling.'

He turned to regard the massed ranks of the spearmen who waited behind him, row upon row of them, all dressed in thick leather jerkins, their crimson shields with brightly burnished bosses hanging from their shoulders. Some wore leather helmets or skull caps, some were bare-headed, and a few – these were the officers – had iron helms with long plumes of dyed yellow horsehair that rippled in the morning breeze. There were twenty rows in all (I counted them) and each row had an officer. Scattered at intervals through the ranks were men with bugles or large drums, who would act as signallers to relay their superiors' orders. Apart from these musicians, every man carried a heavy black spear a little taller than himself, so that from a distance they seemed to be standing beneath a forest of steel-tipped shafts. Lying on the ground in about the middle of the formation was a great tree trunk, trimmed of all branches, which they would use as a ram to break down the gates.

'Not long,' Cei said to Eleuther, who had come to join the others on the knoll.

Eleuther shaded his eyes and gazed at the open space his men must cross to reach the gate. His lips moved, as if he were reckoning something to himself, and he glanced back at his men, then straightened. 'At your command,' he said.

'Look!' cried Llacheu. He pointed towards the ramparts.

A figure had climbed onto the wooden palisade so it stood precariously balanced atop the wall, fully exposed to us, waving its arms.

'What is it?' demanded Cei, squinting in that direction.

'A man, I think,' said Llacheu, puzzled. 'He seems . . . His head is out of proportion to his body.'

'I cannot tell whether it is man or woman,' said Wulfstan, his voice grim. 'He is wearing a full length cloak with a high collar, and his head is the head of a dog.'

'Dog? A dog?' Cei roared with laughter. 'Is that the best the pagan filth can manage?' He took half a pace forward and bellowed across the field: 'A gold brooch to whoever brings that creature down!'

At once a hail of slingshot flew toward the figure. We could see the missiles striking all around it, raising clouds of dust on the earth rampart, gouging white splinters from the timber palisade.

The figure itself remained unharmed. Now that Wulfstan had told me what it was I could see the head was that of a great hound, even see the white teeth glinting in the open jaws. Slowly the figure stilled, as if it had found its balance, and the head seemed to rise upon the neck.

'What now?' Cei growled impatiently.

Something flashed in the morning sun, something metallic. I stared, not understanding, and Wulfstan – whose sight must have been as keen as Cei's was poor – said:

'He puts a tube to his lips.'

Again, once he had explained what was happening I could see it for myself. The man had lifted the mask so he could set a small horn to his mouth.

Silence fell across the field, spreading like the ripples from a stone in still water. All of us stopped whatever we were doing and waited in the bright sunshine, holding our breath. Even the wounded, whose groans were so much part of the background I no longer noticed them, were suddenly quiet. Far away I could hear a horse whinnying, and gulls screaming over the water.

The horn blew, a vivid unearthly sound unlike the brazen shriek of the war trumpets; blew again, before the echo died; blew a third time, hard and strong.

I do not know what I expected. Something like Joshua's exploit at Jericho perhaps: only instead of the fortress walls shuddering down upon themselves, it would be the besiegers' tents, our tents, which would fall, our weapons which would break in our hands, our horses which would stampede. Fire and lightning might fall from the sky, or perhaps the waters of the river Worith would break their banks and wash us from the face of the land.

The final echoes faded. We started, gazed around us in surprise like men awakening from a dream.

'Begone!' shouted a voice, and the cry was taken up by others: 'Begone! Begone!' Heads appeared along the ramparts, till it seemed every able-bodied person within the walls must be waiting there to greet us. 'Begone, begone!'

The shouts became a chant. They were beating on the timber palisade with their spear shafts, and the rattle carried to us, building faster and faster: a daunting sound to the men who must cross the open space. I could sense the ranks behind me shuffling uneasily, hear the faint rustle like the wind in corn as they murmured doubtfully to one another.

'Let the Gododdin have their fun,' growled Cei. He turned, called to the waiting ranks:

'Who are you?'

The reply was ragged, uncertain. 'The men of Eburacum.'

He was like a bull was Cei: a giant of man, solid as an oak, immovable, invincible. He ran a hand through his greying hair, and laughed aloud, not with amusement but with the beginnings of his battle fury.

'Who are you?' he bellowed.

He seemed to have grown in stature, to have become more solid, if that were possible. Eleuther moved away from him, as one might move away from any dangerous and unpredictable beast, scrambled down from the knoll and rejoined his troop.

'The men of Eburacum.'

The response was firmer now, and the men had stopped muttering among themselves. I listened while Cei played them like an instrument, rousing their fury as he roused his own, forcing them to answer him until they drowned the rattle of the Gododdin shafts on the walls of Eidin.

'Whose land is this? Llew's land, Llewthiniawn, the land of the golden youth who was master of all arts. And who fights with you this day? Llacheu, Arthur's son, the golden youth who like his father is a master of every art of war. And you, you are the unbeaten, whose name is a byword for constancy in battle.' The Long Man's deep voice rose to a roar. 'Who are you?'

'The men of Eburacum!' The sound crashed from the massed throats. Cei drew his sword, the long blade gleaming grey in the brilliant sunlight, and waved it over his head.

'Then forward!' he cried, and swung the blade to point at the ramparts, holding the pose for a long moment.

The bugles blew, raucous and demanding. The drums began to beat. The shields dropped into place and the men marched, moving as one to the rhythm of the drums, row upon row of them, tramping towards Eidin with a steady stride that shook the very earth.

Beside me Wulfstan let out a whistle of admiration.

'I have never seen the like,' he said.

'Neither have I,' and it was true, I had not, though I had seen Arthur's Household on the parade ground at Caer Cadwy.

The Legions of old, which conquered all the world, must have been like this: rank upon rank upon rank of hard men, trained men, marching in unison, each drawing strength and courage from the presence of his neighbours, knowing that whatever there was to be faced he would not have to face it alone.

'They will overwhelm them by sheer weight.' Wulfstan shook his head in wonderment. 'How many?'

'Half a thousand,' said Llacheu. He was grinning with excitement. 'They will push through the first wall and keep going towards the citadel. You and I, my friends, will follow and clear the ramparts in their wake.'

'Timing is everything,' said Cei as the last of the ranks marched past us. 'You must give them long enough to breach the wall, then quickly follow.'

Wulfstan was still watching the spearmen. 'Was there ever such an army in all Britain? By the gods, what a thing it would be to lead such a force.'

I nudged him, pointed. 'Then here is your beginning.'

He looked behind him, raised an eyebrow in disbelief. His followers awaited him, together with those of the Companions who had accompanied Cei and Llacheu to Eburacum and had elected to fight on foot. The Companions were smart enough, wearing red tunics under mail or leather so that they had a uniform appearance, but the Saesons were a motley crew despite their leather caps and jerkins. No two were dressed quite alike, and they shambled rather than walked, or leant idly on their spears chattering like slaves in the marketplace rather than disciplined troops about to make a planned assault.

One of them saw their leader staring at them, called something. The others laughed.

'What did he say?' I asked, seeing that Cei and Llacheu were smiling.

'He wants to know if I have finished gossiping with my friends. He says he would have stayed later in bed if he had realized it would take this long to come to business.'

'They need no speeches to encourage them,' Cei said approvingly.

In the meantime the men of Eburacum were halfway across the open space. Our skirmishers melted aside as they came, giving them free passage, and formed on their flanks, maintaining a steady bombardment of the wall. A horn blew, and the spearmen performed one of those manoeuvres which seem so simple when you see them done well, but are in fact incredibly intricate and can reduce a formation to chaos unless every man knows his part.

They had advanced in twenty lines, as I said, across a broad front. Now, as they came within easy range of the archers and slingers on the wall, they changed from line to column, reducing their frontage to a mere ten men. The drums kept time, and the bugles blew again, shrill, insistent. A motion like a wave went through the newly-formed column as the shields moved and interlocked.

'Testudo!' Cei said with satisfaction.

I had never seen this before, and it was indeed like a tortoise. The inner files had raised their shields above their heads to create a kind of roof, while the men around the edges kept their shields facing outwards, like a wall. From where we stood on the knoll, slightly off to one side from their line of march, the formation seemed impenetrable. I could see the arrows taking root in the raised shields without doing any harm, and the slingshot bouncing off to no effect.

'Why did they not do that earlier?' demanded Wulfstan. 'Why wait to do it in front of the enemy?'

He was obviously thinking that if anything had gone wrong with either manoeuvre the spearmen would have been cut to pieces by a quick sally before they had a chance to recover.

Cei heard him. 'To terrify the enemy with their prowess. Watch!'

The hail of missiles from the ramparts was dying away. Our own slingers were concentrating on the area around the gate, either clearing the wall or at least forcing the defenders to keep their heads below the level of the palisade.

The drums beat faster. The bugles sounded again. Another ripple passed through the formation as the ram was passed forward to the men at the front. They were moving at a quick walk now, gathering speed as they approached the gate, their shields still locked except where the tip of the ram protruded.

The impact drowned the rattle of the drums. A second and third boom followed in quick succession, then the wielders settled to a rhythm, relentlessly pounding the gate. After a few moments we heard the sound of splintering wood, and the ram's note changed, became less deep as the timbers cracked.

Suddenly the gate burst open and the spearmen flooded through with a roar of triumph.

Cei made a face. 'They were fools to stand against us.' He turned almost wearily to Llacheu. 'Give them time to pass through the gate, then follow.'

The young prince nodded, eager for the fray.

Cei laid a hand on his arm. 'Offer them a chance to surrender. Most of them will not be warriors but herders and farmers brought to this by the foolishness of their lords.'

'Never fear, Cei.' He smiled reassuringly. 'I shall. I have no wish to slaughter the helpless.'

It was the only time I ever heard him call the Long Man by name.

You know what it is like. A mad dash, everybody shouting and screaming. Some of your companions fall, whether because they have tripped or because they have been struck you have no means of telling.

The heat is merciless. You are parched before you even reach the enemy, the sweat matting your hair and trickling into your eyes, stinging and blurring your vision. With the others you funnel into the narrow gap, hurdling the wreckage of the gate.

A man lies on his back, his shield prickling with arrows.

The spearmen are marching on up the hill in a cloud of dust, driving for the middle rampart. You ignore them, hasten to your right, searching for a way up onto the wall. A man plummets heavily to the ground beside you, and you notice his face is a mass of blood, then you are past him and scrambling up the bank, your feet slipping and sliding on the dry earth.

A frightened boy screams at you, thrusts feebly with a spear. You let it pass you, step in and slice down onto his left shoulder, aiming diagonally across to his right thigh, pulling the blade so it will cut but not wedge in his body, and he falls away even as you swing the blade back at hip height into the next man, who squeals and tries to run, too late.

A moment to draw breath. Wulfstan is beside you, his Gyrwe scrabbling up the bank to join you on the walkway.

'Where's Llacheu?' you scream at him.

'There!'

He points, and you see him, the young prince, dancing the dance of death, the long blade lethal in his hand with a life of its own as he twists and ducks and leaps, moving so fast nobody can touch him, fair hair flying in the breeze, and he is like a god, a god of war, bright in the summer sunshine, laughing as he slays his father's foes, and all the while he is shouting:

'Lay down your arms! Surrender! You will not be hurt.'

A foolish few do not believe him, or in the confusion do not comprehend what he is saying, and they continue to come against him while you race to reach him.

Wulfstan arrives first, hurling himself into the melee without a

371

care for his own skin. You are close behind, using your war-board to batter a path through the dazed and damaged creatures the young prince has left in his wake, not bothering with your sword when a shield boss will serve.

A party of tall men in mail shirts appear from nowhere. You register their faces are painted blue and red, their shields are small and square, engraved with strange designs, and then you are among them, your sword weaving a simple criss-cross pattern for you have neither time nor space for subtlety, your feet darting back and forth as you present one shoulder then the other, creating the illusion of great movement though in fact you are standing on the spot, holding your ground as they batter at you, catching their blades on your sword and shield, opening gaps through which you strike, and you are never still, always in motion, flowing with the earth and heavens, and you know every move they will make before they make it, and the world tastes of salt and you can smell the sea on the breeze.

Suddenly it is over. The enemy have gone. You collapse against the palisade, gasping for breath, and Llacheu flings his arms around you and embraces you, while Wulfstan watches, leaning on his sword, a new respect in his eyes.

They said afterwards I broke the force of the defenders' rally, that had it not been for me they would have flung us from the ramparts. Flattering, but not I think entirely true. Wulf-stan's Saesons were at our backs, and had the counter-attack surged through or past us I think the Saesons would still have held it.

We drew breath, shouted for the water carriers, then took stock.

The outer rampart was ours. Most of the defenders had surrendered once it became clear they had lost this stage of the fight. A handful had escaped inwards, where they would presumably be pulled over the second wall on ropes, since our spearmen were busy before the gate.

Nothing like as much time had passed as I had thought. The men of Eburacum were still pounding at the second gate, and I doubted if it was any stronger than the first. Peering over the palisade I could see Cei and his advisers just leaving the knoll from which they had watched the beginning of the fight.

'What next?' I asked.

'We repeat the performance,' said Llacheu. 'This time Wulfstan can take the lead.'

'Thank you,' the Saeson said drily.

We knew, all of us, that the assault would grow progressively more difficult as resistance stiffened, unless the enemy could be persuaded to surrender. So far we had only breached the outer rampart: what remained were the more complex inner defences, which made better use of the lie of the land.

On this approach to Llech Ysgar the ground, as I have said, rose in a long and gentle slope like a tongue, falling away suddenly on either side. We had passed through the outer bank, which was simply an earth-and-rubble wall built across the base of the tongue, not connected to the inner defences. Now the road ran like an invitation, leading up the hill then curving left to expose an attacker's unshielded side to the waiting slingers on the next wall, which doubled on itself to make a narrow passage like a deep gully between the second and third gates.

Our task was once again to clear the wall. This time the fighting would be continuous, for when we were through the second entrance we could – in theory – pass along the rampart to the third gate without descending to the ground.

'The space will be crowded,' said Llacheu. He squatted in the dust and drew a V on its side. 'The spearmen will not all be able to enter the passage between the walls.'

He indicated a point near the angle of the V, then one near the top of the other arm. 'Here are the two gates, do you see?'

Wulfstan and I nodded.

'Once inside the first our people must pass between the walls to reach the second. It will be like being at the bottom of a ravine, with enemies on both sides.'

'I understand,' the Saeson said impatiently.

Llacheu smiled, but his eyes were hard and steady as he glanced up at Wulfstan. 'Good. Now, some of the spearmen will scale the wall to the right of the first gate and remove the archers and slingers. Our own slingers will follow, and give a covering bombardment over the passage. We, on the other hand, will go left and force whatever barrier the enemy have set across the angle of the V.'

'Yes,' said Wulfstan. 'Then we sweep round and clear the inner rampart.'

'Exactly,' said Llacheu.

373

'Not hard,' said Wulfstan, and he began to whistle softly to himself.

The young prince straightened and brushed off his knees. The Saeson avoided his gaze, pointedly staring up the hill to where the men of Eburacum pounded on the gate.

'They are through,' he shouted suddenly.

'Then we must follow,' said Llacheu, waving his followers forward.

Wulfstan wiped his forehead. I saw his adam's apple bob twice as he swallowed. My own mouth was dry, and there was a hollow in the pit of my throat. The Saeson slashed the air with his sword, like one testing a strange blade, checked the bindings on his shield, looked at me and shrugged.

Llacheu was by this time halfway to the wall, travelling at a swift trot, hemmed around by the Companions of his bodyguard, who were making their own version of the testudo with him at its heart, the pearl within the shell.

'Come,' snarled Wulfstan. 'Let us fight this Emperor's war for him.'

We went forward in a rush, Wulfstan and I and the other Saesons, without any pretence at protection, relying on speed and good fortune to see us safe, spreading into a ragged line as we overtook the slower moving formation of the Companions. Arrows struck the earth around us, thrummed in our shields. A javelin took the man ahead of me in the throat, sent him spinning sideways.

We came through the shattered gate and into the struggling mass of men beyond, for the defenders were clambering down the outer rampart and hurling themselves onto the testudo, trying to break it apart. A boulder crashed onto the locked shields, brought a dozen men to their knees. Some of our spearmen had reached the right-hand walkway and were pushing the defenders back, step by step. The noise and the heat were horrendous.

To the left was a gap where a few wounded wandered aimlessly. A flight of wooden steps rose from beside the ruin of the gate, guarded by a dozen nervous youths. Wulfstan burst among them, sword in constant motion, and they scattered.

'Up!' I shouted.

He jostled past me with a growl, taking the steps two at a time. His Saesons levelled their heavy spears, added their weight to his as he teetered at the top. Somehow he avoided the blows aimed at him by the defenders, staggered and regained his balance. Then we were all on the walkway, pushing him forward into the enemy, and he was cursing and screaming, wielding sword and shield in concert, and they were first giving ground and then in full flight.

'Keep going!' shouted Llacheu behind me. A hail of slingshot from the inner wall rattled around us.

We saw that to pause and draw breath was to die. My tongue was stuck to the roof of my mouth and my throat was clogged with dust. I faltered despite myself, fighting for air, holding my shield over my back to give me some cover.

'On!' screamed Llacheu, and he leapt up beside Wulfstan. The pair of them ran towards the barrier of hurdles which divided the two walls.

'Spears,' I croaked, gesturing to the Saesons.

I do not know whether they understood me or whether they would have acted in any case. They moved forward (one crumpling as a slingshot hit him in the temple) and thrust their spears through and over the hurdles, forcing the defenders back so Wulfstan and Llacheu could dismantle the barricade.

In retrospect it sounds easy, and I suppose it was, though it did not seem so at the time. Once the hurdles had been cast aside we were able to cross to the inner bank, and then it was simply a matter of clearing the walkway. Some of the Gododdin men surrendered, but most leapt clear, jumping down into the enclosure before the fourth and final wall.

Our spearmen broke through the third gate, and the true battle for Eidin began. All we had achieved so far was to take the outer defences: what remained was the Dun itself, the fort proper with its grey wall of stone and wood hugging the line of the hill. Here the ground rose more steeply. The earth had been dug away to make a ditch, everywhere except in one place where a single spine of rock rose to the base of the wall. Into this rock steps had been cut, winding to the left so the uninvited visitor would climb them with his unshielded side exposed. At the top was the fourth and last gate.

The Men of Gododdin and their Pictish allies did not wait for us to come to them. The gate stood open, and a horde of armed men poured down the steps to join those who stood below. This space between the walls was Gurfelling's parade ground, or one of them: the place where his household troops drilled and practised their weapon play. It was almost square in shape, bounded on two sides by a collection of timber barns and granaries. More men waited within these barns, waited to attack the flanks of our spearman as they engaged the main body of troops.

I sat down on the parapet, my legs dangling. Llacheu stood over me, one hand on my shoulder, and we watched the fight unfold. We could hear the beat of the drums again, which had been lost in the confusion of the passage between the ramparts. A horn sounded, and the column peeled into two halves, like a piece of kindling being split by a handaxe. The foremost ranks stayed still, and soon a line three deep had formed upon them, a line which stretched across the square.

'They are tiring,' said Wulfstan.

'Do you wonder?' There was a bite to Llacheu's voice.

'No. But now they must shove with all their strength.'

He was right, of course. Fights between spearmen on foot always come down to this: the side which can push the hardest wins. It is a struggle between massed ranks, not individuals, and there are no great feats of prowess, only the steady endurance of men trained to march and move in step, to push with their shields on the back of the man in front, adding their weight to his.

Eleuther's standard floated above the formation, rising and falling with the sway of battle. Those of the enemy who had concealed themselves in the barns sprang out and attacked the flanks, whooping and shrieking. Their cries ululated across the square, making a noise far beyond their actual number. From our vantage point we could see the lines contracting, shrinking in upon themselves despite the steady stream of new bodies joining them from the rampart we had just taken.

Llacheu's grip on my shoulder tightened. The drumming stuttered to a halt. Our men began to give ground. The standard wobbled as the flanks were nibbled away, and suddenly a long drawn wail of despair went up. The standard toppled, fell; the Gododdin warriors surged into the gap, and suddenly instead of a neat formation there were only isolated groups of men standing against the full host of Eidin.

'Eleuther's down!' cried Llacheu. 'To me, to me!'

The rampart below the parapet was steep but not sheer. He plunged down the slope without waiting to see if we were following. Wulfstan leapt after him, his Saesons in his wake. I held back to ensure our comrades farther along the wall had seen what was happening – they had, and a rain of bodies was hurtling over the edge – when my eye was caught by a movement opposite.

A tall man appeared in the sunlight at the top of the steps leading to the grey fortress. His hair was spun silver and gold, his mail-shirt augmented with patches of brass, his cloak a brilliant blue. Behind him was a stocky man whose dark hair was wild disarray – so wild it had to be deliberate – wearing a brown cloak with a high collar.

These two stood poised for a moment, taking in the scene below, then ran down the steps. The Gododdin men raised a shout, welcoming their lord to the battle, and the cry was echoed on three sides of the square: 'Gurfelling, Gurfelling! Gurfelling of Eidin!'

There was the sound of victory in those voices. They had broken the men of Eburacum, who would have fled if they could, but were trapped by the narrows of the gate and passage behind them. A handful might escape, but only a handful. At any instant the real killing would begin, the massacre of the Army of the North. Once the Army was destroyed, Arthur's reputation and thus his rule would be so badly shaken they would never recover.

It seemed the Empire of Albion would die here, in the heat and dust of Eidin, a mere three years after its birth.

'Will you gawp all day?' said a deep voice beside me.

Cei had come.

For all my arrogance and self-belief, for all I was a seasoned warrior who had distinguished himself upon the field that day, I was a child beside him. I could feel myself blushing like a youth, like a young girl, as he turned his reddened eyes upon me. The top of my head reached no higher than his barrel chest, and his arms were almost the width of my thighs. He could have snapped me in twain with no more effort than I would use to snap a twig. He was like one of the wooden idols of the Saesons come to life: inhumanly big, inhumanly powerful, terrifying.

'Atlendor! Take the Peryth to the right. Clear the barns.'

Atlendor saluted and ran along the rampart. The Peryth, fair men with their swords slung over their backs, trotted after him.

'Where is the young prince?' Cei's voice was harsh, demanding.

I stared down into the struggling mass of bodies. It was hard to make out individuals, and the din of weaponry, war cries and screaming wounded made it impossible to think. I found Wulf-stan and his Saesons, no longer moving forward, trading blows with those around them. Llacheu and his Companions were not far distant, separated from the Saesons by a heaving crowd, the men packed so tightly they could barely raise their arms.

'There!' I said.

'Then let us make an end!'

He jumped, cloak flying free as he cast it aside, struck the sloping bank once with bended knees, and sprang among the enemy, bowling them over with the force of his landing. I followed with the rest, shrieking with fear and exultation as I slithered down the bank, my speed growing as I lost all control, running faster and faster to keep my feet.

Cei rampaged like a great bear, cuffing his foes aside with his steel claws, and we lesser mortals stayed in his wake, dealing with his leavings. Like an arrow he went for where Llacheu was embroiled among the Gododdin men, and soon a space opened up around him, a space into which none dared venture. The two of them met in the midst of the enemy and turned back to back, fighting as a pair, the youth slim and slight beside the weathered giant.

Llacheu called: 'To me, to me!' and the scattered spearmen began to coalesce around him. Cei was silent at first, saving his breath for the struggle, and then he called Gurfelling's name, shouting it at intervals, his great roar ringing across the square.

A strange silence fell over the field. The noise of the fighting faded away, leaving only the background wailing of the wounded. My opponent, who had been battering my shield with his war-knife, suddenly withdrew into the crowd. I could feel the man beside me, one of Wulfstan's Saesons, relax and slump against my arm. We waited, all of us.

Cei shouted again, his voice belling like a king stag issuing his challenge in autumn.

Gurfelling was a brave man. He walked through the press in answer to the Long Man's cry, his followers opening up to allow him passage, a bloodied sword in his hand, his buckler gashed and broken where he had been in the thick of the fighting. Hard on his heels came the man in high-collared cloak, leaning on a short spear. As they came near I saw that this man's face bore a spiral tattoo, done in green, on either cheek, and I knew who had worn the hound mask, who had tried to turn us back at the beginning of the battle.

'Enough, Gurfelling,' said Cei. 'Sufficient men have died to satisfy all our vanities. You have acquitted yourselves with honour. Surrender to me, and we shall make peace.'

The Lord of Eidin bowed his head. In years gone by he had fought as Arthur's ally, and I still believe (as did Llacheu) that this war had been none of his choosing, that he had found himself trapped by fate and circumstance. He wiped his blade upon his sleeve, careless of the fine linen, sheathed it, tugged at his mail-shirt to settle it on his body.

'What terms?' he said.

'A forfeit of goods, a payment of reparation to those whose land and lives have been disrupted.' Cei leant upon his sword, became less menacing. 'No more bloodshed. We are Arthur's Men, all of us; friends not foes.'

He would have said more, but Gurfelling shook his head and opened his mouth to accept. He knew he could trust Cei, that the Long Man would not suddenly betray him after his followers had laid down their arms.

'No!' screamed the tattooed man. 'Treachery!'

Afterwards people claimed that Cei, or Llacheu, or an anonymous warrior, moved to strike Gurfelling, to silence him before he could reject the offer of an honourable peace. It was not like that. I saw what happened.

The tattooed man shoved Gurfelling aside, sent him sprawling, straddled his body with levelled spear. For once Cei was caught by surprise. He made no effort to defend himself as the spear thrust forward at his groin.

'For my father!' screamed the tattooed man.

Cei came to life, too late, tried to sidestep. Llacheu pushed in front of him, tripped, and took the spear in the chest as he fell. The tattooed man drove down hard upon the shaft, twisting the blade in the wound, and leapt back with a grin of triumph.

'Our vengeance begins!' he cried, and Cei's sword took off his head at the shoulders, sent it bouncing into the dust, where it lay with the smile still on its face.

The Gododdin men returned to the attack with renewed vigour, hurling themselves at us with no thought for their own safety. To their minds appeared that we had murdered first Gurfelling and then his chief adviser, and they wanted vengeance. Cei was quickly surrounded, and it seemed to me he must fall, for no one man could hold for long against so many, but I had no

379

time to watch or try to reach him, for the enemy were upon me, and all my attention was given to staying alive.

As I fought, falling into the rhythm of exhaustion, repeating the same simple strokes again and again, a silly pun, a bit of wordplay, ran through my head: Llacheu died at Llech Ysgar; llech and llecheu; stone and stones. I could not believe he was dead (yet he had to be: nobody could survive a thrust like that) and took refuge in nonsense phrases instead: rock and stone, rock and bone, Eidin's fold, Gurfelling's hold. For a brief space I was close to madness. Wulfstan told me afterwards the tears were running down my cheeks as I fought, and that all the while I cursed my opponents, cursed them for murdering fools who knew not what they did, so that after a while the Gododdin men avoided me and chose a saner foe with whom to match strokes.

Thus I won through to a respite, was able to pause and take note of what was happening.

The day was nearly done. Unnoticed, the sun had sunk low in the sky, throwing a rosy glow across the walls of Eidin which I might have found beautiful in other circumstances. Now it reminded me of blood, of blood spilled and irreplaceable, of all we had lost this day.

Then I saw Cei, that I had thought was dead, rising head and shoulders above those around him. Even as I watched he seemed to grow, to become impossibly large, his long greying hair which had been bound back in the morning now loose about his face. His sword moved in a red and blue blur, was never still, and he waded through the enemy as a man might wade through a pack of hounds, flinging aside those that clung to him. The champions of Eidin, of Gododdin, of Pictland, came against him, and he treated them all the same, sending them down into the dark. They assaulted him with swords and with knives and with spears, and he brushed through them all, forging his way inexorably for the steps leading to the citadel. They were brave men, the men of Gododdin, and they died in their prime, for no mortal could stand against Cei in his wrath.

He reached the foot of the stair, and the defenders on the wall cast down rocks upon him, huge boulders which should have crushed him but merely bounced from his upraised shield, and step by step he climbed that stair, hacking his way through his foes, until at last he came to the great gate at the top, which they had closed against him, and he laid his hands upon it and it burst open, and that was the end of the siege of Eidin.

They surrendered, once the final gate hung broken on its hinges. Somebody dragged Gurfelling to his feet, bruised and battered by the pummelling he had received while he lay upon the ground, and he called upon his men to put down their weapons. Most were glad to obey, and the few who were not did not last long.

We gathered, those of us who could yet stand, round Wulfstan where he cradled Llacheu's body, his arms red to the elbow with the prince's blood. Another Saeson stood over them, trying to keep off the flies, fat and lazy, which crawled and hovered everywhere. The spear was still in Llacheu's chest, protruding obscenely from the splintered mail-shirt. Incredibly, the prince's eyes were open.

'Hurts,' he whispered. 'Pull it out.'

Wulfstan shook his head. He was weeping, the tears cutting runnels through the dirt on his face. 'I dare not, my prince, I dare not.'

'Then find a man with more courage, Saeson.' He smiled, closed his eyes as a great shudder of pain passed through his body.

'If I pull it out the life may leave you with it,' Wulfstan said desperately.

Llacheu groaned, shifted in Wulfstan's arms. 'Fool! Do you think I will survive this?' He gestured weakly at the spear. 'Let me go free, for friendship's sake.'

Around me men were praying, victor and loser alike, for none of us had intended this. I could see Gurfelling, the proud Lord of Eidin, beseeching that mightier Lord who rules us all to have mercy, to spare the prince. Even then I knew such prayers were futile. There was a feeling of inevitability about it, a feeling that everything which had happened during the weeks since the original raid, all the riding and marching, all the fighting and killing, had been leading to this moment, when we stood united in our grief and horror.

Slowly, slowly the crowd parted. Slowly, slowly Cei came through them, swaying like a drunkard, his shoulders slumped, seeming diminished in stature, older and weaker, a man exhausted to the point of collapse. Hands reached out to guide him, for he staggered like one blind, urged him on to where the young prince lay.

'Eidin is ours, my lord,' he said. His legs gave way and he fell to his knees beside Wulfstan.

'Uncle,' acknowledged the prince. 'Well done.' Another spasm of pain passed through him and he stifled a moan. 'Release me. It is not seemly that the Amherawdyr's son should lie crying on the battlefield. Set me free.'

Cei's great head bent close to the prince's body. His hands, his huge bloodstained hands, moved gently around the wound, probed the place where the solid shaft entered the flesh.

'Please, Uncle.'

Cei straightened and looked about him. His face was set and grim. We avoided his eye, gazed at the ground and shuffled our feet, let the burden of the decision fall on him and him alone.

Llacheu screamed aloud as the true agony hit him, a long high-pitched wail that hurt the ears. He fought for control, drawing breath in short shuddering gasps.

'In my father's name! Have mercy, old one.'

The Long Man leant forward and kissed his forehead.

'Go with God,' he said.

He struck with such speed none of us could have prevented him even had we wished. Somehow there was a knife in his right hand, though the hand had been empty an instant earlier. It passed across Llacheu's throat, and in the same moment he jerked the spear free with his left hand.

A sigh went up from those present.

Cei waited till the blood had stopped flowing, then rose to his feet.

'It is finished,' he said, and walked away.

4

The night was strange. Normally we would have sacked the Dun, held a great feast in the Hall, sung songs of triumph, celebrated the victory and our feats of arms. The prisoners would have been herded together and stripped of their finery, Gurfelling himself perhaps forced to wait upon us. There would have been women and wine and mead, laughter and much boasting.

We did none of those things. We were all stunned with shock.

The prisoners swore an oath of loyalty to Arthur and we released them, to go where they would, though most remained. We had no fear of treachery: nobody had either the will or the energy.

Had Cei been the one who had fallen we might have slaughtered the captives in vengeance, but as it was the thought never occurred to us. The men of Gododdin's grief was as real as ours, and besides, killing them would not have brought Llacheu back. Nothing could do that.

Subdued, we sat in small groups, bandaging our wounds and repairing our equipment. Few people spoke, and if they did, it was softly, so as not to disturb the others. Once I heard a man start to giggle, but the sound was quickly cut off, whether by himself or another I cannot say. We slept fitfully, uncomfortably, waking at intervals to wonder where we were, to the sight of unfamiliar shadows, to the creak and crack of unknown timbers cooling in the night air.

At last the dawn came and we greeted it with relief. Menw and Atlendor organized food and drink for us, then set those fit enough to clearing away the bodies and the debris. Of Cei there was no sign.

Most of the dead went into a common pit. Eleuther's body we placed upon one side for his people to bury with honour, and some of the greater Gododdin lords were claimed by their kindred. We burned the corpse of the tattooed man, without the head, which had been lost in the confusion.

We did not know what to do with Llacheu. Wulfstan and I laid him out, washed him clean as best we could, and waited for instructions.

At about midday we heard shouting from the heights of the Dun.

We left Llacheu in the charge of his Companions, and climbed the stone steps to the fort. From the north wall we looked out at the estuary of the Woreth, at the Sea of Iuddew, and saw the white wings of a ship coming into the harbour.

She was a Roman ship, not the skin coracle of a Pict or the long keel of a Saeson. Wulfstan grunted contemptuously, forgetting his dislike of salt water, assessing her lines and finding them lacking.

The sails furled and she dropped anchor. 'Lot of movement on board,' grunted Wulfstan. I shaded my eyes against the glare of the water, but the detail was lost to me. A small boat put out from the shore, and I saw a flash of colour as people prepared to clamber over the side of the ship.

'It is the Amherawdyr,' asserted Wulfstan.

I laughed, knowing this to be impossible. Arthur was in Caer Cadwy, far to the south.

'It is the Amherawdyr, come for his son.'

'Don't be foolish. How could he . . .?' I did not bother to finish. The argument was absurd.

'Let us go down,' Wulfstan said heavily. 'You can show me how to ride properly, and I will tell you what is wrong with yonder floating barrel, why it is no true ship.'

We descended through the silence of Dun Eidin, a silence made all the more intense by the presence of so many people, found horses and trotted along the track to the harbour. It was a relief to be away from the dun, to smell the clean sea air.

Cei was already at the wharf, waiting with bowed shoulders for the boat to reach the shore. He was pale and shrunken in the bright sunshine, a man defeated by the ravages of fortune. Gulls screamed mournfully overhead, and I could have wept for the sorrow of it, that the greatest of heroes was reduced to this.

The waves lapped gently against the timbers of the wharf. Wulfstan and I kept our distance, standing with the honour guard, the survivors of the Companions who had accompanied Cei. Nobody spoke.

The boat drew nigh the strand, and I saw that Wulfstan was right, that Arthur was aboard, and Gwenhwyvar with him, their faces set and grim. The rowers shipped oars, the boat glided the last few feet and touched against the stage. A man leapt out, handed the Lady ashore. Arthur followed, and the two of them came arm in arm along the wooden wharf, Arthur limping more badly than I had ever seen.

'Amherawdyr,' said Cei. 'Lady.'

She reached out and touched him.

For a moment he straightened, became his old self. Then his whole body slumped.

'Cousin,' said Arthur, but Cei would not meet his gaze.

They mounted on the horses the Companions had brought for them, and we rode back across the marsh and meadows to Dun Eidin, where their son awaited them.

He lay, pale and bloodless, as we had left him. We had cleaned his mail and sewn together the buckled rings where the spear had

384

entered, arranged a scarf around his neck to hide the gaping wound by which Cei had released him, washed and combed his hair.

Gwenhwyvar knelt gracefully beside him. In her hands – and I suppose she must have been carrying it all along, though I had not noticed – she bore something which caught the midday sun and shone like burnished fire, reflecting the light back to the light, so dazzling I could scarcely bear to look, yet could not help myself.

'What is it?' whispered Wulfstan in my ear.

'The chalice of Sovereignty,' I murmured. It could not be anything else.

'Why is it broken?' he said.

At first I did not understand what he meant. I could see only the brightness, and the pale after images it created within my vision, so that I could not even have said what shape the object had.

Gwenhwyvar placed it reverently on Llacheu's chest, over the spear wound, and sank back on her haunches. Everyone, even Wulfstan, held their breath.

I closed my eyes, opened them again, concentrated. The ghost images floated across my sight, left to right, vanished and reappeared. I stared at the object on Llacheu's body, focused my whole being on seeing it truly.

The glare diminished, dwindled to a sun-reddened glow. I still could not make out its shape, but I could see a hairline crack of darkness deep within the light.

We waited for a long time. After a while Arthur made to step forward. Gwenhwyvar shook her head without turning, and he froze, as did we all.

Nothing happened.

I think – I know – she had believed, had hoped, she could call him back. It was a long while before she would admit defeat, but at last she allowed Arthur to help her up. Her face was wet as she wrapped the chalice within her cloak. She spoke then, the first words she had spoken since she came to Eidin, her voice very calm and clear, ringing across the open space.

'Once I had two sons. Now I have none.'

There is nothing more to tell, really.

Llacheu was buried under Llech Ysgar, his grave marked by a pillar of stone.

Gurfelling was allowed to remain as Lord of Eidin, and his heirs rule there to this day. Gododdin never again rebelled against the Amherawdyr's rule, and they say a small contingent marched south to aid him at Camlann, though they came too late for the battle.

Wulfstan – and this may surprise you – became the leader of Gurfelling's warband. He prospered and did well, bred many strong sons, and for all I know may still be living.

And I, I was offered everything I had ever wanted. My actions on the outer wall of Eidin had been noted, my reputation assured.

But it was too late. Without Llacheu there was no point. I asked to be released from my oath, and returned home to Dumnonia, sick at heart, to spend the rest of my days teaching more young men how to kill, and how to die.

God have mercy upon our sinful souls.

5

The torches had burned low by the time the Abbot finished speaking. He stood with his head bowed beside the embers of the fire, and a murmur passed along the benches, which were crowded, for only a few people had left the hall tonight when the meal was done.

From where he sat Nai could see that some of the women were weeping openly, the tears glistening on their cheeks.

Angus lifted his head, gazed about him. 'Yes,' he said, so softly Nai had to strain to hear him, 'it is a great grief. A great grief indeed, my friends.'

The gathering stilled. They waited, and Angus seemed to wait with them, staring up into the gloom of the rafters.

'We had fourteen years of peace after that day. Fourteen years. Such a thing had not been known in my father's lifetime, nor his father's. Now it seems unimaginable. I tell you, for fourteen years a man might ride alone from Penwith Point in Kernow to Blathaon in the far north, and other than a few bandits, none would molest him on the way.' His teeth flashed in the gloom. 'Or so the bards boasted.'

A ripple of laughter spread through the hall.

'And yet, what a price was paid! That peace was bought with Llacheu's blood. For consider, my friends: the King is shepherd of his people. In times of trouble, it is his strong arm which defends them, he who is first to face the danger on their behalf.'

Angus changed position so his face was cast into shadow, yet it seemed to Nai that the Abbot was staring straight at him.

'There is something more that a shepherd may do when his flock is endangered. Sometimes he may sacrifice himself, that his people may go free. That is what the bards tell us Llew did, long ago, in the land of Gododdin. Perhaps that is only a story. But we know it happened once, for it is what the greatest of all Kings did, not for one people or one time but for all people and all time, on a hill outside the most holy of cities. He too was a son: the Son.'

Some of the monks and nuns shifted uncomfortably on their benches, sensing blasphemy. Nai thought to himself that the Abbot would lose them in a moment if he was not careful. Angus must have felt it too, for he did not push the analogy any further.

'If Llacheu had not been slain, if the siege of Eidin had ended when Cei and Gurfelling met, then I believe war would have broken out again within a few years. The Men of the North never accepted Arthur's rule as wholeheartedly as we in the south, and their rivalries are old and intense. But Llacheu's death shocked them into silence. By his death Arthur's son bought us peace.'

He bowed his head and said in a very different tone: 'Let us pray. Let us pray those days of peace may come again, that we may once again be subjected to orderly government, that the civil wars which rend our realm may cease, that we may have an end to corrupt priests and unchaste deacons, and that the light of God may shine upon us.'

And all those gathered joined their voices to his.

CHAPTER NINETEEN

The morning was cold. Shreds of grey cloud rolled across the moor, hiding and displaying the folded land. The wind tugged at Seradwen's cloak and caught at the hood, which she had left dangling down her back in anticipation of further rain rather than tucked away inside. A patch of sunlight fled across the nearest hill and vanished. She shivered, glanced back in search of some sign of the monastery they had left a while ago, but all she could see was Regin on his restive horse, trailing some ten or fifteen paces behind, and beyond him the emptiness of the moor. She turned before he noticed her, looked instead at Nai riding silently in the lead, his shield on his left arm and a spear in his right hand, his head constantly swivelling as he scanned their surroundings.

The nature of the land was deceptive. Every fold in the ground seemed to hide a miniature coombe, every rising slope a succession of false crests pocked with granite outcroppings that thrust though the thin soil like bones through flesh. Once they passed an old barrow mound set just under the skyline, so that from the valley below it appeared to dominate the heights, while from the top of the hill it merged into the background, and for a time she mused upon who might have been buried there, and what deeds they had performed that their people saw fit to honour them in this fashion.

She woke from her reverie to find Nai had stopped. She followed the direction of his gaze and caught a flash of yellow against the pale brown of the moor. Mischief shifted beneath her, sensing her unease.

'What is it?' demanded Regin when he drew level.

Nai pointed wordlessly with the spear, and as he did so there came a second flicker from amidst the white grass waving in the wind. Whoever it belonged to was concealed in a hollow a few hundred paces away.

'Picts?' said Regin. He pulled nervously at his nose, his eyes darting from side to side.

'Somebody.' Nai's voice was harsh.

'What do we do?'

Nai smiled. 'Your sword and my spears, bard. Remember?'

The wind ruffled the ponies' manes. The bard swallowed, and Seradwen became aware of the dryness of her own mouth, the taste of iron on her tongue, the hair bristling on the nape of her neck. They were exposed and very vulnerable here on the open moor.

'Or we could run,' Nai said softly. His dark eyes met and held hers, and he gave the smallest of smiles, a mere relaxing of the muscles around his mouth, but it heartened her beyond all measure.

'Let us try that first.' Regin patted his horse's neck, straightened in the saddle. 'How many do you think they are?'

'At least two. And they showed themselves deliberately.'

They eased the ponies into a rapid trot, riding in a line abreast with Seradwen in the middle. Their pursuers kept position behind them, allowing the nature of the terrain to widen the gap.

'There!' Regin called suddenly, and swung his horse's head to the right, waving his arms as if to frighten off whatever he had seen.

Seradwen followed, thinking it important they should stay together, and heard Nai curse to her rear. Coal flew past her in a thunder of hooves; there was a flurry of movement up ahead and what might have been a horse and rider disappeared over a ridge.

'Left! Quickly!' shouted Nai, and the three of them turned onto their original course, all of them moving at the gallop now. They pounded through the empty land, skirting dark puddles and reed-fringed pools, moving faster and faster beneath the vast sky till they raced to beat the clouds and shadows, their saddles and leathers creaking, the wind in their faces and hair; and Seradwen forgot why they were galloping, forgot her fear of their pursuers, forgot everything except the exhilaration of the moment as she allowed Mischief to outdistance the others.

She came to a halt on the crest of a hill. Below were the silver threads of two moorland streams flowing side by side before they met, their banks marked by stunted trees, twisted and gnarled against the gales. She glanced back, saw her companions a hundred or so paces behind, slowing to a walk. Nai was berating the bard, who by the set of his body was abashed.

Mischief caught his breath and she took him down the slope at a walk, guiding him to a place where the waters broadened into a ford. They splashed across, the pony hauling himself up the bank in a spray of droplets. To her left, on the peninsula between the two rivers, willows, rowans and dwarf oaks struggled for life among the grey rocks; to her right was nothing except a flat expanse of reeds and marsh grass stretching away to the horizon hills.

She shuddered, flung back her head and stared into the sky until she felt dizzy. They were at the bottom of a great bowl, and all the world was cloud and sky, continually in motion.

Behind her she could hear the bard making some protest, and Nai's voice overriding him, crow harsh. 'We stay together. Or you go your own way.' She dismounted, unsure of the ground on this rough tongue of land, and led Mischief downstream in search of a place to cross, studying the stream banks with a dreamlike intensity she recognized as a reaction to her recent fear.

Rushing brown water foamed over green and grey lichened boulders, babbled in tongues. She heard voices, calling her name, calling her husband's name, the illusion so strong she stopped and glanced about her to see who had spoken.

She did not like this place – or it did not like her. In summer the peninsula would probably be pretty enough, but at this time of year one could see the hardness of the land. Hidden among the boulders was the carcass of a sheep that must have crawled there to die: a few dirty hanks of grey wool, some yellow bones. The place was barren, and whatever spirit lived here did not care to have its rest disturbed.

'They were waiting for you.'

Some trick of the land made it sound as if Regin were beside her. Startled, she looked back and saw the others had only just forded the first stream.

'Of course,' said Nai. 'They have been watching us all morning.'

Regin's next remark was drowned by the noise of the water, but Nai's reply came with perfect clarity. 'Cat and mouse.'

The men seemed content to leave her the lead. She remounted and crossed the second stream a short distance above the confluence, the bank soft and treacherous under Mischief's hooves. The pony heaved himself awkwardly out of the channel, and Seradwen gave the animal time to regain his breath while she took stock. This side of the river was marshy, and she saw no easy way to reach the higher ground. She turned unhappily in the saddle, aware they were trapped against the water, which was in spate and looked to be impassable further down its course.

For a moment she contemplated turning back and trying the other bank, but the slope there was steep and boulder strewn, and the hillside was in any case a mass of silver brooks and rivulets. Their present route seemed the lesser of two evils.

She went forward, the pony's hooves scraping on the granite bedrock. The weather was closing in, the cloud turning to mist, veiling the horizon. The valley narrowed, the far slope becoming higher and almost sheer. A few scraggly trees clung to the hillside. The river grew broader and louder, its waters foaming around the boulders.

Then with a great leap of the heart she saw a line of riders sitting on the skyline watching them. They were perhaps half a mile away, on the same side of the river with only the marsh between, their outlines blurred by the mist so she could not be certain how many there were. They moved, keeping pace, vanishing and reappearing over the ridge, and she wondered whether they were using the old trick of changing position in the line when they were out of sight, to give an impression of more than their actual number.

She reined in, her hands stiff and cold even through the gloves, and waited until the men reached her.

'What should we do?' She could hear the quaver in her voice.

Nai smiled at her. 'Ignore them.'

'What lies ahead?' asked Regin. He tugged at his wind-tousled hair, hunched deeper into the saddle. 'How long until we are clear of the moors?'

'Not long,' Nai said calmly.

The bard cleared his throat. 'If you wish, I could try to parley with them.'

'And what would you say to them?'

Regin shrugged, glanced at Seradwen for support. 'I am not certain. I could ask what they want with us, see if we cannot reach some compromise.'

The horses shied at the sound of Nai's laughter. 'I already know what they want. If you wish to speak with them on your own account, go ahead.'

The bard stared doubtfully up the slope. 'No thank you.'

'Then let us continue.'

Nai gestured and Seradwen took the lead again, holding Mischief to a walk. Their shadows stayed on the ridge, weaving in and out of the mist, keeping pace with them but making no effort to come closer. Twice they turned away from the swollen river when the ground grew too soft for safety, and each time the riders made no attempt to prevent them.

Little by little the ground rose and they climbed away from the water. The line of trees that marked the river thickened, became the beginnings of a wood. Below them the valley deepened into a ravine. Seradwen could hear the roar of the water, see the wind-blown spray drifting above the treetops.

They came to a plateau littered with grey boulders, and there they paused to see what their shadows would do. The ponies browsed noisily on the grass, which was greener here than on the high moor. They were close to the edge of the wasteland, almost back in habitable lands. In fact, as Seradwen looked around she saw they were in the remnants of an old animal pound or something similar: the boulders had once been piled in a rough wall, and over to the side were the foundations of a herdsman's hut.

'How did they find us so quickly?' she asked.

'Somebody told them.' Nai's face was expressionless as he gazed at their followers, and she marvelled that he could seem so unmoved by their danger.

'Who?' demanded Regin.

'Does it matter?' Nai's shoulders lifted wearily. 'Eri, the Abbot, any of them.'

'Not Angus.' The bard sounded shocked.

An old track led from the animal pound, skirted a thicket of blackthorn and vanished around the hillside. Seradwen glanced up at the waiting horsemen. They had stopped when their quarry stopped, and sat slumped in their saddles, their ponies' manes and tails trailing in the wind. At this distance, five hundred paces or more, it was difficult to be certain, but she thought their mounts looked tired, as if they had been ridden hard and long.

'What are we going to do?' She could feel the panic rising within her.

'Keep moving,' said Nai, his voice very steady. 'Regin, you go first along the path.'

The bard licked his lips. 'What if there are more of them ahead?'

'That is why I want you in the lead with that blade of yours.' Nai's tone was patient, but it brooked no argument.

Regin drew his sword. A chorus of jeers came loud on the wind at the sight of the dull blade. The bard rose in the saddle and shook his free fist at the skyline; the men whooped and laughed. Two kicked their mounts down the slope, waving their spears above their heads. They seemed to Seradwen to be charging straight at her, but long before they came within javelin range they wheeled aside in a shower of sods and rode to the edge of the plateau.

She could see the flesh of their hands and faces, oddly bright against the smoky colours of the ground, and she thought how easily Nai with his own dark hair and skin could pass for one of them, except that he was taller and lighter of build than either of these. Aloud she said: 'They ride like peasants,' and then, 'Why do they not all have tattooed faces?'

'Perhaps only the chieftains are allowed to wear them,' said Nai, and motioned her forward.

The rump of Regin's horse was disappearing behind the blackthorn. She urged Mischief along the track, aware of Nai close behind, the ponies' hooves scraping on stone, and the land seemed to rise like a swell of the sea as she rounded the thicket. The wind caught her, thick with moisture so her hair and lashes at once felt damp, and then, suddenly, the air around her turned wan with rain.

'Go, go!' called Nai, and she wondered at his confidence, for she knew this country was as strange to him as it was to her.

She reached the crest in Regin's wake and saw that they had come to the end of the moor. The ground fell away before her, revealing mile upon mile of leafless winter woodlands with the mist floating through them, stretching to the grey blur of the horizon.

The track ran down the hillside and disappeared into the

gloom of the trees. Regin had already started down the slope, elbows flapping as he struggled to control his mount, which seemed close to bolting.

'It feels his fear,' Nai said beside her. 'Come. Their horses are tired, and ours are nicely rested by the stay in the monastery.' He bent over Coal's neck so his face was between the prick ears and whispered something.

Regin's horse was barely under control, slithering on the greasy grass where it had missed a bend in the track, hooves gouging lumps of mud as it fought to slow its breakneck descent.

She blinked the rain out of her eyes and studied the path. The slope was steeper than she had first thought, almost sheer in places, and the path had been eaten away by rain water so it looked more like a stream bed then a track. Under normal circumstances she would have dismounted and led Mischief down.

Behind her she heard guttural voices calling back and forth. More of the Picts had joined the pair on the edge of the plateau. Seven or eight of them sat their horses in a widely-spaced line. Every few moments one would surge forward a length or so then wait for the others to draw level, like children playing a game of dares.

'Come on!' Regin bellowed. His shout startled the birds and brought a pair of does bounding from a thicket.

Nai grinned crookedly at her and swung his mount to face their pursuers.

She set her heels to Mischief's flanks and chose a slanting course across the slope, ignoring the track. She let the pony go on a loose rein, but held ready to tighten up if he showed signs of needing support. All her concentration was given to the task of bringing him down safely, though she was vaguely aware of the Picts shouting challenges behind her.

Mischief stepped daintily, picking his own path as if he made this kind of descent every day, while Seradwen tried to hold her weight to free his hindquarters and thus help his balance. She could feel a triumphant grin spreading over her face: the two of them were working together in complete harmony, each trusting the other to do what was necessary without prompting, and Mischief was making a perfect controlled descent, unlike Regin's horse which had gone down in a wild rush.

Not until she neared level ground did she look back. Nai was coming by the same route, his face taut with concentration. His left arm seemed oddly crooked, the elbow bent beside his head as if he were clutching his neck. Something thin and grey fell through the colourless rain, landed on the muddy grass and skittered down the slope.

'Come on!' Regin shouted again. 'Under the trees!'

Coal stumbled, regained his balance. Nai's teeth were bared, and she realized he was holding his shield to cover his back. A second spear landed point first ahead of him, shivered a moment and slowly toppled over. Coal shied, and Nai shifted in the saddle to compensate.

'Seradwen!' The bard's voice sounded frantic. It had lost the deep richness she had once found so attractive, cracked like that of any other man in the grip of deep fear.

Still she waited, unable to move until Nai and Coal had completed their descent. The Children of Menestyr gathered at the top of the slope, their cries unintelligible, more like a pack of hounds than human beings. One had piled his hair in a topknot through which he had thrust a bundle of feathers: the plumes nodded damply in time with his movements. Another cocked his arm to throw a javelin. He leapt high in the air and cast: the missile sailed through the rain, wobbled as the wind took it, and plummeted harmlessly off to the left. His fellows screamed with contempt.

'They are playing with me,' called Nai as he reached the bottom. He lifted the shield over his head and into its normal position, surveyed the track ahead of them. 'Now we ride; fast and hard as we can.'

Regin wheeled his mount impatiently from the shelter of trees. 'We keep to the path?'

'For now.' Nai glanced at the slope, at the silhouetted figures waiting on the rim. 'Let us see if we can lose them.'

The bard managed a grim smile. His sword was back in its sheath and the reins were wound through his bare fingers. He flicked his pony into a trot, then a canter, ducking beneath the outstretched boughs, riding cautiously like one who expects an unpleasant surprise at any instant.

'Faster!' growled Nai.

Seradwen gave Mischief his head. Soon she was pressing close upon the bard's heels. The woodland was open at this time of year with the branches leafless and the thickets shrunk in upon themselves. She drew aside from the path, swerving around the trees and jumping a fallen oak, and so took the lead, forcing Regin to abandon his caution in order to keep pace.

She heard a rising scream that broke to a series of painful whinnies, and she shuddered, knowing one of the Picts' ponies had fallen on the hill. A man shouted in anger and frustration. Then all was left behind as she wove between the trunks, dodged the low branches and crashed through the undergrowth, the mist advancing and receding around her, the trees looming and vanishing.

Mischief splashed across a small stream and up the far side, the ground dry and firm despite the rain, and came to a clearing. Here Seradwen halted to let the others catch up. The land stretched before her in mile upon mile of black and leafless trees occasionally broken by the deep green of firs or hollies, rolling waves of dark woods reaching to the horizon.

At first glance the forest seemed trackless, but when she looked more closely she could see the lighter lines of paths running between the trees, with flashes of silver marking the water courses. The longer she stared the more colour she saw, so that what had seemed a single dark mass acquired a hundred shades of brown: auburn, chestnut, tan and russet, all mingled together and no two shades the same.

'Will you gawk all day?' cried Regin. His face was pale with excitement, and his clothes were streaked with froth from his horse.

'Easy, easy,' soothed Nai, patting Coal's neck. 'We must preserve our mounts.'

The rain glistened in his dark hair, highlighting the threads of grey at his temples. His brow furrowed in concentration as he surveyed the country ahead. 'We want to strike the Isca road before too long,' he murmured.

'They will guess,' objected Regin.

'No doubt,' he answered lightly. 'But at present they are a nuisance rather than a menace. This way.'

They moved off again. Although Seradwen was aware the pursuit was some distance behind, the feeling that the tattooed men were with them never left her. From the corner of an eye she would glimpse odd shapes hidden among the trees or buried in the undergrowth: a crouching form that on their approach steadily merged into part of the trunk behind which it waited;

an arm or leg, hastily withdrawn into the shadows where it became a stick; even leering faces, dappled brown and green, which resolved into a trick of the light when she came near.

She could smell the danger, smell it in Regin's unnatural excitement, in Mischief's nervousness, in the flurries of wind that tossed the old dead leaves through the brittle undergrowth, in the chattering of the birds among the branches. She carried no weapon except the simple knife at her belt, and that was more working tool than weapon, but she found herself shifting the sheath on her hip so she could reach the hilt more easily.

Only Nai remained calm, controlling their pace so they moved rapidly yet always with time to rest the horses. For all the emotion he showed he might have been riding through the farmland around his home at Din Erbin.

'How will you deal with them?' she asked as they walked the ponies through drifts of dead leaves.

'They are like children,' Nai said quietly. Regin, almost lost among the tendrils of mist that writhed among the trees, glanced round at the sound of their voices, then looked away so resolutely it was obvious he was trying to overhear.

'Their desires war within them,' Nai continued, ignoring the bard. 'On the one hand they want to kill me because I have slighted their clan. On the other they need me alive, because I may lead them to Bedwyr and thence Gwenhwyvar and the chalice. So they relieve their feelings by letting me know they could kill me if they wished, that I am in their power and cannot escape them.'

The rain had slackened, but water still dripped from the branches. Seradwen twisted in the saddle to avoid a shower of droplets. 'What will you do?' she demanded as she regained her balance.

Nai shrugged, and for a moment his face looked old and worn. 'What can I do? Keep running, and hope something changes. When they decide I am no longer useful they will attack in earnest.'

'There are three of us,' she said with more determination than she felt.

He lifted an eyebrow. 'Are there?' he said softly, and she followed his gaze to the mist-shrouded figure of the bard.

Their progress slowed during the latter part of the afternoon as they crossed the grain of the land. Nai lost count of how many icy streams they forded. Once they were forced to retrace their steps when they found themselves trapped in a marshy valley, to scramble up the steep slope they had so carefully descended and cast around for an alternative route.

The light was fading by the time they reached the road, a rough track running along the ridge that divided the great forest of northern Dumnonia from the southern moors. The birds were gathering, flocking and wheeling in the sky before flying low to their roosts. The air smelled of rain and frost, and a chill wind blew out of the north.

'We should find shelter,' the bard called anxiously.

'Soon,' growled Nai, who had hoped to be near the town of Isca by nightfall. He pushed Coal into a trot.

As they completed the ascent of a long slow hill Regin tried again. He indicated a shape lying a little way back from the road. 'What about there? It is growing too dark to see. We shall need a fire for the night, and the walls will hide the glow.'

Nai grunted sourly. He was impatient to be moving, but the bard was undeniably talking sense. Reluctantly he turned Coal's head towards the ruined building, which he had not noticed until Regin pointed it out.

'What is it?' he asked, not expecting an answer.

'What *was* it,' corrected the bard. 'Now it is nothing, a relict of times past.'

Nai snorted and dismounted. His legs were stiff, and he moved awkwardly through the wet grass, trailing Coal's reins behind him.

The building was a small oblong, the straight lines of the stone walls blurred by a heavy growth of ivy. There was something cut on a plaque above the single doorway that he could not quite discern in the dusk. The door itself was long gone, as was the roof, though its skeleton remained in the form of the ridge beam and a few thin rafters. The floor was scattered with debris.

'Kindling,' said Seradwen, who had followed him inside. 'I will see to the horses if you two make a fire.'

'I'll bring in the bags for you, then fetch fuel from the copse,' Regin said from the doorway.

Left to himself, Nai gathered the drier bits of wood and used his knife to make shavings. He struck a spark, and on his third attempt – which he took to be a good omen – coaxed a tiny flame to life. He fed it tenderly, careful not to choke it before it was grown, and by the time Regin returned with an armful of branches he had a respectable blaze.

The bard sighed with relief and held out his hands to the fire. 'Praise the Lord for his gifts: a hot fire on a cold night.'

The wood crackled and the flames leapt. Nai arranged his cloak so he could sit comfortably. 'We should stand watch.'

'I was afraid you would say that.' Regin leant lazily against the wall. 'There is a farm in the valley beyond the copse. I heard the dogs barking as I was gathering fuel.'

'A large one?' Nai asked drowsily, not very interested in the answer.

Regin shook his head. 'No. I went to the edge of the trees and looked. I could just make out the shadow of the embankment, like a great wormcast on the slope of the hill. While I watched the dogs howled and a door opened so light spilled across the enclosure. They have guests this night.'

'Ah,' said Nai. The old stones were starting to sweat where the fire had warmed them. Regin brushed the dampness at his shoulder and moved away from the wall.

'A party of horsemen. I could not tell who they were, not in the dusk at a distance, but who else could they be?'

'I had hoped they were not so close.'

They were silent for a while, studying the flames, then Regin stretched and yawned. 'Shall I take first watch?' he offered, and without waiting for Nai's assent, added: 'Seradwen will take her turn?'

'I expect so. Ask her for yourself when she has finished with the horses.'

'Mind you,' muttered the bard, 'if your friends did nothing during the day, they are not likely to do anything during the night.'

'We should be ready all the same.' Nai gathered his legs under him and stood, shaking off his lethargy. He cleared a space around the fire, scuffing aside the debris that had fallen from the roof or blown through the doorway. While he worked he glanced round at the walls and floor.

'What do you suppose this place was?' he asked for the second time.

The bard rubbed the hook of his nose. 'Roman work, for sure. Only the dead could tell us, I fear. A safe refuge for travelers, perhaps? Or maybe nothing more than a storage barn. There are no windows, and the Romans usually put windows in their dwellings. Or it might have been a shrine to some wayside god.'

'Would the Romans build a barn from stone?'

'They might have done. They shaped stone as easily as we shape wood.' Regin pounded the wall with a fist. 'Like wizardry, the way they worked it. So solid, so eternal, every stone a statement of their intent to span the years. Whereas our wooden houses live for the life of man and no longer before crumbling back into the earth from which they came, the houses of Rome leave their mark upon the land for generations. I have been in the old quarter of Verulamium, and seen the foundations of the houses poking through the grass four hundred years after they were built. Nothing we make will ever last so long.'

'Yet the Men of Rome are gone now,' said Nai, 'and they will not come again.'

'No, they will not,' the bard said bitterly. 'The world has changed. Much of what they did and thought is incomprehensible to us. They would think us barbarians, you know, though I am accounted a learned man in my homeland.'

'Well,' Nai said consolingly, 'they would be right. We are after all camped among their ruins, and that is what barbarians do, is it not?'

Regin laughed. 'True.' He ran a hand through his hair. 'Tell me, my friend. How long will Seradwen accompany you?'

A log burned through and fell in a shower of sparks. Nai poked the charred remnants with a stick, pushed them towards the flames.

'For as long as she wishes.'

'A dangerous life for a woman. I mean no offence, but you seem to have no clear idea of where you are going or what you are doing.'

Nai raised his head from the flames and peered at the bard. 'While you do?'

Regin shrugged. His cheeks seemed pink, though it might have been a trick of the light. 'Mine is a wanderer's life by choice.'

A brief squall blew over the broken walls. The droplets of rain hissed when they struck the fire. The smoke swirled in the down draught, made Regin cough as it caught his throat. Then suddenly the smoke cleared and the flames leapt high again, touching every discontented line and wrinkle in the bard's face.

'We should eat,' said Nai.

'Of course, living as she did, she cannot have met many suitable men,' remarked the bard.

Nai heard Seradwen soothing the horses outside, the wind blowing in the trees, the steady drip of rain.

'Life is always difficult for a widow,' Regin added.

Nai took the middle watch, thinking that if anything was going to happen – which he doubted – it would be then. He woke of his own accord, to the dim glow of the banked fire, to the faint and companionable sound of Seradwen breathing beside him, and eased himself out from under the spare cloak they had shared.

Outside, away from the fire, the air smelled damp and fresh. Regin had chosen a post a short distance from the building, where he could watch part of the road and the slope of the hill down to the copse where he had gathered wood. The ponies were browsing quietly on the long grass behind him. As Nai approached, Coal raised his dark head to see what his master wanted; after a long moment the head sank and he returned to his grazing.

'Nothing,' murmured Regin.

Nai glanced around him. The bard had chosen well, given the difficulty of one man keeping guard on all directions. A determined attacker could creep close by using the building for cover, but that was unavoidable. From outside there was no sign of the fire. Only the horses betrayed the fact someone was here, and again, there was nothing one could do about that.

'Go sleep,' he said, dropping to his heels.

The bard nodded and eased away into the darkness.

Nai had brought a pair of spears and his war-knife with him. He laid the spears down on the grass and drew the knife, testing the edge of the blade on his forearm. After they had eaten and Regin had left, he had spent the evening sharpening every blade he possessed, spears, knife and sword, while Seradwen watched, eyes anxious in the firelight. He had not told her what the bard had said, knowing she would find it hurtful; and to him it did not matter why she had come, only that she was here with him, and he was no longer alone.

The sky was cloudy and there were no stars, but at least the rain had stopped. His night vision was slowly coming; already he could see further than when he had left the ruin. The little wood down the slope must belong to the farm Regin had found. He could see the outline of the trees, the thick stumps and thin shoots where the branches had been cropped for fuel or building materials. He was once more travelling through prosperous country, the wilderness of the moors left behind. It would be hard to move unnoticed, and he wondered how Bedwyr had managed to evade his hunters for so long.

A fox barked in the copse below him and he stiffened, rocked back and forth on his heels. The bark came again and again, sounding like a small dog wailing for its owner. He waited, uncertain, scanning his surroundings for movement. A roebuck stepped across the hillside, its rump a dirty white against the darkness, hesitated and darted away.

Nai lowered himself little by little until he was flat on the ground under his cloak. The grass was damp with rain or dew. The faintest of mists was beginning to curl from the earth. An owl hooted, launched itself from the copse and sailed silently overhead.

From behind him came the angry murmur of rooks disturbed in their sleep. He eased back until he could look in that direction without the movement being obvious. The mist was thickening knee high above the grass. A black shape landed on the ragged wall of the ruin, shuffled sideways, preened itself. Moments later a second arrived and took up station beside the first.

He turned his attention to the ponies. They had senses beyond his and were probably better sentinels. Coal was standing still, staring towards the copse, occasionally shaking his head. The other horses had moved closer to the ruin, away from whatever it was they perceived as a threat.

The mist swirled across the black grass, gathered in the hollows. A gust of wind from the north tore through the grey, opened brief swathes of darkness. Nai lifted his head, peered into the shadows. The night was silent now, and his feeling of oppression stronger.

Coal neighed.

Nai rolled to one side, letting the momentum swing his legs over and pull him to his feet, spear clutched in his right hand. The pony neighed a second time, shook his mane furiously.

A pipe was playing, either very softly or very far away: a thin, plaintive sound that snared Nai's attention. The mist was waist high, undulating. In places he could still see through it to the grass, but elsewhere it had thickened. The music was everywhere and nowhere, a lament for all that was lost and gone, for individuals and tribes, lovers and children, knowledge and power.

He squeezed the spear shaft in his hand, felt the thread he had bound around it to mark the point of balance cut into his palm. The music faded as another gust disturbed the mist, returned stronger than before.

A rook cawed, harsh and unforgiving. He glanced at the building, saw there was something different about the walls under their ivy, looked again and realized that dozens of birds were perched all over the ruin.

'You have much magic,' said a voice from out of the mist before him. 'Too much for us. All the omens tell us we should leave you, and yet, and yet.' The voice trailed away, returned more strongly: 'There is blood between us, and blood is hard to forgive.'

'It was not of my choosing,' he answered.

A grunt came out of the mist. 'Three of our young men meet you. Two are slain and one will never be the man he was. We hunt you with the aid of our allies, guessing where you will go, driving you as the boar is driven onto the hunter's spear, and another of our kindred dies. Word comes you are no longer needed alive, and we laugh, for you are trapped in the old farm, easy prey.'

The voice sighed. 'The oldest of magics, the simplest of magics, is raised against us, and we are powerless, for we are become strangers here, though it was our kind who raised the stones and mounds that define the land, in the long ago when the world was new.'

'Your kind?' Nai searched the mist for a thickening of the darkness, for anything which would betray his enemy's whereabouts. 'They were my kind, my ancestors, who made this land.'

The voice chuckled. 'Perhaps. You have the look of a half-breed of my kindred. And the cunning. You escape the farm in the turmoil of the storm, bringing the woman with you. Again we think you trapped when you enter the wasteland as a blizzard begins. He must turn, we think, and then he will come to us. But no, you do not come, though we dance the hunter's magic and impale your image on the ground, call you to us with blood and bone even as we call the deer to their dying.'

This time the whistling was tuneless, breathy. It seemed to

come from all around him, though he was certain the Pict was alone, suffusing the mist with its shrill discords.

'What do you want?'

The noise stopped. 'You disappear into the wasteland and we think the crows will eat your flesh, the wolves and foxes quarrel over your bones. Instead you come to *his* place.'

'His place?' said Nai, unable to identify the emotion in the voice. 'The Abbot, you mean?'

'The old spider weaving his webs. This confuses us. One day you seem powerful, protected by great spirits, mighty guardians. The next you are powerless, wandering like a child into the grasp of your foe. And when you leave you bring with you his hound, his ally's whelp.'

Nai laughed. 'If you are telling me the Abbot and the bard are no friends of mine I already know.'

'Then why do you let them close to you?' The voice seemed genuinely curious.

'Because it is time to make an end.' As he spoke Nai knew the words were true, and a sense of relief went through him.

'Sa, sa,' mused the voice. 'You would bring them all to a place of reckoning? Then your powers must be even greater than we thought.'

'They are,' Nai said recklessly, and lifting his hands above his head he clapped them together.

The effect was startling, even to him. The sound of the report was flat and muffled by the mist, but it was enough to wake the birds roosting on the ruin. They leapt into the air as one, shrieking wildly, a great black swirl that spiralled above the building, filled the sky with a cacophony of crowing. He heard Regin shout above the noise, saw the horses shy and bolt across the grass, heard Seradwen whistling them back, and suddenly a face loomed out of the mist before him, ugly with scars, lips writhing, and he realized the man was begging him to stop.

He lowered his hands and gradually, as if at his command, the birds settled, some returning to the ruin and others scattering into the night. He could see the bard peering in his direction and he waved to indicate all was well, that he did not need help.

The man settled on the grass in front of Nai. He drew a deep breath, calmed himself. 'We were a great people once,' he said.

Nai inclined his head.

'Our enemies named us Attecotti, the Old People, for we were here in this land before all others. We raided south and east and west, by land and by sea, winning wealth and honour. The Romans were helpless before us, and many of their kin became our slaves. The Caledonii, who called themselves Hard Men, begged to be allowed to join us on our raids. The Scotti, the sea raiders, were proud to follow our lead. We were feared through all Prydein and all along the coasts of Gaul. Even the Saesons sought us as friends.'

'I have heard tell the Attecotti were a mighty people,' Nai acknowledged.

'Were,' said the man. 'Were.' He spat into the darkness. 'In the days of our glory we were mighty indeed, and in those days one clan, one family, was greater than any other. Our pre-eminent chiefs, our most skilled druids, all came from the Children of the Cupbearer. That kindred lay at the heart of all our councils.'

'And their leader was Pedrylaw Menestyr,' Nai said quietly.

'Even so,' said the man. His teeth flashed against the darkness of his skin. 'The Skilled Cupbearer. But the last to carry that name died at the hands of the Long Man, and since that time our powers have dwindled.'

'They dwindled long before,' murmured Nai.

The man hissed, moved forward on his haunches. Nai shifted also, studying the scarred features, trying to decide whether this was Peythan mab Menestyr who had sworn to drink his blood, or another of the kindred.

'We had withdrawn from the world. But many still sought our advice or our magic men to guide them before embarking upon their endeavours. Increasingly we chose to act through others. Our influence was as great as ever. Then the woman betrayed us.'

'Teleri?'

'The same. The chalice was ours. We were the rightful sovereigns of Albion, by virtue of our blood, by virtue of our descent from those who named the land and gave it form. She allowed an outsider to claim our birthright.'

'An outsider?' From the corner of an eye he saw Seradwen and Regin leading the horses towards the ruin, and he waved to show that he was still all right.

'A stranger. To us you are all the same: Saeson, Roman, Belgae, Peryth – whatever you call yourselves. One by one you have come across the sea and dispossessed the People, driven us deeper and deeper into the forests and the mountains, the wild lands nobody else wants, the margins of the world.'

'Weidhel,' said Nai, remembering Regin's story.

'So they called us once. Weidhel, Feni, the people of the edges.' The man coughed, and his voice was seized by a haunting quality. 'The chalice is ours, warrior. This land was given to us by the Lady the Mother. The chalice is her sign. Without it we are nothing. Our sons have been taken from us. Where once we were many now we are few, and the old ways, the true ways, are dying. Too often our magic fails us. Our children die before they reach full growth; our women are barren; our men age early and are like dry husks with all the seed sucked out of them. Every winter finds our people weaker – and the winters are harsher in the north than here in the soft south. The Lady has turned her face away from us since we lost the chalice. With every year our hold upon the lochs and islands lessens. We are squeezed between the Scotti and the tribes of the north. Our neighbours are greedy, where once they were keen to call us allies.'

'God does not give us things forever,' Nai said gently. 'God gives us life but we do not live forever. So it is with land. We hold it for as long as we wish to keep it, then others come.'

The man's face distorted. 'We want our land.'

'Then why waste your men in this far country? Take them home and guard against your foes.'

'Give us the chalice.' The man's voice was soft, insinuating. 'Give us the chalice and we can go home. Give us the chalice and we can live.'

'I cannot,' said Nai. 'It is not mine to give.'

There was a long silence. A wolf howled in the distance and the hairs prickled on the nape of Nai's neck. Regin and Seradwen were waiting by the entrance to the building, their faces pale blurs in the darkness. The bard had drawn his sword and the blade gleamed a dull red where it caught the light from the embers of the fire.

'We lost a horse today. The rider broke his leg. The signs say we should follow you no further.'

'Then go.' Nai sought the other's eyes in the shadows, found only the weals of the tattoos around the deep sockets. 'Go in peace.'

'Last night I dreamed strange and turbulent dreams,' the man said absently. 'When I woke I found this lying by my cheek.' He

406

fumbled in his belt pouch, thrust something at Nai, who took it without thinking.

His eyes still fixed on the other, Nai let his fingers explore the softness of the web and vanes, the fragility of the quill. Finally he looked down, and despite the darkness he saw without surprise that it must have belonged to a rook or crow.

'You are my death,' said the man. His voice seemed to come from very far away. 'You were my son's death, and you will be mine.'

'Go home,' urged Nai.

The man smiled wearily. 'I cannot, any more than you can give us the chalice.' He rose to his feet, placed the pipe between his lips and blew a single blast. The ground mist writhed as if in response. 'We shall not follow you so closely now. I shall not let the young men cast their spears at you in play. When we meet again it will be for the last time.'

He backed away into the night and was gone.

There is a language in buildings, thought Nai, gazing up at the plaque above the doorway of the ruin. He had asked Seradwen what the letters meant, but they were too worn for her to read. The carved figures, though, were clear enough: a triple-headed dog surmounted by a raven, the shape of the beak unmistakable. Until he had seen the plaque in daylight, he had thought of the building as a barn, a casual resting place for the night. Now it seemed a different kind of resting place.

'A mortuary!' exclaimed the bard. Shuddering ostentatiously, he drew his cloak around his shoulders. 'I am not surprised we had a disturbed night. Did your friend tell you anything interesting?'

'He gave me this,' said Nai, holding the crow feather between thumb and forefinger. 'By the way, who is your father?'

Regin's face went very still. 'My father?' He rallied, sketched a smile. 'Surely you did not pass the night discussing my family?'

Nai waited, silent.

'My father is not an easy man,' Regin said after a while. He kicked a tuft, sent silver droplets of dew showering across the grass. 'All my life I have quarrelled with him.'

Seradwen joined them, carrying a saddlebag. She made to speak, stopped when she when she saw their expressions.

'He sent you?' said Nai.

A bird sang sweetly in the coppice down the hill.

'Yes.' Regin turned towards Seradwen as if seeking her understanding. 'My father is . . .' His hands wavered in the air and he frowned.

'Tell us,' she prompted, glancing uncertainly from one to the other.

'I do not know where to begin.'

'Tell us who he is.' Nai's voice was harsh, implacable.

'You know *who* he is, or you would not ask me.' The bard stepped away from the shadow of the building, out into the weak morning sun. 'I will tell you *what* he is.'

'Should we not be on the road?' Seradwen asked anxiously.

Nai shook his head. 'We have time.' He tapped his thigh impatiently. 'Speak, bard.'

'My father is a difficult man to deny,' Regin said slowly. He lifted his face to the sunlight. 'He is a powerful man, domineering, one who expects to have his lightest command obeyed upon the instant. We – his children – all fear his wrath.'

'A monster,' Seradwen said lightly.

The bard spun on his heel. 'I am not joking, woman.' For a moment he stared at her angrily, then dropped his gaze to the ground. 'A monster,' he said in more normal tones. 'A monster, or a great man.'

He rubbed a hand across his face. 'Last summer he had dealings with a band of Scotti reivers, and needed to give some guarantee of safe conduct to their leader. He chose me to be the hostage, the one held by the pirate crew while they waited for their leader to return.'

Nai guessed what was coming.

'At one point during their meeting the Irishman reminded my father that if anything befell him my life was forfeit. My father laughed and said: "I have many sons."'

Seradwen's breath burst from her in a hiss that startled the ponies. Nai touched her arm, prevented her from moving forward.

'I tell you this not because I object to my father's behaviour, but so that you will understand the difference between us.' Regin's skin was stretched across his cheeks, his nose more prominent than ever as he turned to them, singling out Seradwen. 'You, who are childless, find his words callous and uncaring; I, who am one of many and have already fathered several of my own, find his words necessary.'

At the mention of her lack of children Seradwen flinched as if she had been struck. Nai tightened his grip upon her arm.

'It was my father who sent me forth, since I have some skill with a harp and a good voice.'

'And a stock of stories,' Seradwen said shakily.

'Yes.' The bard inclined his head. 'A wide stock, many of which had never been heard in Dumnonia until my coming. Custennin enjoyed them, and so did most of his household warriors.'

'Did Vortepor choose them for you?' asked Nai.

'Vortepor?' repeated Seradwen.

'His father,' said Nai. 'Vortepor of Dyfed.' He released Seradwen's arm. 'Vortepor who sent Eremon and his Scotti raiders in search of Bedwyr and the chalice. Vortepor, who thinks himself fit to take Arthur's place, who by blackening the reputations of Arthur and Gwenhwyvar hopes to persuade us that he, a man so much their inferior his name should not be mentioned in the same breath as theirs, is a possible successor to the Amherawdyr.'

'We need a strong ruler, or we shall wither and die,' shouted Regin, his face suddenly mottled with red blotches of anger. 'Who else is there?'

'We do not need a man whose name is a byword for treachery.' Nai regarded Regin through narrowed eyes, expecting the bard to reach for his sword at any instant. 'Did Vortepor encourage Angus in his rebellion against Custennin?'

Regin whirled on him in a storm of rage and shame. 'Yes! Of course he did! A weakened Dumnonia would be to our advantage. But Angus lacked the necessary ruthlessness. He did not act quickly enough, and Custennin forestalled him.'

'And what is your part in this?' Seradwen asked quietly.

The bard laughed. 'Why, to let you lead me to Bedwyr and thence the bitch queen herself.'

'And if we did?' Nai said curiously. 'What then? I take it Angus would have the chalice for himself, would raise himself up as a new warlord. The Children of Menestyr intend to return it to the north and restore their people's fortunes. You would carry it to Dyfed. I assume Custennin has no part in this, but if Isgofan or Eri are loyal to him after all, you have a fourth problem.'

'No,' said Regin. 'Custennin knows nothing of this. All he did was grant the strangers permission to seek a healer for their king's son.'

'So how will you reconcile these three desires? The Children of Menestyr made their distrust of you plain last night.'

Regin smiled to himself. 'I shall find a way, never fear.' He straightened, his anger spent. 'Well, I shall not say it was pleasant travelling with you, but it was certainly interesting. We will meet again, I am sure.'

'No doubt,' said Nai.

The bard gathered his possessions and saddled his pony, whistling nonchalantly. He swung himself up onto the horse's back, adjusted his sword belt so the hilt was to hand and fiddled with the harp case until he was satisfied it was safe. The pony walked across the grass towards Nai, who did not move.

'You are going to your death.' Regin leant down so his face was close to Nai's. 'At least send the woman home.'

Nai slapped the pony's rump. It leapt into a run, and the last they saw of Regin was his straight back disappearing down the hill they had climbed the previous night.

'He is right,' Nai said when the sound of hooves had died away.

'That you are going to your death?'

'That you should go home.'

She regarded him steadily. 'My dear, if you are going to die I have no intention of wasting what will be my last chance to be in your company.'

He gestured helplessly. 'It is not my death I fear.'

'Good,' she said briskly. 'Now, where are we going?'

'Caer Cadwy.'

'Why there?' She stepped into the shadows, began to pack their belongings.

'Because that is the obvious place to start.' He knelt beside her in the dew laden grass, fumbled with the fastenings of a saddlebag. 'If we find nothing there, we can try the convent outside Lindinis.'

'How did you know Regin was Vortepor's son?'

He folded his spare cloak and crammed it into the bag. 'The Pict told me last night. He called him the whelp of the Abbot's ally. That had to mean Vortepor.'

'The Pict seems to have been talkative.'

'He was.' Nai grinned. 'Amongst other things he made it clear he was not Teleri's man, which means the Abbot lied. And if the Abbot lied about such a simple matter, then it is likely he

410

acquiesced in the lie Eri had been told about Bedwyr torturing a youth in Lindinis. And that is a great relief to me.'

Seradwen saddled Mischief, pulling the girth tight. Nai handed her a bag and she lashed it into position, her tongue protruding as she tied the leather thongs to the bronze ring on the saddlecloth.

'The birds last night,' she said when she was satisfied the bag was firmly attached. 'They were something to do with the Pict?'

Nai turned and stared at the plaque above the doorway of the ruin, at the raven surmounting the three-headed dog, clearer now as the low morning sun illuminated the lines.

'No,' he said. He closed his eyes, saw again the black cloud swirling above the building. 'They were mine.'

CHAPTER TWENTY

They came to the turning as the light began to fail. For once it was not raining, and there was a stillness to the land that made the emptiness around them seem vaster than ever. Nai reined Coal to a halt and studied the track, then glanced along the straight line of the old road stretching away to the north-east.

'We could keep riding,' he said. 'On to Caer Vadon, or the Saeson lands.'

'We could,' she said, drawing level with him. 'And I wonder how long they would follow us.' She jerked her head in the direction of Lindinis.

Although they had seen no sign of the Children of Menestyr or the bard, neither of them doubted that their pursuers were not far behind.

'Ah well,' said Nai, and turned Coal to the south.

The track ran between high earthen banks, and they both found it a relief to be out of the open. Ahead of them was the great hill, looming through the thickening light. They could see the pale scar of a road leading to the summit, with darker patches which were surely buildings clustered along its length. The ramparts looked untouched: they would not have been surprised to see the heads of the sentries poking over the top of the palisade.

'"Nine hundred men to defend the walls of Caer Cadwy"', quoted Seradwen. 'Isn't that what the poets say?'

Nai grunted. 'Only if you were fool enough to place them side by side. You could defend it with a hundred if you had to.' He pointed. 'Look at the way the stumps have been left on the slope, there, under those saplings. Do you see? Any attacking force would lose its formation long before it reached the walls. If you were defending, all you would have to do is hold your men in reserve and switch them to the danger points as they were needed. Nobody could attack the entire length at the same time.'

She grinned at his enthusiasm. 'Nobody ever tried,' she said quietly.

The way grew steadily more difficult. They were obliged to dismount and lead the horses through one place where the bank had collapsed, spilling across the path. Nai paused and examined the soft earth for tracks.

'Someone has been here recently,' he said. 'Before the last rains, but not that long ago.'

'Do you think it was Bedwyr?' Seradwen glanced around her uneasily. The darkness was closing in rapidly, and the way they had come was shrouded in the dimness.

Nai shrugged. 'It might have been. I doubt if Caer Cadwy has many visitors these days. Most people would think it haunted.'

'You mean it isn't?' she murmured, but he affected not to hear.

It was cold in the shadow of the hill. The road led them around the outer defences, the grassy bank and its breastwork tall above them. There were gaps in the beams, and a few stones had been dislodged by rain or frost, but the barrier was still formidable.

Looking closely in the half-light, Seradwen could see that some of the exposed stones were older than the rampart. They bore the faint impression of the columns or capitals of which they had once been a part – a spoked wheel here, a faded leaf there – worn smooth by the passage of the years.

'So many ghosts,' she muttered.

A chill breeze greeted them as they approached the entrance tower. The tunnel was very black, like a a great mouth waiting to swallow them.

'I am afraid,' Seradwen said shakily. 'Tomorrow is the shortest day. Not a good time to disturb the dead.'

'I am afraid too.' Nai was solemn. 'But it was Arthur's fortress, and I do not think Arthur would harm us.'

He urged Coal into the tunnel. The pony's hooves were loud in the confined space, echoing off the walls so that for a moment Seradwen thought he did not ride alone, that somebody had been waiting for him in the darkness. Her lips moved in an unformed prayer, a wordless plea for protection, and before she had time to consider what she was doing she touched Mischief into a trot.

The houses lined the road as it wound up the hillside. She could smell the rotting thatch, could see where the plaster had fallen from the walls to expose the wicker frames beneath. There were more buildings than she had anticipated, spreading from the main road in a maze of lesser streets, and trees grew among them, so that in summer it must have seemed to the inhabitants as if they were living in open country rather than a fortified town.

'Why!' she exclaimed suddenly. 'It is beautiful!'

And it was, with the twilight disguising the worst of its imperfections, so that if she narrowed her eyes, ignored the smell and used her imagination she could pretend that it was still peopled, that all around her was the rush and buzz of crowds on their way home after a day's work in the fields or the workshops, children being summoned to their beds by their mothers, the smell of supper cooking on the fires, woodsmoke drifting on the evening air.

'A change of heart?' teased Nai.

'Yes,' she said firmly. 'You were right. There is nothing to harm us here.'

They followed the road up the slope. As they climbed the night formed behind them. The trees beyond the ramparts blurred into a single dark outline; the meadows merged back into the land-scape. Here, high above the surrounding country, it was light a little longer; far away in the west the clouds along the horizon were still tipped with a final hint of molten gold.

Coal pricked up his ears and nickered deep in his throat. His whole body quickened with interest.

'What is it?' demanded Seradwen.

'I think –' Nai winced as Coal tossed back his head and neighed. 'I think he has found an old friend.'

An answering whinny came from above them and a shaggy coated pony appeared on the crest.

'Broad-belly,' said Nai.

'What?'

'Gorthyn's horse.' He shrugged at her expression. 'Well, you can see why he called him that.' He swung himself from the saddle and let the horses greet each other.

Seradwen remained mounted, surveying the plateau. The hall was the dominant feature, over twenty paces in length, saved from seeming austere by the entrance porch a third of the way along its straight frontage. Even from a distance one could see the hall was shabby and neglected, nearing the end of its life. The porch sagged, and the last of the light showed the dark patches where the shingles were missing on the high roof. Yet sufficient of its former glory remained to hold her entranced, so that she did not notice the figure which emerged from one of the lesser buildings until she heard Nai's sharp intake of breath.

'Bedwyr?' he called doubtfully. 'Bedwyr?'

The figure came closer. It moved slowly, like an old man, picking a route across the grass as if its feet were following a path that was no longer visible.

She did not know what she had expected but it was not this. From Nai's remarks she was aware Bedwyr was not a tall man, and the songs had always made it clear that though sinewy he was not heavily muscled. But the figure before her seemed slight, insubstantial, clad in a dirty cloak and tunic that needed darning. He reminded her of her grandfather just before the end: the once-strong frame fallen in on itself; the incisive mind wandering in its dotage; the formerly fastidious dresser careless of his clothing.

Then the eyes met hers from under bushy brows. 'Welcome, Lady.' He bowed with a sudden grace, turned to Nai and clasped him in a hug. 'Cousin,' he said, and thrust the other out at arm's length to examine him. 'Cousin. At last! How did you find me?'

Nai flushed. 'It – it just seemed obvious, somehow,' he stammered. 'You have shaved your beard.'

'Yes, and trimmed my hair.' Bedwyr patted Nai's back. 'Come, let us see to the horses, and then you must view my quarters. I hope you brought some food with you; my own supplies are running low.' He held out his hand to Seradwen. 'Lady, will you dismount?'

'Gladly,' she said, taking his hand and feeling the strength of his grip. 'And we have food in plenty, courtesy of Abbot Angus mab Connor. But we should warn you that we were followed here. Our foes are not far behind us.'

Bedwyr released her as she touched the ground and she saw that he was not so very old after all; or at least, that though he was old he was far from his dotage.

'We have time,' he said steadily. 'They will not come tonight.'

*　　*　　*

'Interesting that Peythan mab Menestyr should choose to implicate both Angus and Regin,' said Bedwyr. He leant back against the wall of the hut, squinted wearily at the fire. 'Their alliance is failing fast. He must have hoped to force matters to a conclusion, and I suppose in a sense he has succeeded.'

'I pitied him,' said Nai. 'Peythan, I mean.' He stared into the shivering colours of the blaze. 'He was afraid of me, yet he found the courage to meet with me alone.'

'Do not waste your pity.' Bedwyr's face was hard. 'Remember what one of his kind wrought last summer at Porthyle. In their prime the Attecotti were a cruel people, and if their power has dwindled, it is largely because they have allowed themselves to be eaten up by their selfish desire for the chalice.'

The fire crackled. Bedwyr fed it another lump of timber taken from the ruins around them. The dry wood burned with a clear flame, and the little smoke it gave off quickly dissipated through the holes in the thatch.

Eventually Seradwen could contain herself no longer. 'Tomorrow,' she said.

Both men turned to look at her, their eyes glittering with reflected flames, their features expressionless.

'They will come, all of them. Isgofan and Eri, the Picts, the bard as well for all I know.' She waited for a response, but neither spoke. 'What are we going to do?'

She heard the horses outside, heavy hoofed and clumsy in the night. The wind soughed across the hilltop, and she huddled nearer to the fire, though it was not cold in the hut.

'It will be all right,' Bedwyr said comfortingly. 'When they come I will go down to meet them. You and Nai can take the horses. Once they have me, they will lose interest in you for a while.' He patted Nai's shoulder. 'I suggest you ride with all speed for Gereint.'

'No!' protested Nai, his voice thick with dismay.

'My dear, I do not intend to fight. Isgofan has already defeated me once.'

'Do you know where the chalice is, then?' asked Seradwen.

'No.' The old man's fingers plucked at a loosed thread on his tunic. 'I have no more idea now than when I left Porthyle six months ago.'

'Then why sacrifice yourself?' Nai was on his feet, bending low under the roof of the hut. 'Let us leave immediately, while we still can.'

416

Bedwyr drew a deep breath, tugged at Nai's sleeve to make him sit. 'Listen, cousin, listen. I have failed. I have failed so utterly all one can say in my favour is that at least while they have been hunting me they have not been hunting Gwenhwyvar.'

He laughed without humour. 'I deserve to die.'

Watching him Seradwen saw the fragility that underlay his strength, and she remembered a remark Nai had made on the day they left the farm (which seemed like years ago). Someone – she thought it was Teleri – had compared Bedwyr to the strings of a harp. Too loose and they would not play. Too tight and they snapped. Yet even when at the perfect tension the strings were still prone to breaking without warning.

'The Abbot,' she said carefully, unsure of what she was doing, 'wanted us to persuade you to surrender.'

'Then he will have his desire tomorrow.' He gestured helplessly. 'Did he tell you what happened in Lindinis?'

'Yes,' growled Nai. 'He also told us the Children of Menestyr were led by the Lady Teleri, which is a lie. He told us many lies, mixing them with a little truth to make them stronger.' He grasped Bedwyr's arm and shook it as if by doing so he could lift the older man's spirits. 'I would hear your version before I judge.'

'My version,' said Bedwyr. He gazed into the depths of the fire. When he spoke his voice was faint.

'I thought it would be easy. I would wait until the fuss over the events at Porthyle had died down and everybody had forgotten about the obscure hermit who had probably been killed in the fighting. Then I would ride to the Convent of St Helena, where I would identify myself and be given a message which would mean much to me and little to anyone else.'

He slumped against the wall, warmed his damaged hand over the fire. It was so thin the light seemed to shine through the flesh.

'Instead I found Celemon, Cei's daughter. She warned me I was an old man playing at being young.' He raised his head, stared at first Nai, then Seradwen. 'She, who was once my friend, was hostile. She accused me, and Gwenhwyvar, of valuing a pagan symbol above the true word of the Lord.' He ran the broken hand through his hair. 'The worst of it is, I am no longer certain she is not right.'

'Abbot Angus does not seem to believe so,' said Seradwen.

'Angus is a Christian because of the time and place in which he lives, not because of any great personal conviction. He would have embraced the paganism of his ancestors with every bit as much fervour if he had been born a hundred years ago.'

'Do you think so?' Nai was startled.

'Ah, God, I am not sure of anything any longer.' He swallowed, lifted his hands despairingly. 'I thought I was safe, do you see? I was old, not a fighting man any more, a monk and hermit trying to make his peace with God, to understand the world around him. I had withdrawn from the currents of life. I was like a twig thrown into a river: first the water takes it, spins it about and buffets it hither and thither, until suddenly, suddenly it straightens out and begins to ride with the flow, smooth and fast, deluding itself it is in control, convinced it is deciding where it will go, what it will see. It might continue thus for many miles. Then it becomes waterlogged, sluggish, heavy, caught by the eddies, and it drifts slowly, calmly, into a backwater, perhaps is left by the waves on a small beach, its voyage over.'

He lowered his hands, added softly: 'I thought my life was like that.'

'And?' prompted Seradwen.

'I thought I would never again have to fight, and as long as I did not have to fight I would not have to struggle against the desire to hurt. Because, my dears, that is my weakness, my failing, whatever you want to call it, which I have never admitted before even to myself. Not the killing, which is what people say of me, that I loved killing, but the need, the want, to inflict pain. To hear them scream.'

Nai glanced across the fire at Seradwen. 'Who?' he asked tentatively.

'Anybody.' Bedwyr's voice was a groan. 'There is the horror of it. Anybody. You see, it was all right while I had Arthur, the Companions. They told me who was a friend and who was an enemy, and while they were around me I could not take a blade or a hot iron to someone because it would have shamed them. The best torturers – and there were times when we tortured people to make them speak, though you will not find them mentioned in the songs – the best are those who do not enjoy giving pain. If like me you enjoy it you go too far. Hurt a man too much and he no longer cares whether he lives or dies, has nothing to gain from talking.'

'So how many people have you tortured?' Seradwen fought to keep her voice level and matter of fact.

'A Scotti raider when I was a youth and we needed to know their plans.' He held up the claw of his left hand. 'In the next fight I received this. I took it as God's judgement upon me. Then there was Gwydawg mab Menestyr. I made him pick up his sword and keep fighting, long after I should have given him a clean death.'

'Two, in a lifetime,' she said. 'We have all done things of which we are not proud.'

'The third is worst of all,' he continued as if she had not spoken. 'The Pict. I do not know his name. I slashed him a little, kept him terrified so he did not know what I would do next but believed me capable of anything. That is all I remember doing, but after they came into the house he was dead and they said I had killed him.'

'Did you?' she asked.

'I do not know!' he whispered hoarsely. He turned his face towards her and she saw that his eyes were wet in the firelight. 'I do not remember it, all I remember is the man huddled in his cloak, hiding himself, waiting by the door as the axes smote it, and that makes no sense, does it, so perhaps they were right, Isgofan and Dirmyg, and I did kill him. Certainly I caused his death by bringing him there. And I cut him with the knife, beads of blood joining in a curtain down his cheeks, to make him talk, when all along he would have talked anyway! He wanted to talk, had been trying to find me by himself, without the others.'

Nai shifted impatiently. 'Surely it is more likely they killed him because he had betrayed them.'

The old man shrugged. 'Perhaps. But I enjoyed it, Nai, enjoyed my mastery over another person, being able to inflict or withhold pain. That is my secret, has been my secret all my life, and I have covered it by pretending to the lesser evil, which in our times is not so great an evil, that I enjoyed killing. "Cei for the combat and Bedwyr for the slaughter," they used to say. Cei enjoyed the contest, the act of pitting himself against others, but he was just as happy using a wooden stave as a sword or spear, or no weapon at all.

'If not for Arthur, I would have become a man like your friend Eremon, or worse. I would have raided and looted and burned and raped with the rest of them.'

There was a long silence. Seradwen held her breath, not knowing what to say or how to comfort the old man, not even certain that she wished to comfort him.

The sound was like the rasp of a file on rusty metal. Nai's chuckle grew louder as he broke a piece of kindling and fed it to the flames.

'Why do you laugh?' demanded Bedwyr.

Nai straightened, wiped his face, flushed from the heat of the fire. 'Oh, no reason. A small joke, which amused me.' He stirred the flames with his foot. 'Eremon in his last hours made a similar claim. If Arthur had not died, if there had been another like him, he would have followed him.'

He leant forward, very serious, massaged the scar on his throat. 'You are not Eremon, nor could you be. Whatever your faults and weaknesses, you have never sought to dominate the land by first corrupting it. You could have run when the Scotti came to Porthyle. You did not. You could have fled Lindinis and hidden yourself far away. You did not. You came here, back to the heart of things, where you must have known they would find you eventually.'

Seradwen could see him forcing his ruined voice to work, to infuse his words with feeling.

'I do not know how Arthur came to choose you. But choose you he did. He made you the first of his Companions. He trusted you above all others. He was your friend for what – thirty, forty years –'

'More.'

' – and at the end he still chose you to command his warband at the last battle. Do you think Arthur was a fool?'

Bedwyr shook his head.

'Neither do I. A man, even the Amherawdyr, must work with the tools he has, but he does not need to raise weaklings or evil men to high positions.'

'Isgofan defeated me like a child,' the old man said obstinately. 'He could not have done that unless I had sinned.'

'Cousin, I have been defeated more times than I care to recall.' Nai bared his throat. 'Look at this! Was God on Eremon's side that day? A monk beat me with a training stick the other day. Does that make me a sinner?'

Bedwyr gathered his knees into his body, put his arms around them so he sat huddled in on himself. Slowly he rocked back and forth. 'Like a child,' he repeated weakly. 'He took my sword.'

Nai was on his feet in a moment, striding across the hut to where they had piled their belongings. 'Have Gorthyn's.'

He fumbled through the pile, pulled the long shape from its place beside his saddle. Seradwen stared as he carried it into the light. She could remember the sword being made for Gorthyn, the long arguments about the respective merits of laminated and pattern-welded blades. She could remember the scabbard when it was new: the leather cover unmarked over the pale wood, the fleece lining pristine white, the bronze chape and neckpiece brightly polished. A decade later the leather was scuffed and peeling, the wood chipped and dark with weathering, the metal dull and tarnished.

The blade, though, had not altered. Nai slipped it a short distance from the sheath, and she saw again the way the woven marks from the hammering wound down its length, remembered Gorthyn proudly drawing it in the summer sunshine at Din Erbin to show her the loving care with which the smith had beaten strength into the metal.

It shone now in the firelight. Nai thrust it at Bedwyr, forcing him to release his knees to take the sword.

'Not so well crafted as your own.' Nai loomed above the old man, his voice harsh. 'But it will serve. We are not quite done.'

Bedwyr's eyes flickered. He clutched the scabbarded blade awkwardly across his body. His face lifted and he regarded Nai with a reawakened interest.

'What did you say?'

'I said we are not quite done,' growled Nai.

The top of his head brushed the low roof so he could not straighten to his full height, but for a fleeting moment Seradwen had the impression of a much larger man standing there, a man whose hair was not crow black but burnished copper. She blinked, and the illusion was gone.

Bedwyr pulled the sword clear of the sheath, hefted it in his good hand above the fire. The flames leapt, licked at its edge, sent ripples of red light along the pattern in the blade.

'Do you have a whetstone?'

Nai grinned. 'I do.'

'Then fetch it.' The old man twisted the blade through the flames. 'I shall be proud to carry my great-nephew's sword. Thank you, cousin.'

He took the stone and set to work, his lips pursed in a silent whistle. Nai winked at Seradwen.

'This changes nothing,' Bedwyr remarked without looking up

from the sword. His voice sounded less faint, much more decisive. 'I shall still surrender myself tomorrow. I have failed to find Gwenhwyvar, do not even know if she wants to be found. I have searched endlessly and all I have seen is a white owl in the hall here at Caer Cadwy. I am glad you are both here, but I could wish that you were not.' He blew on the edge of the blade. 'Why are you here?'

Nai shuffled his feet. 'It is hard to explain,' he said slowly. 'I was drawn here. Summoned, if you like; summoned without my grasping that I was being summoned.'

Bedwyr grunted. His good hand moved the whetstone faster and faster along the blade until the newly-exposed edge shimmered in the firelight. The noise grew louder, whirring through the hut, biting into Seradwen's skull.

Suddenly she could bear it no longer. 'I shall check on the horses.'

The cold night wind was pleasant after the heat of the fire. The ponies were dark shapes grazing contentedly on the edge of the plateau. A scattering of stars glimmered where the cloud cover had thinned. The long grass whispered around her as she walked away from the hut and the shadows of the ruins, out into the open.

The lights of a farm gleamed in a valley to the south. With a start she realized it was nothing like so late as she had thought. They seemed to have been closeted in the hut for most of the night, but in fact very little time had passed since full dark. Other lights twinkled in the vale before her, and she imagined Gwenhywyvar or Celemon standing where she stood now, gazing down upon a similar sight in bygone years. Except that in those days this area of the hillside would have been a blaze of lamps and torches on a winter's evening, and the surrounding countryside would have been rendered almost invisible. The hall would have dominated, of course: she could picture the lanterns dangling from the porch, the cressets burning along the path.

A door opened behind her and she turned from her reverie to see Nai silhouetted against the fire. He walked towards her, following her trail unerringly through the long grass.

'I cannot dissuade him.'

Seradwen sighed. 'It has been for nothing then.' She touched his shoulder. 'He was badly shaken by what happened in Lindinis.'

422

She felt rather than saw his nod. 'He does not trust his memory. Did I tell you, he hit his head when they were shipwrecked on their way to fetch the chalice? He lost his mind for a while, and says he has gaps in his memory to this day.'

'Yes,' she said. 'Yes, you did.'

Nai put his arm around her and she smelled the familiar smell of him: sweat and old leather, horse and damp wool. 'I thought he would be better after eating,' she said absently. 'If he was a pony I would feed him a hot mash.'

She turned in Nai's arm so she could see the pale shape of his face. 'What does he mean when he says all he can find is a white owl?'

'He scries.'

'He does what?'

'He scries,' repeated Nai. Seradwen felt him studying her. 'I thought you understood. Bodgath would understand. He gazes into water or a polished surface and his mind floats free. He sees things.'

'What things?'

Nai shrugged uncomfortably. 'Past, present, future.'

'And he has searched for Gwenhwyvar by this method?' she murmured, thinking aloud.

'So he said.'

'Is it reliable?'

Nai lifted his hands, palms upward. 'Ask him.'

'I shall.'

She strode to the hut, vaguely aware of Nai on her heels. Bedwyr was sitting in the same position by the fire, the sword across his knees. He raised his head at the sound of her entry, and she thought he looked tired and old with the white bristles in the creases of his skin. His eyes sparkled with what might have been tears, although opening the door had caused the fire to smoke a little and a grey eddy clung to him before vanishing into the roof.

Seradwen hunkered down beside him. 'Tell me about scrying.'

'Scrying?' He spoke listlessly. 'What do you want to know?'

'How is it done?'

He blinked wearily, half smiled, and she saw that the strength was still there under the despondency, if only she could rouse him. 'You empty your mind,' he said quietly. 'The mirror – which can be any reflective surface – is only an aid. Teleri told me she could summon visions simply by closing her eyes.'

'And then?'

'Then you cast yourself upon the deeps.'

She waited, but he said no more.

'Is it always successful?' she asked.

He frowned. 'One always sees something. Whether or not it is useful is another matter.'

'I mean, is it always true, what you see?'

He considered a moment. 'It is always a possible truth.'

She thought he was going to expand on his answer, but the effort seemed too much. 'So,' she said, 'if you search for Gwenhwyvar and keep seeing a white owl in the hall at Caer Cadwy, it must mean something?'

'Yes. Gwenhwyvar – the white phantom – a white owl. There is a connection. As to meaning –' He spread his hands in despair.

'The hall at Caer Cadwy. You see it as it is now, not as it was in Arthur's day?'

He nodded.

She grinned at him triumphantly. 'Then the answer is as plain as the nose on your face.'

'It is?' he said, staring at her with the beginnings of hope.

'Of course. If Caer Cadwy is what you see, then Caer Cadwy is where she is.'

Bedwyr had allowed himself to stir from his lethargy. Now he slumped again. 'But she is not.'

'Not literally, no. She is somewhere close.'

'Close,' he said stupidly.

'Look,' she said. 'If you want to hide something, the best place to put it is in plain view. You conceal a stolen horse in a herd of other horses. You put a stolen sword in an armoury.'

Slowly his eyes widened. 'She went home.'

'Exactly! What could be safer? If she went north or east, she would stand out. Her accent would surely betray her as a southerner, an outsider. It is not easy for a woman to lose herself in this world of ours.'

'Not easy for a man,' he murmured ruefully.

'Far worse for a woman,' she said sharply.

Nai shifted his weight impatiently. 'So where is she?'

'She went home,' Bedwyr muttered to himself. 'By God, of course she did.' He laid the sword aside, rose to his feet. 'Celemon and that bitch of an Abbess cast her out. Who could she trust, in the bitterness that followed Camlann?'

'Who?' demanded Nai.

The old man flung the door wide and stepped out into the night. Seradwen and Nai exchanged a glance then went after him. He ploughed through the long grass, aiming for the high point of the plateau by the ruins that clustered around the hall, the remnants of the kitchens and the guest houses.

'These were *her* lands originally,' he cast over his shoulder as the others panted in his wake. 'Her lands, before they were Arthur's. She came from here, was born within sight of the hill, grew up at Ogrvran's hall within half a day's ride of what was then a deserted dun.'

He paused to let them catch him, the wind stirring his short grey hair. 'Now it is deserted once more. The wheel turns, eh?' He chuckled without humour. 'But she had friends, friends who could not be bought or bribed, friends whose father had suffered on her behalf, who could be trusted to keep their silence.'

The wind caught a loose board and set it creaking. Bedwyr spun, his back to the ruins, waved wildly at the darkness below them and the scattered lights like stars upon the deep. 'Glewlwyd the Gatekeeper. You have heard his tale, how he allowed Arthur to steal Gwenhwyvar on her wedding day?'

'All the world knows that story,' said Seradwen.

'Yes. I thought of it, when I was here before, tried to pick out which of the farms was the one given to his family as recompense for his loyalty. I even debated riding down for the night, knowing they would welcome me.'

He laughed, shook his head, leant forward suddenly and kissed Seradwen on the cheek, taking her by surprise. 'Well done,' he said. 'A fine wit to untangle the web I had woven about me. Well done.'

The loose board groaned and squealed. The grass tossed like the sea, covering and revealing the long line of their footprints.

'Then tomorrow we go in search of this farm,' asserted Nai.

Despite the darkness Seradwen could see the leap of a bushy eyebrow as Bedwyr adjusted his tattered cloak. 'And fetch them down upon her? I think not. No, no. This changes much but not so much as that.' The breath hissed between his lips. 'Rather we must bring her to us.'

'Here?' questioned Seradwen, startled.

'Yes, here.' Bedwyr drew a deep breath. 'Here. It is right. Can you not feel it? We must lay our plans with care, but it seems to me we possess one great advantage we must not waste.'

'What is that?' asked Nai.

Bedwyr's teeth gleamed as he ushered them back in the direction of the hut. 'Why, cousin, this was Arthur's place. Where better to confound his enemies?'

CHAPTER TWENTY-ONE

Seradwen saw them first, just as she was beginning to think they would not come at all. The long grey day was waning into late afternoon when she touched Bedwyr's arm and pointed to the road.

'Two groups,' he said. 'Good.'

She could see nothing good about it. As they came closer she was able to distinguish individual figures. She tried to count them, and abandoned the attempt with a shudder when she reached twenty.

'What if I am wrong?' she said.

The old man smiled. 'You are not wrong. She is there, in one of those farms.' He trapped and held her hand. 'It is time to make an end. They have been hunting these last ten years, and now they can sense they are near to the truth. Sooner or later one of them will make the same leap that you have made, and then they will find her.'

'But –' She opened her mouth to protest, closed it again. There was no point: the old man was set upon his course. Useless to remind him that the principals were not here – with the possible exception of the Children of Menestyr, about whose leadership they could not be certain. If Bedwyr's plan succeeded (which seemed to her increasingly unlikely as the enemy approached) then Angus and Vortepor would simply send more men.

The horsemen disappeared under the ramparts near the south-west gate. There was a long pause when nothing happened, though it seemed to her she could hear voices, very faintly on the wind that ruffled the grass.

'They have mistimed it,' Bedwyr said with satisfaction.

One group came through the tunnel under the gate and halted on the flat ground by the wall. Some dismounted to stretch their legs; others talked and laughed among themselves.

Despite the greyness of the day the air suddenly seemed very clear. She could see Regin with the lump of the harp behind him, lounging in the saddle as he exchanged a remark with the man beside him.

'Eri,' she said.

'Isgofan's friend? It would make sense. They must have had him with them the other night for that farm to have given them shelter.'

She was not listening. The horsemen carried lances, heavy poles that towered above their heads, tipped with pale metal. She closed her eyes, imagined the wicked blades tearing into flesh with all the weight of mount and rider behind them.

'Do not think about it,' Bedwyr said gently. 'You should be safe if you run for the rampart once the fire is alight.'

'I was not thinking of myself,' she snapped, with mingled shame and anger, because it had been her flesh as well as Nai's she had pictured.

'Ah!' said Bedwyr in a different tone. 'There!'

The second group had appeared beyond the walls. They were following the rough track which led to the north-east gate, riding in a long line, strung like scattered beads on a necklace.

'At last they close the trap,' the old man said cheerfully. 'I must go. Remember, light the fire when they pass through the gate.'

He moved down the slope, keeping to the cover of the buildings, and she wondered at the contrast between his behaviour today and his despair of the previous evening. Since the moment they had returned to the hut he had been confident and incisive, planning their every move, refusing to admit the possibility of defeat. The only time she had seen him hesitate was when Nai had mentioned Isgofan. His face had stilled, and after a long moment he had said:

'I cannot fight him.'

Nai had looked taken aback. Bedwyr's mouth had tightened, and after another pause he had expanded. 'Oh, I can fight him, but he will win. I must avoid him for as long as I can. If it comes to it, you must put a spear through him.' He had gazed at Nai wistfully, reminding Seradwen of a disgraced hound pleading with its master for forgiveness. 'I am sorry, Nai.'

Nai had shaken his head, indicated it was not important, and passed on to other matters.

Her hands were trembling as she walked towards the hut where they had passed the night, staying in the shadow of the ruins as Bedwyr had done. The loose board was clattering again, somewhere on the hillside above her. Birds were singing in the trees off to her right, chattering cheerfully as if this were just another day.

Behind her she heard Bedwyr's voice, raised in a mighty shout. The two men had debated whether they should give their enemies one last chance to withdraw, and neither she, nor she suspected they, were altogether clear about why they were doing so. Honour was a part of it, but fear was also important, and she thought that what Bedwyr was saying might well frighten the already demoralised Children of Menestyr, even before Nai made his move. The others though, the urbane Regin and the hardened warriors that supposedly served Custennin but gave their first loyalty to the abbot who had trained them, were less likely to be impressed.

'Who comes to Caer Cadwy on the shortest day of the year?' bellowed Bedwyr. 'Who disturbs the Amherawdyr's peace?'

The birds hushed. The wind soughed though the ruins. If there was a reply, it was inaudible.

'Get you gone from this place, lest the Amherawdyr's wrath fall upon you. Cursed will be the names of those who draw sword or knife against the Amherawdyr's men.'

'Come down, old man, and surrender,' somebody called, and she thought it might have been Regin.

'A final time I tell you. Go!'

The birds fluttered from the trees at the thunder of his voice.

Hugging the dilapidated wall of an old storeroom – the eaves thick with cobwebs waving in the breeze – she peered down the gentler slope to the north, at the dark mouth of the tunnel through which the second group of riders would come. The hillside was empty, apart from a weasel flickering through the long grass down by the entrance. Suddenly it rose on its haunches, stared at the gate, was gone in a flash of brown.

The darkness of the tunnel shifted, changed. A man astride a horse emerged from the shadows, head turning, spear poised in his hand. Long fair hair flapped in the wind. The tunnel spewed forth more riders. They spread in a line, leaving two of their number to guard the gate, and walked their horses up the slope, unhurried and confident.

She ran, feet slapping the ground. Last night's fire still smouldered in the hut. She seized the brand they had left ready, thrust it into the red embers, blew frantically until the end caught. Then she raced from the hut to its neighbour, which she had spent the morning piling with dry kindling and old thatch. Somewhere she heard the jingle of harness, and voices calling like gulls. The brand smoked: greasy, acrid. She pushed the brand deep into the jumble of broken planks and twigs, fell to her knees and puffed with the last of her breath, feeling something tear in her chest, puffed again, struggling to coax the fire to life.

The voices and the jangling sounded closer.

Nai waited in the ruins beside the south-west gate. He leant his head against the rough plastered wall of the alley, smelled the damp and decay. A few more years and these buildings would be gone without trace. He loosened his cloak and hung it over a splintered doorway, flexed his arms. Hooves scraped on the roadway beyond the alley mouth, and he tensed, feeling Coal in turn tense under him, ready for the signal.

Now he must rely on Bedwyr. For the old man's sake he hoped Isgofan would be among this group rather than the party that skirted the ramparts to enter by the northern gate. Coal fretted, and he ran his hands over the pony's neck, soothing him, listening as Bedwyr's challenge floated across the hill.

'A final time I tell you. Go!'

He could hear them mumbling, out on the road he could not see. A man laughed, loud and forced.

'He is ours, I tell you!'

Eri. Had Isgofan accompanied his partner, or had they divided? He would know in a moment. Bedwyr was waiting until the enemy had reached the point in the road they had marked, and then he would speak for the last time, thus:

'So be it. We ride, we ride, Amherawdyr!'

Horse and rider burst from the alley mouth like a thunderbolt, the pony's motion settling to a smooth run as they reached the cobbled road. The enemy were spread in single file along the track, the foremost of them at the point where the way curved as it started to climb.

Lifting his body, Nai braced himself against the hard horns of the saddle. He loosened the reins in his shield hand, let Coal stretch his neck and lower his head. The nearest of his enemies was before him, back exposed, unaware of the danger, and the next in line was barely beginning to turn to investigate the sound of galloping hooves.

Nai flung the spear in his hand, reached down to the quiver behind him and caught the butt of another, his grip sliding along the shaft till it found the twine marking the balance point, raised and threw.

A second man toppled from his horse, screaming. The air was full of howling. Ponies collided and gnashed at each other with yellow teeth. As Coal raced along the shattered line, Nai lost himself in the relentless rhythm of draw, aim and release. Men shrieked, plucked at their chests or backs where their bodies blossomed with strange fruit and blood flowered across their tunics, but it had nothing to do with him. From the corner of an eye he saw Eri tugging his sword from its sheath, and he had time to think dispassionately that the warrior was making a bad choice, a spear would have been better. Then Coal was veering sharply to the right in response to the shift in his weight, and they were hurtling down the last of the narrow alleys before the high ground, his shield brushing the wall, and behind them was chaos waiting for his second pass.

The fire would not catch. Seradwen blew with all her might, used her hands to fan the smouldering brand. The voices were coming closer. She fed the smoke with dead leaves, with lumps of dry moss, anything she could find that might serve as tinder. The leaves charred but refused to take flame, sulked obstinately.

She cursed under her breath, almost sobbing, debated running back to Bedwyr's hut and starting afresh with a new brand. The sweet jingle of harness sounded as if it were directly outside the door. A spark flared in the moss, vanished. Dizzy, she puffed and puffed again, willing the flames to come.

A man laughed. Hooves thudded on the turf. A gull wailed on the wind. Another spark, quickly fading from life. The moss darkened, crumbled. A thread of smoke spiralled from a stick.

Suddenly the brand flared, scorched the wood around it. A

black sheen spread across the sticks, growing before her eyes. Then the flames leapt with a roar that singed her brows.

'What was that?' demanded a voice.

She peered through the doorway at the empty grass. Her knife was in her hand, though both Nai and Bedwyr had told her not to fight, to surrender at once if she was trapped.

There was a crash from the direction of Bedwyr's hut as somebody kicked in the door, cried in triumph: 'He was here!'

The fire was burning well now, with a red glow at its heart. The old thatch she had piled on top of the wood was beginning to smoke, filling the room with acrid fumes. In a moment she would have to leave, regardless of the fair man and his warriors.

'Mice in the house,' laughed a voice. She caught a glimpse of a horseman trotting towards Bedwyr's hut, waited until his back was turned, and seized a burning branch from the fire.

Then she was through the door, running around the side of the building – warm where it brushed her shoulder – and pounding across the open space to the dilapidated row of storerooms. She tossed the branch onto the nearest roof and kept running until she reached the end of the row.

Flattening her body to the wall, she slithered around the corner. Nobody seemed to have noticed her. The guards left with the horses were staring up the slope, and she followed the direction of their gaze.

Thick grey smoke billowed from the hut she had set ablaze. The riders milled purposelessly about the building, coughing and choking as the smoke swirled around them. The fair man cantered across, shouting.

'What are you doing? Find the old man!' He waved a hand, indicating the hilltop, and she saw the dull glint of metal on his fingers.

The horsemen dispersed, reluctantly reformed their line while the fair man berated them. 'Where is Loarn?' he bellowed suddenly. The riders twisted in their saddles, and one pointed down the slope to their left.

A horse was running loose through the ruins. A great cry went up and the line of riders plunged down the hillside, some racing in pursuit of the pony, others angling in the direction from which it had come.

With a howl of rage the fair man – she assumed he was Isgofan – went after them, cursing them for their lack of discipline.

Seradwen waited until she was sure none of them were going to look back. The roof of the first storeroom was smouldering nicely now. In a moment somebody would notice and come to investigate. She sprinted along the row, paused to catch her breath (the air tainted with smoke), and ran to the place where Bedwyr had issued his challenge.

Less time had passed than she had thought. The roadway was filled with the dead and dying, men and horses alike. Nai was a flickering shape riding through the maze of alleys that wound among the ruins. She recognized Regin's horse, wheeling in panic-stricken circles while its rider struggled to bring it under control. She felt a touch of sadness – though no surprise – that the bard was indeed among their enemies, and remembered she had intended to remind Nai that the Abbot had said his first wife was from Dyfed. *Connections*, she thought, *so many connections, all interlaced like some complex piece of weaving*, and then Nai had cleared the ruins and was out on the roadway again, Coal's neck outstretched in full gallop.

Nai's right arm rose and fell inexorably, never varying its pace, and though it did not seem to her that he could possibly have time to aim almost every spear struck a target. His foes tumbled over each other in their eagerness to escape, and those who would have fought back were trapped in the whirlpool of confusion as pony reared and lashed at pony and men tumbled from the saddle.

Seradwen crept forward on the brow of the hill, relying on the ever-thickening smoke to hide her. Nai moved among them like an angel of death, a dark rider on a darker horse, and it came to her then that he had been utterly serious when he had claimed the black birds above the mortuary house had been his.

She shuddered and looked away.

Smoke eddied over the plateau, veiling the Great Hall. A grey pillar rose into the sky, red flames licking at its base. In years gone by, Bedwyr had told her, Caer Cadwy had formed part of a signal network reaching for miles in every direction: to Ynis Witrin and thence the Severn Sea; to Caer Vadon and thence, ultimately, clear across the country to Lindum and beyond; to Sorbiodunum or Durnovaria. Now, she prayed, it would work as efficiently to rouse somebody much closer. She did not think the second group of horsemen would be taken by surprise as easily as the first, and

433

she feared for Bedwyr, of whom she had seen no sign since parting from him on the hillside.

Bedwyr sagged against the wall, panting. Now they knew he was here, in the least damaged part of the town, they had dismounted and were hunting him on foot. He could hear their leader shouting instructions in the background. It sounded like Isgofan, and he was thankful the man had not elected to lead the search in person. The two he had killed so far had both been Picts – the first, he thought, was one of those he had faced in Lindinis – and neither had given him any trouble though he was aware he lacked the speed and strength he had once possessed.

He had to keep them occupied a while longer. Help would not come at once. The smoke was thick above the summit, and surely she would come in response, but it would take time. (What would happen if he and Seradwen were wrong, if Gwenhwyvar were nowhere near, was something he preferred not to dwell upon.)

A heel scraped on stone at the end of the street. They were hunting in pairs now, which was wise, but they seemed to have no sense of how to proceed. He had watched one couple a moment ago scuttling through what had once been a garden and was now a tangled wilderness, using the trees and undergrowth for cover without any consistency, first exposing themselves in one direction then another.

The final indignity, he thought, to be hunted by fools.

He shifted from shadow to shadow, smelling the burning on the air, twirling the blade around him, letting it assume its own life as he heard them drawing near. They were close, very close, their sheep faces waiting unwitting for the horror that would fall upon them as they rounded the corner, *now*, and their lives ended like *this* in blue steel whistling from nowhere to nowhere leaving a trail of red droplets.

Shouts from behind him. Answering cries from ahead. He faded through the open doorway, his sleeve catching and tearing on a nail (give them a path to follow) and he was out into the garden where he had seen the scuttling pair and over the wall in a slow rolling vault that jarred his ankles as he landed, and he cursed being old.

'Bedwyr!'

Isgofan's voice, echoing flatly among the deserted houses.

'Bedwyr. Why do you kill so freely? What harm have we done you?'

434

A body crashed through the undergrowth. Fingers scrabbled on the stone wall he remembered being built to mark the boundary between quarrelsome neighbours. He waited, sword poised.

'Bedwyr! All we want is to talk.'

The fingers showed, disappeared. He could hear a whispered conference in the garden, the sound of someone trying to ease quietly along the far side of the wall.

'We are all Britons, Bedwyr. We are all citizens. Let us save our energies for fighting the outsiders, the Saesons and the Scotti.'

Now there were two sets of fingers scrabbling on the wall: one immediately before him, the other several paces away.

'We want what is best for our country. A strong ruler. An Amherawdyr, to be the bulwark of our nation against its foes. Is that unreasonable? Is it not the very cause to which you devoted your life?'

A face appeared above the parapet, framed between two hands, a knife clenched in its teeth. He laughed aloud at the expression in the eyes as the face registered his presence and the sword sweeping up towards it; and then it was gone in a scream and a flurry of blood.

'God forgive you, old man,' yelled Isgofan, 'for I shall find it hard to do so.'

The second man dropped to the ground, recovered at once and rushed at Bedwyr, long blade licking the air between them. Bedwyr moved forward, whirling his sword in a complicated sequence of slashes, cuts, and thrusts that wove around him the fabled web of steel beloved of the bards, shifted his weight to his left foot and let the other's blade whistle past him (slicing the fabric of his sleeve on the way) and finished his sequence with a blow that lifted his opponent from his feet and flung him against the wall.

A shower of sparks fell around him. He glanced into the sky and saw wisps of burning straw floating on the wind. The smoke was growing thicker, catching at his throat. He heard feet pounding across the mud and grass of the garden beyond the wall. The man he had struck moaned in agony, clutched the ruin of his chest.

Bedwyr backed away into the house behind him, a part of his mind trying to recall the name of the man who had lived here (Owain? Padarn? something very ordinary) and a part alert for the rest of his foes.

'Bedwyr!' Isgofan's cry sounded despairing. 'Surrender! Put an end to this bloodshed! We want only what is best for our land!'

You and a thousand like you, thought Bedwyr. I have seen your best, and it is tyranny, the rule of the strongest. God knows we had our faults, but at least we were honest.

'Give us the chalice, or give us Gwenhwyvar. Then we will go, and leave you to your ghosts.'

'You demand where you should entreat.' He muttered the words, resisting the temptation to shout them in reply. 'You come as conquerors where you should come as supplicants.'

He slipped through the house and out onto the street, searching for a sign of the enemy. The mouth of an alley beckoned; he ran across the open space, ready for the cry of recognition, and waited, fighting for breath, wondering what had happened to Nai, whether the dark man was still alive.

This time Nai came at them from a different angle, riding the route he had so carefully plotted that morning, the thunder of the horse's hooves magnified and confused by the ruins around him.

The air was very clear. He could see the details of the painted design on one man's war-board standing out in stark relief, the feathers bunched in another's hair nodding in the breeze. One of the Picts had been flung into a wall which had collapsed around him: the timbers were honeycombed with wormholes.

Again he threw and threw, his right hand moving without thought in the pattern it had practised so often. A spear skidded from his shield; something thumped against the horn on which his right leg was braced and fell clattering away. Eri rode at him, brandishing his sword, and Coal carried Nai aside, granting him space to plant a javelin in the burly man's throat. A tattooed face howled in anguish, scythed with a war-knife as he came past; he struck down with the rim of his shield and felt bone crack.

Over the screams he heard the beat of hooves, fast closing behind him. Everything happened at once. Nai settled in the saddle and slowed Coal to a shorter stride, used his shield hand on the pony's neck to signal a turn. Coal checked and swung right, so sharply Nai would have lost his seat had he not been expecting it. His opponent cursed, plunged past on a dun pony. At the same time as the turn began Nai lifted himself against the horns, twisted his torso to the left as Coal's head rose, and cast his spear. The other was seesawing the reins as he sought to imitate

436

Nai's manoeuvre, his guard down, believing himself momentarily safe from attack. He howled as the javelin struck hard between his ribs, swayed and fell from the dun pony in a flurry of limbs. It was Peythan.

Exultant, Nai gave Coal his head as they dived into the shelter of a passage between two tumbledown booths and rounded the corner to race parallel with the road. His hand checked the quiver where his last remaining shafts rattled, moved to loosen his long knife in its sheath.

He was shouting as he came into the open, his throat raw and his voice rasping, shouting like the old crow Bodgath had named him, shouting a single word over and over: 'Arthur, Arthur, Arthur.'

His enemies were a confusion of fallen steeds and tangled bodies, men and horses entwined in a mass that blocked the road. Two were still mounted, surveying the dead and wounded as if they did not know whether to help or flee. At the sight of him they reached a decision. Although they were trembling with strain and terror they lowered their lances and kicked their mounts into a charge.

He threw and missed; threw again and hurt one enough to send him swerving away. Nai barked hoarsely: the second man screamed and let his lance point dip. Nai pushed it away with his shield, the impact flinging him back against the rear horns of the saddle, and hurled his final spear into the man's side as his horse carried him past.

Suddenly it was finished. The wounded lancer was galloping for the gate; three more figures were lurching after him on foot. Only the dead and wounded were left, strewn across the road and open ground.

A tattooed man writhed near Coal's hooves, a broken spear shaft protruding from his belly. Nai slid from the saddle, knife in hand, and bent over him. The reek of stale sweat and animal grease filled his nostrils as he turned the man, trying to examine the wound. The man quietened at Nai's touch. His head lolled, his face pleading under the tattoos as he plucked feebly at the shaft.

'There is nothing you can do for him.'

Nai spun at the sound of Regin's voice. The dying man clutched his arm and he struck down hard with the knife, giving the man the release he sought. The bard laughed.

437

Regin was lying with one leg trapped under his fallen horse. Beside him a Pict laboured jerkily for breath, rusty blood smeared across the blue and green tattoos. Around them others moaned or struggled to staunch their wounds, each locked in his own world.

Nai bent and tugged a spear from a body, wiped it on the stained tunic, picked up a second from the churned ground, discarded a third as too damaged to be of further use.

'Have you come to scavenge the dead?' mocked the bard.

'A wise man goes armed among his foes,' said Nai.

'You croak like a carrion crow.' Regin fumbled behind him. With a grunt of effort he drew his sword, held it out before him.

Nai swallowed a laugh and skirted around the horse to where Eri sprawled in the mud. The bard twisted to watch, keeping the blade between them.

'People are smaller in death,' Nai remarked as he levered the javelin from Eri's neck. 'Did you wish to fight?'

'Damn you.' Tears rolled down the bard's cheeks. 'Look what you have done.'

Nai glanced at the dead and dying. The blood-smeared Pict vomited and groaned. His head slumped and after a moment his chest ceased its struggle for air.

'You have broken my harp.'

Nai stepped behind the bard, knocked the sword aside with his knife, grabbed the man's collar and heaved. Regin screamed as he slid out from under the pony.

'Find yourself another mount and go,' Nai said coldly. He waved a hand at the dead. 'Harps can be mended; these cannot.'

The bard's eyes rolled and he fainted. Nai moved through the fallen, gathering spears until he had sufficient to restock his quiver. Last of all he came to Peythan, lying alone on the cobbles while his horse grazed peacefully on the verge. Nai stirred the body with his foot.

'I am sorry,' he said.

He collected his cloak from the place where he had hung it and remounted. Coal was lathered with sweat but still eager. Nai raised his eyes to the hill. Grey smoke roiled across the slope, hiding the summit. He lifted the waterbottle from the saddlebow and rinsed his mouth, spat the contents to the ground. Then, taking a deep breath, he urged Coal up the road and into the smoke.

*   *   *

A flaw at the heart of everything, thought Bedwyr as he moved through the deserted town, wind blown sparks drifting around him. A flaw in them all and in him especially; a flaw in the great realm of Albion.

It grated within him like the ends of a broken bone, the darkness he thought he had subdued and tamed in his years as monk and hermit.

He skirted a collection of tumbledown huts and and a man came at him from around a corner, seemingly as surprised by the encounter as he was. The man opened his mouth to call for help, twisted aside as Bedwyr struck at him, backed into the shadows of the broken walls with a spear levelled before him, jabbed and thrust, jabbed again.

Bedwyr felt as if he had stepped outside himself. He noted how his body responded to the danger, anticipated his opponent's movements before the man himself had decided upon them and shifted the barest minimum to allow the spear to pass without doing damage, as if everything were preordained and his body had the power of reading the future. And yet he was also aware that once his body had done this far more gracefully and efficiently, that he was operating now with only a small part of his former power, that if this man had been a better fighter he would be dead.

He tugged his blade free and wiped it on the man's tunic. Around him he could hear voices calling, mingled with the cries of gulls and the cawing of crows. A raven watched him bright eyed from a nearby stump.

'Was I right?' he asked aloud. 'Or have I brought us all to our deaths?'

Iron rang on iron in the direction of the north-east gate. He cocked his head on one side and the raven mimicked him.

'She has come,' he said, and his heart leapt with fear and joy.

The raven rose in a flurry of wings and flew over the ruins, a ghostly outline in the smoke that boiled across the hillside. Bedwyr sheathed the sword – Gorthyn's sword, but his now he had blooded it – and ran in pursuit, his feet slipping on the grass, winding in frantic haste between the buildings long after the raven had vanished.

Distracted by the need to remain hidden, Seradwen did not notice the newcomers until they had passed through the gate. Neither

439

did the sentries, whose attention was entirely given over to the deserted town to their left. The newcomers, stocky men on foot, formed into a group and approached the nearer of the two guards, calling a challenge.

The light was failing. Seradwen could not see exactly what happened next. There was a cry, and one of the newcomers fell. The sentries wheeled their horses and galloped towards the town, shouting the alarm. The newcomers made no attempt to pursue them. Instead they gathered around the fallen man, lifted and carried him to the mouth of the tunnel. A taller figure wrapped in a hooded cloak bent over the body.

After a long pause the group moved again, leaving the body behind. They advanced across the grass until they were at the point where the slope steepened. Here they halted, spears and shields at the ready, and seemed to debate what they should do next. Some pointed up the hill at the source of the smoke which had presumably brought them here, others indicated the houses to the east where the sentries had gone.

Seradwen bit her lip. From where she stood she could see what was hidden from the newcomers: the fair man astride his horse in the open space by the road, rallying his followers. They limped out of the town like a defeated army and hauled themselves into the saddles of the ponies they had left tethered by their leader. Several horses remained unclaimed.

She did not know whether to run down to the newcomers or stay where she was. While she dithered, unable to decide, Isgofan led his men at a gallop around the side of the hill. The wind eddied and smoke enveloped the hilltop, blinding her. The fumes bit at her throat, filled her nostrils with the reek of old straw and rotten wood. She wrapped her cloak around her face and plunged unseeing down the slope.

When she reached clear air and wiped her streaming eyes, things had changed. The spearmen were falling back on the gate, leaving two of their number lying on the grass. The riders had divided into two groups: one circled behind the newcomers to cut off their retreat; the other pressed home the attack.

The spearmen strove to stay together, to keep the formation which was their best defence against the riders. One of them went down, and the horsemen were through the gap at once. Suddenly the contest became a mass of individual struggles. Some of the riders dismounted, the more easily to close with their foes, and the fighting spread across the space before the ramparts. Watching from above, it appeared to Seradwen that some slight advantage still lay with the newcomers despite the collapse of their formation. They were strong men (one wrenched a rider from the saddle with his bare hands) and hard to kill.

'Hold!' cried a great voice. 'Hold, I say! I have the woman. Hold!'

Isgofan, his fair hair ruffled by the wind, stood holding a long knife to the throat of the cloaked figure. Gradually the fighting ceased as the warriors turned to stare at him, and an uneasy silence fell across the field, broken by the murmurings of the surviving spearmen.

'Now,' he said when he had their attention. 'Let us have an end to this foolishness.'

'You will not leave here alive!' snarled the largest of the spearmen.

Isgofan laughed. 'It may be so, it may be not. But I have more allies on the hill.' He raised his head and called: 'Eri, come down!'

The wind blew through the grass. Behind her Seradwen heard the loose board clattering on the hillside, and weaving with it the sound of a pony's hooves on the cobbled surface of the road leading to the Great Hall. The smoke swirled across the slope, stinging her eyes, and when her vision cleared there beside her was a dark man on a black horse. For an instant he seemed a stranger; then she blinked, and he was Nai, features set and grim, and very weary.

'Isgofan mab Banon,' he cried in his raw and ruined voice. 'Eri is not coming; nor Regin; nor Peythan. Set the lady free.'

Even from here she could see the dismay flash across Isgofan's face. But the fair man quickly recovered.

'Nai mab Nwython. And the woman beside you must be the farmer's widow with whom you have been dallying.' Isgofan waved one of his followers forward, carefully handed him both prisoner and knife.

'So you have slain poor Regin, have you? I confess, I had thought your reputation overblown, but perhaps I was mistaken. Will you come down and fight?'

Seradwen's stomach tautened.

'To what purpose?' demanded Nai.

'A simple bargain,' said Isgofan. He strolled to the foot of the hill, and Seradwen saw that he wore two swords, one at either hip. 'You may be the lady's champion. If you defeat me, my men will withdraw. If I defeat you, the lady will deliver the chalice and return with me to my master.'

Seradwen thought she was going to faint, here on the hillside with all of them staring at Nai beside her. He could not win, not with a sword, and Isgofan would insist upon swords.

'Wait.' The voice was clear and sweet as a bell. 'Surely I have the right to choose my own champion?'

Isgofan turned in surprise. 'Of course. Forgive me. If you had sooner have one of these spearmen, then by all means let it be so.'

She spoke as if there were no knife at her throat, as if she were not held in the crook of a stranger's shield arm, as if she and Isgofan were alone. 'Then I choose Bedwyr.'

'Bedwyr?' The fair man's laugh was raucous. 'I have already defeated Bedwyr once. This, Lady, is his sword. Do you not recognize it?' He drew the blade and brandished it before her.

Seradwen could not see the lady's expression, hidden by the hood and her captor's shield, but she could hear the certainty in the voice. 'He is my champion.'

He came walking through the long grass, a small and shabby figure with his head bowed, his short hair the colour of the smoke billowing around the hill, and it seemed to Seradwen then that the plans they had laid the previous night were like the daydreams of young children, because everything depended now upon this old man and his skill with the sword against a younger opponent who had already, with the greatest of ease, humiliated him once.

'Are you sure, Lady?' Isgofan's tone was mocking. 'Choose again. I swear to you, that though it will make little odds in the end, you would do better with Nai or one of those you brought here.'

'Why,' the lady answered lightly, 'if it makes no odds, it makes no odds. I shall have Bedwyr, and none but Bedwyr.'

Seradwen put her head against Coal's flank and closed her eyes in despair. Nai bent and touched the crown of her head.

'Let us go down,' he said.

They descended the hill together, her hand on his leg. As they approached the bottom Nai leant over and whispered: 'Courage!' She forced a smile onto her lips, and met the curious stares of the crowd, who had gathered in a rough semicircle about the champions.

Isgofan grinned at her: an insolent, confident grin. Bedwyr's gaze was fixed upon the younger man; he did not look round at their arrival.

'It is not too late, even now,' he said. 'Take your followers and go.'

The fair man roared with laughter. 'You amuse me. Tell me, would you like your own sword for this final bout?'

Bedwyr shook his head. 'The one I have will serve. It belonged to a kinsman once, and has always been carried with honour.'

'Then I shall leave this here.' Isgofan laid the sword he had taken from Bedwyr in the grass near one of the Picts. 'What about a shield?'

Again Bedwyr shook his head.

Isgofan sighed. 'Blade to blade then.' He bowed to his audience, section by section, to the lady last of all. 'This will not take long.'

'Bedwyr.' The lady's voice was clear and cool. 'This time you will have to win.'

Both men drew. Isgofan leapt forward, his blade describing patterns in the air, and beat down upon Bedwyr's guard. The older man staggered, gave ground, his sword ringing beneath the dreadful force of the blows as an anvil rings under the hammer.

Listening to the sound Seradwen feared his blade would shatter. Isgofan's sword was of the finest forging, but the other had been made by Gereint's smith, who had never been renowned for the quality of his blades. Nai must have been thinking similar thoughts, for his hand reached down and clasped her shoulder, so tightly she could feel the bruises forming.

Bedwyr reeled, nearly fell. Isgofan cut him on the left arm, once, delicately, grinning all the while, pulled back a step to let him recover.

'Come, old man. Surely you can do better than this?'

Bedwyr swayed. All the strength seemed to have gone from his legs. He had hoped, when he heard Gwenhwyvar's voice, that this time things might be miraculously different, but it had never been much of a hope. Isgofan stepped away and he felt the blood trickling down his arm. It would be a slow death then, like the one he had inflicted on Gwydawg mab Menestyr in vengeance for the murder of Cei. It was no more than he deserved.

His vision blurred and for an instant he seemed to swim through fields of infinite gold. He heard the boom of Cei's

443

laughter, heard the strong sane voice of his friend saying: 'Oh, nonsense! We swore an oath, remember? Honour it!'

His sight cleared. Isgofan frowned at him, puzzled. 'Are you still with me? It was only a scratch. The first of many.'

'I think not,' he said. The world was very bright, much more intense than he remembered, the colours more radiant, the outlines sharper.

Isgofan drifted towards him and he swayed aside, not even deigning to lift his sword, from which light flowed, running like water down the patterns in the blade.

'Yes!' said Cei, his breath hot on Bedwyr's neck. 'Yes!'

He glanced at Gwenhwyvar while Isgofan floundered past him in surprise, and saw that she was no longer alone, that another was standing beside the one who held her (whose grip had relaxed in the excitement of the fight): a tall man, with auburn hair that shone red in the dying sun. The man looked at him and smiled, and he felt his heart lift within him and the joy come bubbling through as Isgofan swung again, fast and deadly. He let the sword slide harmlessly away and reached with his left hand to help Isgofan after it, fascinated by the visible rush of energy between them. Isgofan flew across the grass, tripping over his own feet, and Bedwyr closed his eyes dreamily, the laughter welling within him, saw mountains of light and strange beasts singing in glowing air, waves of liquid sunshine rolling like the never resting sea. He opened his eyes, found Isgofan coming at him once more, shifted so the fair man wallowed past, said:

'Here? You would threaten Gwenhwyvar and try to kill me, here in Arthur's own place?'

'Arthur is dead!' screamed Isgofan.

'Is he?' His gaze met and held the Amherawdyr's. Arthur nodded, and Bedwyr spun on his heel to face Isgofan, seeing the fear leap in the other's eyes. He struck once, mercifully quick. As Isgofan's body began to fold he allowed the weight of the sword to carry him round and forward to where the man held Gwenhwyvar imprisoned, and with the tip of the blade he flicked the knife away from her throat.

'Run!' he roared at the surviving Picts, and though Arthur and Cei were no longer present, it seemed to him their voices joined with his.

*   *   *

444

Gwenhwyvar stepped away from her captor. For a long moment nothing happened. Nai waited, seeing the stunned disbelief on the faces of the crowd. His fingers were crushing Seradwen's shoulder, though she made no protest. He loosened his grip and shook his shield into position, Coal tensing beneath him, both of them preparing for whatever would happen next; and as he did so the echo of Bedwyr's shout returned, reverberating from the walls of the ruined town like a dozen voices shouting the same single word.

'Run!'

Isgofan's followers fled. Those who were still mounted rode at once for the gate and its dark tunnel. The rest scattered, some diving for the nearest horse, others simply running as fast as their feet would take them. A tattooed man was struck by a panicked pony: Nai saw his arms wave wildly in the air, and then the man was down under the hooves, trampled into the mud.

Nai unfastened his shield, slung it over his back. Seradwen stirred beside him, said:

'Did you kill Regin?'

'No.' He looked at her upturned face, smudged with dirt and sweat, at the tangled mess of her hair. 'I broke his harp, though.'

She laughed, suddenly, and he laughed with her, glad that he had not killed the bard. 'He will not like that,' she said, and went off again into peals of laughter.

He swung himself stiffly from the saddle and dropped the reins over Coal's head. 'I suppose these are Glewlwyd's kinsmen,' he remarked, peering at the strangers.

'I suppose so,' she said huskily and wiped her eyes.

The survivors moved among the dead and wounded, helping where they could, rearranging the fallen to grant them some dignity where they could not.

'Nai, Seradwen,' called Bedwyr.

They turned at his summons. The old man was standing protectively beside the woman – Gwenhwyvar, thought Nai, not altogether believing it – cleaning his sword on a piece of rag. He beckoned with the claw of his left hand, the rag dangling bloody in the stiffened fingers, and they walked towards him.

'I knew you would win,' said Gwenhwyvar.

From someone else it would have sounded foolish, a ridiculous assertion made after the event. From her it sounded like a simple statement of fact.

She flung back her hood, revealing silver hair and a face of such worn beauty that Nai caught his breath.

'A woman of fair light form like summer sunshine.' The poet's line ran through his head as he approached, and he saw that it was still true, even after these many years and the great tragedies of her life.

'Lady,' he said, and bowed his head.

'Thank you.' Her voice was melodious. 'Thank you for all you have done, both of you.'

'I think we have finished the Children of Menestyr,' said Bedwyr. 'That was Dirmyg who was trampled under the pony as they fled.' He nudged Nai, who was staring at Gwenhwyvar. 'Did you deal with Peythan?'

'What?' Nai roused himself. 'Yes, and Eri.'

'Good. They will not come again,' Bedwyr said with satisfaction.

'As bloodthirsty as ever,' commented Gwenhwyvar, but there was fondness in her voice. 'They have been sniffing closer and closer for more than a month now. Sooner or later they would have descended on the farm and subjected us to a proper search. Then they would have found me.'

'Does that mean it is finished?' Seradwen burst out, unable to contain herself any longer. 'What about Abbot Angus? And Vortepor of Dyfed?'

Bedwyr exchanged a glance with Gwenhwyvar. He smiled wistfully. 'My dear, it never ends. The best we can hope for is a brief respite, time to lick our wounds.'

'It grows dark,' Gwenhwyvar said briskly. 'We should away to the farm. Your arm needs dressing, and these youngsters look exhausted.'

'A moment,' said Bedwyr. He sheathed Gorthyn's blade, limped across the grass to where Isgofan had left the other sword, the one he had taken in Lindinis. He raised it in the failing light, slashed the air reflectively, frowned. Then he knelt by Isgofan's body to unbuckle the belt and scabbard, tugged it free and walked towards Nai.

The old man halted a few steps short and proffered the hilt across the crook of his arm. Nai stared, not understanding.

'I would like you to have this.'

Nai felt the heat rise in his cheeks. 'Me?' he stammered. 'No, no. That one is yours. Besides, the sword is not my weapon.'

446

'I shall teach you.'

Bedwyr thrust the hilt at him. Nai reached out and grasped it without knowing what he was doing, feeling the weight in his hand as Bedwyr moved away. 'I cannot,' he murmured. 'I am not worthy.'

'You can. You are.'

Together they went down from the fortress in the twilight, among the fading wisps of dusk, the first stars trembling through the gaps in the cloud, the wind at their backs pursuing them with the smell of charred wood, and as they wound into the tunnel under the ramparts a great white owl took flight above them, rising high into the darkness on the sweep of its wings, beating against the night until it was lost among the clouds.

NOTES ON THE
BACKGROUND TO THE BOOK

～

By about the twelfth century, the Arthurian legend had developed
two distinct strands: the Continental and the Welsh. In the
Continental tradition, Arthur's son is called Loholt. In some
versions Gwenhwyvar is his mother, in others Lissanor. The
only tale told of him is that of his death: having bravely slain
the Giant Logrin, he was murdered by the jealous Cei, who stole
the credit for overcoming the Giant. This is a common folk-tale
motif – the monster-slayer killed by a trusted companion, who
then claims to have performed the feat himself.

In the Welsh tradition, he is called Llacheu. References to him
are brief, implying a greater knowledge on the part of the listener
than any we now possess. The images are fleeting and evocative: a
warrior fighting before blue spears in the company of Cei on the
heights of a place called Ystafinion; a brave youth, dying in battle
below Llech Ysgar, where the ravens croaked over blood.

Llech Ysgar means something like the rock stronghold, the
fortified rock – Castle Rock. The twelfth-century bard Gwalchmei refers to a place of that name in Powys, and there were
doubtless others, since it seems an obvious description. But there
is one Castle Rock which was important in the fifth and sixth
centuries, which is still famous in our time, and which has a long
association with Arthur.

The lines about Llacheu making slaughter in the company of

Cei on the heights of Ystafinion are taken from a tenth- or eleventh-century poem known as *Pa Gur*, or The Dialogue with the Gatekeeper. In order to obtain entry to a court, Arthur sings the praises of himself and his chief warriors. Twice he mentions Eidin: two heroes are said to have 'defended Eidin on the border', while Arthur himself fought champions 'on the mountain of Eidin'.

One of the earliest references to Arthur comes in the *Gododdin*: 'Gorddur used to bring black crows down in front of the wall of the fortified town – though he was not Arthur.' (Koch's translation.) The *Gododdin* is a collection of heroic death songs which survives in a thirteenth-century manuscript. Traditionally the work is ascribed to the sixth-century bard Aneirin, and some parts of it may well date back that far. It is not a narrative poem like the *Iliad* or *Beowulf* (to both of which it has been compared), but there are repeated references to a battle at Catraeth. The attacking warband came from Dun Eidin, or Eidin Ysgar.

I have used the *Gododdin* as a source in *The White Phantom* and *The Last Companion*. Nai mab Nwython, Gorthyn mab Erfai, Addonwy and Cadlew are all among the heroes commemorated in the poems. For many years the only English edition of the Gododdin was that of Kenneth Jackson, but lately two more translations have been published: one by A.O.H. Jarman and one by John T. Koch. Koch's version is unashamedly controversial, and amongst other things provided the germ of the idea for Regin's story about Llew and Grugyn.

However, Angus's description of Eidin is not intended to be an accurate portrayal of late fifth-century Edinburgh. Neither is Caer Cadwy meant to be a precise reconstruction of South Cadbury – though I have once again borrowed heavily from Leslie Alcock's *Arthur's Britain*. These and the other places in the book are my inventions, not archaeological sites.

Strictly speaking, horses and ponies are not the same thing, but I have used the terms interchangeably as a reminder that fifth- and sixth-century cavalry were not mounted on modern thoroughbreds or heavy horses – though there is no need to go to the opposite extreme and imagine them charging into battle on the equivalent of a Shetland pony. Horses had played an important part in British warfare since before the time of Julius Caesar, and the *Gododdin* and other early Welsh poems attest to the continuing use of cavalry by the British aristocracy. We know the Romans bred mounts for the purpose; the sub-Roman British must have done the same.

Four-horned saddles, which went a long way towards compensating for the lack of stirrups, were used by the Roman cavalry, who probably inherited them from the Celts. Since several Roman cavalry manoeuvres (petrinos, toloutegon and xunema) have Celtic names, it seems likely that these also were inherited. Nai's original in the *Gododdin* is said to have been skilled at the xunema – throwing a spear at a fixed target while the horse is turning at speed – so it seemed appropriate to have him perform this feat in the closing pages of the book.

We do not know how the laws of inheritance worked in early sixth-century Dumnonia. Gildas, who wrote in the 540s, complained that the judges of his day did not follow 'the rules of right judgement', by which he meant they did not uphold the laws of Rome. Roman law classified a person by their status and domicile, but medieval Welsh and Irish law classified a person by their kinship, and made careful distinction between family property – land and houses – and personal property – livestock. The similarities between Wales and Ireland suggest that this was a survival of ancient Celtic custom, which may well have held sway in rural areas throughout the Roman period, regaining ground with the collapse of urban authority – to the horror of people like Gildas.

The Ogham script came into use in Ireland during the third or fourth centuries AD, if not earlier. It consisted of twenty letters, represented by strokes or notches set at different angles on either side of, or crossing, a vertical line – often the edge of a stone, piece of wood or bone. The signs were arranged in consonant and vowel clusters based on the phonetic principles established by late Roman grammarians. Inscriptions were usually read from bottom to top.

One theory is that Ogham developed from the use of notched wooden tally sticks. Another – and the two theories are not necessarily mutually exclusive – is that Ogham originated as a finger and thumb sign language used by the druids in Gaul as far back as the fifth century BC. Whether or not this is true, Ogham certainly lends itself to secret signalling, and the fourteenth-century *Book of Ballymote* describes both nose and shin Ogham.

Since Vortepor of Dyfed's memorial stone at Castell Dwyran was inscribed in both Latin capitals and Ogham, it seems reasonable to assume that a son as well educated as Regin would have had a good knowledge of the Irish script.

There is at long last a good general survey of this period: Christopher Snyder's *An Age of Tyrants: Britain and the Britons AD 400–600* (Sutton Publishing, 1998).

The three editions of the *Gododdin* are:

Jackson, K.H., *The Gododdin: The Oldest Scottish Poem* (Edinburgh 1969).

Jarman, A.O.H., *Aneirin: Y Gododdin – Britain's Oldest Heroic Poem* (Llandysul 1988).

Koch, J.T., *The Gododdin of Aneirin – Text and Context from Dark-Age North Britain* (Cardiff 1997).

GLOSSARY OF
PLACES AND TRIBES

Albany Roughly, a term for what is now northern Scotland. (Later applied to all Scotland.)

Albion Earliest recorded name for the island of Britain.

Aquae Sulis Bath.

Armorica Brittany.

Attecotti 'The Old Folk'; inhabitants of the Western Isles and Western coasts of modern Scotland. I have assumed they were a confederation of some of the older Pictish tribes.

Bannog Southern boundary of Pictland; the ranges of hills between present-day Stirling and Dumbarton.

Britannia Roman name for Britain.

Bryneich Bernicia: Durham & Northumberland; later came to include much of southern Scotland.

Caer Cadwy South Cadbury in Somerset.

Caer Llywelyth Carlisle.

Caer Vadon Bath.

Caer Weir Chester-le-Street.

Calchwinyth 'The limestone (or chalk) hills.' The south midlands, including Dunstable and Northampton.

Camlann Arthur's last battle: site unknown. I have placed it on the edge of the Somerset Marshes.

Catraeth Catterick.

Cerdicesora   Seat of the Saxon Cerdic at top of Southampton Water, near Netley Marsh.

Corinium   Cirencester.

Dewr   Roughly, East Riding of Yorkshire.

Din Erbin   Fortress on eastern side of River Dart, Devon.

Dumnonia   Cornwall, Devon, Somerset and part of Dorset.

Dun Eidin   Edinburgh.

Dunoding   District of Gwynedd.

Durotriges, land of   Dorset, with parts of south Wiltshire and south Somerset.

Dyfed   South-west Wales.

Eburacum   York.

Elmet   Region in and to east of the Yorkshire Pennines, including Leeds.

Glevum   Gloucester.

Gododdin   Region running from the Firth of Forth to the Wear in Country Durham.

Gwent   One of several minor kingdoms in the south-eastern area of modern Wales. Caerwent was its capital.

Gwynedd   North-west Wales.

Gyrwe   Germanic tribe to which Wulfstan's followers belong.

Iardomnan   The Western Isles and parts of Western Scotland.

Ierne   Ireland.

Isc, or Ux   The Rivers Axe and Exe.

Isca   Exeter.

Iuddew   Stirling.

Iuddew, Sea of   Firth of Forth.

Kelliwig   Near Padstow in Cornwall.

Kernow   Cornwall.

Lesser Britain   Brittany.

Lindinis   Ilchester.

Lindum   Lincoln.

Llech Llew Tuath   The Rock of Llew's People: Castle Rock, Edinburgh.

Llech Ysgar   'The fortified Rock, the Rock stronghold', thus Castle Rock, Edinburgh.

Llew's Seat   Arthur's Seat, Edinburgh.

Llewthiniawn   Lothian.

Loidis   Area around Leeds.

Manaw   District of Gododdin: the area around the head of the Firth of Forth, including Stirling.

Mona or Mon, Isle of Anglesey.

Oak, River River Dart in Devon.

Penhyle A settlement at the head of the Porthyle estuary.

Peryth Literally, 'the lords'. The Parisi: a pre-Roman tribe living between the Humber estuary and the North Yorkshire moors.

Picts Collective name for tribes living north of the Forth-Clyde Isthmus.

Porthyle An estuary in South Devon.

Pritdein The land of the Picts.

Prydein Native name for Britain.

Rheged Roughly, Lancashire and Cumbria.

Saxons, Saesons General term for Germanic invaders of Britain.

Scotti Irish sea raiders.

Strathclyde South-western Scotland between the two Roman Walls.

Summer Country Roughly, Somerset.

Weala Saxon term for a foreigner, particularly applied to the native British.

Wectis The Isle of Wight.

Worethia, or Woreth The River Forth.

Ynis Witrin Glastonbury.

Ytes The Jutes: one of the invading Germanic peoples.